The Survivors

Book II: Autumn

V. L Dreyer

Copyright © 2014 V. L. Dreyer
All rights reserved.
ISBN: 978-0-473-27436-8

Dedication

To my mother, Glenys Dreyer, for her unfailing support of me, and her absolute trust that I can succeed no matter how challenging the task may be. Thank you for always being there for me, even in my darkest hour.

I love you, Mum.

Abigail Hawk

THE IMMORTELLE
The Immortality Clause
At First Blush

V. L. Dreyer

THE SURVIVORS
The Survivors Book I: Summer
The Survivors Book II: Autumn
The Survivors Book III: Winter
The Survivors Book IV: Spring

Table Of Contents

Chapter One	1
Chapter Two	10
Chapter Three	35
Chapter Four	47
Chapter Five	70
Chapter Six	84
Chapter Seven	99
Chapter Eight	107
Chapter Nine	122
Chapter Ten	137
Chapter Eleven	152
Chapter Twelve	162
Chapter Thirteen	177
Chapter Fourteen	203
Chapter Fifteen	222
Chapter Sixteen	239
Chapter Seventeen	250
Chapter Eighteen	264
Chapter Nineteen	280
Chapter Twenty	298

Chapter Twenty-One	329
Chapter Twenty-Two	344
Chapter Twenty-Three	357
The Cast	377
Kiwiana Language Guide	379
Credits	381
About The Author	383

The Journey So Far

I still haven't quite wrapped my head around how my life managed to change so much in such a short period of time. Ten years ago, I lost my family and all of my friends to the devastating plague that came to be known as Ebola X. I've spent the last decade running for my life, always alone, constantly afraid, with nobody that I could trust.

This summer, everything changed. I met a group of good people. For the first time in my adult life, I've started to feel like I belong again. Like I'm worth something. I've found my long-lost sister, alive and well after all this time. I've found friendship, with Ryan Knowles, Doctor Cross, and even little Madeline. I've even found love, with a man named Michael, who makes me feel like there could be so much more to life than just surviving day to day.

Everything was going so beautifully, until disease caught up with us again. Except this time, it's not Ebola X. This time, it's listeria poisoning. The victims it wants to take? My sister, and her unborn child...

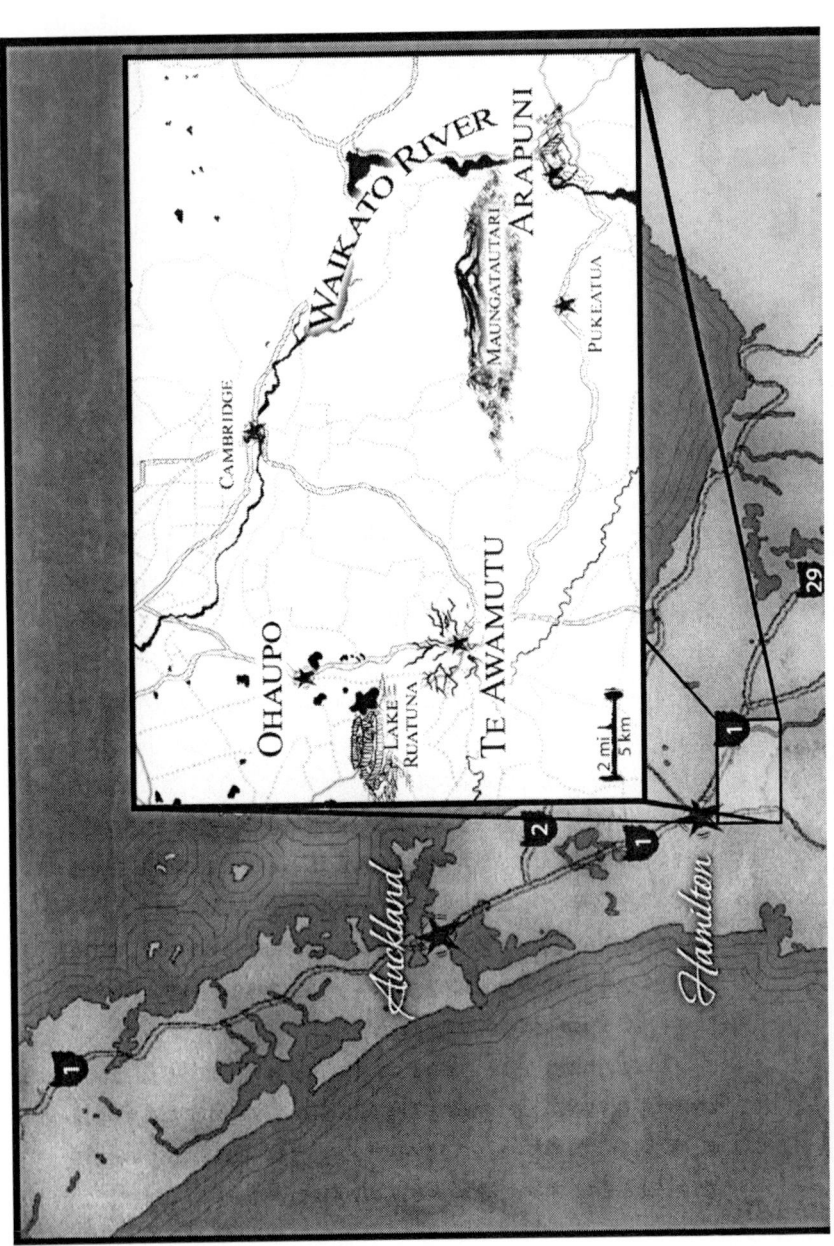

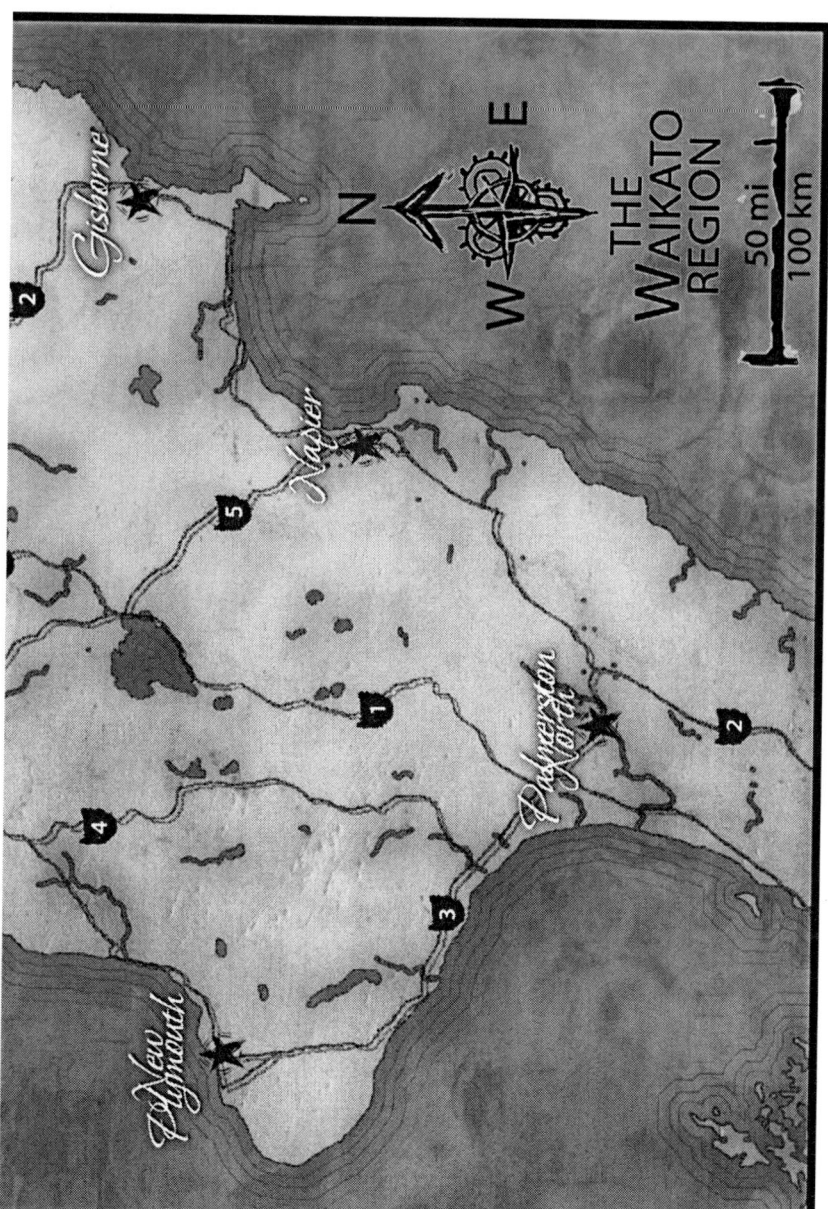

Foreword

The Survivors series is set in New Zealand. In order to preserve the authenticity of the setting and the heroine's voice, this novel has been written in New Zealand English.

New Zealand English (NZE) is an off-shoot of British English, but the geographical isolation of the country has given rise to a quirky sub-dialect that is neither entirely British, nor Australian.

I have attempted to make this novel as easily accessible as possible for readers around the world by providing contextual explanations for most words. However, as the language variations are subtle and frequent, it is not always possible to do this.

A more in-depth article on the language used in this book is available on my website, where you also have the facility to ask me questions.

http://www.vldreyer.com

Chapter One

    I had been through a lot of bad days in my twenty-eight years of life. Terrible, painful days. The kind of days that no human being should ever have to go through. But today felt like the worst.

    Even the sky wept as we lay her in her grave. Despite the rain, the ground had been baked hard by the long, hot summer. It was like digging through rock. It was a struggle to dig her grave deep enough to protect her body from the elements, and from pests. We had no choice, though. We couldn't just leave her to rot in the sun and be eaten by rats. She was family.

    When we finally deemed the grave deep enough, the sweating men climbed out of the hole. All except one: Ryan Knowles. Our friend. He was only twenty-two, but he had been so ready to be a father. Now, it was like someone had stripped the life right out of him. His face was expressionless as he reached up for the tiny body. The light was gone from his eyes.

    Skylar looked reluctant to surrender her baby's body to the earth. She was even younger than Ryan was, just eighteen years old and barely more than a child herself – but like her fiancé, she had been so ready for that baby. She had so much love to give. Now, she wouldn't have the chance. She could still have another baby in the future, but I understood the look in her eyes on some instinctive level, both as a woman and as her sister. No other child could ever replace her firstborn, lost to a miscarriage.

She held the tiny body for a moment longer, then leaned down to place her daughter in Ryan's outstretched arms.

He took the child and looked at her stiff little face, his jaw clenched in silent tension. He didn't say anything, but my imagination filled in the blanks about what he was probably thinking. That face should have smiled and cried, laughed and loved along with the rest of us, but now she would never have that chance. In a heartbeat, her innocent life had been snatched away from us. We'd been excited to welcome her into our little family; now, all our hopes for her had been dashed. Her life had been taken from us before she had a chance to learn how much we loved her.

Ryan leaned down and kissed the baby's forehead, then he placed her in the little box we'd found for her. We had buried other members of our family before, but it felt wrong to just put her into the dirt. She was so tiny, helpless and fragile that even in death, we wanted to protect her.

I knelt beside my sister on the edge of the grave and put my arm around her for support. She'd cried so much over the last few days that her tears had run dry; now she just stared into the hole in the ground, looking wrung-out and heartbroken.

Her baby. Her firstborn child. Gone, just like that.

Skylar trembled beneath my touch, but she didn't seem to have the strength to cry anymore. A part of her was in that hole, her flesh and blood. A piece of her had died along with her baby. We'd already lost so much; losing one more piece was devastating to us all.

All we had was each other, just the six of us against the world. There used to be more people in the group, but they'd lost little Sophie just before I arrived, and Dog not long after. We should have been nine by now, but we were only six. Six people living in the ruins of a civilization that had collapsed a decade ago beneath the weight of a deadly plague. Six people in a country that used to house more than five million, before Ebola X had decimated the entire human race.

Humankind was on the verge of extinction. It wasn't just one tiny baby that we were burying, but a part of the future. Now that there were so few of us, every life was integral to the survival of our entire species. Forget the whales and the tigers; now homo sapiens were on the critically endangered list.

It seemed to take forever for that hole to fill. The rain fell steadily and plastered our hair to our heads, like a constant reminder from Mother Nature about the burden of grief that lay upon us. Even those of us who didn't share a blood relationship with the baby felt a bond with her. They suffered just as much as we did.

I looked at Michael, the man who had once been a police officer and was now my lover and my friend, and I found his face solemn and stern. I knew him well enough to understand that he blamed himself for the baby's death, even though there was nothing that he could have done to predict Skylar's fever. Beside him, Stewart Cross, our doctor, looked just as grim – I suspected that he felt the same way.

I didn't blame either of them. No one had suspected that Skylar's headache had been the symptom of an infection that would have the strength to take her baby's life, and almost take hers as well. There was no way we could have known. Surviving after the fall of mankind meant that we only had access to rudimentary medical supplies, so we didn't have the means to test for listeria poisoning. The doctor had figured it out just in time to save Skylar, but by then it had been too late for the baby.

The poor baby. She should have had her whole life ahead of her. She didn't deserve such an undignified end.

Grief surged within me, and I closed my eyes to try and fight it off. Like my sister, I'd already cried so much that I wasn't sure I could cry any more. Beside me, Skye clung to a tiny pink teddy bear that I'd scavenged for her as a gift. My intention had been to cheer her up when she wasn't feeling well, but now it could only serve to comfort her in her time of mourning.

We watched as the last of the soil went back onto the grave, and the men gently smoothed it and patted it down. It was a mud pie. We'd buried my only niece in a mud pie. A tangled web of emotions surged within me. I wanted to laugh and cry and scream at the top of my lungs until my throat was raw. I'd barely had enough time to accept that I was going to be someone's auntie, and now she was gone.

Michael held his hand out for the wooden grave marker I was holding, his face set in an expression that looked just as wrung-out and exhausted as I felt. I handed it to him without a word; he took it and drove it as deep into the dirt as he could, to make sure that the wind wouldn't knock it askew.

Kylie Knowles-McDermott
We loved you before we knew you.

I read the marker again even though I'd read it a dozen times before, struggling to fight back the surge of emotion that threatened to overwhelm me. It was true, so true. The loss of that baby made me feel like someone had ripped a hole in my heart.

Michael came and sat beside me once his work was done, while the doctor stood with his head bowed beside the tiny grave. None of us could bring ourselves to say anything, so we stood and sat silently, each of us wrapped up in our own grieving process.

We were so focused on ourselves that none of us noticed when Ryan left, and no one saw where he went.

***

The storm turned violent, forcing us to leave the graveside and seek shelter. We were wet and bedraggled by the time we filtered back into the old motel we'd refurbished and converted into our home, but we were all too wrung out to complain. Skylar disentangled her hand from mine and headed off towards her room. The doctor took his little granddaughter, Madeline, off towards theirs.

Michael stayed with me, though he was silent and solemn. We stood hand-in-hand on the upper walkway that overlooked our garden, and watched the sky roiling overhead. A cold wind blew past us; I snuggled against his side, comforted by his warmth and stalwart strength.

Lightning split the heavens. We smelt the tingle of static discharge in the air. The thunder came a few seconds later, a deafening rumble that seemed to reverberate around and around until it shook us to our very cores.

Michael nuzzled his face against the curve of my neck, seeking some way to comfort me. I knew without words that it upset him to see me in pain. Although we had only known each other for a short time, I'd come to depend on him so much. I touched his cheek, and he kissed mine in return, while the cold wind swirled around us.

"I feel so helpless," I admitted softly, not sure what else to say. There was nothing I could do, for my sister or her child.

"Let's go inside." He hugged me gently, his deep

voice barely audible over the storm. "A hot drink will make us feel better."

It wouldn't, but I gave him credit for trying. I nodded and let him lead me down the stairs to the ground floor. We went through the lobby and back out into the cold, passing by the garden that we had planted together. I glanced at it, wondering if our precious little plants would survive the weather.

And what about Skylar? Would she be strong enough to weather the emotional storm she was going through? I worried about her constantly, but no matter how hard I tried I was helpless to protect her. She was my only sister, the one person I had left from the days before the disease came. Our mother and father had died years ago, and we had been separated then. Now, a decade later, a miraculous freak of fate had brought us back together. The thought of losing her again was more than I could bear.

Michael and I retreated into our communal kitchen, and there we found Skylar sitting at the table as though reading my thoughts. There was a note in her hands: a scrap of damp paper that looked like it came from a notebook. I stared at it. What was she doing with a scrap of paper?

She looked up at us as we entered, her expression haunted.

"I found this on my bed," she said, her voice barely more than a whisper, then she looked at me with huge eyes and held the note out towards me. Although her rudimentary reading level was more than enough to handle a simple note, now was not the time for me to push her to read it herself. I took the note from her and sat down opposite her, while Michael went off to make our drinks. I had to read the note three times before it made sense to me.

I looked up and stared at my poor sister, with dread twisting in my stomach. The last thing I wanted to do was break her heart again, but I had no choice. I read the note out loud to her, fighting my own raging emotions to try and keep my voice steady for her sake.

Dear Skylar,
I can't stay here right now. I don't know where I'll go but it can't be here. I don't know if I'll come back. Maybe one day.
 I'm sorry.
 Ryan.

When I finished reading, my eyes shot up to my baby sister. Her expression would have been unreadable to the uninitiated, but I could see the emotional collapse that took place behind her eyes. Although her face stayed neutral, I saw her falling apart like a house of cards on the inside. Ryan had been the one constant in her life for ten years. He had been her companion, her lover, and her pillar of light and support for more than half of her life. Just like that, her baby was dead, and her fiancé had left her as well.

"It's my fault." Her voice was shockingly harsh in the silence. "I did it. I killed my baby, just like you said I would. I didn't mean to. I don't know what I did, but it's my fault."

"No!" I exclaimed. "You heard what the doctor said: it was food poisoning. It's no one's fault, least of all yours."

I tried to grab her hand, but she pulled away from me. She wouldn't make eye contact, and she wouldn't answer. Trepidation washed over me like a rising tide when she rose and left the room, but Michael held me back when I tried to follow her.

"Leave her, Sandy," he whispered. "She needs time."

I turned on him, tears blurring my vision. "But—what if—"

"Hush." He swept me in close against his broad chest, and drew me back into the security and warmth of his arms. "When she needs us, she'll let us know. This is your sister we're talking about, remember?"

I didn't have an answer to that. He was right. My little sister was stronger than all of us put together. I just had to hope that it would be enough to get her through.

So, we left her alone, and sat together drinking tea and listening to the storm raging outside while I struggled to cope with the internal storm that raged within me. Ryan's departure had brought us down to five: two experienced fighters, an elderly man, a child, and Skye. His departure not only cost Skylar her mate, but it cost the entire group one of its few able-bodied defenders. I wasn't sure how we were going to survive.

Chapter Two

The pallor of death hung over our household like a palpable force in the days that followed. We decided by universal consensus to put Skylar on suicide watch, just in case. She was so quiet that it shook me to the very core, and if it hadn't been for Michael's gentle strength, I probably would have fallen apart as well.

As far as we could tell, the grief and self-loathing seemed to have been too much for Skylar's young mind. She shut down completely and retreated deep within herself to somewhere the rest of us couldn't reach her. Although we stopped in and checked on her regularly, she had nothing to say to any of us; if I asked her a question, all she did was nod or shake her head. My little sister was usually so verbose and argumentative that seeing her like that was a real shock to the system.

Her depression was infectious. At night, I curled up in bed beside Michael and cried myself to sleep, and every morning I awoke feeling exhausted. Neither of us could summon any interest in the love-play that had filled our evenings not so long ago. We were just too tired, and it seemed inappropriate somehow.

It wasn't all bad, though. More than once, I had gone to check on Skye and found Madeline sitting beside her. The child possessed intuition far beyond her years, and seemed to have taken a great interest in helping Skylar to get through her grief. Once, I even caught them playing together. It was a sight that filled me with hope. There was something about Maddy that seemed to be able to reach people in a way that no one else could.

As the week passed, I gradually began to recover. There was only so much grief that one person could bear before she either killed herself or clambered back out of the deep, dark hole and got on with her life. With Michael's unwavering support, I eventually dug myself free. It was not in my nature to sit around and mope, so he encouraged me to find active things to do.

To keep myself occupied, I decided to improve our fortifications. I'd managed to install a ladder up to the roof, but the weather had been intermittently foul all week and hampered my plans to build a railing around the edge. The general idea was to provide a safe area where we could position a watcher, to keep an eye out for danger or visitors.

On the seventh day after the baby died, I climbed up to sit on the roof of the motel and watch the sun rise. The morning was clear, but I sensed more rain to come. I'd spent a good deal of time living off the land over the years, and had developed a keen nose for the natural world as a result. Still, even knowing that the rain was coming back, the sunrise was beautiful. The deep clouds along the horizon glowed pink when the dawn's rays struck them, and sent creeping tendrils of rose and gold across the arc of the sky.

The sound of someone climbing the ladder behind me attracted my attention, but I wasn't concerned. The ladder could only be accessed from inside the motel, which meant that the climber had to be one of my companions. Sure enough, it was.

"I was wondering where you went," Michael said as he clambered up onto the roof.

I glanced back over my shoulder and watched him pick his way cautiously across the slanted tiles towards toward me. "Yeah, I didn't feel like sleeping in today."

He sat down beside me, then jerked in surprise when he suddenly discovered that the roof was wet. I hid a smile behind my hand and struggled not to laugh.

"Ah, damn – these jeans were clean." He shot me a mock glare, but I could see in his eyes that there was no real anger behind it. "You could have warned me."

"Oh, it's just a little water. They're still technically clean."

He smiled at my joke, even if it wasn't really a very good one. My gaze lingered on him, studying the contours of his profile in light of dawn. I'd heard that sunrise was referred to as the photographer's golden hour, and I could see why. The gentle light softened the hard angles of his face and made him look almost angelic. Emotion surged up within my chest, an overwhelming wave of affection towards the man that had worked so hard to save both my life, and my humanity.

"Michael," I whispered his name and reached over to take his hand.

His gaze shifted to me, a faint smile on his lips and a quizzical look in his eyes. "Yes?"

Ah, he was such a good man. Such a sweet, kind, wonderful man. What on earth had I done to deserve someone like him? I snuggled against him and reached up to trail my fingers along his jaw. For once, there was no stubble there; he must have shaved just before he came looking for me. I found myself just the tiniest bit disappointed. I had grown fond of him with a touch of scruff. I'd grown fond of him in a lot of ways, really.

He watched me with those dark eyes of his, as if he was trying to figure out what I was about. I smiled cryptically up at him, and his brow furrowed. "Are you feeling okay, Sandy?"

I couldn't help but giggle. I was feeling a little giddy, actually. A little girlish. A little silly. I hadn't felt that way about someone in a very long time.

"I feel a bit peculiar, actually," I said, then quickly finished my sentence before he started worrying about me. "Like maybe I might be in love. I think I am, actually. I think I'm in love with you, Michael Chan. I'm not sure if I should offer you congratulations or condolences."

He stared back at me while my words sank in, so many different emotions flickering across his face that I couldn't keep track of them all. Finally, just when I was about to start getting concerned, the tiniest, sweetest little smile crept across his face, and he hugged me tight.

"Congratulations, definitely." His voice was even huskier than usual and hardly more than a whisper. One gentle hand caressed my jawline, and then he planted a tender kiss on my lips. It lingered for just a moment before he drew back to speak again. "I love you, too. And... thank you."

"Eh? For what?" This time he had me confused.

"Well." Suddenly, he seemed very interested in looking anywhere but at me. "When I told you how I felt last week, and you didn't say it back... I was worried. I thought perhaps I'd misunderstood your intentions, and that I was the only one who felt like that. I thought that maybe you didn't..."

He trailed off, and my heart just about broke looking up at him. In a sudden flash of overwhelming emotion, I threw my arms around his broad shoulders and hugged him as tight as I could.

"Oh, no." I squeezed his firm body with every ounce of my strength. "No, no, no. I just needed time. You know how I am."

He laughed and squeezed me back; the sound of his laughter made me feel a surge of happiness that I hadn't experienced since before Skylar's illness. With it, came a feeling of hope. With Michael at my side, it felt like somehow everything *had* to work out in the end.

***

After we finished our sappy moment, Michael volunteered to help with my project while the weather was still fine. I was glad for the assistance, not just because that it would get the work done faster, but also because it gave me an excuse to spend time with him. That, and he had twice my physical strength, which was handy in construction projects. A girl had to be practical in our day and age.

With his help, we managed to get a railing up around half of the south-eastern side of the roof before the weather started to close in again. I barely heard the distant rumble of thunder over the sound of my own hammering, but Michael did.

"Storm's coming back," he informed me as I wriggled out from beneath the construction we were erecting. He helped me to my feet, and together we watched the clouds gathering in the distance.

"Looks like a bad one," I said. He nodded his agreement. A strong gust of wind blew, almost knocking me off my feet. All of a sudden, I was glad that I'd put a few extra nails into the new railing.

"We should get everything that's not nailed down inside," Michael suggested.

"Yeah, and let's do it fast," I agreed immediately. After ten years on my own, I'd learned to read the weather like a book, and this one had the smell of trouble all over it. It was late summer heading into autumn; while we often got storms at that time of year, this one felt different.

We both hurried to gather up our tools and the left-over wood, and raced back down the ladder to the relative safety of ground level.

There, we found the doctor had anticipated our next step and was in the process of covering up our little garden with a frame I'd made for just that purpose. We tossed our tools into the safety of one of the downstairs storage rooms, and then ran over to help him. We had the garden battened down and protected by the time the first of the rain started to splatter down around us. Thunder rumbled ominously, getting closer with each passing moment.

Michael froze and looked over his shoulder towards the lobby. "Wait, what was that noise?"

"What noise?" I followed his gaze, but didn't see anything.

"I could have sworn I heard engines," he mumbled, half to himself. He headed off towards the front door to check, so I followed him. The wind caught the door as soon as he opened it, forcing him to put his weight behind it to get it to open all the way.

I shoved my hair back out of my face as the wind tried to blind me with it, and peered off into the distance. "I still don't hear anything."

A blur of tabby fur bounded past us as Tigger took the opportunity to escape from the incoming storm. She danced between our feet, and then vanished into the depths of the motel.

"I'm sure I heard something." Michael frowned, leaning heavily against the door to keep it open.

"I really don't—" Then I paused and tilted my head,

straining to listen. "No, wait, you're right – I hear it too. That sounds like farm bikes."

Sure enough, it was. A pair of figures on little motorcycles skidded around the corner a heartbeat later, struggling to keep their balance against the surging winds. I waved to them and beckoned them towards us as soon as I recognised the riders as friends: Anahera and Hemi, members of the Maori group that lived not far away. They came to a stop a half-dozen meters from the entrance. I hurried out of the safety of the building to help Anahera with her bike.

The leader of the Maori tribe was bundled against the weather in a heavy anorak with the hood pulled up over her head, but the wind was so strong it tugged her glossy black curls in every direction. I fell in beside her and helped her wheel her bike into the safety of our lobby, with her son close behind us. Once we were all safely inside, Michael eased the door closed and bolted it shut behind us.

"We may have underestimated the weather," Anahera said, sounding out of breath as we rolled her bike over to a corner and leaned it against the wall. Once it was safely stowed, she leaned back and heaved a sigh, plucking a few long strands of hair out of her eyes.

"No kidding," I answered dryly. Like a good little hostess, I offered her a hand to help her get out of her coat, which she accepted.

"I hope you don't mind that we arrived unannounced." She shot an apologetic glance towards me. "We hoped to consult with your doctor on something, and if we waited then it would only get worse."

"The doctor?" I frowned at her, feeling a stab of concern. Although we had only met once before, I considered Anahera and her son to be our friends. She'd shown herself to be a good, loyal person and had helped me at my lowest point; I felt a sense of gratitude toward her that I wasn't sure I could ever repay. "Of course, Anahera. You're always welcome here. What's wrong?"

"Ah, my boy has gone and gotten himself hurt." Anahera sighed and shot a look at her son, drawing my attention to the young man; for the first time, I noticed he was moving strangely, favouring his left side.

"Aw, mum! It's not like I did it on purpose," Hemi protested, but his mother wasn't having any of it. She stomped over to him and yanked up the hem of his shirt to show us the blood-soaked bandages beneath.

"Ouch." Michael grimaced at the sight of the blood. "What did you do, lad?"

"Someone took a pot-shot at me from the bush while I was out possum hunting. Tane and Iorangi chased him off, but we didn't get a good look at the bastard." He flicked a sheepish-looking glance at his mother. "Sorry, Mum."

"It's fine, dear. I understand." Anahera patted his arm, then turned and looked at the two of us. "I suspect it was an air rifle rather than the real thing, but it got him at a bad angle. We don't have the tools to get the pellet out without doing more harm than good."

"I'll go find the doctor," Michael said, then shot a glance at me to make sure I was okay with being left alone. I nodded and gave him a reassuring smile; he smiled back and hurried off, leaving me to tend to our guests.

"Let's get you somewhere comfortable." I beckoned them both to follow me and led them off toward the room next to the kitchen, which we'd converted into our communal living room. The rain pelted down on the courtyard as we passed, and a gust of wind rattled the windows and doors so hard that it made all of us flinch.

We reached the living area safely, despite the weather's best attempts to fling things at us. Once we were back indoors, I hung Anahera's coat over the back of a chair and cleared a pile of assorted junk off one of the couches so that Hemi could lie down. He protested weakly as his mother stripped him of his jacket and shirt, but by the time Michael arrived with the doctor in tow, we had his bandages laid bare.

"Hey, Doc," Hemi greeted him with a lopsided smile.

"'Hey', indeed. Let's get these bandages off and have a look at you." Doctor Cross frowned deeply at the youth and settled down in his chair beside the couch. Michael and I took that as our cue to leave. We filtered back outside, with Anahera trailing behind us.

"You want a cuppa?" I offered, gesturing towards our kitchen.

"After being out in the storm, I certainly wouldn't say no," she answered agreeably, running her fingers back through her damp hair. I nodded and led the way to the kitchen, where I set about making tea while Anahera and Michael sat at the table.

"How's your sister?" Anahera asked me in her usual pleasant way.

I froze for a second, halfway through setting a pot of water on the stove to heat up, then I turned slowly and stared at her. The last time she or any of her tribe had visited us was before the sickness, when Skylar had been heavily pregnant but more or less happy.

Actually, come to think of it, the last time I'd personally seen her was when she was beating the living shit out of the man who had brutally raped me years ago. Needless to say, there was a damn good reason that I was fond of her.

Anahera wasn't stupid. She knew from the look on my face that something was wrong. Her brow furrowed. When I didn't answer, she looked at Michael instead. He drew a deep breath and looked down at his hands. There was no nice way to say what had to be said.

"She lost the baby," he murmured, so quietly that I could barely hear his voice. I didn't have to, I already knew. Anahera, however, went wide-eyed and her hands flew up to her mouth.

"Oh, no... how?" she whispered, tears gathering in her hypnotically-beautiful dark eyes.

"Skye got sick," I spoke up at last, to help break the

bad news. "Really, really sick. We think that she got listeria poisoning from something she ate."

"Is she...?"

"She's alive, thank goodness." Michael frowned and shook his head. "But the doctor couldn't save her child."

"Oh, the poor dear." Anahera heaved a long sigh and closed her eyes. "She must be devastated. How long ago did it happen?"

"About a week ago." I sighed as well – and then jumped in surprise when a gust of wind rattled a boarded-up window beside me ominously. No one had it in them to laugh at my jumpiness today, not even me.

"May I speak with her?" Anahera looked from Michael to me, as though seeking permission from us.

"You can try. She hasn't been very talkative recently, but..." I looked at her thoughtfully. "Perhaps she would respond better to someone who is a mother."

What I meant but didn't say, was that my sister might respond better to a mother who had already lost most of her children, and understood the pain of losing a child better than any of us could. I didn't need to say it though; Anahera seemed to know exactly what I meant.

"I'll go see her now." She rose from her seat, just as an almighty bolt of lightning flashed outside. The lights flickered and then went out, leaving us in semi-darkness. I grunted in annoyance and reached over to switch off the stove.

"So much for tea," I muttered, and then I pointed Anahera in the right direction. "Upstairs, second door on the left. She'll be in her room, where she always is."

Anahera nodded and left without another word. I looked at Michael and he looked back at me, then lifted a brow that I could barely see in the dark kitchen.

"You know, this would be a great chance to go spend some quality time together, if we weren't all so depressed." He flashed me an impish grin, just in time for his face to be illuminated by another flash of lightning. The humour got a smile from me.

"Well, it is good snuggling weather," I agreed, shifting the pot of water to a safer spot. The rain was so thunderous that it masked the sound of his footsteps coming up behind me, so when his arms wrapped around me he took me by surprise.

"Let's go have a snuggle, then," he suggested, nuzzling the side of my neck. The nuzzle was followed by a nibble, then a kiss, and I was putty in his hands.

"Sure, why not?" I smiled to myself as he kissed his way up and down the curve of my neck. "Snuggles are, um... very good for the soul. I think I could use a healthy dose of snuggles."

"I think we could all use a healthy dose of snuggles," Michael answered, then he gave me a smile, took my hand, and led me out of the kitchen.

***

We settled for his bedroom, where we had a bit of privacy but also could keep an eye out for trouble along the upstairs landing. The wind howled around our little fortress, yanking our hair aggressively as we made our way up the stairs and headed for his room. Well, it yanked at mine, since my hair was long; it barely ruffled his.

"You know, I've been meaning to ask." I looked at him as he stripped off his t-shirt and flopped down on his bed. "How on earth do you keep your hair so neatly trimmed without the benefit of a barber? I can barely keep mine brushed."

"A mirror, a pair of nail scissors and a hell of a lot of patience." His grin was so playful that I couldn't figure out if he was telling the truth or joshing with me. Luckily, my curiosity flew right out the window when he stretched out languidly, in just such a way as to make his taut muscles ripple beneath newly-tanned skin. After that, I completely forgot whatever I was thinking before, enraptured by his teasing.

It never failed to impress me just how quickly he'd learned to push my buttons, considering that he'd never had a girlfriend before. Not that either of us had used the boyfriend-girlfriend words just yet. Between the two of us, we had the emotional maturity of a fourteen year old boy – and that was only if you added us both together and rounded up generously. We'd get there, though. We were learning and growing together every day, and that was what mattered.

He grinned and patted his stomach invitingly. He knew I couldn't resist, so I didn't even try. The breath exploded out of him as I leapt on him in a mock tackle, and we both went head over heels in a mass of tickling silliness. A few minutes and a couple of muffled squeals later, we finally remembered that we were supposed to be adults. Michael flopped on his back with an arm tucked under his head, and I snuggled up against his belly to enjoy the warmth of his skin.

Even though he was out of breath from our play, I could hardly hear his panting over the roar of the wind. It was getting stronger by the second. I rolled onto my belly to rest my chin on his firm stomach, and watched the storm rage beyond the open door.

A disembodied branch crashed into the wall beside his door. It wasn't a big one, but it hit hard enough that the sound of its impact made us both jump.

"Geez, it sounds like it's turning into a cyclone out there." Michael frowned, absently rubbing his chin. "Good thing we brought all that junk in."

"It's going to take hours to clean up this mess tomorrow." I sighed heavily, rubbing my cheek against his stomach. "I hope Ryan isn't out in this."

"I hope he is," Michael spat the sentence with a vehemence that startled me. He was a gentle man by nature, and I rarely saw him angry. For him to wish suffering on someone was unexpected. My brows rose, and I lifted my head to regard him quizzically. He didn't make eye contact with me, but he looked pretty steamed up.

"Aren't I the one that's supposed to be furious at him?" I eased myself up to plant a tender kiss on his throat, right in the spot that I had learned through trial and error was his most vulnerable.

A sharp exhalation of breath was my reward, followed by the feeling of a strong arm sneaking around my waist. "I'm surprised that you aren't."

"Oh, I am." I nuzzled and nibbled at that tender spot, until his head tilted back to give me better access. "I haven't forgiven him, but I understand that he had to go."

"Mnngh..." He murmured inarticulately as I kissed a trail down the side of his throat and across his collarbone. "He abandoned the love of his life when she needed him most. I'll never forgive him for that."

"If there were more men like you in the world, then there would be a lot more happy women," I told him, and then promptly distracted him with a play-bite, right on the nipple.

Michael yelped and stared at me with wide eyes, covering his 'wound' with his hand. "What was that for?"

"For being you." I grinned up at him, and then leaned down to plant a playful kiss on his stomach. Anticipation made his breath catch in his throat, but for now the kiss was all he got. That, and a snuggle when I nestled back up against his side. "I've got to mark you as mine somehow. Unfortunately, people aren't cats; no matter how much I rub my face all over you, it just doesn't work."

That got a laugh from him. "No, it probably wouldn't, but you're more than welcome to try."

I gasped and feigned injury. "You're just trying to

get me to rub you in all the interesting places. I see what you're up to, sir."

He gave me such a wicked grin that I broke down giggling. The wind took the opportunity to yowl mournfully and rattle our windows, sending an ice-cold gust tearing through our little nest. I shivered and cuddled closer to him. It was so dark I could hardly see him in the gloom, but just knowing he was there was enough for me.

"I wonder what the others are up to," I considered aloud, and felt more than saw Michael shrug beneath me.

"Honestly, I'm not entirely sure what *we're* up to, let alone the others."

With a laugh and a poke in the side, I rolled onto my back to stare at the murky ceiling above us. "We're snuggling, remember?"

"Ah, of course." His smile softened to one of affection, and I felt his fingers stroking my hair. I relaxed and closed my eyes, enjoying the sense of closeness.

"You know, in retrospect I'm really glad I didn't shoot you." I sighed and reached up to capture his fingers in my own.

"I'm glad I missed."

I stretched out languidly, listening to the sounds of the storm raging all around us. All the window panes were rattling, and I heard something creaking ominously. A moment later, the sound of glass breaking downstairs made me jump, but Michael restrained me from rushing off to investigate.

"It'll just be one of the downstairs windows," he soothed, drawing my fingers up to his lips for a reassuring kiss. "They're boarded up on the inside, don't worry about them."

"It could be one of those mutant zombies taking advantage of the storm," I protested, but he dismissed the notion with a shake of his head.

"Even the mutant zombies aren't stupid enough to be outside in this weather. They'd just end up cartwheeling down the street." His voice was so dry, and the image was so amusing that I couldn't help but smile.

"You're always so calm and collected; I don't know how you do it." I sighed heavily. A thought struck me then; I turned to look at him quizzically in the semi-darkness. "You did bring your uniform with you when we moved here, right?"

"Of course." He peered down at me, perplexed. "Why?"

I smiled to myself – he really had no idea about the power that uniform had over me. I gave him a long, sideways look, and then I hid my face against his tummy before he could see me blushing. "Oh, no reason."

Why no, I didn't plan to make him wear it when we finally got over our... hurdle. Call me a sucker for a man in uniform, but it looked fantastic on him. Of all the cops I'd seen in my life, none wore it better. Michael grunted inarticulately, like he didn't quite believe me. He always seemed to know when I was up to no good.

Cop instincts or something, I guessed.

Oh, but what about the...?

I sat bolt upright like a meerkat, and made him jump in surprise. "I don't suppose you kept the hat as well, did you?"

"Uh, I think so. It's probably in there." He pointed to a corner of his room, where a couple of bags were still waiting to be unpacked. Part of me wanted to scold him for waiting all this time to get settled in, but part of me understood completely – you never quite knew when you were going to need to pull up roots and run. We had settled in nicely, but there was no guarantee that we could stay in our motel forever.

Hell, there was no guarantee either of us would live out the week. Life was fickle, and far too short to spend the entire time being serious.

I sprang over him and dived into the corner, to root around inside his bags in search of the hat. Although I heard him protesting, he made no attempt to actually stop me from digging through his belongings. It was only fair, after all – he'd gone through mine on several occasions, looking for something. We were close enough that he knew I was no threat to his possessions, just like I understood that he was no threat to mine.

Socks and shorts went flying as I turned his bag upside down, until I finally found what I was looking for, right at the very bottom.

"Victory is mine!" I yanked out one slightly crushed, navy blue police officer's cap. I dusted it off, popped it back into shape and plonked it on my head. There was a muffled snort behind me. I turned and gave him a look of wide-eyed mock innocence. "What?"

"What on earth has gotten into you, Sandy McDermott?" he asked. I bounced back over to join him in bed.

"Me? Oh, I'm just feeling a bit playful, is all." I gave him a grin, to which he responded by snatching the hat off my head and placing it upon his own.

"You're just trying to cheer me up, aren't you?" He peered at me from beneath the brim of his cap, his smile fading away.

I heaved a sigh and flopped back down with my head on his chest. "Pretty much, yes. Trying to cheer myself up, too. It's been such a miserable week."

"I know." He ran his fingers through my hair, stroking a few golden-blonde strands back away from my face. One finger hooked under my chin and tilted my face up towards his so that he could look me in the eye. "It's been a rough couple of months for everyone."

"It's been a rough decade." I broke eye contact and looked away. "I need a vacation from being miserable before I go crazy."

"You and me both." He nodded his agreement and wrapped an arm around my waist to draw me closer against him. Then he kissed me, softly and tenderly; suddenly, it seemed like everything was going to be fine after all. The kiss lingered for long minutes as we both tried to lose our worries in one another. It was a moment of warmth and comfort, the kind of moment shared between two people who had suffered so much and only had one another to fall back on.

We were so wrapped up in one another that we didn't hear the footfalls of someone approaching, nor did we notice the presence in the doorway until Anahera cleared her throat pointedly and knocked on the door frame. Startled, we jerked away from one another and stared at her.

"Sorry to interrupt." She was obviously trying very hard not to laugh at the expressions on our faces. We looked at one another, half-naked with hands in all kinds of interesting places, then promptly started frantically disentangling ourselves. By the time we were straightened up, both of us were blushing furiously, and Anahera could barely keep a straight face.

"Um, sorry." I felt the need to apologise as I straightened my t-shirt, but she just shook her head.

"Don't be, dear. I was your age not that long ago; I remember what it's like to be in love." Her smile faded, and I felt a stab of guilt when I remembered how she had lost her husband to the plague. "Just make the most of him while you can. And you–" She pointed at Michael. "–take good care of her as well. Or else."

Michael flashed his cheeky smile and saluted her, which looked a little ridiculous considering he was still dressed in his policeman's cap.

"Don't just stand out there in the wind, you'll get hit by something." He gestured towards the chair in the corner of room with a flourish, inviting her inside. Somehow, he even managed to sound nonchalant about it. "Come in, sit down. How's Hemi?"

Anahera accepted the invitation and stepped inside, closing the door behind her to keep out the wind. It was getting loud outside, so I thought nothing of the gesture; with the door open we could hardly hear ourselves think.

"He's fine, thank you," she answered as she settled in the chair by the window, adjusting her clothing about her to get comfortable. "The good doctor has removed the pellet, and given him some antibiotics to ensure it doesn't get infected." Her lips twisted into an appreciative smile. "It seems we owe you gifts once again."

"Oh, there's no need for that." Michael shook his head and gave her a smile in return. "Friends help friends, that's all that matters. I'm sure you'd do the same for us if we needed help."

"Absolutely," she agreed amicably, then shifted her gaze to me. "I spoke with your sister."

My heart leapt into my throat. "How is she?"

"She's in a great deal of pain, but she is healing." Anahera sighed heavily. "It will take time and support, and the love of the people around her. She told me that her man left her as well, and I fear that has only compounded her grief."

I felt an arm creep around me and turned to look at Michael; the expression on his face was one of deep anger. Anahera seemed to notice it as well, but she said nothing.

"I don't know how to help her," I admitted, turning my attention back to our visitor. "I've forgotten how to be a sister. We were separated for a long time, and only found one another recently."

Anahera nodded understandingly. "This is a strange world we live in, but I think there is more to your bond than just time spent together as adults. Just knowing that you're here for her is enough."

"How do you know?" I looked down at my hands, feeling helplessness hit me in the gut all over again. "I don't know what she needs."

"I know because she told me as much," Anahera said. I looked up to find her regarding me with an expression that spoke of fondness. "She told me that if it weren't for you, she would have nothing left to live for."

"Oh." I looked back down and leaned against Michael for support. "But I haven't even done anything."

"You don't need to, dear. You're her sister. That's all that matters." I could hear the smile in her voice without looking up, and found it reassuring somehow.

"Is there anything we can do to help her through the grieving process?" Michael asked.

"Perhaps." I heard her shift in her seat, and glanced up to find her staring out the window at the raging storm. "I was going to suggest that some time away from the place where her baby died might help her. Of course, it is difficult to find somewhere safe in this world, so I thought some of you might like to come and visit my group for a few days. After the storm passes, that is."

"That sounds like an interesting idea." Michael gave me a squeeze. I looked up at him, staring deep into those kind eyes of his. "What do you think, Sandy? Shall we go for a visit?"

I stayed silent for a moment to consider the question, then looked back at Anahera, regarding her profile thoughtfully as she watched the weather.

My first instinct would have been to say no, to stay safely holed up in our little fortress with the people I knew I could trust, but I knew that feeling stemmed from cowardice. Anahera was a good person, as was her son Hemi. I liked them both and felt that I could trust them, especially after I had seen the way Anahera reacted to finding out one of her brethren had been preying on women and girls for years before he'd joined her tribe.

She had evicted him from her tribe without hesitation, mutilated him and thrown him out into the wilds as punishment for his crime. I didn't have to go through a lengthy trial, recount my ordeal in great detail, and suffer through the horror of being judged by a jury. Nobody had tried to tell me that I'd been asking for it because of my gender or my state of dress, and nobody tried to pass it off as a misunderstanding. She had listened to me and confronted him, and when he was found guilty, her punishment had been swift.

In a way, I felt like I had gotten more justice from Anahera than I would have gotten in a court of law. I trusted her. With that thought in mind, I nodded my consent and we began to make plans for the nearest thing to a vacation that any of us had taken in a very long time.

Chapter Three

The storm raged for almost a day, tearing branches from trees and uprooting any plants and fixtures that were not lucky enough to be protected from the winds. Every so often, we'd hear the sound of something breaking or being thrown around, but we were safe within our precious haven.

No one even considered sending Anahera and Hemi back out into the storm. It just wasn't an option. Their chances of making it home safely on those little farm bikes would be slim to non-existent. Luckily, our hotel had plenty of spare bedrooms and furniture that had survived the years, so we set them up with beds and insisted they stay the night. I wasn't terribly surprised that neither of them protested.

Without power, lunch and dinner were solemn events. I did my best to cheer everyone up by assembling a salad with canned meat for protein, but I lacked my sister's flair for creative cooking.

Skye didn't leave her room the entire day. At mealtimes, I braved the weather to bring her food, but she barely even looked at me. Each time I checked on her, she was just sitting on her bed, staring out her window at the raging storm, clutching that tiny pink teddy bear. She ate the food I left for her, but never made any comments.

Night seemed to fall earlier than normal that evening, because the sun was obscured by the roiling clouds. I left the others to finish cleaning up the kitchen by candlelight, and went back upstairs to bring Skylar a little lantern for her room. For some reason, the thought of leaving her brooding in the dark made me feel sick to my stomach.

She was still sitting in exactly the same spot when I arrived, her eyes a million miles away. When I set the lantern down and turned it on, she stirred a little, as though coming out of a dream. Her head turned towards me. I looked back at her, and found her watching me with eyes that were sunken and hollow from grief. My heart lurched at the sight of the sorrow etched on her face.

I sat down beside her and wrapped my arm around her slender frame; she felt tiny and fragile now that the weight of her pregnancy had begun to fade. She'd always been slender and small-boned, but now it felt like I could break her if I gripped her too firmly. I wondered if that was how Michael felt, all those times when he held me as gently as if I were a porcelain doll. Now, I understood the feeling.

"Anahera invited us to stay with her clan for a couple of days." I found myself talking to her automatically, even if she was away with the fairies. "So we're going for a trip once the storm is over. Just for a little while. Anahera says it'll be good for us to get away for a bit. I think she's right. What do you think?" I wasn't expecting an answer, so when I got one it just about gave me a heart attack.

"I think… I'd like that." Skye shifted and snuggled up against me. "She's really nice."

"Yeah, she is," I agreed, fighting to contain the flood of relief that poured through me from the simple fact that my little sister was talking to me again. "She's downstairs with Hemi and the others. We were thinking of playing a game to pass the time. Why don't you come and play with us?"

"A game?" She stirred and looked up at me with those big blue eyes, set into a face that looked so hauntingly similar to my mother's that it made my gut twist. "What kind of game?"

"Well, I found a few different ones while I was out exploring the other day. We could play a card game, if you want?" I suggested. She wrinkled her nose and shook her head.

"No, card games are boring." She pulled a face, but apparently I had her attention now. Sometimes I had to remind myself that she was only eighteen. Our relationship had become a bit peculiar. To me, she'd gone from being an adorable eight-year-old to being a grown, very capable young woman without me having a chance to watch the change happen naturally. I was still struggling to work out how to cope with that.

Sometimes I didn't know whether to treat her like an adult or a child. Luckily, she seemed to understand how jarring the transition was for me, and was generally patient with me.

"What about a board game?" I suggested. "I found Cluedo, Monopoly, and Scrabble. Take your pick."

"Oh, I remember Monopoly." Her eyes lit up. "We used to play that with Mum and Dad."

"Yeah, that's right. I don't remember the rules, but I'm sure we can figure it out." I gave her a squeeze and held her close until she finally smiled and nodded.

That was all the permission I needed. I grabbed her hand and dragged her off for an evening of frivolity before she could lose herself in depression again.

The others joined us in the common room, and helped us to set up the board. None of us really remembered how to play and the instructions were faded with age, but between us we managed to figure out enough to get the game going. The pieces were dirty and tarnished, and the old paper money was wrinkled, but no one really minded. Although I offered to play with my sister as a team, she rejected the help with a stubborn determination that made my heart swell with joy. That was the Skylar I knew. Her personality was coming back at last.

We played long into the night by lantern light. Eventually the doctor retired and took Madeline off to her bed, leaving five of us to battle it out. I fell quickly to my sister's brutal wiles, and Michael and Anahera soon joined me in bankruptcy.

Defeated, we sat back to watch the two youngest members of our groups battle it out, their faces masks of intense concentration. Then it all came tumbling down, when one unlucky roll of the dice made Hemi's little race car land on Mayfair. It was stacked high with Skye's motels, so that was the end of him.

"I can't believe it. Beaten by a girl," Hemi complained jokingly.

"And I'd beat you again, too," she retorted, leaning over to smack his arm.

"Hey now! You're not allowed to hit me," Hemi protested, holding his hands up in mock defence. "That's not fair, since I'm not allowed to hit you back."

"Seems perfectly fair to me." Skye grinned wickedly at him. "You think I'm *only* a girl. I'll show you!"

A crack of thunder so loud that it made the windows rattle punctuated Skylar's sentence, and made us all jump. We exchanged looks, and then melted into communal laughter at our own expense.

"Okay, children; off to bed," Anahera commanded once the levity subsided, making shooing motions at Skylar and her son. I expected protests, but neither of them said a word. They stood obediently and departed, still teasing one another as they went out the door.

I watched them go, then turned and looked at Anahera with a raised eyebrow. "You know, if I tried that I'd probably just get jeered at. What's your secret?"

"My secret?" She laughed and shook her head. "I'm old enough to be both their mothers. Mum will always be Mum."

I heard Michael chuckle behind me, then felt a hand run across my shoulders. "Hear that? You're just too young to be the boss."

"Hey!" I pouted at him. "You're only four years older than me. That means you're too young to be the boss, too."

"You're both youngsters." Anahera peered at us with a peculiar little half-smile on her face. "Therefore, I am the boss."

"This entire conversation is silly," I announced, sliding down off the couch to start picking up the game pieces and putting them away. There was a soft grunt as Michael slid down beside me to help, while Anahera watched on from her armchair.

"Yes, it is," she agreed thoughtfully, absently crossing her long legs. "A little levity is good for everyone, though. I am glad you convinced Skylar to join us. This was a wonderful idea."

I glanced up at her, and she smiled at me, a smile so beautiful that it made my heart do a somersault in my chest. There was just something about that woman that was so strong and so charismatic that her praise made me feel like a puppy who'd gotten a treat. I smiled back, shyly, and looked back down at the strewn game pieces.

"Thanks. I'm just glad that she agreed. I was really worrying about her." I absently reached out to touch Michael's hand as it happened to pass by me while gathering up motels. He hesitated, then gave my hand a squeeze, understanding my need for contact.

"We were all worried about her," he said quietly in that deep, grainy voice of his, then shot a glance towards Anahera. "There were a few days where we thought that she might…"

He trailed off and looked at me, leaving me to finish the sentence. I did, but only with great reluctance. "…kill herself."

"Ah," Anahera murmured. She thought about it for a second, then shook her head. "I don't think you need to worry about that. Your sister is a very strong and determined young woman. She just needs time to sort through her grief and find her own strength again. The two of you are much alike in that manner."

"Me?" I looked up again, bewildered. "You must be kidding. I'm the biggest wimp in the universe, just ask Michael."

"Wimp? Hardly." Michael laughed. He grabbed my shoulder and gave me a light shake. "You just have a warped sense of your own self-worth, sweetheart."

"He's right," Anahera agreed, amusement flickering across her face. "How long were you alone out there? A decade, was it? You went through terrible things all by yourself, with no one to support you, no one to fall back on, and no one to keep you grounded. And yet, here you are, alive and well, and forming bonds with other people. You have had to learn how to have friends and how to trust all over again, and you're doing very well at it from what I can see."

I felt my cheeks grow hot with embarrassment, but

when I opened my mouth to protest Michael cut me off.

"Oh no, I know what you're going to say," he scolded gently, sliding an arm around my shoulders. "Don't you even think about it. She's bang on the money, and you know it."

Tears sprang into my eyes. Suddenly, I found myself fascinated by the tiny game pieces in my hands, unable to meet their eyes. "I don't feel like I'm doing very well."

"You are." Anahera joined us on the floor, and reached over to take the game pieces from my hand. She set them aside, and then wrapped her hands around mine. "Darling, I know that you struggle. I saw the way you looked at me when we first met, and I know that look. You have been trapped for a very long time in a prison fate made for you, and now you're learning to cope with the world outside that prison." She reached over and cupped my chin in her hand, forcing me to meet her gaze. "You are doing very well, and I want you to remember that. Promise me."

I wasn't sure what to say to that so I mumbled something inarticulate. She smiled and shook her head but let it pass. She eased herself back into her chair, leaving me to resume picking up the scattered toys.

Michael was never one to leave me to sulk when he knew I was feeling a bit down, so he distracted me with a playful pinch on the bottom. I squealed in surprise and leapt away from him, then laughed and gave him an equally playful slap across the shoulder in return.

"Ow! I was just about to point out that it's been

weeks since you hit me, too. So much for that," he teased. I flung a tiny metal shoe at him in retaliation. He yelped as it bounced off his arm and tumbled away, then went scrambling after it. When he found it, he flung it right back at me. It missed me and hit Anahera in the shin instead.

"Hey now, you two," she scolded us with amusement, leaning down to grab the fallen toy and toss it into the box with the others. "I thought you were supposed to be the responsible ones?"

"Me?" I snorted indignantly and flapped a hand. "God, no. He's the responsible one. Did he tell you he used to be a police officer?"

"He did mention it, yes." She gave Michael a long, pointed look. This time, it was Michael's turn to look flustered by her scrutiny.

"I was a constable, yeah," he admitted. "I guess that's why I feel like I'm responsible for protecting these troublemakers. Or arresting them, I haven't decided which yet." He shot an impish grin at me, and I laughed.

"Yeah, right," I scoffed. "If you arrested me, where would you put me?"

"Oh, I have some ideas..." he teased right back, and then gave me a wink that made me start blushing all over again.

Anahera watched with amusement, clearly enjoying the sight of our youthful exuberance. Then, out of the blue, she hit us with a question that stunned us both. "So, when are you two getting married?"

I stared at her, and then glanced at Michael to find

him looking just as dumbstruck.

"Er... well, but we've only known each other for about six weeks..." he stumbled awkwardly, absently rubbing at the back of his neck. As I watched, I saw a flush of colour rise in his cheeks and the side of his throat, mirroring the rush of heat I felt in my own face.

"Life is short and brutal in this day and age," Anahera said with a shrug. "You two are clearly besotted with one another. God only knows how much time you'll have together. You should make the most of it while you can."

"But, we haven't even... you know, done 'it'," I stumbled, feeling completely out of my element; I'd never discussed my personal issues with anyone besides Michael.

Anahera's brows shot up. "Really now? I never would have guessed." She paused to think about it, then a flicker of understanding passed through her eyes. "Ah, but I suppose I should have. Alas, that is something I cannot advise on."

"It's okay." I looked down at my feet, pretending to be fascinated by anything that didn't involve making eye-contact with anyone. I heard rather than saw when Anahera stood up and stretched, in a rustling of cloth and denim.

"I'm sure the two of you will resolve that matter in your own time, when you're ready," she said in a gentle, maternal tone. "For now, I believe I shall retire. Assuming the storm passes by morning, we have a journey ahead of us."

Then she was gone, stepping around our mess to leave Michael and me both feeling awkward and trying very hard not to look at one another. After the door clicked closed behind her, it left the room nearly silent. The only sound was the shuffling of paper and the clicking of metal and plastic pieces, barely audible over the raging storm outside.

Once we put the last of the pieces away, I slid the lid back onto the box and shoved it into a corner where it was out of the way. Finally, I glanced up and found Michael watching me with a look of pure confusion on his face. Our eyes met for a fraction of a second before he looked away, studying his hands with great interest. Neither of us knew what to say.

Finally, he broke the silence. "Do you... think she's right?"

"No, I don't think so." I drew a deep breath and let it out as a sigh. Marriage? Good God, I barely knew the man. "It's way too soon. I mean, yes I love you, but... I think we need to give it time. We have no idea where this might go. Marriage is a huge commitment, and we have no idea what will happen once the hormones wear off."

"Yeah..." he trailed off, staring thoughtfully down at the ground. Suddenly, he looked up at me with the strangest look on his face. "But the possibility is still open for the future, right?"

My heart just about broke at the expression on his face. I smiled and shuffled over to cuddle up against him. "Definitely still open, when the time is right."

His expression relaxed, and his arms slid around me to hold me close. "Okay. Good. You know, one day. Just in case."

"Right." I hid a smile against his broad chest. Sometimes he could be such a little boy. Sweet, but completely transparent and utterly without guile. It was all part of his charm, though. Thirty-two years old and built like a brick shithouse, but so emotionally inexperienced that I could see right through him. At least I had the experiences of my rambunctious youth to fall back on. As far as I could tell, he'd never even kissed another woman unless you included his mother.

As though reading my mind, I felt strong fingers cup my chin again and then his lips closed over mine. He had learned a lot in the time since we'd met, and apparently he was determined to show me just how much. I definitely wasn't complaining. Practice makes perfect – and we were getting a lot of practice.

Chapter Four

We spent a noisy night huddled in our room, hiding from the storm's wrath. Every so often something would bang, or crash, or rattle and wake us up, so by the time morning came none of us felt like we'd gotten much sleep.

The sunrise was a beautiful thing, though. The world took on a rosy pallet that cast tendrils of colour across the arc of the heavens. Clouds still marred the sky, but the sunrise turned them from grey to pink, and made them seem impossibly beautiful.

I awoke nestled in Michael's arms, like I did every morning, except this time the dawn light had painted our room in lovely colours. I stretched and rolled over, studying Michael's profile in the vivid dawn light. He looked so peaceful when he was sleeping, so young and vulnerable. A surge of hot emotion welled up in my belly; I found myself struggling to stay in control.

I lay my head back down on the pillow beside him, watching him sleep. With one hand, I reached up and trailed a finger along his jaw, feeling the fascinating roughness of his stubble beneath my fingertip. He grimaced in his sleep, wrinkled up his face and mumbled something I couldn't hear, then let out a deep breath and relaxed again. Something deep inside me quivered.

Soon, I promised it, and this time I really meant it. For all the pain I'd suffered, no matter how broken my psyche was, I really did love that man with an intensity that almost hurt. We lay together in sleep, nude and yet innocent, comfortable with one another in a way that I'd never experienced before.

I slipped a hand beneath the blankets and trailed my fingers down his chest. His skin was so smooth, with a light dusting of dark curls in just the right places. My fingers drifted lower, tracing the line of hair that adorned his belly just below the navel. Thoughtful and inquisitive, I followed it lower…

I suddenly realised that he was aroused, and the discovery sent a flash of heat tingling through my limbs. Was he dreaming about me? I often dreamed of him, of all the wonderful things we would one day do together. Equally often, I woke confused and excited, with my most basic animal instincts at war against learned behaviour.

Oh, but he wasn't asleep anymore. His dark eyes were open just a sliver, watching my face. He shifted and drew me closer, burying his face in the curve of my neck.

"Taking advantage of me in my sleep again?" he murmured, his voice so soft and deep that it sent a shiver down my spine. Suddenly, his arms tightened and he had me on my back, belly to belly, chest to chest. His lips closed on mine, a hot, deep kiss that told me so much more than he meant it to. I understood intuitively that yes, he had been dreaming about me.

I had no chance to answer his accusation; my breath was stolen away by the passion of that kiss. He had me pinned, his hands roving across my body, and yet I felt no fear of him. My policeman, my lover. He would never hurt me. I could feel his body pressed against me, but true to his word, he resisted every one of his natural impulses and held himself back until I could tell him I was ready for him.

His lips left mine and drifted lower, seeking out that sensitive spot just below the corner of my jaw. Nibbling, kissing, driving me wild. Oh, I was so ready for him.

I struggled to draw the breath to tell him that, but just as I did, I opened my eyes–

–and found myself face to face with the most enormous, horrifying insect I'd ever seen in my life, squatting on the pillow right beside my head with its talons waving threateningly in the air. The breath I had drawn to surrender myself to him completely turned into a bloodcurdling scream. Poor Michael just about levitated off of me and ended up on the floor, while I fled to the far end of the bed and had myself a nice little heart attack in the corner.

The weta – a huge native insect that resembled nothing so much as the offspring of a gigantic cricket and the Devil himself – was not impressed.

Michael shoved himself up off the floor in a tangle of blankets, trying to figure out what had me so horrified. He spotted the enormous insect immediately, and then flopped right back onto the floor laughing himself silly at my expense.

"That is so not funny!" I was almost in tears, huddled up at the end of the bed. Then it hit me all of a sudden. It was just a bug. I'd seen them a hundred times before. It wasn't really dangerous, despite its horrifying appearance. The worst it could do was draw a little blood. Okay, it was slightly funny.

I burst out laughing, the romantic mood completely gone. I hurled one of our non-bug-covered pillows at Michael. It hit him square in the face, but it was only a pillow so all it did was make him laugh harder.

With great difficulty, he pried himself out of his tangle of blankets and snatched up his hat from where we'd left it the day before. Naked as a jaybird and armed only with a hat, he captured the offending insect, then yanked open the window and flung the creature outside. I joined him at the window just in time to see the huge bug hit the ground below and roll a couple of times. A second later, it was up and off at a run, uninjured but horribly offended by our rude behaviour. Michael looked at me and I looked back, both of us still struggling to control the urge to laugh.

"Fear not, madam! Captain Bugcatcher is here to protect you," he announced, flailing a playful salute.

I'd had about as much as I could stand, and that

crossed the line. I dissolved into hysterics and collapsed back into bed, laughing until tears rolled down my cheeks and my stomach hurt. It was clearly not going to be a morning for love-making, but at least we both got a good laugh out of it.

***

Later, dressed and finally back under control, we descended the stairs to the kitchen. There, we found Anahera, Hemi, the doctor and Maddy sitting around the table, while Skylar stirred something savoury-smelling on top of a bench-top gas cooker.

"Power's still off?" I queried, fighting down a wave of relief at the sight of my baby sister back in the kitchen. Not only did that mean she was feeling better, but she was the best cook we had. All our bellies welcomed the sight of her with a spatula in hand.

"Yes," Anahera answered, then she turned and gave us a strange look. "Glad you could join us. When we heard all that screaming, we were concerned someone was getting murdered."

"All that... oh." I stared at her, unsure what to say. Although I could feel the heat rising in my cheeks, I couldn't fight the uncontrollable urge to start laughing all over again. Luckily, Michael found the willpower to answer while I was still in stitches, with an enormous grin on his face.

"She woke up to the biggest weta I've ever seen, on her pillow," he explained, using his hands to indicate the size of the beast. "It scared the hell out of us both.

I guess it must have come inside on one of those branches that got blown about yesterday. Fear not, good citizens! The demon has now been evicted from the building."

He promptly struck a heroic pose, and soon everyone was laughing right along with me – except for little Madeline, who sat regarding us with eyes that said she thought we were all crazy.

Breakfast was a cheerful affair in comparison to the solemn meals we'd shared the day before. The storm had passed, and although the wind still whined around our building, it left us feeling like we'd survived a disaster.

After we'd finished eating our scrambled eggs, we went outside to inspect the damage done by the storm. Our little garden had survived mostly intact thanks to our forethought, but the outside of the building was a disaster zone. The remains of one large tree lay uprooted across the road, and down the street we could see another, smaller tree leaning up against the side of the building next to it at a drunken angle, its roots partially dislodged from the earth.

Leaves and debris were strewn everywhere, including large shards of broken glass that threatened our feet as we picked our way around the motel to inspect it. Our building had survived mostly intact, and I was amazed to see my haphazard construction on the roof was still standing strong. It'd take a bit of effort to clean it up, but only a couple of boards were missing completely.

A few of the other buildings in town had suffered far worse than ours. Michael nudged me and pointed at a portion of a roof that lay slumped across an overgrown lawn a short distance down the road, reducing the jungle to a crushed mess.

"Glad none of us were under that," I murmured to him. He nodded, but I saw the look on his face. He was thinking the same thing I was: Ryan may have been out in that weather last night. As angry as he was at Skylar's former fiancé for abandoning her, no one deserved the full force of nature's wrath.

I reassured myself with the thought that he'd survived just as many storms as I had over the years. He would know the warning signs, know when to go find shelter, and what kind of buildings would be sturdy enough to survive the weather. New Zealand was an island, and we were all Aotearoa's children. Our country had been subjected to many different kinds of storms over the years, not to mention the geological activity, floods and even tidal waves. You couldn't go anywhere without seeing some kind of natural damage.

Years ago, I'd honestly thought that my number was up. I had been travelling near the centre of the island when an earthquake struck that was ten times more violent than anything I'd felt before. I had fallen to the ground and hadn't been able to get back up for what felt like forever; in the distance, a massive plume of ash had shot up into the sky.

To my eternal relief, I later discovered that it had only been Mount Taranaki venting its red-hot disinterest at the world, as it did on a semi-regular basis. The eruption had caused little damage beyond light ash fall. Nature was a fickle mistress, and she scolded us often; we'd all survived it before.

He's probably fine, I reassured myself, then took Michael's hand and led him back towards the others.

***

Anahera and her son stayed long enough to help us repair some of the damage to our home. Our motel was low, squat, and solid; the work mostly involved clearing debris, so that it wouldn't endanger us in the future.

The wind blew in brief but violent gusts as we worked, yet it only took a few hours to clear up the worst of the mess. There was nothing we could do about the tree that blocked the road without putting all our people at risk, so we decided to just leave it where it was. At least it meant convenient firewood nearby, or a makeshift barricade in a pickle.

Surprise, surprise. The barricade idea was mine. It's not that I'm paranoid, per se. I just like to be prepared for every contingency. That was the same thing that I told Anahera when we were debating whether or not to bring our weapons on our trip west to visit her home.

"It's not that I don't trust you or your people," I explained to the group as we stood around the kitchen, making plans, "but there are a lot of dangers between here and your place that we should be able to defend ourselves against."

"I don't think it's necessary," Michael protested. "We're only going for a short vacation, and it's just a few hours walk away."

"Hemi was only a few hours from home when the pig found him," I pointed out. The youth grunted in agreement.

"She's right, man," Hemi said, then pointed at his bandaged side. "Don't forget about the bugger that's out there taking pot shots at us, too."

The others looked undecided, but it was Anahera who broke the tie.

"I agree with Sandy. You should bring your weapons along." She looked at me and smiled. "However, I appreciate you making the effort to ask my permission before you made the decision. Thank you."

"Of course," I stammered; her praise always left me feeling a little flustered. "You don't bring a shotgun to a mate's house without asking first. That's just bad manners."

"Your mother clearly raised you well." Anahera's smile broadened.

"Well, it's settled then," Michael finally agreed reluctantly. "Everyone go get your things, we'll leave in fifteen minutes."

Those of us who were going filtered out to collect our packs, and left the doctor to chat with our guests. He'd decided to stay behind with Madeline rather than come with us, protesting that our gardens still needed care and someone should protect our home base. I assumed that he just didn't like being out of his element, but I hadn't said anything. If Michael hadn't been so determined to go and Skye wasn't so clearly in need of an adventure, then I would have stayed home as well.

Home. It felt funny using that word, particularly to describe a run-down old motel and a tatty former video store. Michael slipped his hand into mine as we walked back towards his room, and I was forced to quickly reassess that thought. Maybe it wasn't so strange after all. Home is where the heart is, and mine was here.

He opened the window to our walkway between the buildings and offered me a hand up, which I accepted. I slipped out onto the damp planks, testing their stability carefully, then I crossed the alley to the top floor of my old video store to gather my things. Michael stayed behind, to pack his own bags.

My backpack lay in a distant corner of my bedroom, slumped sadly against the wall like an abandoned toy. Unlike Michael, I'd taken the time to clean out the drawers in my room, and replaced all the former occupant's belongings with my own. I didn't have much in the way of personal possessions, but I had acquired a few and it felt nice to have them organised in my drawers.

During my original expedition through the area, I'd spent a good deal of time exploring the town and scavenging anything that looked like it might fit me. When I had returned from Hamilton with my new friends in tow, my prizes still waited where I left them.

Over the course of the last few weeks, I tried everything on and sorted the ones that fitted from the ones that didn't. My sister benefited from anything too small for me, and everything else went into storage. You never knew what you'd need to use for trading one day.

I pulled my drawers open one by one and added enough clean clothing to my backpack to last me three days. Our plan was to stay for a couple of days then head back home, so I doubted that I would need any more than that. If our plans changed, so be it. It wouldn't be the first time I'd had to go a bit longer than preferable without a change of clothing.

I had started to relax my usual dress code recently, too. During the decade I spent on my own, I'd usually worn military surplus, which was abundantly available if you knew where to look. It wasn't pretty, but it was hardy, long-wearing and easy to clean. Settling into life with my group had made me reassess my priorities. I found myself wearing casual civilian clothing more and more. It was mostly jeans and t-shirts, but I did have a few nice outfits that I'd hidden away to surprise Michael with one day. It amused me to imagine the look of shock on his face if he ever saw me wearing a dress.

I pondered that fact as I changed into my travel clothes: my old cargo fatigues, paired with a dusky grey tank top. Would I even know how to get dolled up anymore? I had gotten a wee bit of experience between puberty and when the plague hit, but a decade had passed since then. Michael had one up on me there. All he had to do was put on his police uniform, and suddenly he was the sexiest man alive. What did I have? Not much of anything, really.

With a hefty sigh, I sorted through the neat row of items sitting on top of my dresser. My GPS went into one pocket, my taser into another, my first aid kit into a third, and my gun went into my backpack. That should be enough for a couple of days in friendly territory, if I didn't give in to my natural urge towards caution.

What's the worst that could happen? I told myself as I picked up my pack and headed back to the window on the landing. *Lake Ruatuna's two hours away at most, over open farmland. If something happens, we'll just come home.*

Famous last words, my inner cynic contradicted, but I decided to ignore it. Michael scolded me regularly for being too pessimistic, so I had made it my personal mission to try and stay positive, for his sake. Positive, but realistic. I wasn't about to let a cheerful disposition get all of us killed.

I eased myself out the window onto the walkway, and closed the window behind me. Although it wasn't locked from inside, someone would have to get through the motel to reach it. That seemed pretty unlikely. I crossed the space between my window and Michael's and ducked back into his room. just in time to be confronted by a very nice pair of tight, manly buttocks.

"Well, hello there," I teased as I hopped off the window sill onto the bed below.

Michael shot a glance over his shoulder at me. "Oh, you're back. That was fast."

"I pack efficiently. Call it a skill." I gave him a smile, then flicked a pointed look down over his body. "Why are you naked?"

"What?" He glanced at me again, and then looked down. "Oh, right. I got distracted. Have you seen my vest?"

I flung myself down on my belly and reached under the bed, to pull out a dark blue body armour chest piece. "This one?"

"That's it!" He brightened as soon as he saw it, then came over and took it from me with a smile. "What would I do without you?"

"Lose things, apparently," I answered dryly. "You put it under there last week. Did you forget already?"

"I'm just not quite used to being here yet," he admitted sheepishly, turning his back to me as he got dressed. As sad as I was to see that delicious bottom covered up, we weren't going to go anywhere without pants. "I lived in that bunker for a very long time. I'm so used to everything always being in the same place, and now it's not."

"You'll get used to it," I said, lazing on my belly to watch him pulling on his boxer-briefs and jeans.

"I know, I know; it just takes time to adapt." He gave me that sweet smile of his, then tugged a close-fitting white t-shirt over his head. Once he'd straightened his clothes, he wandered over to plop down on the bed beside me. I felt the warmth of a hand on the small of my back, followed by inquisitive fingers slipping up beneath the hem of my top. "You understand that better than anyone."

"I guess I do," I agreed, rolling onto my back to look up at him. His hand slid over my skin, until it came to rest on my belly. He stared down at me thoughtfully, trailing gentle fingers over the smooth curve of my stomach, as though considering moving them higher. If he did, the chances of us setting off on time were slim to none.

He let out a long, deep sigh and reluctantly removed his hand from beneath my clothing. Self-control could be difficult at times, even for the best of us, but he was a good man and tried so hard. I felt a sudden rush of affection towards him and popped upright to plant a kiss on his cheek.

Michael's brows shot up at the gesture. Suddenly, before I knew what was happening, he caught me in a playful embrace and bore me down onto the bed. I found myself pinned down by strong, gentle hands, and could only squeal helplessly while he planted kisses on my belly. He released me a few seconds later, but it was so sudden and unexpected that it got me laughing all over again.

"You're so weird," I scolded him, giggling; he just grinned right back at me and went about strapping on his vest. It was only then that I realised he'd been looking for it because he intended to wear it for our trip. My levity oozed away. "Wait, you didn't want to bring the guns, but you're going to wear that?"

"I thought about what you said downstairs," he admitted, tugging a strap tighter against his skin, "and I realised that you were right. I don't think Anahera's *whanau* mean us any harm, but anything could happen. We should try to be prepared."

"I've trained you well, my pet," I teased him. While he was busy, I wriggled back over to close the window above his bed, so the rain and insects couldn't get in while we were away. "We'll make a proper survivalist out of you yet."

"I hope not," he answered dryly, then he reached over to poke my bottom while he could reach it easily. "Positivity!"

"Hey, hey, what's with the poking?" I spun around and poked him right back. "I keep telling you, there's a difference between negativity and realism."

"Ah, but there must be a balance, grasshopper," he told me sagely.

"So you're the Yin to my Yang, Officer Chan?" I asked, moving back to the edge of the bed to sit beside him.

"Something like that, except it's the other way around. Yin represents the feminine and yang the masculine." He gave me a quirky sideways smile, and started putting his socks and boots on while we were talking.

"No, I'm pretty sure I meant exactly what I said," I countered dryly. A little too dryly, apparently; it took him a second to cotton on to what I'd said. When he finally put two and two together, he shot me an amused glance.

"Really now? I'm pretty sure that *I'm* the one with

the—"

"Maybe so, but which one of us hits like a truck?" I waved a fist at him playfully.

"Okay, you win that point," he conceded, laughing.

Dressed at last, Michael rose to his feet and stretched languidly. Although the action was quite innocent, it distracted me from our conversation; I watched with interest, admiring his physique. He really was a remarkable man: mentally, physically, and emotionally. Suddenly, I felt a little inadequate by comparison.

Michael glanced over his shoulder at me, as though sensing instinctively that something was amiss. "What's the matter, sweetheart? You're being quiet. It worries me when you're quiet."

"It worries you?" I couldn't help but laugh at that comment. "I'm quiet by nature; why would that worry you?"

"No, you're not," he said, reaching out to take my hand. With that wonderful, gentle strength of his, he drew me up to my feet and wrapped one arm around my waist to hold me up against him. "You're quite gregarious by nature, love. The only time you're quiet is when you're scared, angry, or sleeping. Or when you're thinking, but I can usually tell when you're doing that because of the smoke coming out of your ears."

"Smoke!" I put on an offended expression. "I'll have you know I was thinking just a moment ago, mister. You're so mean to me. Just because I'm blonde doesn't mean I'm dumb!"

"You know that I love your hair, and that I don't think you're dumb at all," he said, his humour fading. With his free hand, he slipped a finger beneath my chin and tilted my face up towards his. "Penny for your thoughts, then?"

Oh, compliments. I still wasn't used to those. Not that I wanted him to stop, but I had no idea how to respond. Feeling the heat rising in my cheeks all over again, I paused for a second to formulate my answer before I replied. "Well... I was thinking about you, actually."

"Me?" He raised a brow, looking curious.

"Yeah, it's just that..." I broke eye-contact and looked away, when a wave of shyness reared its ugly head. It had been a long time since I'd talked to a boy about my feelings. Hell, it'd been a long time since I had a boy to have feelings about.

No, not a boy, I corrected myself. *A man. A wonderful, sweet, loving man who deserved to know he was doing a good job.*

"You're just so perfect, Michael," I admitted, staring at some point beyond his right shoulder as I tried to organise my thoughts. "You're so kind and generous, and you always know just the right thing to say. I just... sometimes I feel like I don't deserve you. I try to tell myself that you must see something in me, but you're just so amazing that I feel like I'm nobody compared to you."

His expression softened, and his arm tightened around me protectively. "Oh, Sandy..."

"I know!" I groaned and rolled my head back, ashamed of myself for feeling that way at all. "I know that it's ridiculous, and that it just sounds whiny and pathetic. I'm a shame to empowered women everywhere. You probably just think I'm fishing for compliments, but I'm really not. I just... don't know how to—"

"Shh." He silenced me with a quick kiss, then hugged me. "You don't have to explain it to me, sweetheart. I feel the exact same way every time I'm with you."

"...What?" I stared at him, stunned. "You feel inadequate beside *me*?"

"Sometimes, yes," he admitted. "I wish that I had half the strength I see in you. Every time I think about what you've been through and survived all on your own, it makes me feel sick for you, proud of you, and envious of your resilience all at the same time." His strong arms tightened around me, not enough to hurt but enough to make me feel safe and secure, while his words made me feel so vulnerable. "It makes me want to be more than I am, for your sake."

I wasn't sure what to say to that. My emotions were a mess at the best of times, and when I felt weak and exposed it only got harder to stay in control. Part of me wanted to laugh, part of me wanted to cry, and part of me wanted to rip his clothes off and have my merry way with him right then and there. Unfortunately, the 'cry' part won. Tears sprang unbidden into my eyes. I buried my face in his chest to hide them as I thought over what he'd said.

Never one to let me mope unmolested, Michael used the opportunity to unleash his wicked sense of humour. He leaned down and put his lips right against my ear to whisper, "Plus, you're fucking gorgeous." Then, he grabbed my bottom in both hands and gave it a vigorous squeeze.

The gesture took me completely by surprise; I squealed like a stuck pig. A second later, I laughed and shoved myself out of his embrace, rubbing my poor, abused bottom. Then his words struck me, and I felt like a teenage girl with her first crush all over again.

"You really think I'm pretty...?"

He'd said it before, but it still felt strange. I'm aware of my physical properties, of course — every person judges his- or herself in front of a mirror at least once in their lifetime — but hearing the words from the lips of someone you adored was a whole other story. It made me feel all twisted up inside, a Gordian knot of tangled emotions.

"No," he chided, which shattered my daydream and took me by surprise, but a second later he smiled and clarified his words. "I do believe I said 'fucking gorgeous'. There's a difference."

"Oh." Man, he was really good at rendering me speechless. Not sure what else to say, I settled for being polite. Mama may have raised a crazy girl, but she didn't raise a rude one. "Thank you, I think."

"You think? Hah!" Michael grabbed both of our bags and draped an arm around my shoulders. "Come on, the others will be waiting."

Unable to resist the allure of his boyish charm, I let myself be led away. Sure enough, the others were waiting in the foyer, ready to depart. Skye took one look at us as we made our way down the stairs and rolled her eyes. "Oh God, Sandy's mutating into a tomato again. What'd you do this time, Michael?"

"He didn't do anything," I said in Michael's defence. By the time we reached them, my emotions had started to settle down, shifting from a turbulent ocean of conflicting pride and self-consciousness into a buoyant sort of happiness. "He was just giving me a pep talk, that's all."

"Sure, he was." Skylar gave me a disbelieving look, but let it drop. Instead, she handed me a small jar, full of what looked like mayonnaise. "Here. The doctor made us some sunscreen. We probably won't need it today, but bring it anyway. You know, just in case." She shot Michael a long, pointed look. The filthy look that he gave her in return made me smile. The relationship between my sister and my lover was an endless source of amusement to me. It was like an antagonistic brother/sister relationship, which was kind of appropriate, considering the circumstances.

"I'll make sure to put some on if the sun comes out," I promised, cutting them both off before the banter could turn into an actual argument. "We should go. I'm not sure how long the weather's going to hold off."

Noises of agreement met my comment, and the

group of us finally pulled ourselves together enough to leave. Anahera and Hemi took the lead, wheeling their light farm bikes so the rest of us could keep pace. Skylar walked with them, looking bright and full of energy for the first time since she'd lost her baby. There was a spring in her step, and she quickly fell into conversation with our new friends.

Michael and I lagged behind. At some point he took my hand – or perhaps I took his, I'm not really sure. It just sort of happened, like it was the most natural thing in the world. We walked together in companionable silence, until a thought popped into my head that I felt the need to express.

"Sandrine."

"What?" He looked at me, one brow raised.

"My full first name. It's Sandrine," I explained. It was a trust thing; I didn't usually tell people my full first name, because it was too painful to hear it spoken out loud. Still, I trusted Michael. He deserved to know.

"Oh." He went silent while he thought that over, staring off into the distance.

"It was my grandmother's name," I elaborated for him, trying to explain why I felt so strongly about it. "I was named after her, but when I was little everyone called me Sandy so there wouldn't be any confusion. She... died."

"And now it hurts to hear her name," he finished for me.

I nodded, looking down at the long grass in front of my feet. "She made me promise, that when she got too sick to speak... she didn't want to become one of the wandering dead. My gun belonged to her, but she gave it to me. I had to... t-to..." I swallowed hard, struggling to get the words out.

Michael shook his head and gave my hand a gentle squeeze. "You don't have to say it, sweetheart. I understand. You had to kill her, because you loved her. Now every time you hear your own name, it reminds you of what you had to do."

Damn, he was good.

I nodded again, fighting back a wave of misery that threatened to bring tears to my eyes. Sweet and intuitive as always, Michael let me have some time to recover from the emotional onslaught.

"I already knew your full name," he finally admitted. Perplexed, I looked up at him, and he gave me a faint smile. "Your sister. She didn't tell me directly, but I overheard her when she was chasing us, back in the bunker."

"Oh, of course. I forgot about that." It made sense, now that I thought about it. Skylar had spit the dummy over something, and I had scampered away and hidden. Somehow, I'd ended up hiding right beside Michael. Of course he had heard. "Well, geez. Way to ruin it. That was supposed to be how I was going to show you I finally trust you with my big secret."

"It still works," he answered softly, his smile growing. "You telling me means way more than overhearing your sister screaming at you. You don't have to worry, though. I won't use it unless you ask me to. I couldn't bear to do anything that upsets you."

"Thank you." I smiled back, relieved that he was so understanding. That he'd known all along and hadn't said a word, even in jest, meant more to me than words could possibly express.

We walked in contented silence for a long time after that.

Chapter Five

Although it wasn't far as the crow flies, the journey took longer than it would have in the old days, even on foot. Ten years ago, you could have driven from Ohaupo to Lake Ngaroto in fifteen minutes, but Anahera told me that the roads were unreliable and overgrown. As we walked westwards, I started to see evidence of what she meant.

The farther we got from Ohaupo, the more wild and unpredictable the route became. Once, the area had been flat, green pastureland dotted by picturesque farm houses, but nature had gone mad in the decade since human supervision ended. The grass stood waist-high in places, and the debris from a hundred storms hindered us at every turn. It forced us to go slowly and carefully, particularly those of us with the bikes – a punctured tyre could turn a useful tool into trash.

Eventually, the grass gave way to young native bush. That came as a relief, since it was easier to negotiate the thin undergrowth than the long grass. That's not to say it was easy going, though; heavy ferns and bushes grabbed at our feet, forcing us to take a twisting path between the trees.

For whatever reason, the herds of feral farm animals seemed to have avoided these parts, letting the plants grow lush and verdant since there was nothing to keep them in check. Birds sang in the trees overhead, fell silent as we passed beneath them, then resumed their songs only once we were out of sight. The familiar, distinctive warble of a territorial tui made me smile.

"Keep an eye out for rabbit," Hemi said, keeping a wary eye on the ground near his feet. "Sometimes they get infected."

I'd seen them before, so the warning came as no great surprise to me, but Michael looked positively horrified. "Zombie bunnies? That's a thing?"

"Yeah." Hemi shrugged helplessly. "Not always, though. Just sometimes. I guess it depends on the bunny."

"Are they violent?" Michael asked. His expression was one of such distress that I felt an overwhelming urge to comfort him, despite the ridiculousness of it all.

"Nah." Hemi paused, then shot us a thoughtful look. "Well, not usually. Sometimes. We usually shoot them if we see them, just in case."

"The poor little things." Michael looked crestfallen. Suddenly, he realised we were all staring at him, and his expression turned defensive. "What? I like bunnies. They're cute. There's nothing wrong with a grown man liking bunnies."

"Whatever you say, honey." I patted his hand, amused. Who was I to judge? I liked bunnies, too. Just not zombie bunnies. Being the shining beacon of diplomacy that she was, Anahera discreetly distracted us.

"The path should be just over there," she said, pointing through the trees. I couldn't see anything, but our guides seemed confident that they knew where they were going. Sure enough, a few minutes later sunlight broke through the canopy and we emerged into a clearing.

My foot struck something solid as I stepped forward. I looked down, and saw railway sleepers nestled beneath the short grass. A glance in either direction confirmed my suspicion: the path continued along a tunnel framed by lush trees, the boughs arching high overhead but not encroaching on the path. Even after all these years, the old railway line was still a solid means of travel. Long after the trains had turned to rust, we could use the scars they left upon the landscape as a walkway. Our boots crunched across gravel as we travelled southwards, but the grass struggled to take root in it.

We travelled much faster once we were inside that emerald corridor. As we walked, I looked around and saw the tell-tale signs of human occupation emblazoned on the local plant life. The tracks left by human feet and small tyres grew in frequency the farther south we went, marking the routes that Anahera and her tribe travelled the most.

An hour later, we left the tracks and followed a narrow path that branched off to the west. This one showed even more obvious signs of human interest in the region; the trees had been cut back and the scrub cleared, to keep the passageway clear. After following the slender green corridor for a few minutes, the trees began to thin out. The sounds of civilization reached us before we saw it: a dog barked, accompanied by the distant murmur of voices raised in good-natured chatter, occasionally broken by the sound of laughter.

We rounded a bend and came to a halt as the camp opened up before us. Raw wooden palisades built atop earthen ramparts formed a wall, built up to a height of at least two metres. In front of the walls, a carefully-planned line of trenches and platforms marked the hillside, forming an impressively formidable defensive position.

Even I recognised the ingenuity of the design. If an enemy force wanted to get close to this village, they would have to negotiate the trenches and platforms to reach the walls, which would slow them down significantly. The heavy gates stood open at the moment, and a ramp had been lowered over the defences to welcome the travellers home.

Within the compound, I saw a mixture of old, pre-plague buildings, and newer, rough-hewn structures made from local materials. Rising high above the walls, an observation platform of carved logs stood silhouetted against the midday sun. I looked around and realised the land had been cleared for more than a hundred metres in any direction, so neither friend nor foe could approach without being spotted.

And spotted we were. The sentry shouted something I couldn't hear and waved broadly at us. Anahera and Hemi waved back.

"More than two hundred years ago, my ancestors fought the largest land battle in New Zealand's history on this very spot," Anahera told us, pride glinting in her eye. She swept her arm out towards the village, and bowed. "This may not compare to the mighty *pā* of my ancestors, but I am proud to call this spot home. *Haere mai*, my friends – welcome."

"Thank you," Michael murmured, his deep voice almost a rumble. "We appreciate being invited."

"You shared your home and your hearth with us; it is only fair that we return the favour." Anahera smiled, and beckoned for us to follow her. "I hope you will forgive us for skipping the formalities. As much as I try to keep my people's traditions alive, I have little patience for ceremony."

I was a little relieved to hear that. You could fit the amount I knew about traditional Maori welcoming ceremonies on the back of a 10 cent piece, and I hated the idea of doing something wrong and upsetting my new friends.

People had begun to gather near the entrance by the time we reached the ramp, a half-dozen men of all ages, shapes and sizes. A couple had lighter skin than the rest, indicating that they had other ethnicities mixed in with their Maori blood, but they didn't seem bothered by or excluded because of that fact. Anahera led us towards them, and as we drew closer I could hear the sound of excited chatter amongst them.

"You're the first women besides me that my boys have seen in quite a while, so be gentle on them." Anahera shot us a wink, and then turned her attention to making introductions.

It took some time for us to learn everyone's names, but they made us feel so welcome that the time flew by. I was relieved to discover that all of them were fluently bilingual, and excited to see new faces. Michael stayed close to me, to help keep me calm with his presence alone. Although I did feel a little uncomfortable at first, Anahera's brothers were perfect gentlemen. In no time at all, their friendliness and manners put me at ease.

Skylar seemed to enjoy the attention immensely. While I was content to let Michael do the talking for both of us, she went off on her own, and seemed happy to chatter to anyone that she could find. There was a natural effervescence to her personality that was finally getting the chance to bubble up to the surface; surrounded by so many friendly faces, she was in her element.

Once introductions were over, we were invited into the tiny fortress for lunch. I discovered to my amusement that the central building of the complex was actually an old yacht club. They had converted it and made it their own, decorating it with intricate carvings cut into the building's wooden framework. There were monsters and gods, men and women, all poised in the distinctively stylized poses traditional to Maori culture. I was fascinated. Handicrafts had been one of my interests since childhood, and the carvings had a professional look to them that surprised me.

"This place is amazing," I whispered to Michael as we were led off to the room they'd converted into a dining hall.

Despite my attempt to be discreet, Anahera overheard and shot me a smile. "Thank you, dear. I'm glad you approve."

I flushed with embarrassment, but there was no sign of sarcasm in her tone. "It is. I mean, these carvings – they're so detailed. Did you do them?"

"Me?" She laughed, and the sound of it reassured me. "Oh, if only I had that kind of skill! No, Ropata is our carver." A stocky man in his early forties looked up from where he had been busy sorting out something lunch-related, but Anahera just gave him a wave and a smile. "He apprenticed as a carpenter in his youth, then went on to learn a variety of other types of woodworking – including *whakairo rakau*, our traditional carving. It's possible that he may be the only master carver left alive."

"I'm glad that someone survived to keep the art going," I answered, pausing to admire a particularly elegant carving around the doorway. "It must be handy to have a proper carpenter in your group, too. I can build something simple and functional, but nothing like this. This is beautiful."

"It is," Anahera agreed. She touched my arm to

draw my attention away from the carvings, then led us to the long wooden table that filled the centre of the room. Instead of chairs, benches flanked its sides. As the guests of honour, she sat us right in the middle, with Michael and me together on one side, Skylar and herself opposite us.

Once we were settled, her comrades came in bearing steaming hot food on a mismatched assortment of platters. The smell of it made my mouth water even though most of the scents were unfamiliar to me. When one of the men set a platter near me, I suddenly realised why.

"Is that fish? Real, fresh fish?" I exclaimed, delighted. I was a poor hunter and even worse at fishing, so it had been years since I'd had any kind of fish except the canned kind. Killing animals for food wasn't in my nature, but I was perfectly happy to eat things that other people had killed for me. No sense in letting a living thing's life go to waste.

"Fresh from our lake. Don't worry, we make a point of fishing far from any of the contaminated parts now." Anahera smiled at us, and then leaned over to point out the different kinds of food as they were brought in. "That's catfish, and this is eel. That one over there is wild duck..."

The list went on. My eyes just about popped out of my head at the bounty before us. There was even freshly-baked bread, made with potato in the Maori way. I didn't care that it wasn't the kind of bread I'd grown up on. It was bread, and I hadn't eaten bread in almost a decade.

I'm not afraid to admit that I gorged myself like a pig, because Michael and Skylar did the same. Our new friends laughed and joked with us, pleased by our enthusiasm for their efforts. For once in my life, I didn't mind being laughed at. The meal was without a doubt the best one of my adult life. Even when I was so full I thought I might pop, I still found room for just one more slice of delicious *rewena* bread, just one more piece of *kumara*, just one more...

It was never just one more.

Eventually, my stomach just couldn't take any more abuse, so I had to stop. With a deep groan of satisfaction, I leaned back on my bench to try and find a position where my tummy didn't ache quite so much, but every angle hurt.

The others, including Michael and Skylar, were still busy stuffing their faces with gusto, but I couldn't possibly eat another nibble. I'd become a bit of a lightweight in the eating game over the years; after spending the better part of a decade on a starvation diet, my stomach had shrunk.

Eventually, Anahera noticed my uncomfortable condition. She hopped off her bench to help me up, and then escorted me down a corridor to somewhere I could rest. It turned out to be a small, makeshift dormitory, little more than a storage room with a couple of old double mattresses on the ground. I wasn't too bothered. I'd slept in far worse places over the years. It was clean and dry, and there were fresh linens on the mattresses.

Anahera helped me to lie down, and then left me to digest in peace. I rolled onto my back and flopped out across the mattress with a groan.

Too full, hurts to breathe, I whined mentally but couldn't work up the willpower to say anything out loud. Not that it mattered, there was no one there to hear it. *Too full. No care. Must sleep.*

My eyes closed and I drifted into a contented doze, soothed by the distant sounds of happiness from the dining hall. I had no idea how long I napped, but eventually I heard the shuffling of feet nearby, then someone flopped heavily onto the mattress beside me. Ever the cautious one, I opened one eye to inspect the new arrival.

Michael. Friend. Safe.

I grunted an inarticulate greeting, and he replied with a groan. Ah, clearly he was suffering the same as me. Good.

Resume sleep mode now, my brain told me in no uncertain terms. I acquiesced without a fight. My eyes drifted closed, and before I could form another coherent thought I was fast asleep.

***

I awoke to the sound of Michael snoring beside me, the only sound in the silence. I rolled over and stretched, then looked around curiously to try and figure out what time it was. I decided that it was still daylight, based off the glow that filtered in between the haphazard curtains strung across the nearby window. A beam of light fell across us, bright enough that I could pinpoint the time at somewhere in the mid-afternoon.

Michael was sprawled on his back with one arm draped over me. He was in such a deep sleep that he didn't even stir when I extracted myself from under his arm and sat up. After so many years of living on a survival diet, where every mouthful was carefully rationed in case it was your last, the chance to actually feast was something neither of our bodies quite understood. It was like ten years of Christmases had hit us all at once. We'd both managed to overload our senses, as well as our poor, distended bellies.

I was feeling better after my sleep, though. It had been ages since I'd eaten that much in one sitting, and all of a sudden I was bouncing with energy and ready to take on the world. So I left Michael sleeping, and went off to explore on my own – and to find a lavatory in quick order.

Luckily for me, I discovered the door next door to mine was the toilet block, so I was able to relieve myself without any issues. Infinitely more relaxed as a result, I went off to wander the halls, sticking my head into various rooms to see what was happening and where.

I found a few people hard at work in rooms nearby, but no one I knew well or felt any inclination to disturb. I left them in peace and moved on. Eventually, I found myself in a large room on the lake side of the building, where several small boats rested. Although I had grown up in an island nation, I knew a grand total of nothing about boats. I saw oars nearby so I presumed the boats were canoes, but that was my best guess. The only thing I was sure of was that there was a gap in the row, so one of the boats was missing or in use.

Beyond the boats, a large concertina door stood half open, which let in a square of daylight and gave me a glimpse of the lake beyond. I moved closer to look outside. The day was still overcast, and it was raining lightly. Beyond the door, a patch of trimmed grass separated the building from the edge of the lake, where a small dock had been built out into the water. Someone sat on the end of the dock with a fishing rod. I could see dark hair pulled back in a braid and a feminine figure, so I assumed it was Anahera.

A distant squeal drew my attention out over the lake. Shielding my eyes with my hand, I stared out across the water at a small boat in the distance, and realised that I could see blonde hair. Although I couldn't see a face at that distance, it had to be Skylar. Curious, I stepped out into the drizzle and picked my way across the damp grass towards the dock. The day was warm despite the weather; the rain was nothing more than a pleasant coolness to counteract the heat.

My feet made a hollow sound as I stepped from slippery wet grass onto wood, which made the person on the end of the dock look up. Sure enough, it was Anahera. She smiled when she saw me and beckoned for me to join her, so I did.

Water soaked through the seat of my cargo pants as I settled on the edge of the dock beside her, but I didn't mind. It was still late summer, so getting wet wasn't an inconvenience. It brought back memories of childhood: like every child, I'd spent many a summer afternoon dressed in my bathing suit, dashing back and forth through the sprinklers in our garden.

"What are they doing out there?" I asked curiously, canting my head in the direction of the distant boat.

"Hemi's teaching your sister to fish," Anahera answered, absently adjusting the slack of her own line. "They bite more when it rains, so now is the best time for it. Fishing generally isn't that noisy, though."

As if to punctuate her sentence, Skylar squealed again. We both grinned.

"She is a little loud," I agreed. On a whim, I shuffled my bottom back away from the edge, and started removing my shoes and socks.

"Just a little," Anahera agreed good-naturedly.

When my shoes and socks were off, I rolled up my pants and slipped my feet into the cool water. It was nice, just hanging out, doing nothing. Like being a teenager before the plague. Even Anahera wasn't trying very hard to catch a fish; I quickly figured out that she was just doing it to relax, rather than to be productive.

Occasionally we chatted, mostly about fishing or the bounty of food the local area had to offer, but primarily we just sat in companionable silence. Skye squealed, laughed, and jumped around, keeping us both entertained with her antics. I was just happy to see her enjoying herself. After everything she'd been through, she deserved a moment of joy. Part of me worried that she'd fall out of the boat or hurt herself, but I wasn't really concerned.

She can take care of herself – and if she gets herself in trouble, Hemi will take care of her, I reassured myself. I was certain he would. They were of a like age and had swiftly become friends. Then, a thought occurred to me. I shot a sideways glance at Anahera. "Does Hemi have a crush on Skye?"

Anahera laughed and nodded, then gave me a long look in return. "I think he has a crush on both of you, actually. But, Skylar is his age and you're clearly enamoured with Michael, so she seems like the logical focus of his ardour."

"That's adorable." I grinned to myself and peered out across the lake. "I'm glad to hear it. After Ryan left her, I wasn't sure how well she was going to hold together. They were together for a long time."

"Hah!" Anahera barked a laugh and shook her head. "I think you underestimate how resilient your sister is. There is a great deal of strength hidden within her. Just give her a bit of time to recover. She'll be fine."

"I really hope you're right." I heaved a sigh, and eased myself back to lie on the dock, folding my arms beneath my head. The rain felt wonderfully cool as it fell on my face. For a moment, life felt perfect.

Chapter Six

We spent our afternoon doing absolutely nothing remotely constructive, and it felt great. Michael eventually emerged to join us, and the three of us talked about all kinds of unimportant things as we relaxed on the dock, watching Skye learn to fish.

When the shadows started to grow longer, Hemi and Skylar paddled their boat back to shore. Skye leapt out of the boat as soon as it was tied off, anxious to show off her catch. She looked so proud that my inner big sister forced me to lavish endless praise on her.

We trailed along behind the teenagers as they carried their fish off to be prepared for dinner, but when Hemi dragged her off to instruct her on how to scale, gut and fillet their catch, we decided to be elsewhere. Of course, by 'we', I mean 'me'. I have a weak stomach when it comes to hurting lesser animals. That was one of my biggest flaws, and probably the reason I'd ended up so malnourished over the years. I just couldn't bear the thought of killing an animal for the sole intention of eating it.

Anahera led us out to the front of the building, to show us where her men were preparing the *hangi* pit for dinner. Although both of us knew the concept, it was fascinating to see the underground oven being prepared. The men laughed as they juggled red hot rocks into the bottom of the pit, and then laid the cloth-wrapped food on top of it.

A second before they were about to fill in the hole to let the food cook, Hemi and Skye came tearing out of the building with their arms full of fish fillets, yelling for the others to wait. The men digging the hangi added the fish to the hole, then filled it in and left it all to cook in the heat.

Later on, when the food was cooked, they dug the hole up again and carried the food inside to the dining room. We all helped to unwrap it and serve it, so that we could learn more about the traditions our Maori neighbours employed in their efforts to preserve their own culture.

Dinner itself was a jovial affair, just like lunch had been, full of boisterous laughter and play. Since we were still full from lunch, my group only ate a little to avoid gorging ourselves unconscious again – but Skylar insisted that everyone had to try her fish. I wasn't lying when I told her it was delicious.

After dinner, we volunteered to help with the cleaning up. As it turned out, washing dishes was exactly the same in both our cultures. Skylar and I took that task while Michael went off to help the men with the heavier end-of-day tasks, leaving us alone together.

I was up to my elbows in hot, soapy water, when Skye suddenly spoke up. "Hey, Sandy? Can I ask you something?"

"Of course. What's up, little sis?" I answered, handing her a freshly-scrubbed plate to dry, then I turned back to grab another.

"What did Mum look like?"

I dropped the dish I'd just picked up, splashing soapy water all over myself. That was a question I hadn't been expecting. I glanced over my shoulder at her, wiping foam off my clothing. "What do you mean?"

"I mean... well, I..." She sighed and lowered her head, staring down at her feet. "I don't remember what she looked like, Sandy. I remember her name, I remember her voice, I even remember what she smelled like and what it felt like to cuddle her. But when I try to think about her, I can't remember what her face looked like. When I dream about her, her face is just... kind of a blur."

"Oh..." Wow, that was an unexpectedly deep question to have to answer while doing the dishes. I chewed my lip while I thought over the answer, and finally decided to go with the most obvious one. "She looked like you, Skye. Just like you."

"Like me?" Skylar echoed, looking bewildered.

"Yeah, just like you," I answered. Her brow furrowed in confusion, so I set aside the dishes to explain further. "When I was little, I used to like looking at Mum and Dad's wedding photos. She was eighteen or nineteen when they got married, so she was right around your age. When I first saw you as an adult, back at the bunker, I just about had a heart attack because you look just like her in those old pictures. The only difference is that her hair was longer, and you have a few more freckles."

Skye stared down at the ground, her young face set in such a look of confusion that I felt the need to hug her – so I did. I grabbed her and squeezed her hard, and she hugged me back.

"Any time you want to see your mum again, all you have to do is look in the mirror," I said softly.

"Thank you, sis," she whispered back, and then gave me one last hug before the topic was dropped, and we resumed washing dishes.

The three of us had to share a room that night, as it turned out that the room with the mattresses was the only spare bedroom our neighbours had. The permanent members of the group each had their own hut built in the space between the yacht club building and the outer wall, made by their own hands and decorated to their tastes, but they rarely had guests.

Skye teased us mercilessly as we settled into our beds, warning Michael and me that there would be big trouble if we got up to hanky-panky with her in the room. She was so silly about the whole thing that all three of us ended up laughing uncontrollably, with tears streaming down our cheeks.

Eventually, though, exhaustion claimed us all, and we each drifted off into a deep slumber.

***

I woke in the middle of the night, jerked out of pleasant dreams by a terrible, gut-wrenching sound: someone was screaming. I sat bolt upright in bed, straining to hear what they were saying, but I couldn't make out the words over a weird crackling sound that was so loud it made it hard to think.

Wait... a crackling sound?

My eyes widened as I came awake enough to put two and two together. I leapt out of bed and ran to the window. My foot hit Skylar's sleeping form along the way and almost tripped me, but adrenaline helped me to keep my balance. With no consideration for the delicacy of the curtains, I yanked them open and stared outside, at a yard turned hellish by the surging heat of flames.

"Fire!" I screamed the word as I leapt back over to my companions, and dragged them from their beds despite their sleepy protests. The fire was huge, and it was close. The smell of smoke was already drifting into our room. My survival instincts kicked in straight away. Before anyone else was fully awake, I had them pulling on clothing and arming themselves. Without a thought for myself, I shoved my taser into Skylar's pocket while she was still struggling to get dressed, and then shoved her baggage into her hands.

Michael had his pants on but was struggling with his shirt. Time was running out. It was starting to get hotter, and a haze of smoke had started to fill the room.

I stuffed the rest of our belongings into our packs, and dragged the baggage with us as we raced for the door.

The smoke was even thicker out in the hallway and left us coughing as we struggled to find an exit. It seemed to be coming from the front of the building, so I led the way towards the rear instead. We burst into the boat room and ran the last few metres to the concertina doors, which had been closed for the night. We struggled with the latch in the semi-darkness, but finally we managed to get it open, and tumbled outside into the darkness.

The air was clearer on the lakefront – at last, we could breathe. Gulping down a lungful of clean, cool air, I dropped our belongings on the damp grass and turned to stare at the burning compound.

The fire was huge. I could see shadowy figures on the other side of the building racing back and forth, struggling to put out the flames, and realised that it must be Anahera's clan. That was a relief. Perhaps we weren't under attack after all. Perhaps it was just terrible misfortune.

That thought lasted for about two seconds. There was a strange sound behind me, followed by a muffled cry from Michael. He hit the ground just as I was turning to see what had happened, his hand clutched over one side of his chest. Blood was leaking through his fingers; it took a second before I came to the horrifying realisation that he'd been shot.

I dropped to my knees beside him, just as Skylar started screaming. There was too much happening, I was too confused; I couldn't see past the fact that Michael was bleeding on the ground. I didn't realise at the time that Skye was trying to warn me, that she'd seen the figures appearing out of the smoke behind me. Michael was in pain, and that was all I could think about.

Then, something hit me in the back of the head, and I blacked out.

***

I came to slowly this time; my brain felt muddled and confused. It took a few long seconds for memory to return, but when it did the sick feeling of dread settled into my belly. Only then did I start to feel my own pain.

The ground was hard beneath my shoulder and sharp rocks cut into my bare skin. I struggled to get up and found my hands were bound cruelly behind my back, with ropes that were so tight my fingers were starting to go numb. I opened my eyes, and my head swam. I discovered that I was lying naked on the ground, stripped of all my clothing.

A small fire burned in the clearing, and a shadow sat in front of it with its back towards me. It was a few minutes before dawn, and the sun was just starting to peek up over the horizon, heralding the start of another day.

Perhaps my last day, I thought perversely, but for once I didn't scold myself for my pessimism. I seemed to be in a pretty bad predicament. My heart hammered in my throat from the force of the adrenaline surging through my veins.

As if reading my mind, the man by the fire turned towards me and I got a look at his face. My stomach dropped to my knees. I knew those tattoos, that blunt, oft-broken nose. The rotten teeth, and scars – and most of all, I knew that terrible smile when he was thinking about hurting me. That smile was on his face right now.

"You're awake. Good. I was starting to get bored," he growled as he rose to his feet, his corpulent body swaying – I could smell alcohol, and realised that he was drunk. I wondered if that was good for me, or bad for me. Probably bad.

"Awfully kind of you, really," he slurred. "All this time, I was thinking that I'd have to come and get you later, once I got my revenge on that bitch at the village. And then what do my boys tell me? Two little blonde sluts showed up this very day, just waiting for us to come and visit? Perfect." He leapt on me suddenly, and grabbed my chin roughly with one enormous hand.

"You brought this on yourself, you little whore," he hissed. I could feel his spittle on my face. His breath was rank, like something had crawled into his mouth and died; the stink of it made me feel nauseated. "You escaped once. You killed my boy. You could have left it at that, but you didn't. Now I'm going to make you suffer so much you'll wish we'd killed you the first time."

He shoved me back down and kicked me hard, sending me rolling away in the dirt. It was only then I realised that my feet were untied. It was a small thing, but enough to give me hope.

Don't be afraid, I told myself silently. *He wants you to be afraid. That's the part he likes best.* My entire body was shaking, either from the cold or fear, but I fought to keep myself under control. I wouldn't say anything, and I wouldn't scream. I would not give him the satisfaction. There was always hope, until you were dead.

When I righted myself, I realised he'd moved away from me and that he was bent over examining something. Then he straightened up, and I saw the glint of steel in his hand – a knife.

Great. Just what I needed.

"That bitch friend of yours cut off my cock, and you're going to pay for that," he told me as he closed on me. I inched away from him warily, my eyes on the knife. "All of you are going to pay. Even that sweet little piece of ass you brought with you. Shame I can't tap that anymore – my boys will have to have all the fun with her. You're mine, though. Since I can't fuck you any more, we'll just have to make our own fun."

Hot pain surged across my breast as he lashed out with the knife. I felt blood flow, but my thoughts were on Skylar rather than myself. Jesus, Skye. I couldn't let them hurt her. I had to do something. He lashed out again and again; I felt the knife bite in, but this time I responded. I kicked out with all my strength at his left knee, and heard a satisfying crack when my blow hit home. The brute yelled and fell back away from me. For a moment, I felt a surge of victory in my chest, but I swiftly realised that wouldn't be enough.

"You bitch. You *bitch*. I was going to play with you a bit before I destroyed you, but maybe I'll just destroy you first and then play with you after!" he yelled at me, hobbling back to the tool kit I could only just see at the edge of my vision. Then he was coming back towards me, with a screw driver and a pair of pliers; a surge of horror lurched through me like a shot of pure ice.

He must have seen it on my face, because he grinned that terrible grin at me. "Yeah, that's right, you little bitch. I'm going to hurt you like you've never been hurt before. I'm going to cut out your fucking tongue, and then tear out every one of your fucking teeth." He gestured at me threateningly with the pliers. "But first... Oh, first, I'm going to cut out those pretty eyes of yours. Let's see how feisty you are when you can't see the pain coming!"

Oh, Jesus. He's sick. Crazy! Panic overwhelmed me and I fought to get up. He kicked me again and sent me rolling, laughing all the while as I scrambled away and tried to flee. Despite the injury to his knee, he caught up with me before I could get up, and pinned me to the ground with one foot – then he lashed out with the knife.

I managed to jerk my face away at the last second; the tip of the blade skidded across my cheekbone instead of taking out my eye as he'd intended. The pain was so intense that I screamed despite my conviction. I couldn't help it. I was going to die – no, worse! Oh God, this was so much worse! But there was no way that I was going without a fight.

I twisted with all my strength and managed to make him lose his balance for a moment; he slipped off of me, dropping the knife into the dirt. I kicked out with as much force as I could, again and again. I felt my blows striking flesh, but all that did was make him laugh. He was stronger than me by a factor of two. The only thing that gave me hope was that by the time he managed to get me pinned down beneath his weight, the knife and the other weapons were gone. Dropped somewhere in the undergrowth, I imagined. It was only a tiny hope, and it wouldn't last for long.

I screamed again when he hit me, a closed fist right across the face with such force that it slammed my head into the ground. His weight was right on top of me, crushing my arms beneath me. I couldn't move, I couldn't reach him with my feet. No matter how hard I tried, I couldn't get him off me. Hope faded as he hit me again, and again. Each blow drew a cry of pain from my battered body, and sent stars dancing across my vision.

I'm going to die. I'm going to die and there's nothing I can do about it. Oh God, but what about Skye? No, no, no – you can't have my sister!

I struggled with all my might, but there was nothing that I could do, and he just laughed at me. He slapped me across the face with an open hand, then drew his fist back to unload another blow.

The blow never came. It was interrupted by the sound of someone else screaming. But this wasn't a scream of pain. It was a scream of rage.

The bastard's head jerked up and he stared at the other side of the clearing. I was too battered to see what he saw, though. My head was spinning from the violence, and blood blurred my vision. But I did hear the roar of a shotgun blast, and I did see the man's head dissolve in a bloody shower of hot shrapnel and carnage. With the last of my strength, I dragged myself out from beneath the corpse before it could crush me, and only then did I see who my rescuer was.

It was Skylar. My baby sister. She strode across the clearing like an avenging angel, her eyes wild, her hair a golden halo around her face in the pre-dawn gloom, the shotgun nestled at her hip ready to deliver more deadly payload should it be required.

It wasn't. Unlike the walking dead, that man was only human. A terrible, evil human, but a human nonetheless. He was dead before she got close enough to check. I, on the other hand, was bloody, broken, but very much alive.

Skylar kicked the body hard, rolling the sack of dead meat away from me, then she came back and knelt down beside me to inspect my condition. Although black and blue from bruises, and bleeding from a half-dozen cuts, I was conscious. She helped me sit up, and used the very same knife that he had planned to blind me with to cut the bonds around my wrists.

My first instinct was to hug her. She hugged me back gently, and then helped me to my feet. A few seconds later, Michael joined us in the clearing and rushed over to help me as well. His chest was bound up in a makeshift bandage, but I could see the blood seeping through it already.

"How...?" I managed to gasp, though my mouth had the metallic taste of blood in it. My lips were cut, but I didn't seem to have lost any teeth.

"Your taser," Skylar explained as the two of them helped me back towards the relative safety of the lakeside fort. "After they knocked you and Michael out, two big men grabbed me and carried me off. They started arguing about which of them was going to rape me first, so I told them that I was still bleeding from my miscarriage and they both got mad.

"They dropped me and started yelling at each other. While they were distracted, I got out your taser and hid it behind my back. When they came back, I hit them with it. They were so surprised that I managed to get them both before they realised what was happening."

"You knocked them both out?" I gasped, amazed at my little sister's tenacity.

"Yeah." She nodded, hugging my battered frame gently. "Then I ran back to the camp and woke up Michael, and we went looking for you."

"I'm so glad you did," I told her, my voice hoarse from screaming and pain. "He was... going to... get his revenge on me by taking my eyes."

Tears welled up, but I didn't bother to wipe them away as they fell. It was too much effort, and I felt exhausted and wrung out. I was safe, I had survived, and even though I had screamed, I hadn't submitted. Michael swore under his breath. I knew instinctively that he felt like he'd failed to protect me, but I didn't have the strength to tell him it wasn't his fault.

Speaking was too hard for all of us, so the rest of the trip back was in silence. When we finally made our way out into the clearing beside the lakefront, the fire had been extinguished, and we found our Maori friends huddled around our belongings trying frantically to figure out what had happened to us.

Someone spotted us and shouted; the next thing we knew, we were enveloped in a friendly mob. Someone got a blanket around me to protect my modesty, then Michael and I were guided off to one of the huts that had survived the fire.

We were put to bed side by side, and our wounds were tended as best they could. Outside, I heard Anahera issuing orders. From what little I could understand of her bilingual shouting, I realised that she planned to take us home as soon as it was safe to move us. She was also sending people out to deal with the brutes my sister had left in the forest.

Beside me, I could hear Michael's uneven breath, and I worried for him more than I did for myself. It was only a small bullet, probably from an air rifle like the wound Hemi had come to us with, but it was in his chest and it could do serious damage.

I squeezed my eyes closed and leaned against him, praying that my love would be okay.

Chapter Seven

By midday, we were on our way back home, each of us on the back of a quad bike with one of our friends driving. Although fuel was precious, Anahera insisted. She wouldn't let us walk all that way in our condition, not after what had happened to us while we were guests in her home. She felt responsible. I understood, but I felt no reason to blame her. It wasn't her fault.

With the bikes to carry us over the uneven terrain quickly, it only took a couple of hours for us to reach our old motel. Hemi and Skylar arrived first. They leapt off their bike and ran to go find the doctor, while the rest of us travelled more sedately so as not to jostle our injuries. Anahera parked her bike beside the door and helped me off, while behind us Ropata did the same for Michael.

Once the adrenaline had worn off, it left me in terrible pain. My wrists were black with bruises and it hurt so much to breathe that I wondered if I might have a broken rib. My sides and back were covered in grazes from where I'd been kicked across the dirt, and I needed a bath something terrible to get the dirt out of my wounds.

The doctor took one look at me and agreed. Skye and Anahera bundled me off to the shower, bathed me, and cleaned my wounds. The water was cold since the power was still off, but that helped to numb the pain.

I didn't even mind being bathed by two women all that much. After what I'd been through, being naked in front of friends didn't feel like the end of the world any more. At least they could reach my back for me – I was so stiff that I could barely move my arms.

Once I was bathed and dried, I was led back to Michael's room, where he lay recovering from makeshift surgery. The doctor knew me too well, and reassured me about his condition before I could even ask.

"He'll be fine," Dr Cross told me in no uncertain terms. "His ribs stopped the projectile, and I've removed it now. Aside from that and a minor concussion, he's going to be right as rain. Now, come here and let me look at you."

Given the extent of my injuries, I had to stay naked while he examined me. That was a more uncomfortable experience than the shower because of his gender, but he was also my doctor. I reminded myself of that every time he needed to fish a piece of gravel or a twig from a wound in an intimate place. I just closed my eyes and bore up to it, reminding myself that I was lucky I still *had* eyes to close. I owed Skylar big time for that.

A couple of the cuts were so deep that they

required stitches, including the one on my face. Dr Cross warned me that I would probably have a scar from it, but I couldn't have cared less. All that mattered to me was that I could still see. I'd come so close to losing the privilege forever. I'd come so close to losing my life.

My ribs were examined by gentle touches, but the news from there was good – I probably had a couple of fractures, but no actual breaks. None of my injuries were life-threatening. Every inch of me hurt, but I still took that diagnosis with a smile. The way I saw it, it could have been so much worse. Despite the pain, I felt buoyant, even joyous.

Once my wounds were washed and dressed where appropriate, he gave me painkillers and put me to bed with firm instructions to rest. For once in my life, I felt no inclination to defy the doctor's orders. Frankly, I felt like a couple of miles of bad road, and all my body wanted to do was sleep.

I snuggled up against Michael's good side, resting my head on the half of his chest that wasn't covered in bandages. I felt an arm slip carefully around me, and the closeness was very comforting.

I slept fitfully through most of the afternoon and into the evening. Often, I woke up and just lay there with my eyes closed, thinking over everything that had happened. When I thought back to my brief captivity, I realised that I felt… nothing. No fear, no anger, no hatred, despite how close I'd come to losing several body parts that were very precious to me. All I felt was relief that it was over, and that everyone had gotten home safely.

At the time, yes, I had been afraid. I had panicked. But, more importantly, I realised now that I'd put up a damn good fight. I had screamed, but I hadn't surrendered. Although I hadn't realised it at the time, my screaming had helped my rescuers to locate me. Screaming saved my life.

Thinking over it logically, I came to the decision that I'd done very well, considering the circumstances. My entire attitude had changed. If this had happened six weeks earlier, I probably would have ended up a blubbering mess and not had the strength to fight back.

These survivors, my friends, had changed me. No, that wasn't right – they'd shown me that I wanted to change myself. I wanted to be stronger, for their sakes as well as my own, and when the chips were down I had been stronger. I was growing, as a person and as a woman. Skylar and Anahera both gave me good role models to look up to after being alone for so long. I was proud of them, and proud of myself. I felt like my mother and my grandmother would have been proud of me, too.

Realising that I'd managed to hold my own in an emergency brought with it a sense of pride, and a sense of personal achievement. I had done nothing to be ashamed of. Even though I hadn't told anyone the details of my ordeal yet, I felt like I could without any kind of shame. Considering how humiliated I'd felt for years after my first encounter with that man and his cronies, that was a vast improvement.

All of a sudden, I realised that I felt good about myself, for the first time in a very long time. More than just that, I came to another conclusion, one that I had to discuss with someone very important to me. I opened my eyes and discovered that it was dark, but I could hear the sound of uneven breathing that told me he wasn't asleep.

"Michael?" I whispered.

"Mhm?" he mumbled, shifting a little beneath me. The moon was full and our curtains were wide open; a shaft of moonlight fell across his face, so I could see his dark eyes watching me.

"I've been thinking," I told him softly, reaching up with one hand to trail my fingers along his jaw. His stubble was longer than usual, rougher, but I didn't mind. We'd both been through an ordeal. I couldn't blame him for being lax in his personal grooming.

"Yes?" He closed his eyes, leaning in to my touch.

God, he is handsome, I thought to myself, studying him in the moonlight.

"We almost lost each other today," I whispered, shifting closer against him so I could press my cheek against his. Understanding my need for closeness, he tightened his grip around me and held me gently against his side. "We live in a world where so much is outside of our control. There's so much danger. We could both die tomorrow. It's never going to be perfect; the only thing in this life that's perfect is the way we feel about one another."

He started to say something, but I interrupted him with a kiss. I wasn't interested in hearing protests or complaints, not this time. We loved each other, and that was all that mattered – I knew he wanted me just as much as I wanted him. We had both been delaying the inevitable out of fear. So I kissed him, deeply and tenderly, to give him something else to think about besides his own nerves. I felt his body respond to it.

When our lips parted, I gazed down at him and saw a mixture of confusion and longing on his face. I understood the feeling well. I'd felt it so often in the recent weeks. Every time I looked at him, in fact – except for right now. For the first time in a very long time, I felt a kind of clarity. My desires and my needs were crystal clear. I knew exactly what I wanted.

"Michael, I don't want to lose you without ever having the chance to show you how much I love you," I told him in no uncertain terms. "I want to make love to you, right now, however imperfect the circumstances may be."

"But... your injuries..." he protested. I snuggled closer against him, my lips seeking out the curve of his throat. He was right, it hurt to kiss him with my split lips, but I didn't care.

"So be gentle. You're very good at that," I whispered huskily, my breath hot against the side of his neck. He loved being kissed there, and I felt him shiver in response.

"Are you sure?" Even though I already had him aroused and I knew he wanted me, he still showed such restraint for fear of hurting me. I knew it, and I loved him all the more for it. Drawing back just enough to look down at him, I gave him an adoring smile.

Then a kiss, and another, and another. A series of hot, quick, playful kisses. He responded instinctively, and I felt gentle hands upon my body. I rolled onto my back and he went with me, supporting his weight on his hands to keep from hurting me. With increasing enthusiasm, he returned my kisses and I felt his body pressing down against mine. His skin was so warm, his belly firm and taut, and his manhood...

Only then did I break the kiss long enough to reply, when I was trapped beneath his strong frame and knew for certain that he was just as ready as I was.

"I've never been so sure of anything in my life," I told him, and it was true. After all this time, after how gentle, sweet, and endlessly kind he had been to me, I wanted nothing more than to make love to my policeman at long last. To return his kindness with pleasure, and to show him how much I'd grown – because of him.

And so we did. Tangled together in bed, with our wounded bodies bandaged and bloodied but our minds finally at peace, we made love beneath the moonlight. I was oblivious to the pain as we fell into a world of our own pleasure, all things forgotten except for my love for the man in my arms.

It felt like that pleasure would last forever, and it was like nothing I could ever remember feeling before. So gentle, so expressive, so... right. I heard myself cry out, but I didn't care; I heard his voice whispering my name, and that was all that mattered in the world. This world was our world, and ours alone. Nothing else mattered here, except for the two of us.

After what felt like forever, we collapsed exhausted and replete in one another's arms, our bodies slick with sweat and our breath racing. He kissed me tenderly one last time as I snuggled up against him, before we both drifted off to sleep.

This time, we both slept deeply.

Chapter Eight

I had often wondered in my youth what people meant when they spoke about true love being the only real source of satisfaction, about unrelenting passion and desire so strong it addled all of your senses. My early experimentation with boys in high school had done nothing to prepare me for what I experienced with Michael that night. When I awoke late the next morning, I felt lazy and satisfied in a way I'd never known before, and felt no desire to move from the position I had slept in. I couldn't even be bothered to open my eyes, lest the wonderful feeling dissipate in the light of day.

It didn't occur to me that Michael might have woken up before I did until I felt gentle fingers stroke my temple, sweeping a lock of my hair away from my face. I opened my eyes and found him propped up on one elbow, watching me with a smile of pure contentment on his face.

"Good morning," he whispered, leaning down to kiss me. My response was muffled by his lips and it wasn't necessary anyway. He knew how I felt better than I did. It felt like he always had. Words were just unnecessary between us; our bodies and our hearts spoke louder than words ever could.

Ignoring the stiffness of my joints, I drew him down atop me once more, and this time he came willingly. All his reluctance was gone when we made love for a second time, in the light of the golden morning sun. I felt such joy that I never wanted to let him go. I'd finally found a place where I felt safe, happy, and welcome, and it was right there with him.

Ever the gentleman, Michael refused to put his own pleasure above mine at any stage. He held himself back with a resilience that amazed me, and focused on pleasuring me instead. His lips touched my throat, my collarbone, and my breast, while gentle hands explored what he could of my flesh around the bandages and wounds. Only once I was satisfied did he let himself join me, and then he finally collapsed with his head upon my uninjured breast, his breath coming in harsh gasps that sent chills across my skin.

Eventually, Michael rolled onto his back and drew me atop him, so that I could lie comfortably in his embrace. Despite our exhaustion, neither of us felt the urge to sleep again. We'd rested for almost a full day now, and were starting to get restless. I heaved a long sigh and stretched languidly, only to get distracted when I felt curious fingers creeping across my belly.

I opened one eye, and I found him grinning at me. The look on his face made me laugh. He looked like the cat that had finally gotten the cream. The fact that he'd been willing to be so patient with me made it feel so much better in the long run.

"Insatiable, huh?" I teased him right back, trailing a few exploratory fingers in interesting places of my own. My touch drew a deep-throated growl from him, but I knew him well enough to know he was only playing.

Unfortunately, our play was interrupted by a knock on the door. We had just enough time to separate and feign innocence before the door swung open, and Skylar entered with a couple of plates of something that smelt so good it made my mouth water.

"Breakfast, you two." She gave us a knowing look, and set the plates down on the small table beside Michael's bed. As she was turning to leave, she added, "The doctor will be up to check on you both shortly."

We exchanged looks at her warning. I cringed, since I knew that we were about to get a lecture for messing up our dressings so badly. As far as I was concerned, it was more than worth it, and if I was any judge of expressions then Michael felt exactly the same way. Still, the doctor had a way of making us feel like naughty children over the smallest misdeed.

Breakfast ended up being more interesting than usual. We had to fight to keep our hands off each other and our food going in the right place, but we got there in the end. I wasn't terribly hungry, but as always Michael cajoled me into eating, and my resistance to his demands was at an all-time low. Besides, I knew he was right. My body needed food to heal, and it had a lot of mending to do.

By the time the doctor arrived to check on us, we'd finished eating. We were just relaxing side by side, chatting casually like nothing had happened. He took one look at us and seemed to know better, but for once he said nothing. Even though we were both braced for a scolding, he didn't say a word – he just changed our bandages, inspected our injuries, then left us in peace.

Michael and I exchanged a confused look, but no answers were forthcoming. I was glad to go without my daily scolding, and content to leave well enough alone. Michael was more reluctant to let it go, until I distracted him to the point that he didn't care anymore.

***

Hours later, we languished abed trying very hard to rest, but I was too restless to relax.

"I want to get up," I complained, absently rubbing at one of my bandages.

"You're supposed to be resting," Michael scolded, and gently grabbed my hand. "Stop scratching. If you scratch it, it'll never heal."

"But it itches," I whined like a spoilt two-year-old, wriggling to try and escape his grasp. Of course, he wasn't having any of that and held me tightly until I finally gave up and relented with a heavy sigh. "Okay, okay, I won't scratch – but I still want to get up."

"Bored of me already?" he said, feigning injury with such conviction that my heart leapt up into my throat.

"No! It's just that I... I..." Then I saw the smile

twitching at the corners of his lips, and realised he wasn't serious at all. "You're just pulling my leg, aren't you? Damn it! You had me going!" I snatched up one of our pillows and flung it at him.

He laughed merrily at my antics, then picked up the pillow and deposited it back where it belonged. "Of course I am. I'm bored, too. We've wasted an entire day."

"So, let's get up then. I'm sure there's something productive we can do that won't put too much strain on our injuries." I leapt out of bed before he could stop me, despite my aching muscles. I needed to move, to stretch and to get my biological engine going before it froze up completely, and there were only so many times I could use Michael for that before he ran out of steam.

"Like what?" he asked curiously, easing himself out of bed with much greater care than me. While he was stretching, I went over to my gear to find clothing. Luckily for me, the others had left my belongings in the room when they escorted me up here, so I didn't have to go far to find what I needed.

"I have no idea." I shrugged. I pulled on my clothing, fighting the urge to curse at the pain. It was a necessary evil, though; I couldn't exactly go prancing around naked. Michael probably wouldn't have minded, but everyone else would. "I suppose we could work on the roof?"

"Nah." Michael shook his head, his back to me while he dressed as well. "Climbing ladders isn't a good idea in our condition. We'll tear our stitches."

"Ugh, you sound like the doctor," I complained, plopping back down on the edge of the bed to put my socks and shoes on. In the middle of the task, I paused to stare at the horrible pink scar in the middle of my right foot.

That scar was the legacy of the injury that had brought me to this group of survivors. Although it was a memory of terrible pain, it had brought me something wonderful in the end: a family, and a lover. Two things I so desperately needed in my life. Now, I couldn't imagine my life without them.

Michael caught me staring at the scar. He knelt down on the floor in front of me, captured my foot in his big, gentle hands, and planted a kiss on the top of it.

"Someone has to make sure you take care of yourself, Little Miss Reckless," he said, surrendering my foot back into my own care. In spite of everything we'd been through together, that little gesture made me blush.

"Says Mister Hero," I retorted, poking a finger in the direction of his wounded shoulder. "The man who took a bullet for me."

"Well, I didn't really take it for you," he said, suddenly looking embarrassed. "I mean, I would have in a heartbeat, but I didn't see the shooter before he got me."

I immediately regretted my choice of words when I saw that embarrassment on his face. I reached out to stroke his cheek, instinctively seeking to reassure him. "I know, sweetie. I didn't mean it like that. It was just a little joke."

"I know." He closed his eyes and leaned into my touch. With a sigh, he lay his head down on my thigh, letting me run my hands through his short hair and over the contours of his face.

For some reason, the moment felt even more intimate than the time we'd spent in bed together. I admired him thoughtfully, letting the contact warm and relax me. A surge of emotion brought tears to my eyes unexpectedly, and I found myself wondering at the feelings that this man could make me experience. It was new and intense. I'd never felt anything like it for anyone else. I wondered if it was the decade alone in the wilderness that made my feelings so extreme, or if it was possible that he was 'The One'. I had so little experience to compare it to. From what my mother used to tell me, it could happen unexpectedly. Sometimes, you just knew that it was meant to be.

Only time will tell, I told myself, turning my attention back to the task at hand.

"Well, there is a place," I said, running my fingers over his nailbrush hair. "In the township. I found a door, but it was too solid to break through on my own. Perhaps between the two of us, we can figure out a way to open it."

"A mystery door?" He lifted his head out of my lap and looked up at me, curiosity twinkling in his dark eyes. "Where?"

"In the old general store, at the back. The rioters tried to get in, but couldn't get past the locks." He sat back on his haunches to give me room to finish putting on my shoes and socks, then I rose to my feet. Michael joined me a moment later. Together we made our way out onto the landing and down the stairs to where we stored our equipment. "I was going to go back and try to pick the lock, but I never got around to it."

"You can pick locks?" His brows shot up, and he peered at me askance.

"Sometimes." I shrugged noncommittally. "I'm okay at opening the older-style locks, but this one was pretty modern. I'm not terribly confident about my chances."

"Hmm." He rubbed his scruffy chin absently, as we crossed the courtyard and entered the storage room. "Why don't we just take off the door?"

"Take off the door? What do you mean?" I shot a curious look at him.

"If the door is on the right way, then we might be able to force the bolts out of the hinges, and lift the whole thing off," he explained. We paused so he could show me what he meant on the storage room door.

I made a thoughtful sound and nodded slowly. "That might work. I don't remember which way the hinge was on. Let's bring a crowbar anyway – we'll probably need it, one way or another."

Okay," he agreed. With a plan in mind, the two of us dove into the boxes of goods we kept stored in case of emergencies, until we found a tool kit and a large crowbar. Armed with those, I led the way out of our motel and held the door open for Michael. Of course, he insisted on being the one to carry the heavy stuff despite the wound in his chest, so I just let him. It wasn't worth the fight, and my muscles were sore enough that I wasn't sure I was up to it any more than he was.

We traipsed down the road towards the town centre, stepping carefully over the debris deposited by the storm a few days before. Every now and then I spotted something potentially hazardous, like broken glass or a downed sign post, and marked it to be cleaned up. A few minutes later, we arrived at the little shopping centre that dominated the centre of town, though Ohaupo was so small that "town" was kind of an overstatement. Since we'd destroyed the function centre complex, there were only a half-dozen shops left, including my tiny video store.

Michael peered around us with interest as we walked, as though seeing everything for the first time. We rarely came this way without a purpose, so he'd only seen it a handful of times in daylight. I, on the other hand, had turned the place upside down over the weeks since my arrival, and knew it as well as any inhabitant.

"Hold your breath," I warned as we approached the creaking doorway of the old general store – and with good reason. The stink of decomposition didn't get any better for being aired out. And even though I'd been in there before, I was never one to ignore personal safety. I had my taser in hand as I stepped through the doorway into the reeking darkness beyond, and kept it armed until I had cleared the building.

Nothing stirred, not even the baby mice that I'd seen last time I was there. That was interesting. Perhaps Tigger had eaten them. I heard gagging behind me, and turned to watch poor Michael with amusement.

"And I thought I had a weak stomach," I teased. He shot me a dark look in return.

"It just... takes a second to get used to it, is all..." He gulped down a lungful of the stinking air, then straightened himself up and put on his best manly airs. I hid a smile and led him deeper into the building.

We passed row after row of dirty shelves covered in rotten produce and shattered glass, picking our way towards the back counter. There, the mysterious door stood waiting for us, as implacable as a gargoyle guarding its treasures. At least, I hoped it was guarding treasures. Otherwise, all the effort we were going to have to put in would be for nothing.

"Huh. That's a tough door for the back room of a little corner store," Michael pondered out loud, rapping his knuckles against the old metal.

"Yeah, that's what got me curious. I mean, it seems like a lot of security for relatively nothing," I agreed, edging around the door to get a good look at it. "At least the hinges are on this side. I think we should be able to get these off."

"I assume that you already checked if there was a back door, or a window?" He glanced at me, then looked back at the door.

"Of course." I nodded and gave him a smile. "What kind of scavenger do you take me for?"

"Well, you never know. Let's get to it then, eh?" He grinned back at me, handed me the crowbar, and set the tool kit down on the countertop nearby. "Feel like making a bet on what's in there?"

"I don't have a clue. Probably money or something equally useless, knowing my luck." I pulled a sour face, but Michael laughed.

"Hey, hey, hey – positivity!" he scolded me lightly, while fishing around in search of a screwdriver big enough to survive the abuse we were about to unleash on it.

"I know, I know." I sighed and gestured towards the hinges. "Have we got any lubricants in there? These are rusted solid; it's going to be a bitch to get them loose."

"Language!" Michael teased me playfully.

"Sorry, Mum," I answered dryly.

He gave me a peculiar look, but I was too amused to explain. Did it make me weird to have spent so much time alone that I had inside jokes with myself? Yeah, probably. Oh well.

Michael shook his head and shot me a lopsided smile, then tossed a can of industrial lubricant to me with a gentle, underhand throw. I caught it easily and popped the top, then covered my face with the neck of my tank top to protect me from the fumes as I lathered the hinges with grease. When I was done, I stepped aside and Michael attacked the hinges with his screw driver, while I smeared lubricant over the locking mechanism as well.

It took all of Michael's strength and a great deal of cursing from both of us before the bolt began to slide up out of the hinge with a blood-curdling, rusty screech. I ducked beneath his muscular arm and sprayed the bolt with more grease. It came up easier after that. After a few minutes of work, the first bolt came loose and we moved on to the next one.

The top bolt was even more difficult than the first one had been, since it required him to clamber up on an old crate to get the angle he needed, but eventually we got it out as well. By the time we got to the bottom hinge, we had our technique down; the last bolt came out easily compared to the first two.

Once we were done, we cast aside the loose bolts and stepped back to admire our handiwork. Now, the door was only held up by the tension of the lock itself, and a decade's worth of rust.

"Honestly, who on earth thought metal doors were a good idea? Really, that's just selfish, if you ask me," I commented. My usual technique for solving any problem involved attacking it with a liberal dose of sarcasm, and this situation was no different. I grabbed the crowbar, then jammed it into the gap between the hinges and the wall. Michael added his strength to mine and we pulled as hard as we could, but all we got was a metallic whine that set my teeth on edge.

"No good," Michael muttered. We released the tension and stood back again.

"The lock's in too tight, I think." I bent down for a

second to peer at it closely, then straightened up and went over to the toolkit. "Give me a second, I have an idea. Ah, here we go." I pulled out the tools I had been looking for, and showed them to him: a hammer and chisel.

"How will those help?" Michael peered at the tools dubiously. "It's metal."

"The door is metal, and the hasp is metal," I answered, then reached over and tapped the door frame. "But this is just wood. I suspect if I dig deep enough, we should be able to rip the whole locking mechanism out of the wall."

"Ahh…" he breathed in understanding and nodded his approval. I set about destroying the structural integrity of that frame with a vengeance. Michael slipped up behind me to brace the door closed while I worked, just in case it happened to come loose. With careful, practiced strokes, I reduced the old wood to splinters, taking care not to risk injuring either myself or my lover in the process.

In due time, I uncovered the base of the hasp buried deep within the wooden frame. My chisel struck it with a resounding clang, which let me know that I'd dug deep enough to reach my goal. I widened the hole carefully until we could see the entire mechanism, then I set the hammer and chisel aside.

"That should be enough," I announced, and looked back at him. "Now we just need to break the screws on the other side. It's brute force time."

Michael nodded his agreement. With another

terrible clang, he drove the head of the crowbar into the gap between the hasp and the wall, and I added my strength to his.

"Brace yourself," he warned, though it was pretty much unnecessary. Both of us knew all about the terrible infections we could catch if we were to fall and cut ourselves in a filthy place like this.

"So much for taking it easy, huh?" I commented. Michael chuckled and nodded his agreement. He planted his feet wide and leaned his weight against the crowbar; once again I pulled with him. The door groaned in protest, but I could feel it moving. We released after a moment, and he shifted the bar to a slightly different point.

"And again," he instructed. I joined him, pulling with all my strength. The door was definitely moving now; I could see it arching and I heard the whine of old metal protesting that it had been left untended for far too long. Then, with a violent cracking sound, the left side of the door came free, with what was left of the hasp still clinging to a shattered segment of the door frame.

Suction kept the door from falling in on us, though. Michael braced himself against it to keep it in place while I took the bar and loosened it around the edges. It creaked and whinged as I chipped away at a decade's worth of rust until, with one last shriek, the entire door came away from the frame.

I lent my strength to help him shift the heavy door to one side, leaving both of us breathless but feeling victorious.

"How's that for teamwork?" he gloated. He grabbed me and gave me a quick kiss, then we turned our attention towards finally discovering what our prize actually was.

I was the first one through the doorway, so when I skidded to a halt without warning, Michael just about bowled me over. Then he saw what I saw and we both froze with shock.

When we finally regained our senses, Michael reached up to scratch his scruffy chin. "You know, all of a sudden I feel this overwhelming urge to arrest someone."

Chapter Nine

"Hell, yes!" I laughed with glee, and broke out my best impression of the Snoopy Dance.

"This shouldn't be here," Michael mumbled to himself, his expression one of intense concern. "This really, really shouldn't be here."

"It shouldn't, but it is," I pointed out happily, bouncing around him like an over-excited toddler on a sugar rush. "And whoever used to own it must be dead, so now it's ours!" There was still a locked grill between me and our findings, but I didn't mind. We had all the time in the world to figure out how to get into that cage, and I was pretty sure I knew exactly where I could find just the right tools for the job.

"You're entirely too happy about this." Michael shot a stern glance at me, then he grabbed my hand and drew me into a protective embrace. "You do realise how dangerous this is, right?"

"Take a second to consider who you're talking to, then ask that question again," I answered dryly, and gave him a long look in return. A faint flash of annoyance rose in my breast at his tone of voice, but I shoved it back down. He was just trying to protect me, and everyone that we held dear. "Of course, I know. I know better than anyone – but I also know exactly how useful this will be for keeping our family safe."

Michael looked at the cage and heaved a long sigh. "I suppose you're right, but I worry. There's military-grade hardware in there, Sandy. Just imagine what could have happened if those thugs that attacked us had been armed with one of those instead of a couple of air rifles. We'd probably all be dead."

He had a point, and that calmed me down. I stared at the cage, where a half-dozen semi-automatic assault rifles of various makes glinted ominously in the half-light, flanked by an assortment of handguns. As much as I had longed for a real gun to defend myself with, he was right – any weapon could be used against its owner.

"We should still take them," I said, then looked back at him. "We can't leave them here now. Let's hide them instead, somewhere that only we can get at them. If those mutants come south, they could save our lives one day."

Michael nodded thoughtfully, his dark eyes distant as he mulled over the idea. Finally, he nodded again, more firmly this time. "Okay. That makes sense. Like you said, we can't just leave them here – anyone could grab them."

"Go fetch the others to help us carry things back," I instructed, reaching over to give his hand a gentle squeeze. "Bring boxes or crates, anything that we can hide stuff in so no one knows what we've found except our group."

"What are you going to do?" He raised a brow and looked at me.

I gave him an impish smile, and flexed my fingers dramatically. "I'm going to get that cage open."

***

I'm nothing if not efficient. By the time Michael returned with the doctor and Skylar in tow, I'd just about finished with my task. The cage was held closed by a small padlock, so I had simply taken a pair of bolt cutters to it. Problem solved. The lock hit the ground with a heavy clang just moments before my family arrived to join me.

"My goodness!" the doctor exclaimed, adjusting his scratched spectacles to get a better look at our find. "I thought you were kidding, but I see you were very serious."

"Wow." Skylar stared at the guns with enormous eyes. "That's a lot of guns."

"No kidding," I agreed, shooting her an amused look. "Do me a favour and check out the rest of this place while we're getting this ready to shift?"

"Sure," Skye agreed readily. She turned and vanished through a doorway nearby, while Michael and I began carefully lifting down each weapon and inspecting it. I wasn't exactly an expert on guns, but I'd learned through trial and error how to disassemble and clean a handgun, and I definitely knew how to shoot one.

Michael seemed to know what he was doing better than any of us. He took each gun I handed to him and lifted it to his eye, carefully sighting down along the barrel. One by one, he inspected them, then either nodded or shook his head when he handed it back to me. Those he judged salvageable, I carefully packed into a crate they'd brought for that purpose. Those that were not, I set aside to be stripped down for parts. Everything would be useful, one way or another.

When we were done with the rifles, we moved on to the handguns, then to the boxes of ammunition stacked in neat columns beneath the weapon display. That was the most dangerous part, but we were lucky. Everything had been safely stored all those years ago, so nothing exploded in our hands.

"Sandy, come and look at this," Skye called through the doorway. I exchanged a glance with the others, then handed the box of ammunition I was inspecting to Michael and went off to see what my sister had found.

The doorway opened up into a tiny, single-room flat, with a decrepit old bed against one wall, and a kitchenette against the other. The entire living quarters was probably no larger than the stockroom where the guns were kept. My sister was bent over staring at something on a dusty old desk at the foot of the bed, but she looked up as I approached.

"This is a radio, right? One of those old-school things they used before cell phones?" She reached out to brush some dust from it, a look of intense curiosity on her face.

"I think so." I shrugged helplessly. "I couldn't tell you for sure, though – you know how I was about communication before I met up with you guys."

Skye heaved a long-suffering sigh, then called over her shoulder towards the door. "Doc? Michael? Do either of you know anything about radios?"

"Indeed, I do." The doctor responded to her cry for help, and came trundling over to peer at the object of our interest, absently adjusting his spectacles. "Well, now. If I am not mistaken, that's a shortwave ham radio kit."

"Ham radio," I echoed, rubbing my bruised wrist absently. "I remember that term. That was amateur radio, the two-way kind – right?"

"Indeed," the doctor agreed, then suddenly lashed out and smacked the back of my hand lightly. "Stop scratching!"

I yelped and danced out of his reach, while my lovely little sister laughed at my misfortune. The sound of my cry attracted Michael's attention, and he stuck his head into the room as well.

"What's going on in here?" he demanded.

"The doctor's beating me," I whined, retreating to the relative protection of his embrace – or at least, I tried to, but he knew me better than that.

"Well, stop scratching then," he teased me mercilessly, and left me pouting to go examine our find. "A radio? That'll be useful. Look, it's even hand-cranked – no batteries required. Good find. Skye, can you gather up all the pieces and take it back with us? Look around and see if you can find any spare components, too."

"Okay," Skylar answered agreeably and set about doing just that, while the men filtered back out to the guns. As soon as their backs were turned, she promptly stuck her tongue out at me and whispered, "Who's finding the cool stuff now?"

If I were a puppy, I'd have had my sad face on for a second there – sometimes sisters were *not* the coolest thing in the world. Then Michael called my name, and I forgot all about pretending to be the injured party as I hurried back out to join him.

***

It took us a while and a good amount of muscle power to get all of our new toys back to base. When the guns were in their crate it proved to be too heavy for one person to lift, so we each took a side and manhandled it back the way we'd come. A few more trips later, we finally had everything safely hidden in one of the downstairs storage rooms, beneath a mound of old clothing and behind a couple of huge sacks of rice.

There was some argument about what we should do with the guns now that we had them. Skylar argued that if we had them then we should use them, while the doctor joined the rest of us on the cautious side of the fence.

In the end, it was decided that we would train everyone to use them but only in the case of an actual emergency. Skye wasn't happy, of course, but she grudgingly accepted our more experienced judgement. She was too young to understand the concept that violence begets violence, but she did understand that we would make ourselves targets if we waved around something so valuable.

The radio was a whole other story. Radios had not been that common before the plague hit; by that stage, they were already outdated and had been replaced by the internet and mobile phones. Now, ten years later, our wonderful modern technology had more or less failed us, which turned a radio into something precious.

Skylar had found an instruction manual squirrelled away in the closet of the person who had once owned the ham radio. She was intensely fascinated by the idea of communicating with people outside of our own group, and roped all of us into helping with her project. We took turns assisting her with setting the radio up and learning to work it, which also gave us an opportunity to help her improve her reading as well.

We spent the next week or so keeping to ourselves. Michael and I divided our time between learning to use our new weapons, resting our injuries, and exploring the bounds of our new romance. Needless to say, we spent a lot of time in bed. And in the shower. And in any other interesting place we could get away with. Call it an experimental phase.

I'd missed out on that phase in my early twenties. Now that I was almost thirty, I felt like I deserved it – we both did.

Skye spent most of her time hunched over her radio, scanning the frequencies for any signs of life. Despite her reading difficulties, she picked up the basics of ham radio swiftly. After the first few hurdles, she only came to us for help on a rare occasion. However, she discovered that there just wasn't much to be heard on the airwaves anymore. I encouraged her to keep trying. After all, anyone on the other end was just another human being. They had to eat, sleep and forage for survival just like the rest of us, so they were unlikely to be sitting there all day waiting for her to contact them.

It was getting late in the season. Summer was almost over, and autumn well and truly on its way. The wind blew cold on occasion, but the sunshine was still warm. Over the course of the week, the weather cleared up. On one sunny morning, Michael and I lay contentedly on the roof, basking in the sun while we could. We'd finished assembling the railing around the edge, and had even added a small shelter at one end, in case we decided to position a guard up there one day. All in all, it was a ratty piece of work but it was functional.

I heaved a long sigh and folded my hands beneath my head, letting the warm tiles soothe me. The sky was a beautiful shade of azure adorned with delicate, fluffy clouds, and the sun shone down with just the right degree of heat – enough to warm, but not to burn. The breeze was crisp but not chilly, cooling us when the sun got a bit much, but not enough to make us shiver. Our bellies were full, our home was secure, and our family was safe. All in all, it was a perfect day as far as I was concerned.

Beside me, Michael made a contented sound and stretched out languidly, then turned his head and looked at me. "We should probably be doing something constructive."

"Nah." I flapped a hand to brush away the idea. "We've done plenty of constructive things. We deserve a rest."

"I like the way you think," he agreed amiably. Apparently, he was in too good a mood to fight over something as inconsequential as being useful. It was a beautiful day, too beautiful to waste on work. Winter would be here all too soon, and then we'd be trapped inside, dreaming about days like today.

So we loitered for a while, sunbathing, as useless as a pair of statues. I wasn't sure how much time passed, and I really didn't care. One of the few benefits of watching civilization fail was that we stopped having to count the time.

The days flowed in an endless stream, with no calendars to tell us what date it was. I didn't know what day of the week it was, or even what month. I guessed from the weather that it was around the middle of March, but more than that was a mystery. We had a vague idea of the year from counting the summers that had passed since we last saw our loved ones, but it really didn't matter anymore.

The days of counting the minutes between work or

school and home were no more. Gone was the daily grind. The watchful eye of society, that had once told me where to be and when, had gone to sleep forever. None of it mattered now. These were our days, and only we dictated how we spent our time.

Once the necessities of survival were taken care of, nobody could complain if we spent our days wisely or not. No one cared if we spent hours lost in books, exploring or even indulging in casual love-making, because there was no society left to judge us.

There was a strange kind of freedom that came with losing everyone and everything that used to matter. Without the shackles of social and moral guidance, each person had only his or her will to guide her actions. I used to hate having no goal or purpose; now that I had others to enjoy it with, the freedom had actually begun to be enjoyable.

I'd always been the type of person that went out of my way to keep myself busy. If I had nothing to do, then I usually ended up getting bored and inventing tasks for myself. I'd done it so often over the years that it had become second nature. Skylar once commented that I was the most proactive person she'd ever seen, but the truth was that I had just gotten really good at keeping myself busy, to avoid having to confront the reality of my world. When you spend a decade alone, you get very good at that. Now, my new family was teaching me the joys of laziness, and I found the process to be quite pleasurable.

The sun was still only halfway to its midday apex

when the sound of a distant engine stirred me from my doze. For a moment, I thought the sound was in my head, but when I opened my eyes to check I spotted a small figure bouncing along the trail from the west on the back of a farm bike.

I nudged Michael. He grunted in displeasure at being woken, but his annoyed expression faded into curiosity when he heard the engine as well.

"Trouble?" he wondered out loud, and glanced at me.

"Nah." I shook my head and stretched, feeling no great sense of urgency. "Looks like Hemi. He's probably just coming to chat up Skye."

Michael chuckled and flopped back down on the warm tiles, draping an arm over his eyes. "Ah, puppy love."

"If that's puppy love, what do we have, then?" I laughed, stretching up a little taller to wave at the kid on the motorcycle.

"Well, clearly we have an extremely mature relationship based on mutual friendship and respect," he answered dryly. His joke made me laugh even louder; the only time 'maturity' belonged in the same sentence as our names was with a thick slathering of sarcasm on top.

Our playful jousting was cut short when Hemi cruised into range, his little motorcycle bouncing under the weight of a heavy basket on the back. The bike swerved as it came to a halt, but Hemi knew what he was doing; he'd been riding that thing since childhood.

The young man shielded his eyes against the sun and peered up at us curiously.

"*Haere mai*," I called down, and waved to him. Although I didn't speak as much Maori as Michael did, I knew a few phrases, and considered it respectful to use them where I could. Our neighbours seemed to appreciate the effort, even if they spoke English as fluently as I did.

Hemi grinned and waved back at me. "Kia ora, mate! What are you doing up there, eh?"

"Sunbathing," I called back. "What are you doing down there?"

"Mum sent me to check on you guys." He grinned even wider and jerked a thumb back over his shoulder. "Plus, we were hoping to do some trading. You game?"

"Sure. I'll be right down," I agreed. I leaned over to nudge Michael and see if he was awake. He grunted and flapped a hand at me, so I let him be. I was happy enough to talk to Hemi on my own. In my mind, the kid had already moved from the 'stranger danger' category into the 'can be trusted… more or less' category. That was a big leap for someone was naturally paranoid as I am. There was also the fact that I was three inches taller than him, which probably helped my confidence.

I crawled across the roof and swung myself onto the ladder, then scampered down to the ground with light-footed ease. I had always been fit and agile, but over the last few weeks I'd spent more time running up and down ladders than the rest of my life combined.

When I hit the ground, I took off at a trot across the

courtyard. Hemi had barely finished parking his bike by the time I stepped out the front door, and he was in the middle of trying to wrestle the basket off his bike without dropping both. I hurried over to help.

"Thanks, mate," he acknowledged with a grateful smile. I took the basket's weight, and braced it against my knee so he could get the straps undone. The youth shot me another one of his impish grins while he was working, and looked me up and down. "You're looking better."

"I'm feeling better," I agreed, watching him worrying the straps to free the basket. "Definitely going to have a scar, though. Alas, my beauty is forever flawed."

"Somehow, I don't think Michael cares," Hemi teased. We both laughed at the joke.

Once the basket was free, he took its weight and carried it inside, with me in the lead to hold the doors open for him.

"How are the repairs going?" I asked as we made our way into the kitchen, where I helped him to lift the basket up onto the table. I'd learned from the others that the tribe had survived the fire physically unscathed, aside from a little smoke inhalation and a few light burns, but the damage to the buildings was extensive.

Hemi blew out a sharp breath and shook his head. "Not well, eh. A lot of our supplies got damaged. We've got plenty of food, but we're running low on construction materials – lumber, nails, tools, that kind of thing. I mean, we got plenty of trees so we can get lumber no problem, but it's hard to cut them down when all our saws are melted."

"Damn, that's rough. I guess that's why you're here, huh?" I gestured to the basket. Hemi nodded and gave me a wry smile.

"We need as many hands as we can get for the repairs, so it's easier to trade than scavenge. You guys are the closest," he admitted readily, then heaved a deep sigh. "Mum thinks that Lee's boys did it on purpose. They lit the fire where they knew it would cause us the most grief, to destroy all the stuff we can't replace. Bastards."

"Yeah, I wouldn't be surprised." I heaved a matching sigh and gestured for him to sit down. "You know, I didn't even know that guy's name until you just said it? We'll help, of course. You want a drink before we get started?"

Hemi nodded, so I fetched him one of the bottles of purified water we kept stocked up on at all times. He took it gratefully, popped the lid and took a swallow before continuing. "Thanks. We're happy to trade food for tools. I brought as much as I could carry, but we'll bring more over time. Even if we can just borrow some tools until we find our own to replace them, that would really save our hides."

"Don't worry, mate. I've got you covered," I reassured him as I settled down in a chair across the table from him. "I've got this place all mapped out so I know exactly where we can find what you need. Did your mum give you a list?"

"Yeah." Hemi fished a crumpled scrap of paper out of his pocket and handed it to me. I read over it quickly and nodded, confident I could find what they needed in short order.

"This is all basic stuff, no worries. You give me a couple of hours and I'll have what you need, okay?"

Hemi nodded enthusiastically. "Yeah, man – sweet as."

"I'll move faster on my own, so you can stay here," I told him as I rose back to my feet. I caught his glance towards the door, and hurried to hide my smile behind my hand. "Go on, then. She's probably in the common room."

"Cheers, mate!" Hemi waved, then rushed off with unseemly haste, leaving me chuckling to myself.

The kid was transparent as glass, but I wasn't complaining. Hemi was a nice boy, and Skye could use a nice boy to help her forget the one that had abandoned her. If there was one thing that Michael had taught me, it was that having someone to love you was a very important part of the human condition. It didn't matter whether it was the love of a friend, the love of a sweetheart, or the love of family – it was important just to be loved.

Chapter Ten

I don't know how Michael managed to find me, but he did. Apparently, that man either had a hell of a nose for his lady, or he was a way better tracker than I gave him credit for. I was bottoms up in the back of a dusty garage at the time, rooting around for a saw that I was sure I'd seen six weeks before.

He managed to take me completely by surprise; I damn near jumped out of my skin when I emerged from the garage with my prize, and came face to face with an unexpected human figure in the doorway. It took me a second to realise that he was just standing there, with a grumpy look on his face.

"Why the long face, sour-puss?" I enquired, picking my way across the overgrown yard to retrieve my sack of miscellaneous goodies from where I'd left it.

"I got pooped on," he answered dourly.

"Eh, what?" I turned and stared at him over my shoulder, then I suddenly realised that he'd changed shirts since I last saw him. "Oh, did a bird get you, sweetie? I'm sorry to hear that."

"That was my favourite shirt, too." He gave me the kind of pout that made me go weak at the knees, then wandered over to help me with my sack of treasures.

"It's just a little poo, it'll come out in the wash," I reassured him with a sympathetic pat on the shoulder, though it was very hard to keep a straight face. "Well, since you're here, you can help. Anahera's group are in need of tools and stuff to help them rebuild. I've already got most of it, but there's a few more things I need to grab."

"I'm always happy to help. Lead on, my love." His grumpy look faded away completely, and he gave me one of his sweet, lopsided smiles. When I leaned down to pick up the sack, he stopped me with a gentle touch so that he could take it instead. "Don't worry, I've got that. What am I good for if I let you carry all the heavy stuff?"

"Well, if you insist. Thank you, honey." I leaned up to press a kiss against his lips, then turned and led the way towards the last stash we needed. Although my inner feminist might have protested that I didn't need a big, strapping man to help me, she was swiftly silenced by the part of me that was just happy to have him close to me. I didn't need Michael's help, I wanted it. That was the difference. I wanted it, because I wanted his company. After spending ten years on my own, who could really blame me?

We walked together in companionable silence, the tromping of our boots across the overgrown fields the only sound that interrupted the birdsong all around us.

The singing stopped when we passed beneath the boughs of a tree, but it started again the moment that we moved on. The sound of it made me smile, but it also made me think.

"I wonder if we'll ever really be able to salvage what we used to have," I pondered out loud. "Do you think one day, in ten or twenty generations, we'll have towns again? Cities?"

"I don't know," Michael said, his deep voice close behind me. "I hope so. I hope that we'll have the chance to learn from our mistakes."

"Which mistake is that?" I asked, shooting a grin over my shoulder. "'Don't take Mother Nature for granted, because she's a vindictive bitch?'"

He chuckled and nodded. "That, and don't take the people you love for granted, either."

"I think that's the most important thing," I agreed, pausing for a moment to step carefully over a few fallen fence posts as we crossed the dividing line between properties. "You never know when you'll lose them. In retrospect, I guess I was one of the lucky ones. At least I had the chance to say goodbye."

"I'd give anything for that chance," he said softly, his voice huskier than usual. I glanced back again, concerned I might have upset him, but instead of tears I saw a wistful sort of sadness in his eyes. When he realised I was looking at him, he glanced up and offered a sheepish smile. I returned his smile, and led the way across an overgrown field that had once been someone's back yard.

With no one to trim it, the grass had grown thick and lush. It was waist-high now and difficult to wade through, but at least the mud had dried up. Come winter, the place would practically turn into a swamp. I silently prayed that I would not need to come through there during the wet season. Mud and I were not close friends.

I ducked beneath a lopsided clothesline and slogged the rest of the way across the yard towards the little shed at the back of the property. It was a small thing, no more than a couple of meters wide and about the same deep, but I had found a treasure trove of tools inside the last time I'd explored the area. The door swung on rusted hinges, squeaking faintly in protest with every gust of wind.

"I thought I closed that," I mumbled to myself, but I shrugged it off – there were doors askew and windows broken all over the place thanks to the storm.

I shoved the door open the rest of the way and quickly checked that there was nothing inside, then made my way into the gloom. Everything was as I left had it. I gathered what I needed without any problems, then picked my way back out to join Michael. I found him looking perturbed, staring down at the ground near his feet with a strange expression on his face.

"What is it?" I asked.

"Blood, I think." He didn't sound entirely certain. When I got closer, I could see why. The patch he'd spotted was old, dry and brown; it was hard to tell if it had been blood or just mud. Whatever it had been, it was large and spread over a sizable area. The grass had been crushed flat in the area, but no trace remained of whatever might have died there except for the blood – if it was blood.

"That's creepy, but it looks old. At least a couple of weeks." I shook my head and then looked up at him. "Whatever did that must be long gone by now. Let's go home."

"Agreed." Michael nodded, then he took my hand and together we left the scene and returned to our motel.

***

We made it home without any issues. I led the way back inside, and headed to the kitchen where Hemi's basket still waited patiently. Michael frowned when he saw it and shot me a look.

"Are you really going to make them give us stuff in exchange for things they need?" he asked, his tone of voice disapproving. I bristled instinctively. I hated it when he used that tone of voice on me.

"I'm not going to 'make' them do anything, but that is how trade works," I said, dumping my armful of goods down on the table beside the basket. "We have something they want, they have something we want, and so we swap. It was their idea to offer a trade, and they've always been willing to trade fairly."

He didn't have an answer to that. When I glanced at him again I saw a strange expression on his face. Once more, I was forced to acknowledge that he was new to the world outside his safe little bunker. I reached out to him, to place my hand upon his arm.

"This is how it works out here, sweetie." I softened my tone and rubbed his arm gently. "Trade and barter. We're lucky that Anahera and her group are honourable, but not everyone is like that. Many people will take whatever you offer them and run, then come back with a bunch of friends who 'need help' as well. They'll take everything you have and leave you with nothing." I ran my hand all the way up his arm to caress the side of his neck, gazing up at him. "If everyone were as generous as you, this world would be a much nicer place – but they're not."

He sighed and looked down, silently acceding the point to me. "It's just... it feels wrong, taking things from people in need. Particularly our friends."

"It's not wrong," I reassured him, trailing my fingers up over his cheek. "They offered us things they have in plenty – they're not going to suffer for losing them. That's how trade works. You save up things you find that other people might need, and when you need something, you barter with stuff you can afford to lose. It's also a little bit about pride, too. Some people don't like accepting charity. They'd rather have a fair trade, or work for what they're given. Trust me, I've been doing this for a long time."

I smiled up at him. He smiled back, nodding his agreement. "I defer to your experience, my love."

"Good." I stepped back so he could set his burden down, and then I started arranging the assorted tools we'd collected on the table beside the basket. "While we're on the subject though, I think we should give one of our walkie-talkies to Hemi to take back with him. It's a long way to run to check on one another, and it would be nice to have some way to connect with our neighbours if we need them, or they need us."

"That makes sense to me," he agreed. "Good thinking, Batman."

I started to reply, but before I could I suddenly found myself swept up in his arms, being cuddled vigorously, and kissed all up and down the side of my neck. The gesture took me so much by surprise that he had me well and truly caught before I had any chance of escaping it. I squeaked in surprise and wriggled in his arms, but I have to admit that I didn't fight very hard.

Of course, it was right at that moment that Hemi came tearing into the room with his arms flailing like a demented windmill, frantically calling our names. He skidded to a halt when he caught us mid-canoodle, staring at us wide-eyed. Michael released me so suddenly that I almost fell over.

"Gah! I don't need to see that!" Hemi yelped, covering his eyes with his hands. Once I recovered from the shock, I laughed merrily.

"Then don't come running in unannounced," I teased him. "'That' is fun, so we're doing it every chance we get."

Poor Hemi made a pathetic whining noise like an injured puppy, but he was a good-natured youth and was soon laughing right along with us. When the levity faded, he suddenly seemed to remember why he'd been looking for us to begin with.

"Oh, oh, I almost forgot. Skye told me to find you guys. She got a signal – come on!" Hemi beckoned to us excitedly then rushed from the room. Michael and I exchanged a look, and then took off after him.

That signal could mean more survivors, or it could mean nothing. There was only one way to find out.

***

The three of us huddled behind Skylar as she struggled to tune in the signal. We could hear the sound of a voice speaking, but it was too faint to make out the words.

"The reception might be better upstairs," I suggested. "There might be something blocking the signal down here."

Skye nodded, leaping to our feet. With our combined efforts, we carried the radio upstairs, along with the little card table and chair she'd acquired to sit it on. Along the way, the doctor stuck his head out to see what we were doing. Soon he and Madeline joined our entourage as well. A few minutes later, all six of us were huddled around the little radio while Skye searched for the signal she'd heard earlier.

This time when she found it, it came through clearly enough for us to understand the words. The signal strength wasn't great, but it was enough.

"—any able-bodied survivors in the Waikato region. Urgent assistance is required. Attention any able-bodied survivors, please respond..."

"He sounds exhausted," I said, glancing at the ring of faces around me.

"Can you answer him?" Michael asked.

"I think so. Let me try." Skye stared at the radio thoughtfully for a moment, then she fussed with it a bit and spoke awkwardly into the small microphone. "Hello? Can you hear me?"

"Affirmative, we can hear you!" The reply came almost immediately, and the voice sounded very relieved. "Oh, thank God. We were starting to think there was no one out there."

"Sorry, we only just detected your signal. It's very faint," Skye replied, then glanced over her shoulder at us. "Where are you located, mate? What's wrong?"

"Arapuni Power Station," the voice replied, then there was a pause. The silence dragged on for so long that we thought we'd lost them, but then they returned. This time, the voice was female. "Please, we need assistance. We've been doing our best to keep the station going, but a tree came down in the last storm and it's blocked the intakes. We had to shut the power station down and we can't clear it alone."

"So that's why the power's still off." I looked up again and caught Michael's eye. He nodded silently, acknowledging what I was thinking. We'd all wondered why the grid hadn't come back online yet.

"Well, if we ever want to have another hot shower again, we should see if we can help them," Skye said. There were nods of agreement all around – even from

Hemi. Michael hurried out to go find our maps, while Skye spoke into the microphone again. "What kind of help do you need?"

"Muscle-power, mostly," the voice replied. "We have all the equipment we need, but we just don't have enough hands. It's just me and my husband here." There was another short pause, and then the woman's voice dropped down low. "We could use medical supplies, if you have any to spare."

There was a fuss in the background and we heard the male voice protesting, but the female ignored him. "My husband broke his arm trying to clear the block. I trained as a nurse, so I've set the break, but we have no painkillers or antibiotics of any kind. I'm concerned about infection."

Skye looked at me for instruction, as de facto leader in Michael's absence. I thought it over for all of half a second before I gave her a nod and gestured to the doctor, who also agreed immediately. Skye clicked the microphone on again, and spoke into it once more. "We have a doctor with us. I'm going to put him on to talk to you, so he can work out if we can help you."

We could all hear the voice thanking us profusely as Skye stepped back, and Dr Cross took her place. Michael returned a moment later, so we filled him in on the conversation he'd missed as we spread out the maps and located the point in question.

"Here. The power station will be close to Arapuni township," I said, my finger falling on a point about 50 kilometres from our current position. "It's a long way, but if we want power back then we have to help. Plus, it's the right thing to do."

Michael smiled at that comment and nodded his agreement. "You're right. They're alone and injured, we can't just leave them."

"And they've been providing us with a service all of these years," I added. "We owe them a lot for that. It seems like a fair trade to me."

"I think Mum will want to help, too," Hemi added, leaning over to inspect the map with us.

"Can you spare the manpower right now?" I shot a worried look at him, but he just shrugged.

"We have to, I think. Like you said, we owe these people a lot, and we want the power back on as much as you do." He flashed us a grin, showing straight, white teeth that contrasted vividly against his smooth brown skin. "Lord knows I need a shower."

"Yeah, you really do," Skye teased him playfully, then squealed gleefully and ducked out of reach when he made a mock charge in her direction.

"Keep it down, you two – Doc's trying to listen," I scolded playfully, amused by their antics. To my surprise, they actually obeyed, though that might have been because Skylar ducked behind me to use me as a human shield.

"I'll go get Hemi sorted with a radio and his tools, so he can head home and speak to Anahera," Michael volunteered, then glanced to me. "Take care of the planning for us? You know the area best."

"I'm on it." I sketched a salute, which made him

smile. He nodded to me and quickly kissed my cheek, then took Hemi and left us to our planning. The doctor was just finishing up with his questions when I approached. He glanced at me and gestured for me to take over. I settled in the chair and drew a deep breath to bolster my confidence. Skye quickly showed me the button to press to make it work, and I did so.

"Hi, I'm Sandy," I introduced myself. "I need to ask you some questions about the terrain en route to your location. Are you able to answer?"

"Hello. My name is Rebecca Merrit and my husband's name is Jim," The female voice replied. "We haven't moved from here in a while, but we'll do our best to answer your questions. Which direction will you be coming from?"

"The west," I said. "Our base of operations is in Ohaupo."

"Ohaupo? That was my home town. How's the place holding up?"

"Not well," I told her honestly; there was no sense in lying. "You really don't want to know what it was like when we got here."

"Oh... I'm sorry to hear that, but I'm not surprised." She paused for a long moment, then pointedly changed the subject. "How many people do you have with you?"

"Five, but that's including children, so we'll only be bringing two adults." I heard Skylar start to protest, but I ignored her. "There's also about a dozen people living on one of the lakes a little further west, too, but I'm not sure how many they'll be able to send yet – they've just had a fire."

"Only two… well, seven hands are better than three. We'll take any help we can get. We've been broadcasting as often as we can all week and you're the first people we've heard a reply from."

"Your signal is very faint," I explained. "We barely heard you at all – we just happened to get lucky. What's the terrain like between here and Arapuni? I've been to the south and the east a bit, and it was pretty wild out there. I have maps and a GPS unit, but I'm sure I don't need to tell you how out of date they are."

"Definitely wild this way, too," the woman agreed. "We have tried to keep the roads clear, but there's only so much two people can do. Keeping the station running takes most of our time. You'll need to take the south road through Te Awamutu. The northern route was blocked a few years back by a rock fall."

"Got it." I followed the route on the map with my finger. "What's the condition of the river? I can't tell from this map."

"It runs through a gorge at Arapuni, and flattens out to the north and south," she explained. "Stick to the road though, and cross at the bridge by the catchment dam. The bush is extremely dense on your side of the river. I don't recommend trying to ford the river if you can avoid it. The current is deceptively strong."

"Noted." I traced the curve of the river to the bridge and tapped it absently with one fingernail. That bridge meant a long detour to the south, but we'd have to do it – I had no intention of getting myself drowned.

"What about the infected in your region? Are they a threat?"

"Infected humans? No. We've put most of them out of their misery already. This is pig country, though, so be careful."

"Ugh, I hate pigs." I sighed and made a mental note to go armed.

"Yeah, me too. They're no good at negotiating steep inclines, though, so at least the terrain works to your advantage." She sounded sympathetic. I filed that bit of information away for future reference. "When you're on the east side of the river, follow the road north. The station is on the centre island, where the river splits. Do you see it?"

"I see it. How do we cross?"

"When you're heading north towards the town centre, keep an eye out for an old walkway that branches off towards the west. I'll mark it for you so you can't miss it. The path will lead you to a swing bridge, and then just follow the path south again."

"So, kind of like a spiral." I considered the map thoughtfully. That was a lot of extra travel, but we didn't have much choice. "Are you okay for supplies? Food, water, clothing?"

"We're fine for the basics, thank you. Arapuni township was well-stocked, and we're pretty much on our own down here. We can feed your people while you're here, too." There was silence for a moment, and then the man's voice returned. "If you've got any vodka, though, I'd kill for a drink."

I couldn't help but laugh, and heard the others chuckling behind me. "I'll see what I can do. It'll take us a couple of days to reach you, so stay safe."

"You too, lass. Mind the pigs. And... thank you."

Chapter Eleven

As soon as I was off the radio, Skylar was on me like a dog on a bone.

"Why can't I go? I'm an adult. I'm useful. I could help!" She smacked me in the arm with one petite fist. "Don't treat me like a baby!"

The doctor took one look at the potential fight brewing and made himself scarce. He muttered something about needing to put the prescriptions together and hurried out of the room. I just rolled my eyes, then turned my full attention on Skylar.

"I have never once treated you like a baby, Skye. I consider you a grown adult, and a strong, capable member of this group," I told her calmly. That answer seemed to surprise her, which gave me a momentary respite to justify my decision. "In fact, that's why I want you to stay. If we took you as well, we'd be stripping all the defenders away from our home and leaving it completely undefended.

"I need you to stay here because I know I can trust you to take care of our home, and Madeline. Doc's getting on in years, and you know that he just about wets himself if someone asks him to fight. If something happens, I want someone here that I know can hold her own. I also need you to manage communications, and you're especially good at that."

Skylar stared at me, her brow furrowed in confusion.

I sighed, and translated into layman's terms. "I need you to talk to other survivors on behalf of the group."

Her expression brightened. "Oh, you mean like Hemi's tribe?"

"Precisely," I said, nodding. "Michael's giving him one of our walkie-talkies, but by the time he gets home we're probably going to be out of range. If they decide to come and help as well, you're going to need to pass the directions on to them. You were listening, right?"

"I remember every word." Skye nodded enthusiastically, her anger forgotten and her eyes twinkling. I knew then that I'd sold her on the idea. Hey, apparently I was getting back into the big sister groove after all, or maybe I'd picked up one or two of Michael's leadership skills..

"Good." I put a hand on her shoulder and gave it a gentle squeeze. "If they decide to go, tell them everything. They're cool, so if they need to borrow anything, then let them, so long as it doesn't put us in danger. I trust you to use your best judgement. Even more importantly, I need you to keep track of things around here, and reassure me you guys are okay – you know how worried I get. I'll call you on the first evening after we arrive, at sunset."

"Okay, I can do that." She nodded again and embraced me quickly, then stepped back and looked up at me. "Sorry I doubted you, sis."

"It's okay." I smiled down at her and gave her a wink. "I'd have thought the same thing in your position. The only reason I selected Michael and me to go is because he's the physically strongest of us, and I have the most mechanical knowledge. You're better at managing people than I am, and you're a good shot as well, so it just seems logical that you hold down the home front."

"Makes sense," Skye agreed, her short blonde curls bobbing as she nodded vigorously. "You can count on me."

Suddenly looking very pleased with herself, Skye spun on her heel and bounced out of the room. I watched her go, shook my head in amusement, and headed off about my own business. My task, as the group's makeshift mechanic, was to make sure our even more makeshift mechanicals were in functioning order before we went anywhere.

I popped into the kitchen to fetch the keys to the Hilux off their shelf, then headed for the door. During my routine check-ups on the vehicles, the utility's engine had been starting to get less and less reliable. Something was wrong with it, but I couldn't work out exactly what it was or how to fix it. It came as no great surprise to me, though. The poor old truck was probably about as old as I was; it was kind of a miracle that we'd gotten this much use out of it.

When I stepped outside, I saw Michael and Hemi working together to load the basket back onto the little farm bike. I waved at them. They waved back, but they seemed to have everything under control so I left them to it and headed down the road towards the old mechanic's workshop. The workshop was clean, dry and spacious, and had all the tools I needed on hand, so it had seemed like a logical place to keep our cars.

The minivan sat abandoned in the yard, waiting to be disassembled for parts. It had died the long death barely two days after we'd arrived in Ohaupo, and no amount of coaxing or cursing had convinced it to return from the other side of the grave. Our prison transport was faring much better than either of the others, for the simple reason that it'd been stored underground for the last decade. Unfortunately, it was ill-suited for our current mission.

I knew the condition of the roads near Te Awamutu, and we'd need a four-wheel drive to get through. My Hilux was the best vehicle for the job, but the problem was that whenever I started her up, she made a bizarre sound, like the cough of a dying walrus. I hadn't found the source of the problem yet, but I knew that was not a good noise for a car to be making.

The temperature changed as I stepped out of the sun and into the cool, dark shadow of the garage. For a moment, I regretted the need to leave the sunshine, but then my internal temperature adjusted and I forgot all about my brief discomfort. I went over to the car and pulled open the driver's door, then stuck the keys in the ignition and turned. The Hilux whined and coughed pathetically, complaining about the need to work.

It took three tries before the ignition finally caught. The engine spluttered to life, but it only did so reluctantly and with an assortment of very unhappy noises. Intent on trying to figure out what was the matter, I went around to the front of the machine and popped up the bonnet. The Hilux was a lifeline for us. It was the only way we had to get from point A to point B without having to travel on foot. I was concerned that losing it would cut off our freedom to move. There were a few other vehicles lying abandoned on the outlying farms that I could probably repair if I had to, but fixing them up would cost valuable time that we didn't really have.

"What's wrong with it?" a familiar, deep voice asked. I glanced over my shoulder and saw Michael's broad frame outlined in the doorway.

"I think it needs a new starter motor, or maybe an alternator," I answered, returning my attention to the engine. "The problem is that I have no idea how to replace one of those, and we don't really have time for me to figure it out."

"I guess we'll have to risk it. If something happens, we'll ditch it and come back for it later," Michael suggested. I sighed, not much liking the option, but it was the only one we had.

"We better pack wisely, then," I said, straightening

up and planting my hands on my hips. Then a second pair of hands joined mine, and I felt a strong, warm body pressing up against my back.

"Mhm... very wisely," he agreed, nuzzling his face in against the curve of my neck. His hands slipped around my waist, sliding up beneath my top to explore my belly; I suddenly realised that I could feel the evidence of where his thoughts had gone pressed up against my back.

"Really, Officer Chan?" I teased him. "Here? Isn't public nudity a criminal offense?"

"It's only an offense if you have a public to offend," he answered, grunting something that resembled a chuckle. His lips were so close against my ear that I could barely make out what he was saying – but for once in his life, his law-abiding nature didn't seem to be at the forefront of his thoughts.

Before I knew it, our clothing had somehow miraculously disappeared, and we were up against the side of the Hilux breaking as many laws as we could think of.

***

Later, once our rampant libidos had been sated and we could focus on the task at hand, I drove the Hilux around to the motel and parked it out the front while we organised our gear. Since we knew that we might have to ditch the truck at a moment's notice and continue on foot, we packed lightly.

One spare change of clothes, plus socks and

underwear for a week. Four days' worth of food and water, GPS unit, maps and a first-aid kit. Camp stove and cooking equipment. Sleeping bags and jackets for night time. Walkie-talkies. Weapons.

Michael and I decided that it was in our best interest to take one of the new weapons with us, since we were going in to pig country. Neither of us had any desire to take on a pig without the proper protection. I took Michael's shotgun, since it was a weapon that I was familiar and comfortable with, and Michael armed himself with one of the M16s.

We added spare ammunition to the pile, on the justification that it was better to be safe than sorry when it came to infected wildlife. Michael volunteered to take the weight, and I was grateful for it. While I was athletic, I had to acknowledge his superior physical strength. It wasn't his success or my failure. It was just a fact of nature. He was biologically hardwired for it.

I found it interesting to observe that one of the side-effects of having to live in the ruins of a dead civilization was that in some ways feminism had died along with it, while in other ways it had grown stronger than ever. Now, every hand was equally important to the survival of the group as a whole, because the strengths of one person balanced out the weaknesses of another. We'd finally achieved equality, but it was through acknowledging and accepting our differences instead of trying to ignore them. The gender dynamic of the human species seemed to have evolved.

Anahera's tribe was a prime example. In her

previous life she'd been a primary school teacher, but now that experience gave her the skills to lead. She wasn't the strongest, oldest, or the most skilled of her group, but no one seemed to doubt her leadership, or suggest that someone else should be in charge. She ordered her men to jump, and they jumped – not because she had breasts, or because she scared them, but because they knew that they could rely on her to keep them all alive.

I had noticed with a detached fascination that the same thing seemed to have begun to evolve amongst the members of my own group. Although Michael had been the de facto leader when I met them, more and more often my group-mates were looking to me for advice, information or guidance – even Michael. No... *especially* Michael.

I rather liked the feeling, knowing people looked up to me. Despite having spent the last ten years as a loner, Michael had been right when he pointed out that I was a social butterfly by nature. The only reason I had become an introvert to begin with was as a defence mechanism to protect me from the terrible situations that I'd found myself in over the years. Fear was a cocoon, to protect the fragile butterfly inside me from the dangers of the outside world.

Michael had once called me gregarious, and at the time I'd denied it. As time passed and I had a chance to mull it over, I'd come to understand what he meant – and more importantly, to realise that he was right. Necessity had forced me to bottle up that aspect of my personality, and bury it so far down in my psyche that I'd forgotten about it. As I spent more and more time more time around good people, I began to remember the parts of me that I'd hidden away: I liked people. I liked being around people. I liked talking and helping, loving and being loved.

That was a trait that had made me vulnerable, and that vulnerability had made me an easy victim for the predators of the world, so I'd hidden it away deep inside where it couldn't hurt me anymore. Now, being around friends and family that cared about me had helped me to dig that trait back up from the deepest recesses of my mind. Not only had I gained a family, but I had also regained a piece of myself.

Once, when we'd lain together in the dark enjoying the easy companionship of being together, Michael had told me how much he enjoyed watching me evolve before his very eyes. He had said it was like watching a butterfly finally emerging from her chrysalis after so many years of waiting.

I had smiled to myself in the dark, thinking that was probably about the most romantic thing anyone had ever said to me, then I'd promptly accused him of calling me a caterpillar. We'd both laughed.

Although it had been less than two months since I had joined the group, I'd come to greatly value the opinions of my little family. I really enjoyed knowing that they looked up to me, and that they respected me for my experience. I was pleased by the thought that they missed me when I went away, and were happy to see me when I came home again.

I guess everyone likes to feel wanted and needed. It's human nature. Even after everything that had happened to me, I was still no different at the core.

Chapter Twelve

It was early afternoon by the time we were ready to depart. Rather than wait for the next morning, we decided to set off immediately and make the most of the hours we had left until sunset. The days were still long at this time of the year, so I estimated we could probably get as far as Te Awamutu before dark.

Skylar, the doctor, and Maddy stood together in a huddle by the door while Michael and I loaded our backpacks into the rear cab of the Hilux. Once we were done, the doctor came over to give us the medicine, and Skylar brought a bottle of something she'd found in our stores.

"I don't know what this is, but I think it's alcohol." She peered at the label and read it out slowly. "Rum... rum? Is that booze?"

"Yes." I laughed as I took the bottle from her, and wrapped it up in my spare clothing to keep it safe. "Well done, your reading is getting much better."

"Thanks." Skye beamed proudly, and then she enveloped me in a hug that lingered just a little longer than it should. "Take care of yourself, sis."

"I will. We'll be back before you know it." I hugged her back, understanding without words that she was worried about us and trying very hard not to show it. I felt the same way, so I held her tight for a minute, then hugged Maddy and the doctor as well.

They waved to us as we headed away from the motel, and I found myself wondering if we'd ever see them again. I felt guilty for lying to my sister when I had told her the reasons I wanted her to stay. While every word I'd said had been true, I'd lied to her by omission. I had failed to tell her the biggest reason I didn't want her along was because I feared that we were walking into a trap. I couldn't stop Michael from coming if I tied him up to the nearest lamppost, but at least if I died then I would die knowing I'd kept my baby sister safe. There would be someone left to carry on my family line, and there would be someone left to remember me.

I took the wheel for the first leg of the journey, since I'd come along the southern road on foot not that long ago. Our plan was to take the same route for a while, then swing east at Te Awamutu. With any luck, that would keep us well clear of the dangerous gang territory further south.

For over a year, I'd used Te Awamutu as a refuge from those gangs. At some point before my arrival, a localized earthquake had devastated the little city, and reduced its buildings to hazardous piles of rubble, shards of glass and twisted steel. Most of the water sources were tainted, and there was little to interest the other survivors when easier sources of sustenance were just a few days away. I was no ordinary survivor.

When I had arrived in that little town, I'd felt just like one of those shattered buildings. I had just escaped from captivity, after being tormented, tortured, and brutally raped over the course of days, maybe even weeks. I had been so wrapped up in my own misery that I'd lost track of the time.

I had limped into that town a broken woman, my clothing in tatters, my hair matted, and my body covered in filth and blood. Most of the blood was mine, but some of it had belonged to the man I'd killed to escape.

My survival had been a matter of sheer luck. The man with the tattooed face, Lee, had left camp with most of his friends, leaving just one man behind to guard me. They'd thought I was too far gone to fight back. I remembered that the guard had been drunk. He'd tried to force himself on me again, but had fallen asleep before he could get it up. I remember the rank stench of his breath as he snored in my face, as clear as day.

They had underestimated my desire to live, and it cost that man his life. I knew where they'd tossed my belongings when they caught me, and the drunk had loosened my bonds when he'd decided to use me. I found my bag, and in it was my gun. The drunk had stirred awake just long enough to see his own death coming. I shot him right between the eyes, with no hesitation and no mercy. God knows they hadn't shown me any.

Then I took my things and I ran, as far and as fast as I could. I ran for days, until my water ran out and my feet were so blistered I could barely walk. But I was clever enough to cover my tracks, and when I reached Te Awamutu I knew I'd found somewhere I could hide. I'd searched carefully amongst the ruins until I found one water source that was still clean. I made my home near it, inside an old shipping container.

Living in the ruins of Te Awamutu had been a humbling and depressing experience, one that reminded me of the destruction of the beautiful city of Christchurch in similar circumstances, almost a decade earlier. Except back then, there had been people. People to recover and rebuild. Te Awamutu had been a ghost town. There was no one there to care for her, or return her to the way she had been.

It was an appropriate place for the shattered soul I had been to cower and lick her wounds. Now, I was going to return, with the man I loved at my side. I had mixed feelings about returning to that place in my life.

"You're scowling," Michael commented softly. I glanced at him, and discovered that he was watching me. He was relaxing in the passenger seat with one arm resting on the edge of the open window, content to let me negotiate the uneven roads in peace. At least, he had been. Now after many long minutes of silence, he was studying me. I suddenly felt uncomfortable.

"I'm just... focused." I tried to brush it away rather than have to explain, but Michael wasn't having any of it.

"No, you're not. I know that face." He absently brushed away an insect that had buzzed inside the cab, and then gave me a faint smile. "Tell me what's bothering you."

My shoulders slumped; I was so transparent, I couldn't even get away with harmless white lies. "It's just... I lived down this way for a while, before I came north. It wasn't a good time of my life. I'm not ready to talk about it yet. I'm sorry, Michael."

I gave him an imploring look, a look that silently said 'if you love me, you'll leave it at that'. Apparently, he did love me. He gave me a long, hard stare, then he just nodded and went back to watching the scenery roll by.

The road directly south of Ohaupo was familiar to me; I'd walked this way once, and then driven around the area a few times to reach the outlying farms. The roads were fractured and overgrown but not blocked, so we made good time to start with. As we left the township, the narrow rural roads widened into a thick strip of dusky grey that wound off into the horizon, the road markings worn away by time and the weather.

Land that had once been all picturesque little farmsteads set amongst tidy green fields had grown into wild, overgrown pastures interspersed with destroyed buildings, fallen fences and the occasional patch of young native bush. Nature's reclamation process was brutal and unforgiving, but it was beautiful in its own way.

I kept our place slow but steady as the road surface grew gradually more erratic. A flash of water through the trees to our left drew our eye momentarily, marking the passing of another lake. Michael shifted the map around and identified it, to keep track of our progress.

A few minutes later, we came across an overturned milk tanker blocking the road, its contents long since evaporated away. I'd walked around it on the way north so I knew that it was coming and had planned my route in advance. When we reached it, I nudged the Hilux far to the left and eased it gently around the wreck. One tyre clipped the ditch on the side of the road and spun for a moment in the gravel, then it caught and we were off again.

Eventually, the road began to narrow, turning into a slender ribbon of cracked asphalt. The bush flanking the road grew thicker and thicker, but it was still young and wasn't tall enough to block out the sun yet. The roots were well on their way to destroying the road itself, though. Grass already peeked up through the cracks. In another ten or twenty years, there would be nothing left of this old highway.

"The storm really made a mess here," Michael murmured thoughtfully, staring out the window. I made a sound of agreement, but I had to keep my attention focused on the road to avoid the very debris that he was talking about. When I had walked northwards, it'd only been a mild inconvenience, but now there were large branches and mounds of leaves scattered all across the road. Our tyres ground over something that I failed to spot in time and made the entire vehicle shudder, but I had chosen the Hilux for a reason. I gunned the powerful engine until I felt us clear the obstruction, and then we were back on our way.

The road began a long, slow curve to the left and the trees began to thin. A few minutes later, they trailed off into an assortment of low, scrubby bushes that allowed us to see the first signs of the devastation. I glanced at Michael, and caught him staring in mute fascination at a low farmhouse to the left of the road. The tremors had hit it with enough force that the little homestead had collapsed like a house of cards.

Suddenly, the truck hit a deep rut in the road. Beside me, Michael grunted in surprise and grabbed the dashboard to keep himself from being flung out of his seat.

"Put your seatbelt on, honey," I warned him. "It's only gets worse from here."

"What happened to this place?" he asked, hurrying to obey my instruction. I belted up as well, then gently nudged the truck forward. Again, we grated over deep furrows in the roadway. The entire truck bounced and shook. Michael leaned out the window and stared at the ground, and I heard his sharp intake of breath.

I knew what he was seeing, I'd walked over it on my way north. The road had ended up rippled like the surface of a pond that had been snap-frozen in the middle of a windy day. In some places, the pressure had been too much for the old tar seal to bear, and it had left behind jagged ridges and ruts. The truck struggled to get over some of them, even with its four-wheel drive.

"Earthquakes. Brace yourself," I explained, and took my own advice as we went over a particularly rough ridge. Beside me, I heard Michael yelp. I shot a worried glance at him as we cleared the lip. He was clinging on with both hands now, a look that was equal parts nervousness and steely determination on his face. "There was at least one big one, possibly more than one, and a bunch of aftershocks I'm betting."

"Jesus. And you lived down here?"

"Yep," I winked at him, then turned my attention back to the road. "Keep holding on. It's only just begun."

***

By the time we reached the outskirts of Te Awamutu, we'd found a whole new meaning for that old saying about five miles of bad road. The Hilux was making even more unhappy noises than usual, and we were in no better condition. The tension of having to brace ourselves for hours against the constant juddering, the sudden drops and peaks, and the occasional ominous screeches was stressful in the extreme.

We passed from farmland into the rural equivalent of suburbia, but the devastation was so wholesale that it was painful to look at. Nothing had been left standing. What the earthquake had failed to flatten had been razed by fire in the aftermath of the quakes, or by storms over the subsequent years.

The frame of a gutted house stood stark against the setting sun, like the carcass of a long-dead monster, its bones blackened by the raging flames of yesteryear. The fire had burned out of control and spread death through the forest for kilometres to the east. Even years later, it hadn't fully recovered. Only a few sprouts of grass and a couple of saplings had managed to sprout from the barren earth. That would be our highway.

"We're going off-road," I warned Michael. I felt him tense up beside me as I eased the wheel to the left and took us down off the edge of the roadway. The wheels crunched as we rolled across the ashen wasteland and slowly headed towards the east. Strangely, it was a smoother ride across the sooty ground than over the broken asphalt, and most of the small obstructions were so badly burnt that they dissolved beneath the Hilux's tyres.

"Didn't you say that she said to stick to the road?" Michael protested. I shook my head.

"Impossible. They obviously haven't been here since before the quake," I explained, leaning high in the driver's seat to eyeball the uneven ground before us. "You think it's bad here? You haven't seen anything like the centre of town. If we cut across here, we should hit one of the back roads soon, and we'll use them to skirt around the edge of town."

"Planning to get us killed already?" he teased, obviously trying to relieve the tension. I gave him a smile as a reward, even if I didn't really feel it. This place was full of memories, and none of them were good.

The ground was spongy with decayed plant matter, but it held out beneath the truck's weight. By the time the sun started to set in earnest, we'd cleared the other side and found a narrow, winding back-country road, one that was little more than a single-lane track. The bush started to get thicker again, to the point where it covered our path with long shadows that made it difficult to see.

There was a low, deep crunch when the asphalt ended, and we found ourselves on a gravel road barely visible through the long grass. In front of us, the trail climbed up a gentle hill, and at the top I could see a clearing. I gently touched the accelerator to ease us up the incline, wary of damaging the truck on something I couldn't see.

As if reading my mind, we hit something with a heavy clunk. I froze for a second, then leaned out the window to check what it was. An old electric fence – electric no more – lay crushed beneath our wheels.

"Oops." I gave Michael a sheepish grin.

He laughed and patted my knee reassuringly. "Oh well, too late now. Keep going."

I nodded and put my foot down again. We cleared the obstruction and climbed the rise slowly. Although it was only a slight incline, the view as we came over the crest was stunning. The hill was just high enough for us to see the landscape for miles in all directions, and it gave us a commanding view of the land we had yet to traverse.

"This seems like a good place to stop for the night," Michael suggested, pointing ahead of us. "In there?"

At the crest of the hill, our path branched off towards a high metal fence that still stood proudly, guarding a large house that had been turned to kindling in one of the quakes. I saw what attracted him immediately. It was a defensible position that we would be able to fortify easily. I nodded and eased the truck closer.

With his gun at the ready, Michael hopped out of the passenger seat and moved to the gate, scanning the area for anything remotely hostile. Once he was done, he turned and gave me a thumbs-up, then he opened the gate so that I could drive through. Once we were safely inside the ring of high metal fencing, he shut the gate and I backed the Hilux up until its tail rested against it, effectively preventing anyone – or anything – from entering without permission.

I put the truck in park, killed the engine, and climbed out to join him with my shotgun at the ready. Between the two of us, we stalked the interior of the compound, guarding one another's backs as we circled the old house to ensure nothing was hiding behind it. Everything seemed safe from a distance, but neither of us were willing to take chances with the life of the person we loved; we'd only just found one another, and I certainly had no intention of putting that love in jeopardy.

The long grass hid few secrets from our watchful eyes. The only things that stirred were the birds in the trees, singing and fluttering from branch to branch as they put themselves to bed. I agreed with that notion; after a long day of travel, I was ready to rest. Although the bare earth might have been softer, Michael and I unrolled our sleeping bags side by side on the cracked concrete of the old homestead's driveway, because it felt safer than sleeping in the long grass.

"We could sleep in the back of the truck, if you want. It'd probably be more comfortable," I suggested as we sat down on our sleeping bags, and began setting up the gear to cook our dinner. The little gas cooker felt like such a luxury when resources were running low, and there were so few people around capable of making things to replace them. We'd found it in a cache before we left Hamilton. If it hadn't been for that, then we would have had to gather dry wood and build a fire the old fashioned way.

"Nah." Michael shook his head. "I think it'll be more comfortable out here. I've always enjoyed the thought of sleeping beneath the stars."

"I think you've been living in a bunker for too long, honey," I told him with amusement.

He gave me one of his quirky smiles and shrugged. "Maybe. I used to like camping in the old days, too."

"I guess it's all fun and games when your life doesn't depend on it," I answered, thinking back to my own childhood. I'd felt the same way. To distract myself, I rooted around in my backpack and fished out the food I had planned for our dinner. In addition to a few other things, I pulled out that old can of mushroom soup that I'd scavenged so many weeks ago. I still hadn't worked up the courage to open it and find out if was edible, but tonight was the night. If it was still good, then it seemed appropriate to share it with someone that I loved.

"Hey, I remember this stuff." Michael reached over and took the can from my hands, turning it over to examine the familiar branding on the label. "Where in the world did you find that?"

"In someone's larder," I answered, leaning over to take it back. "I've been hanging on to it for a while. You up for a gamble, honey?"

He gave me a smile and leaned over to brush a strand of hair off my cheek. "I took a gamble on you, didn't I?"

"You have a point. Okay, cross your fingers – and hold your breath." I took my own advice as I reached for the pop-tag that opened the tin; I knew as well as anyone that when canned soups decided to go rancid, they did so in a spectacular fashion. After weeks of anticipation, I was almost afraid to end the wait, but it was time. I squeezed my eyes shut as I thumbed open the tag. There was a creak as the lid rolled back and then... nothing.

I opened my eyes and stared down into the can, astounded to discover that the food was actually still edible. After all the build-up, I'd been expecting a congealed black mess.

"Hey, looks like we win," Michael commented, eyeing the contents of the can. Then he leaned over and planted a kiss on the side of my neck, along with a little playful little nuzzle. "Are you planning to share that with me?"

"'Course not," I teased, putting on an offended face just to mess him. "What kind of girl do you think I am, sharing my food with creepy old men? Go get your own, this is mine!"

I wasn't being serious and he knew it, but he made a show of whining like a neglected puppy and trying to steal my soup away. By the time we were done playing, I found myself giggling like a schoolgirl and feeling surprisingly refreshed. After spending hours travelling through the devastated countryside, his good humour helped to elevate my mood.

"Okay, okay, you can have some. Now, give me the pot, you silly man," I scolded playfully. Grinning, he fished the little steel cooking pot in question out of his pack and put it in my hand. I dumped the contents of my precious can into it and set it over the gas cooker to warm up. While it was heating, I added some more water to thin it, then a packet of dried noodles and some smoked fish to turn the soup from a light snack into a proper dinner.

"Now, this is food I approve of," Michael commented, leaning over my shoulder to watch me curiously while I was cooking.

"But there's no vegetables," I complained.

"Caveman need no vegetables, only meat." He

made a few silly grunts, then caught me around the waist and pulled me up close against him. "Meat and pretty lady. Pretty lady looks tasty."

I squealed in surprise when he unleashed a teasing love-bite on my neck, followed by a string of kisses and even a little light tickling. When he was done, we both collapsed in a panting, laughing heap, exhausted but happy just to be in one another's company.

Once the food was cooked, we ate together, enjoying the delicious savoury taste of mushroom and fish, then we curled up to sleep in one another's arms.

It may not have been the most comfortable camping trip, but having Michael there with me made it a hell of a lot more pleasant than the last time I'd slept beneath the stars. Before I knew it, I was fast asleep, nestled cosily in the crook of my sweetheart's arm.

Chapter Thirteen

I awoke to the savoury scent of eggs cooking in the pre-dawn gloom. Disorientated by waking up in a strange place, it took a second before my brain warmed enough to connect the sounds and scents to reality

"Good morning." Michael looked at me over his shoulder, his ever-present smile resting comfortably on his lips. "Did you sleep well?"

"Well enough, I guess – but I miss my bed," I said, stretching to get the stiffness out of my joints. After six short weeks, my body had decided that it didn't care for sleeping on the ground any more. Or maybe I was just getting old.

"Your bed, or my bed?" Michael teased, leaning over to give me a quick good-morning kiss.

I returned it happily, and then gave him a grin of my own. "Your bed is my bed; I claimed it. Communal beds, that's how we roll."

He chuckled and went back to scrambling eggs. "That's true. I don't know how I'd sleep without you snoring away beside me."

"What?" I froze, staring at him. "I don't snore, do I?"

Michael looked away and didn't answer, which instantly made me suspicious. He turned even further as I crept around to get a look at his face, trying in vain to hide his smile.

"Ah-hah, I knew it!" I exclaimed, hopping up to my feet. "Pulling my leg again, you big meanie? You can't talk. You snore worse than I ever will."

"Eh?" He shot me a started look. "I do not!"

"Yes, you do – but only when you sleep on your back," I informed him cheerfully, and then I skipped off to the bushes to relieve myself, leaving him to mull over that new revelation.

By the time I returned, breakfast was ready and waiting for me. We settled down together to eat straight out of the pot, leaning against one another for warmth in the early-morning chill. We were both ravenous, and devoured our scrambled eggs in record time.

The sun had only just begun creeping over the horizon by the time we were done, casting golden threads of light and long, angular shadows across the landscape all around us. Michael went off to take his turn in the bushes while I cleaned up our breakfast utensils and packed our cooking equipment back into our bags. He returned in time to help me roll up our sleeping bags, and then we were off on our voyage once more. Or rather, we would have been... if the Hilux hadn't died in its sleep.

I turned the key in the ignition. The engine spluttered and whined, making sad, sad noises. I tried pumping my foot on the accelerator to give it a little more juice, but all it did was whimper and click unhappily. Michael stood outside the driver's window, waiting for me to move the truck so we could get out, but the truck refused to play ball.

"Well, this is a fine time to cark it." I climbed out from behind the wheel, and jogged around to the front. I lifted the bonnet up and set it on its little arm, then leaned over the engine and peered at it. "Honey, can you please try to start it?"

"Sure, one second." Michael put his gun down on the roof, then leaned in and tried the ignition again. Nothing.

"It's dead, Jim," he quipped morosely, shooting me a sad look. It had been so long that I couldn't remember where the quote even came from.

I examined the engine for a few minutes longer, then heaved a long sigh and leaned back to stretch my spine. "I think it's the starter motor. There's nothing I can do unless we can find a replacement. Let's just go, I'll keep an eye out for spare parts along the way. Maybe we can get it going again on the way back."

"And here I was, hoping to give my poor feet a rest," Michael complained, but he was still smiling. I had figured out weeks ago that he was just a glass-half-full kind of guy; I think that was part of the attraction. He was quite literally the polar opposite of me, so we stuck together like magnets.

I also suspected that personality trait had helped him to keep it together in the wake of his beloved niece's death. It'd been almost two months since he held her in his arms as she died, but he seemed to be coping well with the grief. Occasionally, he lapsed into a dark mood, but they were rare and I could usually coax him out of them.

My other suspicion was that our relationship helped him to cope as well, since it gave him something new and exciting to cling to instead – and it also meant that he had someone to help him through the grieving process. Sometimes I wondered if our relationship had begun because we both needed someone to cling to, and I worried that when we had both finished healing I'd lose him.

Well, if there was one thing Michael had taught me, it was not to let my self-doubt get me down. Whenever thoughts like that crept up, I slapped them away and contented myself with the fact that I enjoyed what I had at the moment. If something happened in the future, at least I would have these wonderful memories for the rest of my life.

"Well, I suppose you have to maintain your girlish figure somehow," I teased him as I wandered around to take the keys out of the ignition. I stared at them for a second, then tossed them on the driver's seat and slammed the door closed. No point adding extra weight to my burden when there was no guarantee I'd get the truck working again.

When I turned back, I caught Michael watching me

with an amused smirk. I blinked in surprise and asked, "What?"

"Sandy…" He seemed on the verge of bursting out laughing, but I couldn't quite figure out why.

"What is it?" I demanded, starting to get frustrated. He knew that I hated being laughed at, even if I knew it was only in jest.

"How are we getting out?" He gestured towards the gate, which we'd pinned closed with the Hilux the night before.

Suddenly, I felt foolish, and I ended up laughing at myself. "I didn't even think about that."

"And here you thought that I was the pretty one, and you were the smart one," he teased; this time, I was equally amused. Somehow, that sweet, silly man always seemed to make every situation funny.

"Nuh-uh. I'm the pretty one and you're the strong one. Get around the other side and push," I ordered playfully, then I yanked open the driver's door, took the handbrake off and set the car in neutral. Between the two of us, we managed to roll the truck forward just enough for us to be able to squeeze out of the gate.

Once we were free, we stripped everything useful from the car, shouldered our packs, and set off on foot towards the rising sun.

***

Saying that it was a long walk was the understatement of the century, but two fit people on foot could travel almost as fast as two in a four-wheel drive in our day and age. It was actually easier to negotiate the uneven landscape without a car – but that didn't mean it was fun.

The sun climbed slowly in the sky as we made our way eastwards. Eventually, clouds began to gather, but they were light and fluffy, not rain clouds. Just enough to keep the sun out of our eyes, for which we were grateful. We stuck to the remains of the old roads for most of the journey, occasionally cutting diagonally across fields when it was necessary to keep us moving in the right direction.

After an hour, we found ourselves skirting around the edge of the outermost suburb of Te Awamutu, avoiding the worst of the destruction. East of the town, we reached the main road towards Arapuni. We followed it until midday.

By the time our rumbling stomachs advised us it was about time to stop for lunch, the sun had burned away the last of the clouds and beat down on us with an intensity that was almost painful. Michael shielded his eyes against the sun and stared at the road ahead of us, then he looked back at me.

"We should stop soon, and wait until the heat of the day passes," he suggested.

"Agreed." I nodded. "My foot isn't too happy right now. This is the most walking I've done since it healed."

"Over there?" Michael pointed towards a huge oak tree that grew close by the roadside. Together, we made our way over to the cool, welcoming shade, and flopped down side by side.

"I may be a little out of shape," I admitted, unlacing my shoes and easing them off to examine my feet. The right one was swollen and sore, so I massaged it between finger and thumb to ease the tension in the scar tissue. Michael made a sympathetic noise and reached over to take my foot in his strong hands.

"Poor little foot," he rumbled softly, rubbing it gently to ease away the aches and pains. "So abused. Your mistress is so mean to you." Then he leaned down and planted a kiss on my big toe, which took me completely by surprise.

I yelped and pulled my foot away, staring at him with wide eyes. "What on earth are you doing? I've been walking all day in sweaty socks, you crazy man."

"Do you honestly think I'm concerned by how you smell when you're a little sweaty?" He raised a brow at me, then grabbed my foot again and resumed massaging it. His nimble fingers kneaded away the tension more effectively than I could do myself, so I let him have it. "You do realise that I've kissed you in far sweatier places, right?"

"That wasn't *sweat*, per se," I sniped back.

He grinned wickedly at me. "Hmmm... true. Perhaps I should find another way to distract you from your sore foot."

I felt a surge of warmth in my belly at the look of lust he shot my way; all of a sudden, I found myself giving serious thought to the possibilities. Even though there was no possible chance of being caught in the act, there was still something inherently naughty about a tryst beneath the open sky. It was... appealing, and more than a little arousing. Not that I had any intention of telling him that; the chase was half the fun.

"Oh, you mean lunch?" I retorted playfully, giving him my most innocent look.

"No, that's not what I had in mind at all," he rumbled back in that deep voice of his, the one that sent chills all up and down my spine. I'd swiftly learned what it meant when he used that husky tone on me, but I still loved to hear it. It made me quiver all over.

"Oh, really now?" I murmured back, enjoying the rising tension in the air. It crackled between us like static electricity; every touch of his hand sent tingles through me.

"Mmhm," he answered inarticulately. He pressed his lips against the inside of my ankle, then he drifted higher, trailing kisses along the inside of my leg. Even with us both fully clothed, my breath began to quicken in anticipation. By the time he reached my stomach, he had me all a'quiver.

"Out here in the open? And I thought you were such a good boy," I commented as his kisses drifted higher; I could hear the huskiness in my own voice, and I felt his body respond to it. He lifted my tank top up painfully slowly, inch by inch, rolling it back to expose a little more skin with each kiss.

"It's your fault," he murmured breathlessly as he finally lifted my top enough to expose my bra. He slipped his thumbs beneath the band and raised it up as far as my chin, exposing my skin to the warm breeze. I gasped as his head dipped down to taste me, and I felt my back arch but could do nothing to stop it.

"Ooh... My fault? How is it my fault?" I was having trouble following the conversation, and yet the conversation was half the fun. The heat in my belly was so intense, I could barely breathe, barely focus.

I felt him unzip my trousers and ease them down off my hips, and then those same fingers were teasing me, with just enough pressure to drive me mad. I couldn't bear it any longer. The chase was over – I had to have him.

His lips found that sensitive spot on my neck while I was still struggling to get his trousers off, and his breath was hot across my ear. "Because you're irresistible, Sandy McDermott. You're irresistible, and I love you."

That was the last coherent thought either one of us had, before we tumbled head-first into the world of voyeuristic pleasure.

***

An hour later, we lay together watching the fluffy clouds roll by, satisfied, exhausted, and energised all at the same time by our brief lunchtime tryst. Michael lay on his back with his hands folded behind his head, perfectly happy to let me doze with my head lolling on his firm belly. I felt safe and comfortable, knowing he was watching over me while I napped.

Eventually, hunger won out over the desire to sleep. I sat up and stretched lazily, absently wondering where my clothing had gone. Then I felt eyes upon me, and glanced over to find him watching me with great interest.

"Don't get any ideas," I teased him. "We'll end up stuck here all day."

"I know, I know." He heaved a long-suffering sigh. As I hopped up to retrieve my trousers from where they'd landed in our frantic haste, I almost missed the slow, self-satisfied smile that crept across his face. "That was fun though, wasn't it? Who knew public indecency was such an enjoyable crime?"

"I imagine all those people you arrested knew, right up until the time you slapped them in cuffs," I retorted, stepping over his prone body to retrieve my tank top from where it adorned a nearby bush. As I passed, I felt playful fingers creep up my leg but I was out of reach before they could achieve anything.

"Well, they should have invited me," he laughed merrily, watching me while I hunted around for my missing undergarments.

"They probably just like being in handcuffs. I hear that's a fetish." I was only kidding of course, but the noise Michael made was somewhere between a low growl and a purr; a sound of intense, animal interest. I turned to him in surprise, and raised my brows. "You? Really? You don't strike me as the kind of man that would like to cuff a girl up and give her a feel."

"What?" He looked equally startled for a moment, and then laughed and shook his head. "No, no, not like that. The other way around."

"Oh?" I peered at him with interest, equal parts

curious and fascinated by the revelation. "Horny young police officer goes to arrest the sexy she-villain, only to get captured in the line of duty? That sounds like the theme of a dirty movie."

"Something like that," he said looking embarrassed, as if he were admitting to a dark secret.

"I'll have to remember that." I gave him a wicked, flirtatious smile. Just at that moment, the wind caught something stuck in the tree above us and set it flapping. The movement attracted my eye. I glanced up, and then gasped in astonishment. "How did my bra get up there?"

"I plead not guilty," Michael answered cheerfully. As if to contradict his statement, a particularly strong gust caught the garment and tugged it free, dropping it right on his face. He was laughing so hard by the time I reached him that he made no attempt to keep it from me.

With a victorious whoop, I pulled on my bra and tank top, and then went back to searching for my underpants. It took me a second to realise that Michael was still laughing. Curious, I glanced back at him and spotted him holding up my poor knickers teasingly.

"You thief!" I accused playfully, leaping on him in an attempt to capture the metaphorical flag, but he laughed even harder as he held them out of my reach. We tumbled together in the grass, both laughing and shouting like silly children, oblivious to how foolish we would have looked to anyone else. Sometimes, the fact that we were almost entirely alone in the world was a good thing.

After a few moments of play-wrestling, I finally got my underwear back and managed to get dressed. It took some coaxing to get Michael to do the same, though; after being cooped up in that basement surrounded by small children for so long, he was enjoying the freedom of his own nudity a little too much.

I wouldn't have minded, if not for the fact that we would need to get moving or we'd never reach the dam. Eventually, the promise of lunch coaxed him back into decency. It was a little bribery on my part, but it worked.

"What have you got now?" he asked curiously, leaning over my shoulder to watch while I sliced and assembled our meal.

"Sandwiches," I told him proudly. It really shouldn't have been so exciting, but it was. After ten years without bread, I relished the thought and the texture of something so simple. The idea had come to me just before we left, so I had found an old Tupperware container in one of our cupboards and packed it full of the fixings of a good sandwich: tomatoes, lettuce, smoked fish and the delicious rewena bread our Maori neighbours baked.

Anahera understood my longing for bread like nobody else, and had sent along a freshly-baked batch when Hemi came to trade with us. Who would have thought that something as simple as bread would become more exciting than cake?

I sliced the bread thickly and carefully arranged the other fixings upon it, with Michael watching over my shoulder the entire time. As soon as he had figured out what I was doing, he was riveted by the idea. Although Michael had been born in China, he'd grown up in New Zealand and that made him just as much a Kiwi as I was when it came to our tastes in food. Ten years of living on rice was a bit much for anyone, so he longed for bread just as much as I did.

The fresh produce wouldn't last forever outside in the heat though, so we had to eat it before it went to waste. I filled the sandwiches full to bursting, then I carefully picked one up and handed it to him, and took the other one for myself.

We enjoyed our old-fashioned lunch immensely, far more than either of us would have liked another boring meal from a can. Although Michael never complained, I knew he must be as frustrated as I was with having to live that way. The introduction of a steady supply of fresh food into our diet had brightened both of our moods almost as much as the new romance blooming between us. It brought back memories of decades past, and made us feel... human again.

After lunch, we waited until the heat died down before we slathered on a fresh coat of sunscreen, picked up our backpacks, and moved off. The wind picked up just after midday, bringing pleasant gusts to cool us, which made the walk much more pleasant. My foot felt a little better for the rest, but I longed to soak it in the cool waters of the Waikato to take the swelling down. It already felt like we'd been walking forever, and we were unlikely to reach Arapuni before sundown. I wondered if we would find somewhere safe to rest before nightfall.

In contrast to what Rebecca had said about the bush being dense in this part of the country, the land directly east of Te Awamutu was flat and pleasant with only a few trees sprinkled along the route. The roadway was narrow and cracked, flanked on either side by gorse bushes that kept all other plant life from encroaching too closely on the road itself. Aside from the long grass that stuck up through the cracks in the asphalt, the walk was relatively easy. Still, the road was so well-preserved that I regretted losing the Hilux – we would have made good time in those conditions.

Beyond the gorse, long grass waved placidly in the wind. We watched it for any sign of trouble, but held our weapons relaxed with the safeties on. If something as large and dangerous as a pig approached us, then we would be sure to see it coming long before it got close enough to concern us.

The road took a bend, and we followed as it wound its way into a small patch of woodlands. A flash of neon yellow amongst the trees caught my eye. I nudged Michael and pointed it out. His expression turned grim when he spotted it, but he nodded and walked on regardless. What I'd seen was an old sign post warning non-existent drivers of the school up ahead.

I had no doubt that we shared the same thought: we both dreaded the thought of finding an infected child.

The trees began to clear as we reached another bend. We looked, and saw the overgrown remains of a primary school nestled within the curve of the road. The playground was rusted and bent by a decade's worth of weather, but what made me freeze and grab Michael's hand was the sight of a small human figure sitting on the swings.

He saw her at the same time I did. I looked at him. He looked back, and I saw my own indecision reflected on his face. I knew that we shared similar feelings about the infected. Despite our experiences with the mutated ones, the regular infected were objects of pity, to be put out of their misery whenever possible.

"We can't just leave her there," I whispered, shifting my shotgun into the crook of my left arm. With my right hand, I drew my taser out of my pocket, and then I looked at him again. He nodded his agreement and adjusted the weight of the rifle in his hands. I understood the precaution. Our encounters with the violent, mutated infected in Hamilton had left us both tense and on edge.

With stealthy footsteps, we crept closer to the young girl on the swings. We were wary, but we'd both done it before. This time, though, something was different. Just as we were closing on the lone figure, I grabbed Michael's arm to halt him and paused, listening intently. He glanced at me in surprise, then seemed to realise what I was hearing: the girl on the swings was singing quietly to herself.

We exchanged looks of shock as we both reached the same conclusion. Either that little girl was some kind of infected that neither of us had seen before, or she was actually alive. Michael grabbed my arm and pulled me back out of earshot.

"Are there any groups of survivors in this area?" he whispered urgently.

"I don't know. I haven't heard of any, but things change." I shook my head slowly, unable to tear my gaze away from the young girl. She had her back to us and hadn't noticed us yet. I couldn't guess her age without seeing her face. I couldn't even identify the language she was singing in.

"Maybe she's on her own," Michael said, and then he looked at me as though seeking my advice. I stared back at him, turning the thought over in my head, trying to decide the best way to proceed. Eventually, I came to a decision.

"I'm going to talk to her. Stay here," I said. I offered him my shotgun, which he took from my hand with a frown of obvious concern.

"Are you sure?" he asked. "I'm happy to do it, if you want me to."

"No, I'm less threatening." I shook my head firmly, my mind made up. "Goodness knows what she's been through. I don't want to scare her. You just cover me, okay?"

Michael nodded slowly, but I could see the worry in his eyes. He knew better than anyone else in the world that my past experiences made me skittish around strangers, but this was different. This wasn't a big, strapping man, it was a young girl. I could handle a young girl. At least, I hoped I could.

Armed only with the taser hidden in my pocket, I circled around the edge of the playing field until I moved into her field of vision. She didn't seem to see me at first; her attention was focused on something nestled in her lap. Once I was fully in front of her, I slowly walked towards her, making no attempt at stealth and no sudden movements. As I drew closer, I could hear her singing again. The words were nonsensical to me, but it didn't take long for me to figure out that she was singing in a foreign language that I didn't recognise.

The girl was young and small, fragile from malnutrition, with long, tangled dark brown hair that hung almost to her knees. She was so thin it took me a while to pinpoint her age at around thirteen or fourteen; her rag-clad body showed a few of the earliest stages of puberty, but not much. In her lap, she nursed what appeared to be a very threadbare teddy bear. At least, that's what I hoped it was. All I could really see was light brown fur.

I did a quick calculation in my head and worked out that she must have been three or four when the virus hit. A surge of sympathy hit me along with the realisation that she would have been hardly more than a toddler when she was left on her own. I wondered if her parents had been immune, or if she'd been completely alone since she was a little child, and somehow miraculously survived all these years without any adults to help her. I wondered if she spoke English, or if she just remembered a song her mother had sung to her as a baby. There was only one way to find out.

"Hello," I said softly, halting about five metres from the swings. The girl looked up sharply, her otter-brown eyes huge against skin the colour of milk chocolate. I recognised her ethnicity as someone who originated from India, but I couldn't even begin to guess which province.

The girl didn't say anything, just sat there looking totally shocked by my unexpected presence. She didn't seem to be frightened so much as bewildered, which made sense since she probably hadn't seen another human face in a very, very long time.

It occurred to me that she might only speak Hindi. Maybe her parents had never had a chance to teach her English – or maybe she'd just forgotten over the years. I raised a hand and waved a harmless greeting, then repeated myself. "Hello."

The girl looked at my hand, then looked at my face, then looked down at her own hands. Slowly, as if uncertain what to do, she raised her hand and waved back at me. The confusion on her face tugged at my heartstrings; her eyes were so big that she looked like a little girl, despite being in her early teens.

In an effort to make myself smaller and less intimidating, I eased my backpack off my shoulders and set it down, then sat down on the ground a few metres away from her.

"Can you understand me?" I asked, speaking gently so as not to frighten her, but slowly and clearly.

The girl stared at me while the question sank in. It was a look I understood better than most; after a decade of isolation, it was hard to think in terms of questions and answers. Conversations were no longer second nature. At last, she nodded hesitantly and found a question of her own. "Are you... real?"

The question confused me a little, but I took it in my stride. "Yes, I'm real. My name is Sandy. What is your name?"

Her brow wrinkled. For a moment it seemed like I'd lost her, but I just waited and gave her time, not rushing her for an answer.

"Priyanka," she said at last. All of a sudden, she was off the swing and kneeling on the ground in front of me, almost close enough to touch. Those enormous eyes studied me through her tangle of dark hair, somehow seeming entirely too large for her little face. "Sometimes I see Mama and Baba in my dreams. Are you a dream?"

"No, I am real and you are awake." I shook my head slowly and extended a hand towards her, palm up, to show her that I was real and she could touch me. To my surprise, she did. The girl grabbed my hand and turned it over, staring at it as though it was the first she'd ever seen besides her own. Up close, I could see that she was a filthy little thing, but I ignored it. Under the grime and the smell was a little girl, and she was all alone.

"Real..." She touched my hand with covetous

fingers, then laid her hand over mine and compared them, looking fascinated by the contrast between her dark skin and my fair skin. Eventually she looked up at my face again, and I saw that her eyes were rimmed by tears. "Thought all people gone. Thought I was only one."

"No, there are still some people out there," I told her, turning my hand over slowly so that I could hold hers. It was so tiny and bird-like compared to mine that I was almost afraid to break it. To my surprise, she not only let me hold her hand but seemed happy for it; she ducked her head down and sniffed at my hand. I felt a spot of moisture on my skin and couldn't tell whether a tear had fallen on me or if she'd licked me for some reason, but either way I managed to keep myself from flinching.

It was a child-like fascination, inquisitive, young. With no adults to care for her, she'd never had the chance to learn anything more. Her education had stopped as a toddler. Even Skylar's education had included the company of other human beings.

"I want," she whispered, nuzzling against my hand like a little child. "I want. I want. No go, please. No go."

My heart just about broke when I realised her cheeks were wet with tears. I found myself stroking her tangled hair without even thinking about it, letting her work through her emotions at her leisure. In my mind, all I could see was a cherub-faced child, toddling the countryside all alone, confused, frightened and hungry.

Without anyone to care for her, it was a miracle that she'd survived.

Over her head, I saw Michael approaching with a look of concern on his face, but he relaxed when I gave him a reassuring smile. I tilted my head towards a patch of grass beside me. He understood that I meant it was safe for him to join us, so he did. He settled cross-legged a little way away and hid the weapons behind his back. The sound of his bulk settling on the grass attracted the girl's attention, though she still clung to my hand as though afraid to let me go.

"This is Michael. He's a friend," I told her, and then looked at him. "Her name is Priyanka. I'm pretty sure she's alone out here."

"Michael." The girl repeated his name, stumbling over the pronunciation a little. Wide-eyed, she looked back and forth between us, then down at her own dusky-skinned little hands. "Different?"

"Our mamas and babas come from different places," I explained, using her own language to help her understand. Her speech was obviously stunted due to limited exposure to other people, but there was no reason to assume she was unintelligent. "People look different in other places. Michael is also a boy, while I am a girl, like you."

"Ah-hah." She made a universal sound of understanding and leaned back on her haunches to examine us both. The movement let me get a good look at the object she'd been cradling; I was relieved to see the fur did belong to a ratty old teddy bear, as opposed to something less savoury. It was so ancient its fur had worn bare in patches, and the stitches around its throat had come loose to reveal the dull grey stuffing within.

Seeking a way to bond with the girl, I pointed at the teddy bear. "Would you like me to fix him? His head is about to come off."

The dirty little girl looked down at her teddy bear uncertainly, then back up to me. "Fix?"

"I can sew his head back on for you. Make him all better. See, his insides are coming out?" I leaned in closer to point out the damage, but made no attempt to take the bear from her in case she misinterpreted the action as a threat. She seemed to understand, though.

"Make better, please," she said, holding her precious bear out to me. I smiled at her manners, and gently took the teddy from her outstretched hands. Priyanka inched closer to watch while I opened my backpack and dug out the tiny sewing kit I always kept with me during long journeys. It was one of those things that had proven itself well worth the minimal weight over the years. Things always tended to break at the least convenient moments.

I caught Michael watching with interest as I deftly threaded a needle and began sewing up the gaping wound in the bear's neck with small, neat stitches. Being a survivor made you self-sufficient; I'd learned the patience required for tidy sewing through trial and error. Fast, sloppy stitches would only come loose again, and force you to do the work all over again.

The girl's eyes widened as the wound shrank, as if I

were showing her an amazing magic trick. I suppose to someone with the life experience of a three-year-old, it was. There were a lot of things she'd been denied beyond just the obvious.

The learning that took place in those early formative years was so much more in depth than just reading, writing and arithmetic, and she had missed out on all of it. I felt pity for her, and sympathy – it would be hard to learn those lessons later in life, but I hoped that she'd be willing to try.

She showed patience beyond her years as she watched me work. I suppose she felt the passage of time much like I had when I was out on my own; the rise and fall of the sun only provided a vague sense of when to eat and when to sleep, but time was more or less meaningless.

Eventually, I closed off the last stitch and bit the thread short, then offered the newly-repaired bear back to the girl. She took it reverently, as if she had just witnessed a miracle, and turned it slowly within her hands. Then all of a sudden, she smiled and hugged the bear to her chest. "All better. Fix."

"All better," I agreed, feeling a flush of pride at the joy I'd brought to her with something so small. I guessed that bear must have been with her for a while, but I doubted she would be able to explain its origins. I tried a simpler question instead. "Where do you live, Priyanka?"

The young girl looked at me thoughtfully, and then stared around herself as though seeking an answer.

Finally, she shrugged and hugged her teddy again. I took her silence to mean she lived wherever she could.

"Where did you sleep last night?" I asked, trying another tactic. That one she could answer more easily; she pointed at the playground, towards a small, sheltered enclosure at the head of the rusty old slide. I nodded my understanding and asked another question. "What do you eat?"

She looked down at her feet and shrugged again, absently plucking at the long blades of grass around her. I felt a stab of sympathy, intuiting that expression meant that she ate whatever she could find. Judging by her small size, it wasn't a lot.

I exchanged a glance with Michael, and he gave me a nod. There was an understanding between us, a survivor's code: we couldn't leave this poor girl on her own any more than Michael could have thrown me out when he found me.

"Would you like something to eat?" I asked her, leaning forward to look her in the eye. Her expression changed so swiftly that I couldn't decipher the emotions. I saw fear, longing, hope, and so many others all twisting together. Her response was another shrug.

I saw right through her mask of nonchalance. She was just a little girl, and she was half-starved. I reached into my backpack again, pulled out the small lump of rewena bread left over from our lunch, and held it out to her.

She stared at it as though afraid that it might be a

trick, and then looked up at me with confusion on her grubby little face. I smiled at her reassuringly and broke a tiny piece off the bread, which I put it in my mouth to show her that it was edible. It didn't take a psychoanalyst to know that she wanted it but was just afraid to take it.

When I offered it to her again, she snatched it from my hand. She seemed poised on the verge of flight, about to leap up and scurry away with her prize like a frightened animal – but something held her back. She looked back and forth between us, uncertain. We sat there patiently with smiles on our faces, watching her indecision.

Eventually, she figured out that we weren't going to take her bread away from her. She sniffed it, licked at it, and then took an enormous bite. The texture of the food enticed her in, and soon the small hunk was devoured. Once it was all gone she licked the crumbs off her dirty fingers, and looked around anxiously for more.

That was the last of our bread so there was none to be had, but Michael followed my lead and gave her an apple from his pack instead. She only hesitated for a moment this time before snatching that from his hand, and devouring it with glee. She wasted nothing, and even ate the core. When she was done she flopped back on the grass with a satisfied sigh.

"Thanks you, thanks you," she whispered, just about breaking my heart all over again with her sweet expression of gratitude. Whoever had been the 'mama' and 'baba' of this young lady, they had done a good job teaching their little one manners.

"You're welcome, Priyanka," I said gently.

"Would you like a drink? Water?" Michael spoke up for the first time, holding up one of our smaller water bottles for her to see. His deep voice seemed to startle her, and it took her a moment to translate his words in her head. When she made sense of them, her expression brightened and she nodded vigorously. He took the lid off the bottle and handed it to her. She drank gratefully.

Michael and I exchanged glances as the girl drank. On his face, I saw the same concern I felt mirrored back at me. We both knew we had to take the girl with us, if she was willing to go. The doctor would scold us for collecting more strays, but we had no choice. No decent human being could leave another in a situation like that and not feel guilty.

"Priyanka." I leaned forward to catch her eye. She stopped drinking, and stared up at me. "Michael and I have to go soon. We have a very long trip to go on, to meet with some friends. If you would like to, you can come as well. Would you like to come with us?"

That may have been the stupidest question of all time. She had no intention of letting either of us out of her sight any time soon.

Chapter Fourteen

Despite her fragile build, Priyanka didn't slow us down at all. Since she had no belongings besides her teddy bear, we were back on the road within minutes of her decision to join us. She skipped along beside us as we walked, singing happily to herself in Hindi. Or at least, I presumed it was Hindi. For once, Michael had no insight to offer despite his usual adeptness as a translator.

A couple of times, Priya's dancing took her so far ahead of us that we almost lost sight of her. Each time, she suddenly panicked when she realised that we weren't close by, spun around, and came tearing back to us as though afraid we would leave her behind.

We wouldn't, of course, but I understood that desperate, irrational fear; I had felt it myself on more than one occasion since I joined Michael's group. Sometimes she latched onto my arm and clung to me like a limpet, but even then I couldn't bring myself to be annoyed with her. Human beings are innately social creatures, and the fear of rejection is almost as strong as the fear of death. Sometimes, it's even stronger.

Each time she attached herself to me, I stroked her hair and spoke softly to her until she calmed down again, like you would with a frightened puppy. Her fits of clinginess never lasted for long. Once the latest one had passed and she'd scampered off about her play, I glanced at Michael and found him watching me with amusement.

"What?" I asked, shooting him a smile in return. His expression turned into a grin.

"I think that girl likes you," he replied, slipping an arm casually around my waist. "I have the sneaking suspicion we won't be able to have any more romantic interludes on this trip."

"Oh, I'm sure we'll think of something," I replied, reaching up to pat his cheek affectionately. He leaned down to plant a tender kiss on my lips. I closed my eyes for a moment to enjoy the closeness. When I opened them again, I found that Priya had returned, and was watching us closely with her head canted at a curious angle.

Well, this was going to be an uncomfortable conversation. How to you explain the birds and the bees to someone with the social experience of a three-year-old?

"You kissies," she commented in her childlike manner, looking fascinated by the discovery.

"Sandy is my girlfriend," Michael explained, heroically leaping to the rescue. "Like your mama and baba."

"Oh." The young girl bobbed her head in understanding and smiled broadly. "You have baby?"

"No, not yet. It's not safe for babies," Michael answered, shaking his head. "Maybe one day, when it's safer."

Priyanka seemed satisfied with that and contentedly skipped off to resume her play. I, on the other hand, found myself all a'fluster. Ever observant, Michael was quick to notice my expression.

"What's wrong, honey?" he asked, gently drawing me closer against his side as we walked. "You're blushing."

"You called me your girlfriend," I answered, stunned and incredulous.

"Aren't you my girlfriend?" He frowned at me, an uncertain look in his eye.

I felt a stab of panic and rushed to reassure him. "No! I mean, yes– I mean, I didn't mean it like that. I mean, you've never called me that before. It just took me by surprise." I was even more flustered now; my emotions darted all over the place, but as always Michael seemed to understand.

"Do you want me to stop?" he asked, but this time a smile danced across his lips instead of a frown.

"Nah." I resorted to humour to cover my embarrassment. "I think it's okay. Hell, you can do it more often, if you want. That might be awesome. I'm not so sure about the babies thing, though."

"I am," he answered, his expression softening as he looked down at me. "I mean, not right now – but one day, I definitely want to have a child of my own. I think I could be a good father. Don't you?"

"God yes, you'd be the best father in the world," I blurted with all the elegance of a rhinoceros in a tutu. "It's me that I'm worried about. I've just, you know, never even thought about it. Two months ago, I couldn't imagine letting anyone touch me, let alone starting a family with someone."

"I know, sweetheart – and there's the worry about the immunity. But one day, when it's safe, then we can think about it." He grinned suddenly and gave me a playful nudge. "You have to admit, we'd make some pretty cute babies together."

I had to laugh at that, and nodded my agreement. "Yeah, so long as they look like you. Chinese babies are the cutest things since kittens in tuxedos."

"Well, if I remember my high school biology right, the eyelid thing is a dominant trait, so there's a good chance they would." His grin turned impish, and he reached over to grab my plaited hair, giving it a playful tug. "It's a shame blonde is recessive. Could you imagine a little girl with your hair and my eyes?"

"Now that's a frightening thought." I laughed even harder at the mental image he conjured up; throw in a big frilly dress, and Maddy would have some competition for the cutest kid on the block. "It could happen, though. Your dad might have passed on a recessive gene to you."

"That's true. Granddad was a Kiwi mutt, like you," he teased. I knew it was all in fun, so I took no offense and teased him right back.

"Hey, I'll have you know that I'm only *half* Kiwi mutt. My daddy was pure Scottish stock, but he moved here when he was two." I flicked back a strand of hair loosened by his playfulness, and gave him a smile. "I'm an actual McDermott. We have a plaid and everything."

"I can think of a hundred other things I'd rather see you in than a kilt," he gave me a flirtatious wink, but with curious young eyes intensely interested in everything we did, our flirting stayed firmly in the realm of decency for once.

***

The landscape we passed through gradually changed over the course of the afternoon. Wide, flat expanses of pastoral land that had once grazed farm animals gave way to fields that had been used to grow crops. As we moved further eastwards, we began to pass by enormous cornfields, gone wild over the years. They stretched as far to the south as the eye could see, their tall stalks swaying gracefully in the breeze.

Michael and I watched the cornfields warily, our weapons at the ready; the perpetual movement and incessant rustling made us nervous, because it could hide the approach of any number of enemies. Priyanka showed no such concern, though. She darted away from us and vanished into the long stalks with a squeal of delight.

I glanced at Michael and shrugged. "I guess now we know how she's survived all these years on her own."

"I guess we do," he agreed.

"We should bring some corn back with us; we could make our own bread out of it. Maybe we could even grow it." I glanced over at him to see what he thought. He nodded slowly, turning the idea over in his head.

Whatever his answer may have been, it was interrupted by Priyanka's return. She scampered back to us at full tilt, her bare feet flashing across the grass. With a prodigious leap to clear the long grass on the verge, she darted back across the tarmac and proudly presented each of us with an ear of corn.

We thanked her, then resumed walking eastwards. Priya and I stripped the husks off our corn, so that we could nibble on it as we travelled. Just as I was about to tuck in to mine, I cast a glance sideways and caught Michael staring at his cob, looking totally perplexed.

"What's the matter?" I queried, amused by the look on his face.

He shot me a helpless look, and shrugged. "I'm a city boy. I've never... opened one of these before."

"Give it here." I chuckled, shoved my cob into my pocket, then reached over to take his. With practiced expertise, I showed him how to snap off the stem and peel back the leaves, revealing the golden sweetness within. "I've eaten a lot of this stuff over the years. It just takes a bit of practice. And... there you go, just like that."

"Huh. Just like that. That was easier than I thought." Michael took the cob, sniffed at it, and then took a bite. He nodded thoughtfully as he chewed, considering the texture.

"Tastes a lot better than the canned stuff, doesn't it?" I asked jovially, pulling my cob back out of my pocket.

"Definitely," he agreed. "Better than cooked, as well. I believe we may be obligated to bring back as much as we can carry."

"Shame it's so far away, or we could just come back here and pick as much as we need at our leisure," I commented thoughtfully.

"If only the roads were functional." He sighed and nodded.

"Where's a bureaucrat when you need one?" I joked, drawing a chuckle from my companion.

Priyanka laughed too, but not because she understood the joke. She laughed because she was happy to hear the sound of people around her after so long alone.

***

Eventually, the fields gave way to long, rolling hills; the further east we travelled, the steeper they became. The forest grew denser as we walked, and the road began a long, slow climb towards the heavens.

My hamstrings protested as we ascended the hill, but none of us said anything out loud. Priyanka seemed less bothered than Michael and me, but her energetic bouncing did slow to a plodding walk. I worried about her bare feet on the uneven roadway, but she didn't seem concerned at all. I could only guess that after ten years without shoes, her feet were probably a lot tougher than mine.

"Have you walked this way before?" I asked her, breathless but curious. The girl looked around herself a bit, then she looked up at me and shook her head.

"Is new place to me. Has you walked?" she asked me in return, equally curious.

I shook my head as well and pointed behind us, to the west. "No. We come from very far in that direction."

"Why we go this way?" she enquired with child-like inquisitiveness. I could tell at a glance that she wasn't complaining, she was just interested in knowing our reasoning. Curiosity was a trait I encouraged in everyone, so I answered her as best I could.

"There are some people that live over there, far on the other side of these hills," I explained. "They called to us for help. We're going to help them."

She made a noise of understanding, but further conversation was interrupted as we crested the hill. Directly ahead of us, the roadway vanished over the edge of a ragged cliff. Once, years ago, a rest area beside the road had commanded a magnificent view of the valleys all around, but sometime in the past the cliff face had collapsed. Now, only jagged edges remained.

The three of us inched closer to the end of the road to peer over the edge; beneath us, a small truck lay smashed upon the rocks. My guess was that its weight had caused the collapse, but that knowledge didn't help us at all.

"We'll need to go around." I pointed to the right of the road, where the verge climbed sharply into a shoulder-height cliff. Beyond the verge, the hill top was dense with forest, but the only other choice was to climb down and up the other side of the break in the road. Although the cliff was only a few metres high, it was starting to get dark, and climbing at dusk seemed like a very bad idea.

Michael nodded without a word and went to the verge, where he cupped his hands to boost me up. I placed my foot in his hands and a hand on his shoulder, and then I was up and over the ledge easily. The two of us helped Priyanka up, and then Michael vaulted up after us.

The bush on the hilltop was dense, dark and threatening; I felt a sense of foreboding just looking at it. Instinctively, I brought my shotgun around in front of me and slipped off the safety.

"Priya, you stay between me and Michael, okay?" I glanced at her as I gave the order. She tilted her head curiously, not quite seeming to understand, but she did as she was told as we moved off.

I led the way, scanning the woodlands around us as we walked. I could hear the faint rustle of small wild things all around us, but in the shadows beneath the canopy I could see very little. Keeping the verge within sight to our left, I picked my way carefully amongst the trees. Leaves brushed at my cheeks and tugged at my hair, forcing me to shove them away impatiently. Although we were far more exposed out on the road, at least I could see any threats coming; in the dense undergrowth, things could sneak up on us much more easily.

The impending twilight was another concern. We were in the middle of nowhere, and the last building we'd seen was several kilometres behind us. Finding a place to stop for the night was becoming more urgent. Although we both carried torches, it was unsafe to keep travelling after dark. The batteries wouldn't last forever, and this far from anywhere, the only other light we had was starlight.

"I think I see the road," Michael whispered; I understood that he felt the need for stealth, like I did. I looked where he pointed, and spotted the flash of grey through the trees.

I nodded and led the way forward. A dozen metres further on, I stepped around a particularly dense bush – and almost fell over the edge of a low cliff. Michael grabbed me and pulled me back, then he held me reassuringly for a moment while I recovered my wits. Two metres below us, the roadway resumed its course.

"Over there," I gasped, my heart racing from my brief encounter with potential injury or even death. A little further to the east, the cliff between the forest's edge and the road was lower and more manageable.

The three of us hurried to the lower spot and scrambled down the bank, back to the roadway. By the time we were able to resume our eastward march, the sun had drifted lower and sunset was beginning in earnest. I glanced back over my shoulder and shielded my eyes from the sun's glare. I estimated that we had about an hour left before we'd be walking in total darkness.

"We should hurry," I told the others. They both nodded in agreement. Even little Priyanka seemed to understand the dangers of being out after dark. For most of the day we'd wandered along at a leisurely pace, but now we all felt a sense of urgency. None of us wanted to be left exposed at night.

***

I had always found it kind of amazing how much ground a human being could cover on foot when he or she put her mind to it. As a child and a teenager, I would never have imagined that I'd be out walking the roads instead of driving, and as such I never stopped to think how long it would take to travel those routes without the benefit of a car.

Dusk cast long shadows all around us as we descended the eastern side of the hill into the valley beyond. The low angle of the sun rendered the landscape in shades of grey and made it harder and harder to see. The trees around us were tall, making the world beneath their boughs seem darker and more threatening.

"I think I see something." Michael was the first of us to speak up. At first I worried, but the tone of his voice was one of relief, not fear. My shotgun held at the ready, I stepped forward to try and locate what he'd seen. There it was, nestled amongst the trees – an old white mailbox. I couldn't see the house though, because the trees were too thick.

"I think we're going to have to risk it," I said. Michael nodded in agreement. He took the lead this time, and we sandwiched Priyanka between us as we picked our way in the direction a driveway had once gone.

With the sun almost down and darkness descending across our wild little world, we could hardly see beneath the trees. We clicked on our torches to light the way, but the tiny beams of light they produced barely penetrated the gloom. I strained my ears but I couldn't hear any threats, just the sound of the birds chattering as they went to sleep, and the sound of our own footfalls.

Between one step and the next, Michael's tread changed in timbre. I recognised the sound of gravel crunching beneath his boots. Ten years ago, I would never have noticed the difference in the sound, but now it sounded like a clarion call to me.

"I see a house." Michael's voice was soft as a whisper, but I heard it clearly in the relative quiet around us. It was so dark that I couldn't see his broad back in front of me anymore, only the sweep of his torch as it swung back and forth.

"Lead on," I whispered back, as much to reassure him that we were still following as for any real need to give him instruction.

Our little convoy picked its way across the old, grass-hewn gravel that had once been someone's driveway. Again I found myself worrying about Priyanka's feet, but she didn't protest at all. The flash of Michael's torch beam cut across timber, and again I heard the sound of his boots change; he was climbing wooden stairs, and then walking across a porch.

As loathe as I was to turn my own torch away from the dark forest behind us, we had to focus in front to make it safely up the stairs. I felt a hand touch my arm gently as I cleared the top step: Michael, reassuring me of his protective presence.

"Watch the door while I clear the house," I instructed. I felt more than saw him nod, then his torch beam cut away from us to scan the edge of the forest.

I found the front door not far away, and when I tried the handle it was unlocked. I could hear Priya's breathing behind me as I stepped inside and scanned the interior of the house by torchlight. The place wasn't large, just a small, cosy home that had seen better days. To the right of the doorway I saw a living room with a couple of fat couches and a fireplace. To the left was a dining room and kitchen.

Directly in front of me was a long corridor that led towards the rear of the house, where I imagined bedrooms must be located.

"Stay with Michael," I told Priyanka, then I crept deeper into the house to check each of the rooms carefully. Nothing stirred in the living room, kitchen, or dining room. I picked my way carefully along the hallway towards the rear of the building. One at a time, I opened doors and checked for hostiles, but I found nothing more threatening than an army of dust bunnies.

At the far end of the hallway, a back door opened into darkness. I closed it quickly and locked it, then I hurried back to the front of the building. I found Michael still standing guard, and Priya hovering uncertainly between him and the doorway.

"We're clear. Get in here so we can lock the door," I whispered to him. Michael fell back on my word, his torch still sweeping the dark forest. The moment they were both inside, I closed the door and locked it. Suddenly, we all felt safer.

I heard Michael heave a sigh of relief, and I grunted wordlessly in agreement. A strange, dark house in the middle of nowhere was not my favourite place to be, but at least we weren't out in the open any longer.

"We've got a fireplace. That should give us some light." I padded across the thick, dusty carpet and knelt down in front of it to see if I could get it going. "Honey, there's a back door at the end of the hall. I've locked it, but I'd feel a lot safer if we could figure out some way to block it, just in case."

"I'm on it," he answered, his deep voice disembodied in the shadows. "Priyanka, come help me? I'll need someone to hold the light."

"Okies," the girl agreed amiably, and I heard their footsteps retreat towards the rear of the house. Soon, there were sounds of things being dragged around, but I ignored them and I focused on getting the fire started.

A stack of old wood still sat nearby, with all the

fixings to get it going. After so many years indoors, it couldn't have been any drier; the fire started easily and stayed burning with minimal effort. It didn't give us a lot of light, but it was enough. By the time they returned, I had the fire burning cheerfully in the fireplace.

"We found some blankets," Michael told me, dumping them in a pile in the middle of the living room. "I'll bring out one of the mattresses as well. We should be able to sleep comfortably."

I nodded my approval, and he hurried off. Priyanka stayed with me this time, settling down on the floor beside me to watch me poke at the flames. Without the breeze to blow away her funk, the smell of her hit me more strongly than ever.

"You need a bath," I told her gently. She tilted her head and looked up at me, clearly not understanding. "A bath – you know, a wash? You're dirty."

I pantomimed scrubbing myself until she finally understood, but she misunderstood my intentions. Tears welled up in her eyes and she looked at me like I'd just kicked her. "I am bad?"

"What? No, no, no – you're a good girl." I swiftly struggled to alleviate her fears. "You just need a bath, so you won't get sick. I'll help you tomorrow, when the sun is up."

"Oh..." The girl absently scratched at herself and looked down. "The dirty is bad, not I am bad?"

"That's right." I reached over and stroked her hair; her expression relaxed at the touch, reassured. "The dirty is bad, it can make you sick. We'll give you a bath, make you clean. Then you won't get sick – and won't be itchy either."

"Itchy," Priya agreed readily, scratching at her arm. Up close, I could see a couple of little sores on her arm, and understood just how desperate for a bath she was. And clothing, for that matter – hers were just rags, so tattered that I couldn't even figure out what they'd originally looked like. She could use a haircut, too. Her hair was so long that she probably hadn't had one since before the plague struck.

"You poor little thing." I sighed as she cuddled up against me, staring up at me with those big, sad eyes of hers. "I promise, you'll feel much better after a bath. No more itchy."

"No more itchy," she echoed. Further conversation was interrupted as Michael returned, carrying with him a mattress pilfered from a single bed. He shoved it up against the wall beneath the windows and piled the blankets on top of it.

"Bathroom seems to be functioning, if either of you want to 'go'," he told us helpfully, glancing back at us as he went about turning the couch and the mattress into functioning beds.

It had been a while, so I did need to relieve myself. I guessed that Priya probably did as well, so I took her by the hand and led her off down the hall, where we took turns using the lavatory. I was relieved to discover that she was toilet-trained. At least that was one less thing for me to worry about.

Afterwards, I showed her how to wash her hands with soap and explained in simple terms how important it was to do so. She was a ready student and didn't argue, apparently content in the knowledge that grown-ups knew best. If only she knew that we were all just making it up as we went along, too.

Illuminated by the narrow beam of my torch, we made our way back to our little campsite in the living room. Michael had put dinner on while we were away, and the savoury smell of fish cooking lured us to join him. The three of us sat in a circle around our cook stove until it was ready, then he divided it up into a bowl for each of us and handed it out.

Priya didn't even bother with a spoon. She just dove right in face-first, to our amusement. Now wasn't the time to try and teach her manners, so we just left her to it while the two of us ate at a more sedate pace and talked quietly about the day's adventures.

"We should probably keep a night watch," I suggested. "We didn't really have a chance to secure this place before we bunked down, so it would make sense."

"I defer to your experience," he agreed, popping a spoonful of fish and rice into his mouth. Once he'd swallowed it, he added, "I'll take the second watch, if you want. That's always the harder one."

"It's sweet of you to offer." I smiled up at him gratefully, since he was right. Waking up in the middle of the night and trying to stay alert was always harder on the body. "I won't say no."

"I didn't think you would." He gave me a playful wink. We finished our meal in companionable silence.

By the time we adults had finished eating, Priyanka was fast asleep. She just curled up on the floor like a sleepy kitten, without a blanket or a pillow. Between the two of us, we moved her to the couch and wrapped her in warm blankets to keep her comfortable, then we settled down on the mattress on the floor.

Michael snuggled up against me with his head in my lap, while I sat upright resting my back against the end of the couch. I ran my fingers absently over his short hair as he fell asleep, feeling a strange sort of contentment wash over me. Although it felt weird to be sitting guard while others slept around me, I felt a strong desire to protect them. Sleep would not come to me while I sat watch, keeping my family safe.

After a while, I got bored with my own thoughts, and dug into my pack for the book I'd stolen weeks before. I'm still not sure what had driven me to bring it along but I had, so I made use of it. Angling the book so the flickering light from the fireplace fell across the dusty pages, I lost myself in a world of foolish fantasy romances and long-dead places.

Every so often, a noise would disrupt my peaceful world. Something outside would creak, a gust of wind would disturb the trees, or an owl would hoot. Every time, it got my heart racing all over again, only to end with me chiding myself for being so jumpy. Once, I heard something that sounded like a footstep, but it faded before I could determine exactly what I'd heard.

At around midnight, I felt Michael stir against me. As though awoken by some internal alarm clock, he stretched and yawned, then looked up at me with those fathomlessly dark eyes of his. "Any trouble?"

"Nothing I'm worried about," I reassured him as we swapped places; he sat up, while I snuggled down beneath the blankets, looking forward to my half-a-night's sleep. Despite the odd noises, I felt content knowing that Michael was watching over me. He would never allow any harm to come to me while I was vulnerable, and that made me feel comfortable and relaxed.

I nuzzled my face against his firm thigh and closed my eyes. Before I had time to ponder another thought, I was fast asleep.

Chapter Fifteen

I slept deeply that night. My dreams were full of knights, princesses, and beautiful young girls with dark eyes and long, Rapunzel hair. I awoke just after dawn, feeling warm and comfortable – until I realised that the firm thigh I'd been using as a pillow was rigid with tension. I looked up, and saw Michael's jaw was clenched and his face was set in a mask of intense concentration.

"What's wrong?" I whispered, jerked fully awake by the look on his face. He started at the sound of my voice, then let out a deep breath, as though he'd been so tense that he'd forgotten to breathe.

"There's something outside," he whispered back. "I've heard it walking around out there for the last few hours. It hasn't tried to get in, though. Seemed safer to wait until dawn before we go see what it is."

"Good thinking," I agreed, easing myself up into a sitting position. "Let's go find out, then."

Both of us had slept fully clothed that night. With Priyanka in the room, it felt inappropriate to disrobe –

and neither of us liked to let our guard down in unknown territory. As reluctant as I was to leave the warm nest I shared with my beloved, necessity required it. We extracted ourselves from bed and found our weapons in the semi-darkness, then we headed for the front door.

I peeked through the curtains that hung over the nearest window and saw nothing. Room by room, we checked each window to see if we could get some idea of what was out there, but we saw and heard nothing.

Michael was ahead of me as we crept down the corridor towards the back. Suddenly, he froze and jerked a hand up to silence any questions I might have had. He tilted his head to one side, silently communicating that I needed to stop and listen. I did so. From the other side of the barricade, we could quite clearly hear the shuffling of feet. I opened my mouth to say something, but an unexpected sound interrupted my train of thought: a faint whine.

We stared at each other in surprise, not quite sure what we were hearing.

"Was that a dog?" I whispered. Michael hesitated and then nodded, probably for lack of any better explanation. For reasons that I couldn't guess at, domestic canines had been a rare sight since the plague hit, but they weren't completely unheard of.

As if to answer our question, a low, pitiful howl came from the other side of the door, followed by more whining and whimpering. We both stared at the door, and I saw my own indecision mirrored in Michael's face.

"If it's hurt, then we should help it," he said, echoing my thoughts. "But, it also might just attack us on sight."

"There's only one way to be sure," I answered, shooting a glance at him. "We have to go look. I think we should go out the front and walk around, rather than move the blockade. That way we can always run back in and lock the door."

"Sounds like a plan," he agreed with a firm nod. Together, we returned to the front end of the house. Priyanka still slept soundly on the couch, so we left her there and we headed out the front door with our weapons at the ready. I led the way down the front steps and swung around the house in a wide arc, treading lightly across the grass-hewn gravel. Now that we were in daylight, I could see that the little bungalow sat in a small, overgrown clearing amidst the trees; to the rear of the building, I saw a large, open shed that backed up to the house. It seemed like a safe assumption that whatever had been making the noise was hiding inside.

Michael fell in beside me as we tiptoed around the edge of the building. I swung out wide to try and get a look inside the shed before we exposed ourselves in danger, but the long shadows of sunrise made it hard to see. I could only just barely make out the outline of the creature hiding within. What I did see was that it was leaning hard against the back door, and I heard it whining pathetically.

It didn't seemed to have noticed us even though I

was standing silhouetted against the morning light. I glanced at Michael, then looked back at the animal and let out a whistle. Its head came up immediately, ears pricked, then it struggled to its feet with some difficulty. With slow, hesitant steps, it limped towards me, swinging its head slowly from side to side.

When it stepped out into the light, I realised that it wasn't sick, just elderly. I'm an animal person by nature, so the sight melted my heart. Michael seemed to feel the same way. He handed me his gun and knelt down, making soft clicking noises and calling the dog until it turned its head towards him.

"Come here, buddy. Come on," he called, snapping his fingers to attract the dog's attention. It came towards him slowly, swinging its head back and forth as if trying to isolate the sound of his voice. A few steps closer, it paused and sniffed the air, then whined again and inched closer with its tail wagging shyly.

Michael held out his hand and let the dog sniff it, which it did. The creature's breath made wuffling noises between whines, and then it licked his hand. Michael took that as an invitation and reached over to rub the old dog's ears, making comforting noises to keep it calm. As soon as he did, the dog's tail started wagging frantically.

"Doggie?" Priyanka asked from behind me, just about scaring me out of my wits. I glanced back to find her hiding behind me, staring at the creature with wide eyes. Her gaze shifted up to me, her expression one of apprehension. "Doggie will bite?"

"No, I don't think he'll bite you unless you're mean to him." I extended an arm out to her. Priyanka ducked beneath it gratefully, and cuddled up against my side.

Together, we watched Michael talking to the elderly canine, ruffling its ears and making comforting sounds. The dog's tail wagged so hard I could practically hear the old joints creaking, but it seemed thrilled to feel a human's touch.

"You know, the doctor's going to kill us if we bring home two strays," I commented dryly.

Michael laughed and nodded, keeping his voice low to avoid scaring his new friend. "But he doesn't have a choice in the matter; he was my first stray and he knows it."

"I am stray?" Priyanka asked, looking bewildered by the comment.

"You were a stray," I corrected her gently, giving her a sideways hug. "But you're not any more. Now, you're our friend."

"Oh... stray means not friend?" Her brows furrowed in obvious confusion.

"Not quite. In this situation, a stray is just a friend you haven't met yet," I tried to explain, using simple terms that her limited vocabulary could understand. "It's a new person, or a stranger."

"Oh." Understanding dawned in the girl's eyes. "Doggie is stray, but can be friend if no bite?"

"Yes, that's right," I agreed. It was close enough until we could expand her vocabulary. Looking pleased at her new-found knowledge, Priya disentangled herself from me and crept over Michael and the dog. She knelt down beside them, staring at the creature.

While Michael took over her education and showed her how to let the dog sniff her hand, I stood guard. I divided my time between watching Michael's paternal instincts coming out, and keeping my eyes peeled for danger.

I had to admit, I was secretly impressed by his adeptness. The years he'd spent raising Sophie, his niece, paid off. Even though I had no interest in having children of my own just yet, some part of me found his skill with youngsters extremely attractive. Despite being so physically large with a deep, powerful voice, neither the child nor the animal seemed to be frightened of him at all.

Eventually, I drifted off into my own thoughts while the others played, staring into the bush surrounding the clearing. Suddenly, a squeal of delight attracted my attention. I glanced back and saw Priyanka hugging the dog around the neck while it licked her face, tail wagging frantically. Michael laughed merrily, and even I found myself unable to resist a smile.

The age of technological and capitalist pleasures was long gone. Now, it was the simple joy of a child's laughter, of fresh food and clean water, and the companionship of lovers, friends, and family that brought happiness into our lives. As much as I missed my parents, I felt like we might actually be better off for it in a broader sense. The downfall of our species brought us back to our roots, to what we were meant to be before the Promethean lure of the modern age had turned us into something else completely.

"Doggie need bath," Priya told me as she disentangled herself from the old sheepdog and hopped up to her feet. "We have bath now?"

"You first," I told her, holding out my hand. The young girl raced over to take it and skipped along beside me as I led her back to the front of the house. Behind us, I heard Michael coaxing the old dog along as well. Soon, the four of us were safely back inside.

***

Bath-time proved to be a noisy and rambunctious affair that ended with water and soap suds all over the old bathroom. By the time I'd peeled Priya out of her filthy rags and gotten her into a tub full of cold water, I'd come to the awful discovery that she was infested with all manner of parasites. Her rags had to go, as did her long, matted hair.

I half-expected a fight, but when I told her that I was going to cut off her hair she seemed more fascinated than upset. As it turned out, she hadn't realised that hair could be cut; her parents had never given her a trim. She waited obediently while I hunted around for a pair of old scissors, then attacked her mane with gentle determination. Lock by lock, her tangled tresses fell away into a pile on the bathroom floor, until all that was left was a short, manageable crop.

"Gone?" she cried happily as she ran her fingers

through her newly-cut hair, looking delighted by the funny feeling of short hair beneath her fingers.

"That's right, all gone. It'll grow back, but we must keep the yucky bugs out," I told her, and then promptly dunked her back under the water. She popped back up again a moment later, spluttering and laughing, then she splashed me playfully in retaliation.

"Yuck, bugs!" she repeated, poking at a patch of floating dirt that had come off her skin. "Yuck, yuck. No more bugs?"

"No more bugs," I agreed, amused. She was a bright kid, and her English was improving with every sentence. "Close your eyes tight, okay? I'm going to put soap in your hair to kill the yucky bugs."

"Okies," she agreed readily, squeezing her eyes closed. I found a few unopened bottles of children's shampoos and anti-nit treatments stashed away in a cupboard, and since the bottles were still sealed I judged that they were likely fine. With a twist, I opened one and then applied a liberal amount to her head.

The pleasant scent of shampoo filled the room as I rubbed it into her scalp. The smell and the feeling of my fingers massaging her scalp drew happy noises from her. When I told her to dunk her head, she obeyed. We rinsed the shampoo off, then applied another treatment just in case.

Once she was done, I drained the bath and put her under a cold shower to wash away the last of the dirt, then bundled her up in a big towel. Shivering and dripping, she followed me happily from room to room as I searched for new clothing that would fit her.

At first, we had no luck; the three bedrooms we found appeared to belong to parents, and a pair of teenagers – one boy, and one girl. Unfortunately, Priyanka was a tiny thing for her age, so their clothing was much too large for her. But in the back of the girl's wardrobe, we struck a goldmine: a box full of old clothing that had been packed away when it no longer fitted, but no one had ever gotten around to throwing out.

Priyanka looked delighted by the bright colours and happy patterns. It took some doing to teach her how to wear underwear and which way the other garments went on, but she was a clever little thing and learned readily. With my help, we got her dressed and picked out some spare garments for her to bring along with us.

In the corner of the room I spotted a faded pink backpack, someone's old school bag tossed aside on that day long ago when the world changed forever. I picked it up, and discovered that it was still crammed with faded school books and homework that would never be graded. Although I felt a momentary pang of sadness for the young woman who had owned that bag, Priya needed it now. I emptied it out, and carefully folded Priyanka's new clothing into the bottom of it.

"This for mine?" she asked while I was packing her bag. She snatched it up as soon as I was done, and hugged it to her chest.

"You mean, 'is this for me?'" I corrected, and then nodded. "Yes, sweetie, that's for you now. The girl who used to live here doesn't need it anymore, so you can have it."

"She dead?" Priyanka asked thoughtfully, looking around the bedroom as though seeking some trace of the person who had once lived there. "She had pretty things. I like pretty things, too. She like me, I think."

"Would you like one of the pretty things to take with you?" I asked, lifting a hand to rest on her shoulder. It seemed like a good time to teach her a few valuable lessons, and to make her happy at the same time. "She's gone now, so you can take something if you'd like. Just remember, you never take things from living people without asking. And if you want to take something from here, you have to carry everything that you pick yourself. Okay?"

"Okies. I want pretty thing. I carry," Priyanka agreed readily. She scampered away from me and went over to the girl's bureau, where she began poking around amongst the various bits of girly nonsense. I decided that she was going to be busy for a while, so I left her to it. I headed back to the bathroom to gather up all the anti-nit treatments that were left, and added them to my pack. Priya would probably need another treatment in a few weeks, and my fastidious nature left me intensely aware of the fact that both Michael and I had been in physical contact with her several times. It was getting later by the minute so there was no time to treat our hair now, but I planned to make sure we both got a dunking as soon as possible, just to be safe.

Once the bottles were safely stowed away, I went

off to check on Michael. I found him sitting on the kitchen floor with his arm draped over his new canine companion; the dog had its muzzle buried in a bowl of dog food. Michael looked up when I entered the room and gave me a shy smile.

"I found some dog food in the kitchen," he told me. "There's some stuff for us as well. I figured, you know, that you wouldn't mind if we brought the dog along, so long as we're not feeding him out of our own supplies." To my surprise, Michael actually looked a little embarrassed, like he thought I would actually say no to the idea of bringing the dog with us.

"Of course, I don't mind if we take him along." I knelt on the floor beside him, and leaned over to kiss his cheek. "Did you honestly think I'd mind? My only concern is that he might be sick, or might not be able to keep up with us."

"Well, I wasn't sure," he admitted, putting his free arm around my waist to draw me up against his side, then his lips captured mine for a quick, tender kiss. In the heat of the moment, any resentment I might have felt was brushed aside by the overwhelming adoration I felt for that kind, strong man. I couldn't possibly be angry with him for making that assumption, and I didn't want to be.

When our lips parted, I chose the moment to tease him, just as mercilessly as he routinely poked fun at me. "Well, okay, you can keep him – but you do have to give him a bath."

Michael's eyes widened as he struggled to figure

out how serious I was. As if to punctuate my statement, a fat flea leapt off the old dog's fur and landed the floor tiles beside us. I was quick enough to crush it with my fingernail, then I gave him a pointed look.

"I bathed Priyanka, you have to bathe the dog. There's flea soap under the sink in the bathroom."

"But... but, I..." he stammered, staring down at the dog with uncertainty. "I don't know how to bathe a dog."

"Doggie needs a ba-ath," Priya called from the far end of the house, catching us both by surprise. A second later, we melted into laughter.

"Okay, okay. Doggie needs a bath," Michael agreed, once the levity had subsided. "There must be instructions on the bottle, I'm sure." The elderly canine had just finished up his last mouthful of food, so Michael stood and called him until the animal padded out of the room after him.

With everyone else busy, I turned my attention to the important task of breakfast. It was an hour past sunrise, and we weren't on the road yet; if we didn't reach our destination soon then my sister was bound to start worrying. Although I had warned her I wasn't sure how far the Hilux would take us, on foot it should only have taken three days at most. In theory, we should have been there before sunset – but that estimate hadn't included being distracted by lost children and stray dogs.

I was sitting in the lounge stirring a pot of canned spaghetti on our little camp stove when Priyanka came looking for me. She was so stealthy in her bare feet that I didn't even notice her arrival until she knelt down beside me.

"What is this?" she demanded, thrusting a small, sparkling trinket into my hand as soon as I turned to look at her. I took it without thinking – she didn't really give me a choice – and examined it thoroughly before I answered.

"This is a bracelet, a charm bracelet. I used to have one just like this when I was your age. It goes like this." I reached out and took her hand, then showed her how to put the bracelet on. It was made of silver and semi-precious stones, but it had aged well. There was only a little bit of tarnish, since it had been kept in a dry, relatively clean environment over the years.

"Bracelet?" Priyanka drew her hand back and shook her wrist, watching the light dance off the sparkling stones. "I remember... Mama wore bracelet. Many lots of bracelet. Went 'rustle rustle' when she cuddled me when I was little."

The thought didn't seem to upset her, but it did appear to interest her. In my mind's eye, I saw her as a chubby little toddler being picked up by a woman wearing stacks of bangles. I found myself wondering, and curiosity got the better of me, as it often did.

"What did your mama look like, Priyanka?" I asked carefully, cautious of dredging up painful memories.

"Pretty." Priya's eyes lost their focus as she thought back, seeking an answer to my question. "Mama was very pretty. She hands same colour as my hands." She held her hands out towards me, as though I might have forgotten what she looked like. "Hair like my hair. Long, long. No bugs, though." The girl pulled a face. I laughed.

"Your hair will grow long again, and this time we'll keep it clean so no bugs get in," I told her with a smile. "Promise."

"Good." She nodded vigorous approval, and then resumed her tale. "Mama like to wore the pretty colours, always pretty colours. Pretty like this." She pointed to a patch of colour on her newly-salvaged clothing. "I no know the name for this."

"Pink," I supplied helpfully.

"Pink?" she repeated, looking up at me with those huge, soulful eyes of hers; I nodded and she smiled. "Pink. Mama wore this colour often. And the colour like the sky, and sometimes the colour like the grass. She wore long, pretty dresses with patterns on them. Not like the dresses in we look at here, other kind of dress. Had a... a thing."

She mimed something, indicating a flap of cloth worn over the shoulder; it took a minute for me to interpret what she meant and dredge the word out of my memory.

"A sari?" I supplied, a little uncertain if I was giving her the right answer, but she nodded vigorously.

"Sari, yes," she echoed, looking happy with that definition. "Very pretty sari. She wore pretty sari that was pink with shiny on it, and very many bracelets. I remember Mama giving me many hugs, and letting me play with her bracelets. She read to me many, many books, all the time. Teach me many things. Mama love me, and me love Mama."

"I think that you are much like your mama, Priyanka," I told her. "You are also very pretty, and you're a good girl."

She visibly swelled with pride at my praise, too young to have developed any sense of modesty yet. I liked that about kids. No false pretences. No pretending one thing when they thought another. They were honest.

"I go look at more pretty-pretties," she announced, springing up to her feet with a pleased look on her face.

"Breakfast will be ready soon," I called after her, but she'd already vanished down the corridor. Shaking my head in amusement, I returned my attention to cooking.

A few minutes later, the sound of splashing and unhappy noises, both human and canine, caught my attention. Priyanka came dashing back into the room, laughing her head off.

"What are they doing?" I asked, trying to push aside my instinctive panic-response. How much damage could an old sheepdog possibly do? Priyanka's gleeful response answered my question in quick order.

"Doggie give Michael bath!" She chortled merrily, and mimed shaking water off herself like a dog would. Then, she suddenly seemed to remember she had come looking for me for a reason, and plunked down on the ground beside me. She pointed at my feet, then held up a pair of sneakers that appeared at a glance to only be a tiny bit too large for her. "Look-look! I found like what Sandy has."

"Hey, that's great. They're called 'shoes'," I explained, reaching over to take the object from her. They were dirty and well-worn, of course, but that didn't matter to us at all. To a survivor, anything that was new to you was as good as being brand new. "Good for walking in so the stones don't cut your feet. See these nice, thick soles? These are good, they'll protect you very well. Now, we just need to find you some socks."

"Socks? Sssssocks. That word is funny." She giggled gleefully, repeating it a few more times for good measure. "What is socks?"

"Underwear for your feet," I explained simply, rolling up the leg of my fatigues to show her mine. "They stop your shoes from getting stinky."

Priyanka stared dubiously at the shoes in her hands. "Shoes already stinky."

"Then they'll stop your feet from getting stinky," I answered with a laugh. "You want some breakfast, Priya?"

"Breakfast? Food?" She leaned over to examine my concoction, and her eyes widened. "What is? Is funny colour."

"It's called spaghetti. Yes, it's food." I gave her a smile and picked up a bowl, filling it with the fragrant orange sauce. "You'll probably like it. Kids always seem to love spaghetti. Now, this is hot so don't try to eat it with your fingers, okay? Do you know how to use a fork?"

Priyanka took the bowl from my hands and stared down at it dubiously, apparently unsure what to make of the substance I was trying to tell her was food. I couldn't blame her; the stuff was so full of food colourings it sure didn't look all that edible, but the smell of hot canned spaghetti could still make my mouth water even after all these years.

She looked up at me and shook her head, bewildered. I gave her a smile and a pat on the head in return, then leapt right on into teaching her how to use a fork and spoon. It was a messy business and took some doing, but by the time Michael finally joined us, our little foundling was well on her way to being competent with utensils.

I made a point of not looking when Michael plopped down beside me, because I was really struggling to hide my amusement. I could tell from the scent and the sound of his movements that he was soaked to the bone. Without a word, I dished up his breakfast and handed it to him, and we sat in a ring around the stove, eating our food.

Or at least, we did – right up until the dog padded out into the living room, and shook himself off, spraying water droplets in all directions.

Chapter Sixteen

A few hours later, we were back on the road, and I found myself pondering the strange turn of events that had doubled the size of our little party in less than a day. Michael and I walked together in the rear, while Priyanka skipped along in front with the dog prancing around her legs. The two of them had become firm friends, and spent most of the morning playing together.

"Penny for your thoughts?" Michael asked. I felt a strong hand slip around mine. When I looked over, I found him watching me. He smiled, and I felt a flush of heat in my belly. I looked away, absently tucking a strand of hair behind my ear with my free hand.

"Oh, you know." I stole a glance back and found his smile was a little wider than before. "I was just thinking that it's kind of amazing the dog can keep up so easily. I noticed that his eyesight isn't great, so I was a little concerned that he'd slow us down. He really isn't, though."

"It is pretty impressive." Michael's gaze shifted to

follow the old sheepdog bounding ahead of us. "Kind of makes you feel like we humans got the bum end of the stick when it comes to sensory input, doesn't it?"

"You're not kidding," I agreed. "I remember when that bastard, Lee, was telling me that he was going to put my eyes out. The only thing I could think of was just how helpless I'd be if he blinded me. I don't think I could bear it."

"You'd still have me," he quickly reassured me, giving my hand a gentle squeeze. "If anything like that happened, I'd protect you and take care of you."

"I know you would, but what if something happened to you and there was no one else around?" I gestured towards the happy dog, who was leaping around Priyanka without a care in the world. "He can find food and avoid danger with just his nose and his ears. I can barely tell when my socks need changing."

"Well, I can tell when your socks need changing," he teased playfully. I responded by giving him a smack on the shoulder, to which he reciprocated with his best impression of a dying walrus. The peculiar sound startled both the girl and the dog. They both froze and stared at us in perfect unison, and the looks on their faces were so priceless that Michael and I burst out laughing.

"Grown-ups are silly," Priyanka told her canine companion solemnly. The dog barked his agreement, then bounded off again with his tail wagging frantically. The girl squealed in glee and chased after him, apparently forgetting all about us again.

***

It was around midday when we reached the township of Pukeatua, a blip on the map that was even smaller than our little Ohaupo. The place was so tiny that it barely even warranted a name.

At first, I didn't even realise that we'd arrived. All I noticed was that the trees thinned out a bit, and then suddenly a clearing opened up in front of us. A handful of road signs sprang from the overgrown verge like a crop of ugly mushrooms as we climbed a low rise, then we crested the hill and saw the ruins of the town sprawled out below us.

Of course, using the word 'town' to describe a place like Pukeatua was taking some liberal usage of the noun; there were maybe a half-dozen houses within sight, in various states of disrepair. There was something off about the place, though. Something that instinctively put my nerves on edge. I cradled my shotgun close against me as we moved further down the road. As if sensing my disquiet, my companions fell silent behind me.

I picked my way carefully past the debris that was strewn across the road, trying to put my finger on what was bothering me. There had to be a reason. My instincts were a little over-aggressive at times, but they were well-honed. I'd spent years living in the bush, always alone. I knew the sights, sounds, and smells of New Zealand like a wild animal.

And then it struck me. It was quiet. Too quiet.

Although the bush thinned out around the town, there were still plenty of trees – but no birds were singing. I held up my hand to halt the others, scanning the road and buildings ahead of us for anything out of the ordinary. I spotted a few dark, ominous shadows dotting the asphalt, like puddles of dried blood. In the distance, I could see spray paint on the side of a building. It was too far away to tell if it was a gang sign, but that was warning enough for me.

"There's something very wrong here," I whispered. "We should leave, now."

Then the dog began to growl, low and deep in his throat.

I had the safety off my shotgun in a second, and dropped into a defensive crouch. Michael flanked me as I took a couple of cautious steps backwards, his expression one of focused intensity that mirrored my own. However, his instincts were honed for urban combat, while I possessed a completely different set of skills.

The footfall sounded like an elephant's tread against the quiet world around us. I spun around, but it was too late; the stranger had one massive hand around little Priya's throat, and in the other he held a very large, very sharp machete. Priya cried out in surprise as she was swept up against the huge man's body like a human shield. She struggled, but he was three times her size – at least four inches over six feet tall, all rippling muscle, and outfitted in full army battledress.

"Let her go," Michael said, trying to negotiate even

though we both had our weapons trained on the massive soldier. "We're just passing through, we mean no harm."

"No harm? Heh..." The man's voice was a deep-throated rumble, but it was totally different to the familiar purr of my lover's voice. His voice was pure threat, and it sent the alarm bells in my head ringing like crazy. "You should have listened to your woman, chink, and left while you still had the chance."

I saw Michael bristle at the use of the racial slur, but I cut him off before he could respond.

"There are two of us, and one of you," I pointed out coldly, calmly; I felt the surge of adrenaline pumping through my veins. Usually it brought fear, but not this time. I had learned something over the last few months, and improved myself. This time, the adrenaline brought with it a detached kind of clarity. "We're well-armed and well-trained. If you hurt her, we'll kill you before you can draw your sidearm."

"Well, aren't you a feisty one?" The stranger showed teeth, but it wasn't a smile. "I have no problem with you. You can leave if you prefer. These two, though... a fucking chink and a curry-muncher? Their kind brought this plague on us. I'll kill them all!"

My eyes did not leave the stranger, but at the edge of my vision, I could see Priya's terrified eyes staring at me, enormous and confused. She didn't understand what was going on, and she was too afraid to fight anymore. I sensed more than saw Michael's readiness, but we were trapped, with that innocent little girl caught between us.

"You're an idiot if you believe that," I told the man coolly. Reasoning with a madman was impossible, and yet I had no choice. "The plague came from monkeys, not people. Any five-year-old knows that."

"Fucking lies, spread by that nigger president in America!" the man roared, his face turning red with fury. For half a second he was distracted, and I saw his grip on Priya loosen.

That half a second was all I had, so I used it. I sprang forward and lashed out, using the butt of my shotgun as a club. The blow struck home with the resounding crunch of bone fracturing; his roar of rage turned to one of pain.

He lashed out blindly with the machete, but I twisted away and caught Priyanka by a fold of her clothing to yank her from the madman's grasp. The hot flash of pain exploded across my ribs, but I barely felt it – my only concern was for Priya. I would worry about my own health once she was safe.

I shoved her away, and felt her fall somewhere behind me, but I didn't have time to find out where; I'd pissed the racist soldier off right royally, and it was right at that moment that I realised he wasn't alone. Although they were hidden out of sight, the intensity of life-or-death fighting put my senses on edge. I could faintly hear the sound of human breathing in the clumps of trees on either side of the road. We only had moments before they would enter the fray, and then we'd be outnumbered.

The behemoth sprang at me, but I was waiting for him. I leapt back out of the range of his machete, and unleashed a brutal kick to the groin while he was off balance. Although he was huge and presumably strong, his size was a disadvantage against someone as comparatively small and nimble as me – particularly since I fought dirty.

The man crumpled to his knees, all the breath gone from him. As he tumbled forward, I jerked my own knee up and caught him in the forehead. He went down hard, like Goliath to my David. I didn't take any time to celebrate my victory, though; we were in intense, immediate danger, and I knew instinctively that that Michael hadn't realised it yet.

"Follow me," I ordered breathlessly as I raced past him. I grabbed Priyanka's hand, and sprinted into the nearest patch of bush without a second of hesitation. A man was waiting there with a weapon drawn, but I took him by surprise. I shoulder-charged him before he could fire, bowling him to the ground, then I leapt over him and kept on running.

I heard heavy footfalls behind me, and a quick glance back confirmed that Michael and the dog were right on my tail. The canine may not have understood the exact nature of the threat, but it had decided to follow us anyway. Michael, on the other hand, just knew me well enough to trust my instincts without question at a time like this. Reassured that he was still safe, I turned my attention back to guiding our flight, deeper into the bush.

My ears were tuned for danger, and I heard all the sounds that happened around me: the heavy breathing of my companions, the crash of my own feet as I cleared a path through the heavy brush, even the alarm sounds of the birds in the trees all around us. Over that, I could hear the furious shouting of our pursuers as they chased us. The behemoth's deep voice rang out above the others like a herald of doom, ordering them to find us and kill us without mercy. Then, suddenly, I heard another sound. It was much closer at hand, and ominously familiar.

In the bushes to our right, I could hear low, deep squeals, punctuated by the thud of flesh striking flesh. Those squeals were the kind of sound that would forever haunt my nightmares, but this time they brought a flash of inspiration. I skidded to a halt and thrust Priya's tiny hand out to Michael, who took it without thinking. He started to say something but I interrupted him. There was no time for questions, no time for thinking – it was time to act.

"I have an idea," I told him, then I pointed him in the direction we had been going. "Stick to the forest. Keep heading east until you reach the river, then follow it south to the bridge. I'll meet you there."

"But—"

"Just go, now!"

He tried to protest but I waved him away. Although I could see the tension in his handsome face, he nodded grimly. A quick kiss and then he was off, vanishing into the undergrowth. I was left alone, between a pair of vicious enemy factions.

The hellish squealing drew me back to the ferns. I peeked through, and saw what I expected to see: two infected pigs were fighting one another, locked in a bloody battle for supremacy. They didn't notice me at first, but that was going to change. I cocked my shotgun, then aimed it from the hip and peppered both their hideous bodies with hot shrapnel.

The shotgun's retort rang in my ears, and sent birds scattering from the trees overhead. I'd given away my position, but that was part of the plan. The two horrid monsters instantly lost interest in one another and turned on me, but the underbrush was too thick for them to charge properly. When I turned and ran, they barrelled after me at top speed, but I was light on my feet and much more nimble than they were amongst the trees.

The creatures were single-minded in their intensity, but they couldn't quite catch me. Although my heart hammered in my chest from the knowledge that a single misstep would spell my doom, I somehow kept myself calm. The adrenaline fuelled me, and again I felt that strange kind of clarity of purpose, the drive to succeed at all costs. It was powerful, and it was addictive. Feeling cool and collected in spite of the danger, I drew ahead of the pigs a little bit, just enough to give me an advantage, but not quite enough to lose them. For my plan to work, the pigs had to stay close. Very, very close.

Suddenly, I saw a human figure amongst the trees.

Although he was shadowed by the forest, his size gave him away as the madman who wanted us dead for no better reason than our ethnicities. I sprinted straight at him, my feet crushing the ferns that flourished in the lightless land beneath the canopy.

The sound of my footfalls alerted him before I reached to him. I tried to dodge past him, but he was quicker than I estimated despite his size. He made a grab for me and managed to get hold of a handful of my clothing, preventing my escape. I felt a momentary flash of panic, but the act of grabbing me spun him around, so he couldn't see his death incoming.

"Oh, so you changed your mind, did you?" he growled and shook me roughly, unconcerned by the weapon in my hands. "You know, I was going to let you stay with me and my boys once I killed your friends, show you what a real man looks like. Pretty, white girl like you? Could have had some fun, you and me – but now I think I'll just kill you as well."

"I hate to tell you, but I've already got a real man," I answered him breathlessly, feeling a surge of victory despite the danger I was in. "So this seems way more appropriate. A swine like you deserves nothing better."

My dark smile must have alerted him that something was amiss. He glanced back over his shoulder just as the huge boar burst through the underbrush, and bowled him over from behind. His grip on me faltered, and I was ready for it. I twisted away just in time, and ducked behind a tree out of the sight of the incoming beasts.

For all his size, the man was only human, while the infected boar was the largest I'd ever seen. It bore him effortlessly to the ground, and then it was on him, attacking viciously. Hidden from sight, I heard rather than saw when the sow joined in the attack, but I could barely hear their squeals over the man's screams.

Suddenly, I felt nauseated about what I'd done. I reminded myself that it was for the sake of my lover and our innocent young charge. That man would have killed them both for no better reason than the colour of their skin. If those bloodstains were anything to go by, we had not been the first victims of his gang. He deserved a horrible fate.

While the pigs were both completely focused on their attack, I ducked out of my hiding spot and ran as fast as my legs could carry me. Even though I'd been the instrument of that man's well-deserved destruction, I could not bear to watch the creatures kill and eat another human being.

His screams rang through the forest behind me as I fled to the east, putting as much distance between myself and the grisly scene as I could.

Chapter Seventeen

I ran like a madman, ducking and dodging through the undergrowth despite the constant risk of personal injury. A few minutes later, I found the road again, far to the east of the little town. I froze and stared all around, listening to the sounds of the wilderness until I was certain that I was alone. Sticking to the road would be dangerous, but I could travel faster if I took that route. It only took a second to decide, and then I was off again.

I ran as hard as I could for as long as I could along that cracked grey ribbon, until my breath seared in my lungs and my heart started making a serious effort to bust its way out of my ribcage. The late summer sun beat down on me mercilessly, and sweat carved rivulets through the sunscreen protecting my skin.

Eventually, I had to slow down to a walk. By that stage I judged that I had probably put three or four kilometres between me and my enemies. I didn't stop, though. I couldn't stop until I knew Michael and Priya were safe. I was alone, but I was well-armed and in my element. My concern was for them, not me.

On my own, I moved much more quickly than I had when I was with the others. Weeks of good food had begun to restore my body to a decent state of health; I felt better than I had in as long as I could remember. My foot had adjusted to the rigors of travel once the muscles had time to warm up and stretch, too. Although it ached, it was an ache that I understood and could safely ignore. I knew it wasn't an injury anymore, just a mild discomfort.

When my lungs had recovered, I eased myself back up to a trot. After a few hundred metres, I slowed to a walk to recover, pacing myself for the long haul.

Water was a concern. Michael had most of our supply in his backpack, and the small bottle I kept in my pocket to sip as we walked was almost empty. I took a swig from the bottle anyway, since there was no point conserving it. If worse came to worst, I could always boil river water. Right now, I was parched and sweating. My body needed water to keep going.

The trees hung low over both sides of the road, granting me a temporary respite from the heat. I paused for a moment to listen, but I heard nothing that indicated a threat. The birds still sang contentedly in the trees, and the wind rustled the branches. Everything seemed safe and calm, with nothing to indicate any danger nearby.

I continued on, guiding myself up to a loping trot for another few hundred metres. As I ran, I found myself thinking that something good had come out of the attack: running for our lives had put us back on track to reach the power station before nightfall.

The thought made me smile. Perhaps Michael's positive attitude was starting to rub off on me after all. I decided that it was best not to think about the other things that had happened; the sun was shining too brightly for me to dwell on morbid thoughts. Instead, I focused on keeping myself alert for danger. I had no idea how many members of the neo-Nazi gang were in the area, so I chose my path carefully in case they decided to track me. Each footfall connected only with solid tarmac; I crushed no blades of grass with my weight, and avoided any patches of gravel that might leave a footprint behind.

It was strange to think that I had learned so much about tracking over the years. I'd begun life as a city girl, raised in pleasant suburbia without a care in the world. But when the plague had come, I found myself on my own and often under attack. I had learned the way of our new wilds, and fast. That was how I'd survived all these years.

I was no genius but I wasn't stupid. Logic dictated that a footprint didn't leave itself, that a healthy leaf or flower bud didn't break without reason. I'd learned to look for those signs, and to listen to the world around me for the telltale markers of something that didn't belong. After spending so much time on high alert, that sense had become second nature to me. For a while, in Hamilton and later Ohaupo, my sense of the world had begun to fade away – but the moment I returned to the familiar places I used to call home, that sense came back to me in force.

Everything I knew I'd learned the hard way, because I had been lucky enough to survive my mistakes. I learned which wild berries I could eat by watching the birds. In the early days, roaming the bush starving and alone, I ate a berry from a tree. It had made me so violently ill that I had been unable to move for hours. While I'd lain in the leaf-litter, recovering, I had noticed that the birds flitting around in the canopy above me avoided the fruit from that particular tree. Instead, they favoured the product of another tree. When my stomach recovered, I tried a few of those berries instead, and discovered that they were safe for me to eat.

I could survive in the bush if I had to, and I wasn't afraid to retreat to the wild places if the urban regions became too dangerous for me. However, I generally still preferred the urban life. It was easier to find food and water, and it was more likely for the amenities to still be functioning in town than it was in rural areas.

But, the bush was safer. There, I could hide and live wild. I had learned to listen to Mother Nature and to trust her, even when she was in one of her more capricious moods. The sights, sounds, and smells were familiar to me, and I generally knew how to respond to them. I could only imagine that was how Priya had survived all these years, too. Trial and error, and learning to trust nature to provide a solution. When it came down to it, we were all Mother Nature's children.

Some of us had just forgotten that.

My mind drifted at random as I travelled east, running a few hundred metres then walking a few hundred. As a teenager, I'd read a book that had recommended that method as the most efficient way for a human on foot to travel without exhausting themselves. That knowledge had served me well over the years. My nostrils flared wide with each breath, drawing air deep into my lungs to power the efficient hydraulics of my body.

It was during one such breath in that I caught a scent on the breeze that was out of place. The wind blew from the east, and it carried with it the acrid smell of gunpowder, and coppery scent of blood. Ahead of me, the road bent slightly and sank down behind a small hill. I slowed to a walk and brought my shotgun up in case I needed it.

As I crept towards the bend, I eased myself into a low crouch-walk, my senses extended and alert. The birds still sang on, aside from the few directly above me. My small size, soft footfalls, and the dark green camouflage print of my clothing meant that I bothered them much less than a grown man thundering through the brush – or worse, a pig.

Of course, there might be someone hiding nearby that was as savvy in the rules of bush-law as I was, but I would not know until I sensed him. Regardless of the risk, I followed the road rather than moving into the underbrush, and stepped carefully around the bend until the source of the smell came into view. A human body lay in the middle of the road ahead of me, blood pooling on the tar seal beneath it.

The corpse was so fresh that the blood had barely begun to congeal in the hot sun. I stared at the brush nearby for a long minute until I was sure there was nobody watching, then I crept closer to the body to get a better look.

It was a man, sprawled on his back with dead eyes staring blankly at the sky. He was clad in battle dress, just as the massive soldier had been, but wore no body armour. That mistake had cost him his life: his chest was riddled with bloody wounds. I judged by their location and the way his body lay that he'd died nearly instantly, in a hail of high-powered bullets.

A fold of his clothing half-concealed something. Curious and analytical, I prodded the corpse with my boot to clear the cloth away. It revealed an empty holster on his hip, big enough to hold an automatic pistol and a couple of spare clips. The holster was empty now, and a quick glance around revealed no sign of the weapon or the ammunition.

I did see shell casings though, small ones, probably from a 9mm gun like the one that this man had carried. In my mind, I turned the physical evidence over and replayed the scene a few different ways until I had a clear picture of what must have occurred.

The dead man had fired first, I guessed; he must have done, as the wounds in his chest were from a heavier weapon. For there to be shells from his weapon on the ground, he must have opened fire before the person with the heavy weapon shot him. The corpse was facing east, and I recognised the wounds in his chest as entry rather than exit wounds.

The scenario crystallized in my head: this man had been following someone heading east. He had approached them from behind and opened fire, and they had in turn killed him in self-defence and taken his weapon. Michael. It had to be.

I had told him to stick to the forest, but it didn't surprise me that he had gotten lost along the way. His sense of direction in the wilds was still developing, which was why I was our guide. I was just relieved that by some dumb luck he'd found the road instead of wandering off in the wrong direction. Even he could follow a road. As far as I could tell, he was going in the right direction.

I left the corpse, not caring if the man was the victim of pests or animals this time. He was nothing to me, someone that wanted to hurt me and my family. He deserved no respect in death.

A dozen metres further down the road, my boot struck something small and sent it tumbling across the asphalt with a metallic chime. I paused to look, and discovered the shell casings from the heavier weapon scattered across the ground. Although I couldn't be sure, I was fairly certain that they'd come from Michael's rifle.

Unfortunately, I also spotted something that worried me. Sprinkled amongst the fallen shells were a few droplets of dark crimson, that were rapidly turning brown in the heat: blood. One of my companions was injured. Which one, I couldn't tell. Spurred on by concern, I picked up to a run and headed eastwards as fast as my tired legs could carry me. It was more than an hour past noon now, almost two, and my friends would be worried sick about me.

I was relieved to see the blood trailed off after only a few metres, meaning it had been staunched rather than left to bleed. That reassured me, but still I felt the overwhelming need to return to them as soon as possible. I longed to feel Michael's arms around me, holding me safe and warm. Then there was Priyanka and her elderly pet; the girl had a smile that could light up the room, and I feared either she or the helpless animal might be the ones hurt.

I could not abide that thought, and it made me feel better about what I'd done to protect them. The guilt would come later, when I had time to brood – but for now I was busy, my thoughts and actions dictated by necessity. There was no time for recriminations or regrets until after I knew my companions were safe.

***

An hour later, I was drawing close to the end of my reserves of strength. My legs trembled with every step, but my resolve held strong. I was almost there, I could sense it. I'd covered many more kilometres, and I could feel the land beneath me beginning to slope gently downwards. The bush grew denser and denser, until I was travelling through dark shade despite it being the heat of the afternoon. The changes in the landscape around me told me the river must be nearby.

As I began to pad around a long, gentle curve in the road, I was startled by the sound of a human voice shouting. Another shouted back, but I couldn't make out their words. Then there were gunshots, rapid and piercing, from several different kinds of weapons. I skidded to a halt as self-preservation kicked in. Until I could see them, I couldn't be sure who was shooting at whom. It could be friends, it could be foes. It could be both.

The shotgun held close against my chest, I pressed myself into the shadows of the undergrowth and crept around the bend at a wide angle. The paved plateau in front of the bridge opened up below me, providing a wide area of open ground that would leave me exposed if I moved much further. There were two bodies there, sprawled out and still twitching, no more than a minute dead.

I glanced around cautiously and saw nothing besides the two of them. My heart hammered in my chest as I emerged from the shadows and snuck towards them to see if I could determine what had happened. Both of the bodies were male, both in battle dress and at a glance I could see that both of them had been killed by a hail of high-calibre bullets.

It was only then that I sensed eyes upon me. I spun towards the bridge, with my shotgun raised automatically to defend myself. I found myself looking at a familiar face on the other side of a longer barrel:

Michael.

Both of us were still in fight or flight mode, so it took a second for what we were seeing to sink in. When it did, we both lowered our weapons and rushed to one another. His longer strides covered the ground more swiftly than my exhausted ones, and he caught me before I made it a half-dozen steps.

Strong arms enveloped me and held me close. I buried my face in his sweating chest, luxuriating in the heat and the scent of his body. A few months ago, I would never have imagined that I could find the odour of a sweaty man to be pleasant, let alone intoxicating – yet now, I did. It was fresh and healthy, and it belonged to the man that I loved with all my heart. I clung to him, overwhelmed by sensations of affection and relief so strong it made everything I'd done seem so worthwhile.

After a minute, I drew back and kissed him, quickly and repeatedly, indulging a need to express my affections as physically as possible. He understood and held me close, returning my shower of kisses with his own until I calmed down.

"I was afraid I'd never see you again," he whispered to me, his arms still wrapped around my waist. His voice was huskier than usual and I detected deep emotion in it that made my heart lurch.

"I know, but... I had to. You know I had to," I whispered back. He nodded, silently telling me that he understood. He always understood. It was the same reckless abandon that had driven him into a violent rage when one of the undead had cornered members of our family, weeks ago. Unlike him, I had not been driven into shock in the wake of my actions, though. I had stayed calm and rational throughout. It felt like it had happened to someone else.

"They're fine. I've got them hiding under the bridge," he told me softly, anticipating my question before I could ask. I nodded and glanced at the corpses for a moment, then I suddenly remembered the blood I'd seen on the ground.

I shoved myself back and stared at him, inspecting his body from head to toe. Sure enough, there was a crude bandage wrapped around his bicep, and another around his left wrist. He didn't bother to put up a fight when I took his hand, and dragged him off towards the shelter of the bridge to get him cleaned up.

"I saw the first body, way back, and I saw your blood on the ground. I've been so worried about you," I admitted as we retreated down the bank and ducked into the dark recess beneath the bridge's span.

Very little plant life grew down there, since it never saw any sunlight. When my eyes adjusted, I spotted Priya sitting on a patch of hard concrete, her knees drawn up to her chest and arms wrapped around them. Her eyes were closed and young face was a picture of misery, but the dog spotted us straight away and alerted her to our presence by letting out a happy yip.

The moment she saw me, her eyes widened. A second later, she had her arms around my waist and was clinging to me like she was afraid that I'd left her forever. Even though I was anxious to see to Michael's wounds, I understood her vulnerability and made no effort to detach her. Instead, I led both of them back over to sit on that patch of concrete, the three of us all huddled in a row in the shadows.

Priya leaned against me crying quietly while I stripped away Michael's makeshift bandages. I inspected the wounds, cleaned them, and then redressed them with proper, sterile dressings from my first aid kit. Although it caused him pain, he clenched his jaw and bore up well to the discomfort. I knew that he trusted me to only have the best of intentions for him, and he knew I would only cause him pain if it was for good reason.

For my part, I was relieved to discover the injuries were only flesh wounds, and none of them would cause him any real trouble unless they got infected. Of course, with someone as attentive as me to be his nurse, there was no way he was getting infected any time soon. At least, I hoped not. I'd had enough of infections to last a lifetime.

Hell, we had barely recovered from the last time we ended up in bandages. That was the last thing we needed. Michael still had a tiny red pucker mark of half-healed tissue on his ribs from when he'd been shot with that air rifle ten days earlier. He still had to cover it, but it was past the danger stage.

Michael had the presence of mind not to ask what had happened. Even if he had, I wouldn't have told him with young, innocent ears sitting right there beside us. A vague reassurance from me that our racist friend wasn't going to trouble us any further was good enough for both of them.

After the wounds were cleaned, the four of us just sat catching our breath for a while. Priyanka finally stopped crying and clung to me in silence, while Michael stared off thoughtfully into space. I sat in the middle, turning over in my mind the strange situation I found myself in this time. I felt so protective of that young girl even though I'd only just met her, and I could see in Michael's face that he felt the same way.

Was it animal instinct that drove us to protect the young, even when she wasn't our child? It was a strange feeling, but it made sense to me. In little Priya, I saw someone who had an entire life ahead of her, one that was so full of promise and potential. Although she'd come from someone else's womb, in that young child I saw the future of my species. We were on the verge of extinction, and yet she gave me hope.

She, and all the other children like her. Madeline, Priya, any children that Michael and I might have one day. They were our future. Without them, there was no tomorrow for humankind.

I didn't realise that I was squeezing Michael's hand until I noticed him looking at me with concern. I gave him a sheepish smile and relaxed my death-grip, but he seemed to understand. He put his arm around me instead and drew me up against him. I contentedly nestled against his side and closed my eyes.

Suddenly, the dog let out a yip and sat bolt upright. Startled, the rest of us looked at him and then at each other, trying to work out what the dog knew that we didn't. I started to say something, but Michael held up a hand to silence me; a moment later, I heard the sound as well. There was an engine coming our way. No, several engines.

"Stay here," I whispered to the others, extracting myself from between their bodies. I crept noiselessly out from beneath the bridge and inched up the bank beside it, keeping myself hidden deep within the long grass. Despite my instructions, I felt the warmth of a large body beside me and knew that Michael had followed me. Side by side, we lay in hiding, waiting for the source of the noise to come into sight.

From the west, along the very same road we'd come down less than an hour before, came a small group of quad- and farm-bikes. The lead bike stopped when the rider spotted the corpses lying in the road, and the others came to a halt in a gaggle behind him. After some discussion, the rider of the first bike hopped off and hurried over to the corpses to examine them.

As he drew closer, I recognised him, and heaved a deep sigh of relief. Shoving myself up out of my hiding spot, I waved to the startled rider until he realised who I was and waved back.

"Kia ora, mate!" Hemi shouted. "Fancy seeing you here."

Chapter Eighteen

It took some explaining to get Hemi up to date on the situation that had led to us being in possession of a number of corpses, an elderly sheepdog, and a small, buzz-cut-wearing teenage girl. Luckily for us, Hemi was good-natured and patient. He listened with interest to our tale, and expressed relief over our survival.

Priyanka needed some time to adjust to the presence of more people in our group. When the others first arrived, she was too frightened to come out of her hidey hole under the bridge. Eventually, curiosity won out over caution. I felt her tiny presence manifest behind me. When I looked down, I found her staring at the newcomers with enormous eyes.

By the time we finished talking, she was standing beside me instead of hiding behind my back, though she still clung to my hand. I glanced down at her occasionally, and each time I found her watching Hemi or one of the other men with intense fascination. I decided that was most likely to do with their physical appearances. Although they were still different to her, they looked much more similar than Michael or myself.

"Priya, this is my friend Hemi. Say 'hello' to Hemi," I told her, trying to introduce her to the young man. The girl stared at me, then ducked her head shyly and hid behind me again. I exchanged a glance with the others and shrugged. "Sorry, she's had a bit of a scary day. She'll come back out of her shell when she's ready."

"Sweet as, man." Hemi grinned cheerfully. He gave the girl a playful wave when he caught her peeking at him again. She stared back at him, her mouth agape and eyes almost as wide as saucers. Everyone chuckled.

There were four men besides Hemi in the group, and all of them were familiar to me from the time we'd spent with the tribe. I was pleased to see that Ropata, the carpenter, was with them, since his skills would no doubt prove invaluable in the task waiting for us.

Tane and Iorangi were there as well. The two men were brothers, who stood tall and imposing, but I'd learned that they were just big teddy bears full of good-humour and fun. Tane was around my age, and wore his hair in long, distinctive dreadlocks. Iorangi was a few years younger, but taller than his brother by several inches.

The last member of the group was a slender, wiry man in his mid-thirties. I knew his name was Richard, but that was about all I knew. We'd only spoken twice before, but he seemed like a nice enough guy. He was just quiet, and usually kept to himself.

Once the explanations were over, we set out on foot to find a better place to sit down and have lunch together. The bridge followed the rim of the catchment dam for the power station down river, but it was bisected in the middle by a small island which was home to an overgrown picnic area. It seemed like a good place to rest for a bit, since it gave us a clear view in all directions in case there were any more neo-Nazis coming after us.

After we had eaten, we gathered our belongings and moved on. The road continued in a long curve, but this time it didn't just span water – it crossed the top of the Arapuni dam itself. That was by far more terrifying than the first half of the crossing had been. The river pooled placidly to our left, while on our right the only thing that separated us from a drop of more than a hundred meters was a tattered mesh fence. When we made it safely to the eastern side of the river, I let out a deep breath to calm my frazzled nerves. I'm not a huge fan of heights.

"Oi, Sandy – we'll give you a ride, eh?" Hemi called to me. I glanced back and watched his group wheel their bikes the rest of the way onto solid ground.

"Sure. We'll cover more ground that way," I agreed. I looked down at Priyanka, who still clung to my hand like a limpet. "We're going to go for a ride, okay? Go sit behind Hemi and hold on tight."

Priya's eyes just about bugged right out of her head. She shook her head frantically and ducked behind me. "Don't wanna."

"C'mon, it'll be okay," I reassured her. "I'll be right there, too. We're going to go fast. You don't want to get left behind, do you?"

Priya stared at me in horror, then looked back at Hemi.

"Go on, sweetie," I said, leading her towards the bike. "It's okay. I'll be right here. Hemi won't hurt you, he's my friend. He's a good boy."

"Good boy?" Priya echoed softly, though she still looked dubious.

"Yeah, good boy." I nodded firmly, and guided her up to sit behind him. "Put your arms around his waist and hold on tight, okay?"

"O-okies," she said, and did as she was told. I smiled and ran my hand over her head, then went to find my own ride. Michael did likewise, calling the dog after him.

Although we were forced to travel relatively slowly so the elderly canine could keep up with us, we made much better time over the last leg of the journey than we could have hoped to do on foot. The nimble little bikes bounded over the tattered tarmac without complaint, their light weight and good suspension keeping us safe from harm.

Seated on the back of Tane's quad bike with my arms wrapped around his waist, I watched the scenery pass in a blaze. Every so often I got smacked in the face by a dreadlock and had to shove it out the way, but I took it with good humour. The last leg out of trip passed swiftly and painlessly compared to the first couple of days.

Within just a few minutes – about ten or fifteen, I

estimated – we were bouncing our way out of the countryside and back into relative civilization. Abandoned buildings sprang up out of the overgrown lawns and gardens on the right, while the left side of the road was lined by heavy bush.

Remembering the instructions Rebecca Merrit had conveyed to us, I kept an eye out for something obvious to mark our path. She hadn't been specific on what she'd be using, though. I could see Michael looking around too, and in the end he spotted it before I did. He shouted and waved, which brought our little column to a halt.

A moment later, I saw what had caught his eye – a bright yellow high-visibility vest tied to a tree, flapping languidly in the breeze. As she'd promised, it really couldn't have been any more obvious. As soon as Tane stopped our bike, I leapt off and hurried over to examine the flapping cloth, with Michael and Hemi hot on my heels.

"I think there's a walkway back here." I reached out and moved aside a branch, revealing a deep, cavernous gloom beneath the trees. It had the look of a tunnel, trimmed back to be easy to traverse on foot, but the branches hung too low for the bikes to pass safely.

"We'll go find somewhere to hide the bikes, and then we'll follow you, eh?" Hemi glanced at me for confirmation. I nodded, so he hurried off. Priya scampered over to join us, looking refreshed and high-spirited after her exciting ride on the back of a quad bike, with the dog close behind her.

With Michael and me in the lead, and Priya behind us, we set off down the dark pathway to see what lay beyond. The passage was so narrow and dark that it felt like travelling through a cave. Behind me, I heard Michael muttering as low-hanging branches tugged at his hair, and even I had to duck on occasion to avoid getting a twig in the eye.

Every so often, a metal pole divided the path into bike lanes; we could feel concrete under the leaf litter beneath our feet. Once, this had been a public walkway and cycle track, for tourists wanting to visit the power station. Now, it was something else entirely. The wilds had reclaimed it. Walking that track was a strange experience but somehow comforting, kind of like being back in nature's womb.

Eventually, I saw filtered sunlight dancing across the end of the path, startlingly bright after the tunnel's gloom. I stepped out into the sunlight, raising a hand to shield my eyes – and drew a sharp breath of surprise.

"Oh, lordy," Michael rumbled as he drew up beside me, staring at the bridge. The walkway terminated in a small, open area that bordered the edge of the Arapuni gorge. A hundred metres below us, the river rumbled over rapids. The bridge that spanned the gap was little more than rails and netting with a narrow walkway down the middle.

I picked my stomach up from about my knees, and took a long, deep breath. "At least the bridge is still intact. No holes... I'm not sure I could handle holes."

"I feel like I should make a joke about that,"

Michael answered, "but I can't think of one right now." He looked at me, his dark eyes unreadable. "Do you want me to go first?"

"No... no, I've got this." I'm not entirely sure if I was trying to reassure him, or myself. Regardless, I swallowed hard and stepped out onto the bridge, expecting it to bounce and sway beneath my weight. To my relief, it didn't.

As terrifyingly exposed as it felt, the bridge had clearly been designed with public safety in mind. The entire length of the crossing was lined by a mesh fence nearly twice my height; if I wanted to fall off, I would have to put some serious effort into it. Unfortunately, I could still see through the mesh, so knowing that I was safe didn't help with the vertigo.

As I stepped out further onto the narrow walkway I felt the bridge swing languidly in the wind, but it didn't bounce or jostle the way many rope bridges did. This one was steel and chain rather than wood and rope. Even the panels that made up the footpath had metal peeking out through the wooden veneer. I let out a sharp breath and tried to relax, reassuring myself that I wasn't going to fall.

When I heard the others filter out onto the bridge behind me, I paused to turn and check on them. Michael was assisting a nervous-looking Priyanka with gentle words, holding her hand as he led her out onto the span. It was only then, when we were fully committed to the bridge, that we heard a voice call out to us.

"Hold it right there!" It was a male voice, and it was shouting. "Do not come one step closer, or I will drop you."

I froze. Those words told me that the speaker was armed, and meant business. Although it was completely against all of my basic instincts, I managed to release my death-grip on the handrails and slowly raise my hands above my head in the universal sign of surrender. Closer to the start of the bridge, I saw Michael do the same whilst discreetly inserting his bulk between the gunman and our young charge.

"That's right. Now, turn around slowly. No sudden moves." The instructions were obviously for me, so I did as I was told. It was difficult to move slowly when every one of my instincts was screaming to get the hell off that bridge and back onto solid land. "Identify yourselves and tell me why the hell I shouldn't shoot you."

"We were invited here," I called back, mentally cringing at how out-of-breath I sounded. My heart was racing more and more the longer I stayed up there. I could feel panic gripping at the edge of my psyche, running icy talons up the back of my neck. "Rebecca Merrit invited us. Check with her, she'll tell you. She said that you needed help, so here we are. My name is Sandy."

My answer was silence.

I realised suddenly that I was trembling all over, whether from adrenaline or basic animal terror; it felt like the chasm was drawing me over the edge even though I wasn't moving. My breathing had accelerated to the point that I was panting, and I felt the tickle of sweat gathering on my forehead. If I didn't get off that bridge soon—

"Why are you armed?" the voice demanded suddenly, interrupting my internal monologue.

"You told us it was pig country," I answered, with a stab of annoyance. They had asked us for help, and yet we were the ones getting interrogated? "By the way, you failed to mention that Pukeatua is neo-Nazi territory. We almost got shot getting here. Come on, Jim – let us off this damn bridge. We've brought rum."

"Rum? But I asked for vodka," the man complained, but my words had the desired effect. He stepped out of the brush where he'd been hiding, a long hunting rifle nestled in the crook of his bandaged arm. "Well, come on then. Hurry up, we don't have all day."

Gun or no gun, I couldn't get myself off that bridge fast enough. As soon as my feet hit solid ground, I nearly collapsed with relief. A second later, Michael and Priyanka joined me, and the three of us clung together for a moment to recover. The dog bounded along after us, showing no sign of being any the worse for wear for his adventure.

"I really don't like heights," I admitted, letting Michael's comforting bulk steady me until I felt better. Then I turned and looked at the portly man that had briefly held us hostage, studying him. He was an older fellow that I estimated to be in his late fifties, but it was hard to tell. A ring of scrabby reddish-blonde curls stuck out over his ears, but other than that he was completely bald. He had the heavy summer tan, rough skin, and beer gut of the typical Kiwi bloke, but there was a degree of intensity about his eyes that the average bloke didn't have.

"You said it was just going to be two of you," he accused. "You didn't say anything about a kid or a dog."

"We found them along the way," I explained. "We couldn't very well leave them behind. However, you'll be happy to know we managed to convince five of our big, strapping friends to join us and help clear up your problem."

"Five?" The man's eyes widened. "Cripes, that's more than we expected. We didn't even know there were that many people left in the Waikato."

"You'd be surprised," I answered sympathetically, relaxing now that I was out of harm's way. Sure, he was carrying a gun, but so was I. Neither of us were aiming at one another. "My group consists of five people, six if you count Priyanka here, plus our friends have a group of eleven."

"Bloody hell." Jim itched at his balding pate with his good hand. "Had no idea. Figured there was maybe a half-a-dozen folks still around, but no more than that."

"You kept the power going all these years for a half-dozen people?" I asked, incredulous and a bit stupefied.

"Well, I've been working here since I was a pup. Keeping this power station going is all I know. I ain't got no family, so when the plague took my mates I just stayed here, kept doing what I've always done." The man absently rubbed his jaw and lifted his good shoulder in a shrug. "Then I found Rebecca in town. She'd had a bit of trouble with a few lads further south, so we decided to get married to keep her out of trouble. Seemed like a good idea at the time."

I chuckled and shook my head. "I'm going to tell her you said that."

"Hah." Jim grunted a laugh as well. "The old bat already knows. Bloody nag, never lets me get a moment's rest." Despite the aggression in his words, his tone was affectionate.

A shout from the other side of the bridge drew our attention. I turned and saw Hemi and his crew gathered on the far side. With a wave, I beckoned for them to join us despite the wary look on Jim's face.

He relaxed once introductions were made. For some reason, knowing someone's name made them seem infinitely less hostile. Besides, we were a generally good-natured crew, and we came bearing booze. When Jim finally consented to lead us off towards the power station, there was a fair amount of joking and heckling going on between us, which seemed to put him at ease.

Michael and I followed Jim, with the rowdy group of lads, Priya and our dog strung out in a pack behind us. I glanced back to check on my small charge, and found her staring adoringly up at Hemi. Amused, I shook my head and smiled to myself. Oh, how quickly her opinion of him had changed.

Suddenly, an arm snuck around my waist, and took

me by surprise. I shot a curious glance at Michael and found him chatting away with our host despite the possessive grip. Though he was still smiling and joking, I could see a strange tightness around his eyes that confused me. It took a few seconds for me to realise that it was nervous jealousy.

That was an emotion I had only seen from him once before, when we'd first met Hemi's enigmatic mother. Although I had no sexual interest in women, I found her fascinating to the point of being hypnotic, and Michael had seemed irked by that fact.

Now, I realised it was the fact that, aside from Priya, we were completely surrounded by men. I could only imagine he felt some basic animal need to exert his ownership over me, as the only adult female in the group. I didn't really mind, per se, but it was a strange feeling and left me a little uncomfortable. The thought of being claimed like a piece of meat was not a happy one, but I knew Michael didn't think of me that way. It was an instinctual thing, and I would probably have felt the same way if we'd been surrounded by a pack of women, and Michael had been the only virile man in sight. Hell, that made me nervous just thinking about it.

All of a sudden, I felt an overwhelming need to reassure him that he had my full attention, and I simply wasn't interested in anyone else. I placed an arm around his waist and leaned against him comfortably, but I didn't say anything. I didn't have to. That was enough.

As it turned out, access to the power station was

not for the faint of heart. Jim led us down the steepest flight of stairs I'd ever seen in my life, a concrete pathway etched directly into the side of the gorge. Through a mesh of overgrown branches, the river valley opened up below us; it was a sight of unparalleled beauty that took my breath away even more than the steep descent did.

The river was the colour of carved greenstone, still running high after the recent storms. It wound between steep hillsides lined with thick bush. I found myself amazed by the fact that the trees and ferns had managed to survive clinging to the slopes, but not only had they survived, they'd flourished. The closer to the riverside that we got, the louder the rush of water became. By the time we reached the landing, it was loud enough that it was getting hard to hear anyone's voice.

If this is how loud it is when the station is off, how do they get any sleep when it's running?

I glanced around the massive concrete platform curiously; the power station was enormous, possibly the single largest human-made structure I'd seen in my life. A relatively narrow concrete walkway ran around the edge of the monolithic structure; although it seemed slender compared to the size of the station, it was easily wide enough to drive two trucks down side-by-side.

There were no trucks, of course. I saw no sign of a road or access-way to the lower portion of the station, so there was no way to get them down there.

To our left, a concrete wall rose ten or fifteen

metres above my head, perhaps more. It was hard to get a sense of scale on a building so impossibly large, particularly when a significant portion of it was buried within the rock wall of the gorge. Enormous windows glinted in the sun, but they were up too high for me to be able to see inside.

Jim opened a door and led us in. I found myself feeling a little like Alice in Wonderland, stepping through a door that looked so tiny compared to the monstrous wall it was set into. We entered a hallway that was of a more normal scale, and were shown about a dense network of old offices that had been converted into living space. The thick concrete drowned out the rush of the water, so it was relatively quiet inside.

"Rebecca?" Jim bellowed his wife's name suddenly, startling me with the volume of his voice inside an enclosed space. "Where the hell are you, woman?"

"In here," a female voice replied through a partially-open doorway. Jim shoved the door the rest of the way open and strode in, muttering to himself beneath his breath.

"Visitors," Jim grunted noncommittally, then promptly left the lot of us in his wife's care and stomped off about whatever business he thought was so much more important than us.

"Welcome, and sorry about my husband," Rebecca greeted us, glowering in the direction her antisocial spouse had gone. Introductions were made, and explanations for the unexpected presence of our new companions.

Unlike her husband, Rebecca Merrit didn't seem bothered. I found myself taking an instant liking to her as she led us through the warren of old offices and storage rooms beneath the power station, assigning us sleeping quarters.

"I'm afraid we don't have enough beds for everyone," she admitted, looking apologetic. "We weren't quite expecting this many people. I've only made up two, but we can probably drag a few more out of storage tomorrow. It's a little hard, what with Jim's arm."

"It's fine," I answered, and gave her a smile. "I think we're all used to sleeping on the ground from time to time. So long as we don't wake up covered in dew, anywhere you can spare is just fine."

"That much I can definitely do," she agreed, smiling back at me.

She was at least a decade younger than her husband, fit and spry with no trace of grey in her long, brunette hair. Although her hair was pulled back in a practical ponytail and she was wearing men's clothing, she was slim, vivacious, and full of life – the complete opposite of her portly, grim-faced husband. The comparison amused me, though I thought it impolitic to mention it to either of them.

"Now, I'm assuming you boys don't mind letting the ladies have the good beds?" she asked, shooting a pointed look at the men trailing along behind us. They'd obviously been well trained by Anahera, so her question was met with noises of consent.

She showed me and Michael to one room, and Priya to another across the hall from us, then left us there to get settled in. The 'good bed' was nothing more than a narrow cot with a thin mattress, but neither of us minded. We'd shared a similar sized bed back in Hamilton. We didn't mind getting cosy for a few nights.

Priyanka, on the other hand, was thrilled at having a room to sleep in with a real bed. "Mine room, for me!" she told us with great glee, bouncing back and forth between the chambers. As relieved as I was to see her happy again, I found myself wondering about the issue of privacy.

"We should figure out how to lock the door," I commented dryly, shooting Michael a pointed sideways look. He instantly took my meaning and laughed merrily.

As though to prove my point, Priya promptly stuck her head in the room to find out what we were giggling about. I burst into laughter as well. Poor little Priyanka just stared at us, bewildered, like all the adults in her life had suddenly gone mad.

There were some things in life that I just wasn't ready to explain to a cloistered thirteen-year-old yet. It was safe to assume someone would have to have The Talk with her at some stage, but today was not the day.

Chapter Nineteen

By the time everyone had settled into their rooms and changed out of their grubby travelling clothes, there were only a few hours left until sunset. We left Jim with his prescription of booze and painkillers, and headed out to inspect the work that needed to be done.

Hemi, Michael and I followed Rebecca, with Hemi taking the leadership role for his group in his mother's absence. It seemed like a natural progression; despite his youth, Hemi appeared to have inherited his mother's organisational abilities, and at least a little of her charisma.

Rebecca led us out of the building, and along a walkway around the edge of the power station. Eventually, we made our way down another narrow set of concrete stairs onto a smaller ledge that ran just above the water line. About half way between one end of the station and the other, Rebecca stopped and pointed at the concrete beneath our feet.

"These are the intake vents." Rebecca knelt down on the concrete and leaned forward. I joined her, and stared where she pointed. "There's a grille over them that normally stops things from getting into the vents, but the storm knocked a big tree over. Somehow, the tree went right through the grille. It's lodged in the intake down there."

The water was clear as glass near the surface, but it lost its translucence just below the surface due to the turbulence of the recent heavy rain. I couldn't see much, just a few branches and a handful of leaves.

"How big a tree are we talking?" I glanced at her, curious.

"Big." Rebecca sat back on her haunches and heaved a long-suffering sigh. "It's an old oak tree, used to grow over the river down by the dam. We found the stump; it looks like it got split by lightning. Even with eight able-bodied people, I have no idea how we're going to get it out."

"You said you had equipment?" I asked. "What kind of equipment?"

"All kinds of equipment, but unless you know how to scuba dive it's not going to do much good."

I looked at Michael and he looked back at me. Sure enough, he nodded. I found myself fighting a smile. "We may just have someone that can help with that."

"What?" Rebecca stared at me, and then looked around at the others. It took a moment before she cottoned on to the fact that she was missing a joke. "You're kidding me, right?"

"Not at all. Michael was a cop," I explained to her. "He's trained in all kinds of different things."

"Actually, I learnt to scuba dive while I was in high school," he interjected helpfully, and flashed me that silly grin of his.

"Or he's just an overachiever. Something like that." I shot him a mock-glare for contradicting me, but that just made his grin widen.

"Well." Rebecca absently rubbed the back of her neck, staring thoughtfully down at the murky water. "I guess that does change things, doesn't it?" A flicker of hope passed through her eyes, and brought a smile to her face. "I guess we have a chance after all."

"Let's hope so," Michael spoke up, then he glanced around at the rest of us. "We'll need to get down there and have a look before we formulate our plan of attack. None of us have any experience with hydroelectric power stations besides you. Which of us can swim?"

Hemi grinned at him. "Man, my boys live on the edge of a lake and take our kai from the water. What do you think?"

"I'll take that as a yes." Michael winked, and then glanced at me. I simply nodded; I didn't swim very often, but I could if I had to. He nodded back, then looked up at the sky to judge the time. "We probably have enough time to take a quick look. Is your equipment ready?"

"One set is," Rebecca answered, easing herself back to her feet nimbly. "I'll go fetch it."

"I'll help," Hemi volunteered cheerfully. The pair of them scampered off, leaving Michael and me alone.

I watched them go, then looked up at him and

playfully raised a brow. "So, if you're going swimming, does that mean you're going to take your clothes off?" I teased impishly.

Michael just grinned at me and waggled his eyebrows.

***

By the time Rebecca and Hemi returned with the scuba gear, Michael had stripped down to his boxer-briefs and given his clothes to me for safekeeping. I folded them up neatly and put them aside, and promptly initiated an in-depth conversation on the weather. No, really. For reasons that I couldn't quite determine, I had started finding it hard to concentrate the moment that he'd undressed, which seemed to amuse him greatly.

"It definitely smells like rain," I commented, shading my eyes against the setting sun.

"You keep saying that, but I don't smell anything." Michael looked at me curiously. "How can it smell like weather?"

"I don't know how to explain it, but I can definitely smell it." I did my best to explain what my instincts were telling me, but he didn't seem to fully understand. "If you draw in a deep breath through your nose and mouth, you can feel a coolness and moisture on the air."

"I can't smell anything." I heard him sigh sadly, and shot a quick, worried glance his way – except that when I did, I caught him smirking and realised that he had deliberately drawn my eye.

"Damn it!" I complained, swiftly covering my eyes. "That's not nice. You know how to play me like a fiddle."

"I think a flute would be a more appropriate instrument, don't you?" he teased mercilessly, then reached out and grabbed me around the waist to pull me into a playful kiss. Suddenly, it was very, very hard to concentrate on the task at hand.

Someone scoffed in mock-disgust. Startled, I squeaked and leapt out of his arms, leaving him looking incredibly amused. With a flash of completely irrational embarrassment and a touch of annoyance, I blushed furiously and stalked off a short distance to cool down while Rebecca and Hemi helped Michael into the diving gear.

"The current is quite strong," I heard Rebecca warning him, "so be careful. The turbines are all off so you can't get sucked into any machinery, but you could get stuck down there."

"I'll be careful," Michael rumbled. The imminent danger distracted me from my strange mood; although I was feeling out of sorts, he was still my Michael and I loved him, so I returned to the group to offer my support.

They hadn't bothered with a wetsuit since the water would be warm, and he wasn't going to be down there for long. Residual moisture left on the tank and mask sent water droplets rolling down his skin like a gentle caress. I tried not to see them, but the more I tried to look away the harder it was to focus. One droplet survived long enough to trek all the way down across his hard belly, to moisten the rim of his shorts; try as I might not to see it, my eyes followed it all the way down.

Thankfully, no one was looking at me as the heat rose in my cheeks again, which was a blessing in disguise. My sister taunted me mercilessly about the blushing thing. My skin was so fair that I turned as red as a tomato at the drop of a hat. Suddenly, I was very glad that she'd stayed at home.

"If you need us to haul you out, tug the rope sharply three times." Oblivious to my distress, Rebecca continued her instructions as she fastened a secure line onto Michael's weight belt with a heavy-duty clasp, and fed out enough line for him to be able to move freely.

He nodded and slipped the mask over his face, settling the mouthpiece within his lips. My heart skipped a beat as he stepped backwards into the water, but he popped up again a moment later and flashed us a thumbs-up sign. Rebecca tossed him a waterproof torch, and then he was gone into the depths.

We were left to feed out the safety line as he needed it, but other than that all we could do was wait. I sat down on the edge of the concrete platform to wait, and slipped off my shoes so I could dip my feet in the river and let the cool water take down the swelling.

I watched the trail of bubbles diminish as Michael moved beneath us; I could imagine his powerful strokes as he swam, even if I couldn't see him. With no other option, I pushed my anxiety aside and tried to relax. Michael was a competent swimmer and seemed to have an impressive assortment of skills. He'd be just fine.

All kinds of different skills. I trailed a toe in the water as I mulled over the idea. *You might even call them talents. He's... a very talented man...*

"Are you still blushing?" Rebecca's comment made me jump. When I glanced up, I saw both her and Hemi watching me with amused expressions.

"No," I retorted sharply and looked away, suddenly embarrassed beyond words.

"Uh-huh." Rebecca did not sound convinced. I could practically hear her rolling her eyes. My embarrassment deepened, and anger rose within me. Michael shouldn't have put me into that position. He knew very well I was shy and cautious around strangers, though he had made it his life's mission to draw me out of my shell.

Embarrassing me in public was certainly not the way. He must have seen them coming and decided to assert his position of ownership over me right when they could see it. It was the only logical conclusion. For once in his life, I felt like he had made a very serious judgemental error. I glared at the water and kicked it absently, gritting my teeth in brooding silence.

I heard the other two wander away a short distance, and then a whispered conversation between them that ended in muffled laughter. I felt sure that I was being gossiped about, and I didn't like that feeling at all. Sulking, I stared off into the water, willing my boyfriend to return so that I could kick his shapely backside all up and down the river for leaving me in this state.

My annoyance grew in leaps and bounds the longer I was left to think about it. Then Worry reared its ugly head, and smacked Annoyance aside. To say that my emotions were at war would be a misstatement; it was more like a vicious barroom brawl going on inside my head. My conflicting emotions were locked in a catfight for dominance.

Concern won for the time being, but I wasn't sure how long that would last. As annoyed as I might be, I loved Michael more than I had any means to express. I worried about him all the time. Even though he was technically still close to me, it felt like he was a million miles away, in a whole other world. I estimated it had been about ten minutes, maybe fifteen. I leaned forward, staring down into the murky water, willing myself to be able to see more than a few feet down.

Something moved, a shadow in the depths. I leaned out further, straining to make out what it was, but I couldn't see it clearly. Then, suddenly, something cold and slippery fastened onto my ankle and pulled; before I could even scream, I was yanked bodily into the cold river. My head went under, then I popped up spluttering and fighting the current.

Michael grabbed me around the waist to keep my head above the surface. It took a second before I realised that he was the one who had pulled me into the water, then I let out an inarticulate shout and smacked his shoulder.

He just laughed playfully and helped me back to the river's edge, where strong hands grabbed me and hauled me back out of the soup. As soon as we were back on dry land, I planted my hands on my sodden hips, and fixed Michael with a dark glower.

"Dammit, Michael; that water is cold, you know," I complained, soaked from head to toe. The breeze chilled me and left me shivering.

"I know, but you made me wash the dog so it's only fair," he answered cheerfully, as he shed his mask and stripped off the tank and weight belt, leaving himself clad only in a pair of distractingly wet shorts.

And with witnesses, too. Annoyance sprang back on the offensive and bitch-slapped Worry with her purse.

Thankfully, Michael knew when to quit. He must have seen something in my face that told him enough was enough, because he settled down and put his serious face back on. Rebecca handed him a towel, but rather than use it on himself he put it around me and rubbed my shoulders to dry me off. The gesture relaxed me a little, but I was still feeling cantankerous and had to bite my tongue to keep from saying something smarmy.

"Let's head back inside," he suggested, glancing at the others. "Once we've dried off and changed, we'll gather the troops and formulate a plan of attack."

They took the hint. Relieving us of the scuba gear,

the two of them hurried off, leaving Michael and me to follow at a more sedate pace. Sensing something was amiss, Michael gathered his clothes under one arm and put the other around me, but I was stiff and unresponsive as the fight continued inside my head. I felt him watching me but I didn't make eye contact. Instead, I glared down at the ground by our feet.

He waited until the others were gone to point out the obvious. "You're mad at me."

I grunted wordlessly; I had no idea how to verbalize what I was feeling.

"Hey," he whispered, trying to catch my chin and tilt it up as he so often did, but for once I resisted him. "Please don't be mad, honey. I was just playing around. I thought you liked the water."

I could hear the hurt in his voice, and that softened my annoyance. He was as new to this as I was, I reminded myself. He had no way to know what would hurt me unless I found some way to articulate it.

"It wasn't the dunking; I was already angry by then," I told him. My voice came out harsher than I intended it to. When I finally looked up at him I could see the pain in his eyes.

"What did I do?" His voice was confused and pleading. For the first time in our relationship, he didn't understand me, but even though I'd hurt him with my sharp tone he was still trying. Guilt suddenly reared her ugly head, and shanked Annoyance right in the kidney. I looked down again, but this time it was for a whole other reason.

"It's just... I... I don't know how to say it." I sighed heavily and closed my eyes; I felt his strong hands on my shoulders, rubbing me gently through the towel.

"Please try?" he whispered, drawing me up against him. "If I've done something that hurts or offends you, give me the chance to make it up to you. You know that I would never, ever deliberately hurt you."

My shoulders sagged as I felt his warm, comforting bulk press up against me, holding me close. He was right, I did know that. I knew it wasn't his fault. He couldn't understand unless I explained it. He was a sweet, kind man, and he didn't deserve the cold shoulder.

"I-I... I don't like it when the others laugh at me, at us. When you get me all, you know, blushing and stuff, and then they're there and they laugh. I feel so embarrassed." Tears stung at my eyes; it all felt so ridiculous, but I couldn't help how it made me feel. "Rebecca laughed at me after you made me blush before. I was so humiliated."

"Oh, sweetheart, I'm so sorry." He brushed away my tears with one hand, and leaned down to plant a kiss on my forehead. "I didn't mean to. I guess I'm just... out of practice on how to behave in public."

"I think we all are," I agreed, snuggling up against him. His skin felt simultaneously warm and cool where the wind had chilled it, and closeness always felt so wonderful.

"What can I do to make it better? Or not do, so it doesn't happen again?" He sounded anxious, far younger than his thirty-two years of age. Like me, his emotional growth had been truncated by the disaster that had devastated our planet. At the age of twenty-two, his world had ended, and he had no romantic experience to fall back on except what he was learning from me. "Would it be better if I didn't touch you in front of others?"

"No," I hurried to reassure him. "I don't mind if you touch me. I like that. It's just, sometimes when you tease me... you know how easy it is for you to get me worked up. I'm vulnerable when I'm worked up. You're the only person I trust to see me that vulnerable."

I heard a soft intake of breath; when I glanced up at him, I finally saw understanding dawn in his eyes. He nodded and offered me a tiny smile. It was then I knew that I had reached him. He hugged me gently and I hugged him back, snuggling my face up against his broad chest as a pleasant sense of tranquillity drifted through me.

We had officially survived our first fight, if you could call that little tussle a fight. At least this time, no one ended up with a cracked jaw. I felt him nuzzle me, the rough stubble of his chin brushing my cheek as he put his lips beside my ear. His voice was a whisper, cool enough to chill my wet skin but warm enough that I only shivered in the pleasant way. "Are we okay, then?"

"We're okay," I whispered back, brushing my wet hair out of the way so that I could kiss him and show him that I still loved him. I felt him relax as our lips met;

his hands were so gentle, it felt like nothing in the world could ever make him want to deliberately hurt me.

All of a sudden, the troubles of our lives seemed so far away, and the only thing in the world that mattered was the man in my arms.

***

Michael and I retreated back to our room hand-in-hand. I felt buoyant, so much better than I had a few minutes before. Despite how recently I'd been in a sulk, I now felt happy and content. More importantly, I finally understood what people meant when they talked about the make-up period after a fight.

I definitely looked forward to spending some pleasant alone-time with him later on in the evening. Hell, I would have dragged him off to bed right then and there, except for a promise I had made to my sister. It was almost sundown, and I'd sworn to contact her on the first evening after we arrived.

When we reached our room, we found a few more towels waiting for us, as well as an old plastic drying rack for our wet clothes. Michael set up the frame, while I peeled off my sodden garments and flung them into a pile on the floor. By the time I was down to my underwear, I realised that I was being watched.

"What?" I shot Michael a look over my shoulder, and narrowed my eyes at him as though I were on the verge of taking offense. This time I wasn't, but two could play at the teasing game.

The poor man looked so tormented that I couldn't

keep the ruse up for long. A smile snuck its way past my mask of indignation, at which point he suddenly realised that I was pulling his leg. His expression brightened immediately, and with it returned his wicked sense of humour.

"Hey, it's not my fault that I like watching you take your clothes off," he retorted, folding his arms across his broad chest. Suddenly, his smile turned impish, and he made an encouraging gesture with one hand. "Oh, don't stop there. The rest of your clothing is soaked as well."

I felt the heat rise in my cheeks at his flirtation, but since we were alone I didn't mind at all. While his cheeky humour had gotten me so upset before, now it struck just the right chord with my increasingly playful mood. I found myself giving serious consideration to whether we had time for a little indulgence before sunset.

Michael snuck up behind me while I was still frozen with indecision, and the feel of his chest against my back made the choice for me. Skylar could wait a few more minutes.

"Here, let me help," he murmured, his lips right behind my ear; I felt nimble fingers unfastening my bra and then a chill as he peeled the wet garment away to expose my skin to the air. A shiver ran right through me, but it was the good kind of shiver; goose bumps rose across my breast.

"Why thank you, sir. How terribly helpful of you," I purred back. I hadn't even realised that I was capable of making that kind of sound until I met him, and it never failed to startle me. Thankfully, Michael distracted me by slipping his hands around my body, his fingers exploring my moist skin.

One drifted down across my belly, drawing me back against his chest, while the other snuck up to cup my breast. His fingertips tickled me in all the right places, and his lips graced the curve of my neck with tender kisses and nibbles. I felt myself responding instinctively to his touch; all thoughts of my sister were gone, lost in the overwhelming, animal desire to mate.

Before I rightly knew what was happening, the flimsy, wet cloth that separated our bodies had been stripped away, leaving us naked in one another's arms. Lost to the moment, I was more than happy to let Michael guide me up against a nearby wall, and take me from behind.

Although we coupled like wild things, never for a moment did that gentleness fade from his hands or his disposition. Never once did I feel any kind of fear, only pleasure so intense I couldn't hope to contain it. I turned my head, seeking his lips with my own; he understood and kissed me with a heat that drove any rational thought right out of my mind.

Each time we made love, I found myself shocked by the intensity of the feelings he stirred in me. Each time, it seemed so impossible that what we had felt before could improve, and yet each time he left me breathless and astounded. I marvelled at just how intense and wonderful it felt.

Although it had been a decade ago and I may have simply forgotten, I had no memory of ever reaching climax through the awkward fumbling of my teenage boyfriends. This was new, and this was special. I vaguely remembered faking it for the sake of their egos; with Michael, I had never once felt the desire to fake anything. He could bring me to the edge of orgasm with the merest touch of his lips or his fingertips.

I wondered if perhaps it bespoke more of my feelings for him than of his abilities as a lover, but I decided it didn't matter. That's not to say that he wasn't gifted, because he was, but I vaguely recalled someone once telling me that the pleasures of sex were always more intense when backed by the emotions of intimacy and love. That certainly seemed to be true.

Our lips parted and I felt the strength drain right out of me, but he caught me before I could slip away. I felt myself bundled up and carried off to bed, where I just relaxed contentedly in the warmth of companionship as I recovered from our brief but potent tryst.

When I regained my senses, I found myself draped across Michael's lap comfortably, while he sat on the bed with his back against the wall. There was a sheen of sweat on his tanned skin, and for some reason I found it fascinating. I couldn't resist the urge to reach out and trace a finger across his chest and down his toned belly.

One of his eyes flickered open at my touch, watching my finger's progress. I looked up and gave him a smile, and he smiled contentedly in return.

"If that's make-up sex, then we should fight more often," he murmured in that deep, husky voice of his. As always, it sent a chill down my spine, but his words made me laugh.

"How about if we skip the fighting and just go straight to the make-up sex every time?" I suggested.

"Good thinking. I like it," he agreed with a languid grin, running his fingertips through my wet hair. I closed my eyes and sighed contentedly, only to have my impending doze interrupted in advance. "Hey, don't go to sleep; you have to call your sister."

I grunted at Michael's reminder, then opened my eyes and fixed him with my best effort at the sad puppy eyes. "Don't wanna."

Apparently, he was much better at it than I was. When I tried it on him, he only laughed. "If you don't, by this time tomorrow we'll have her on the doorstep freaking out."

He did have a point. Knowing Skylar, she'd probably do exactly that.

"I'm up, I'm up." I sighed heavily and straightened up, perching myself coyly on his knee. "But, if I have to get up then so do you."

His sigh echoed mine as he slowly sat up as well. One big hand ran up the length of my thigh, and then shifted up to cup my cheek. I turned my head willingly as he guided me into another kiss – a tender one this time, soft and affectionate, the kind of kiss I wished that I could curl up in and live inside forever. Alas, it was not to be.

All too swiftly, he broke the kiss and gazed down at me, absently stroking the curve of my jaw with his calloused thumb. "I know, my love. I have to go rally the troops. This will just have to do until bedtime."

"Bedtime isn't very far away. I'm sure we'll manage." I smiled up at him, feeling a surge of hot emotion through my chest as I gazed up into his handsome face.

"Oh, we'll manage," he agreed, "but tonight…"

His words trailed off with an entirely different kind of heat, one that made my belly go all quivery at the mere sound of it. I bit my lip and looked down for a moment, then flicked my gaze back up to regard him. "Is that a promise?"

"No," he answered with his usual razor wit and wicked grin. "It's a threat. Now, put your clothes back on and go call your sister."

I gave him a pout of course, even though he was right. The sun was just dipping below the horizon, and I had promised to call.

Chapter Twenty

It took a while to track down Rebecca and get her permission to use their radio to contact home, but once I found her she agreed right away. She led me to the radio and briefly showed me how to use it, then hurried off to gather everyone else for dinner.

I tuned the radio carefully to make sure it was fully in the band, then pressed the submit button and spoke into the microphone. "Arapuni Dam to Skylar McDermott, come in Skylar."

There was no answer. I waited a few moments then tried again, tweaking the tuner a little to the left and the right. Again, no reply. I frowned and twiddled the buttons, trying to boost the signal without really knowing for sure what I was doing. Thankfully, I got lucky; on the third try, I received a reply.

"We receive you, Arapuni; this is Skylar. Who is speaking?"

I smiled with relief and sat back for a moment to let my concern flow away before I replied. "It's me, sis. We arrived safely a few hours ago."

"Sandy! Thank God, I was worried." Skylar's reply was crackly, but the signal was strong, "How are you? How was the trip?"

"We had a few hiccups, but we got there in the end. You're not even going to believe what happened, though," I answered, and then I took a deep breath and launched into the story. I told her about losing the Hilux but gaining a little girl and a pet, and about the ambush at Pukeatua. I glossed over the more gruesome details, though. There was no need for anyone to know those but me. I told her about meeting up with Hemi's tribe, and about the situation at the power station.

"Wow, you did have an adventure. I'm glad everyone's okay," she answered quietly, but then there was a pause. A distinctive kind of pause told me something was wrong at home. "There's... something weird going on around here..."

"Weird?" I echoed, furrowing my brow in concern. "What kind of weird? Good-weird? Bad-weird? Weird-weird?"

"Weird-weird," she answered, sounding a bit uncertain. "It's Maddy. The last two nights since you guys left, she's been having nightmares. She keeps waking up in the middle of the night, screaming that her bed is on fire. The doctor says it's just a phase, but I don't know. Maddy's..."

"...special." I finished the sentence for her, understanding exactly what she meant. Although she was only seven years old, Madeline Cross had shown intuition well beyond her years on a number of occasions. I'm usually the biggest sceptic on the planet, but Maddy had proven that she was anything but an ordinary child.

"Yeah. I don't know, sis. I feel like maybe we should listen to her. What do I do?" It wasn't often that my sister sounded lost, but right now she did. I thought about it for a moment before I answered.

"Well, it's better to be safe than sorry," I said decisively, and then I started issuing orders. "There's a bunch of fire-fighting stuff in one of the downstairs storage rooms. If I remember correctly, there should be three or four small fire extinguishers and half-a-dozen hoses in different sizes. What I want you to do is put one of the little fire extinguishers in your room, one in the doctor's room, and one in the kitchen under the sink.

"Then I want you to take the hoses and spread them out as well. Put one in each bathroom and one in the kitchen. Make sure everyone has one of those little plastic adaptors on their tap so the hose fits, and check the hoses all work.

"Lastly, I want you to take the biggest hose and hide it under the porch of the house across the street. You know, the one with the fallen-down tree in the yard? If there are any spare fire extinguishers, put them there as well. Okay?"

"Okay," Skye agreed, sounding relieved that someone was taking her concerns seriously. "I think we should move the you-know-whats, too. Just in case."

"The... oh, right, the you-know-whats." It took a

second to click that she was talking about the guns. "Yes, absolutely. Put them in the downstairs room of my apartment. I left you the keys. There's a little office at the bottom of the stairs that can be locked from both directions." I thought for a second. "Come to think of it, put some spare food and water in there, too. Enough to last all of us three days. Some spare torches and batteries, and one of the first aid kits – you know, emergency supplies."

"Good idea, sis. I'm going to go do that right now, before it gets too dark." Skye heaved a heavy sigh. "Talk to you at sunset tomorrow?"

"Yeah." I paused for a moment, searching for the right way to phrase what was on my mind. "Before you go, though... how are you, little sis? Are you holding up okay?"

There was silence on the other end of the line for a while. When she spoke again, her voice was subdued but determined. "I'm coping. I'll be okay, I just need time. I've been spending a lot of time playing with Maddy, to keep myself distracted."

"I'm glad to hear it," I answered. It wasn't a lie, either; I worried about her, but she was stronger than I gave her credit for. She'd always be my baby sister, even now that she was grown up. That was my problem though, not hers. The last thing she needed was me hounding her to express her feelings. "If you ever need to talk, just let me know."

"Thanks, sis. I better go before it gets dark. Good luck with your tree."

We signed off then, but I sat for a few minutes longer staring into space as I thought over what she'd said. I found myself way more concerned than I probably should have been under ordinary circumstances – but Maddy was special. It was more logical to think that she was just a little kid having nightmares, but as I'd told Skye, I felt that it was better to be safe than sorry.

Besides, the precautions were all logical and reasonable. Anything could happen. It made sense to be prepared. Scout's motto and all that. Once I calmed my nerves, I focused on the task at hand. The sooner we got that stupid tree out, the sooner we could go home and keep an eye on things personally.

I rose from my seat and went looking for the others, following the sound of their noise through the maze of passages. After living in the bunker, it was familiar and comforting to hear the echo of human voices through cold, concrete tunnels, even if the tunnels themselves were new to me.

When I found the other survivors, they were gathered in a noisy mob around a small office-turned-dining-room. There wasn't enough seating for everyone, so Rebecca had put on a buffet instead. My friends stood around or sat on the floor, eating and talking to our hosts. The food was nothing to write home about, but it was hot and filling. After ten years living as scavengers, most of us weren't all that picky anymore.

I slunk through the mob and filled up a plate of

my own, then wandered over to join Michael. He was sitting on the floor in a corner with Priyanka and the dog, talking to the girl while they ate. They both glanced up at my approach; I was both amused and flattered to see their eyes light up at the sight of me, though for completely different reasons.

"Hey guys," I greeted them, as I settled down on the floor beside Michael. Priyanka waved happily and showed me the utensil in her hand.

"Look look! I am forking," she told me proudly. Michael snorted with laughter and almost choked on his mouthful of food.

"You mean, 'I am using a fork'," he corrected her gently once he managed to swallow his food, his eyes shining with good-natured fun.

"Ooh." She stared at him for a moment, and then beamed at me again. "Look, I am using a fork!"

"What a good girl you are. Well done," I praised her, reaching over to give her an affectionate pat on the head. She positively glowed at the commendation. My heart would have melted, if it hadn't already been a big, soppy puddle of goo for that kid. She was so sweet that I had no kind of resistance against her charm. She even made me feel a bit maternal, which was unusual for me in all kinds of different ways.

"How's everyone at home doing?" Michael asked.

I glanced at him and shrugged. "Maddy's been having nightmares about fires, so Skye was pretty freaked out. I've got her out right now fireproofing the motel, just in case."

"You think it's a premonition?" Michael looked as dubious as I felt.

"No, of course not – but there's no harm in being prepared. I mean, look what happened to Anahera's tribe." I shrugged absently, shovelling a forkfull of food into my mouth. After swallowing I added, "Having a plan in place in case of fire is a good idea."

"Yeah, that's true. It's not like we can call the fire department anymore." Michael nodded slowly and leaned back against the wall. "Well, I suppose I should go get this meeting started."

"Probably a good idea, before they get into the rum," I agreed with a smile, then I leaned over to touch his hand reassuringly. "Good luck."

"Thanks." He sighed heavily and levered his powerful frame up off the ground. He returned his plate to the receptacle that waited for soiled dishes, then he clapped his hands loudly and yelled over the noise. "Okay, guys. Shut up for a minute."

To my surprise, the din settled down and all eyes turned to him straight away. Michael took the opportunity while he had it, and went over to stand in front of an old whiteboard that still hung on the wall from the days when this room had been used for business. He picked up a marker that was miraculously still working, and began sketching on the whiteboard as he spoke.

"I think everyone knows why we're here, but

just in case anyone's unclear, there is a tree stuck beneath the power station," he explained as he illustrated the situation underwater. "I went down a few hours ago and had a look. It's wedged in the first intake, which is basically a big rotating fan. To get it out, we're going to need to get down there and cut off all the branches, then winch it out.

"Rebecca says they have enough scuba gear here for three people, so I'm going to need volunteers to learn to dive." He paused and glanced around. Hands came up from most of the people in the room. "Okay, good. Hemi and Iorangi, you're in; the rest of you will need to be on the river bank to clear the debris we bring to you. I may swap you out later, depending on how it goes.

"Sandy and Richard." He shifted to look at me, and gave me a faint smile. Someone in the room wolf-whistled, but they were silenced by jeering before I could figure out who it was. When the room quieted down again, Michael continued. "I have a special project for you two. Jim tells me there's a small boat kept in a shed a little way down river. It's designed for this and has a winch on the back, so we're going to need it. I want you to find it and figure out how to get it going."

I nodded reassuringly, even though I knew nothing about boats. Over the years, I'd learned enough to jerry-rig most mechanical things back to life for a little while, so I had confidence I could at least get the engine going. Richard could deal with the 'boat' part of the equation.

"I'm sure all of you want to get home as soon as possible," he continued, to grunts of agreement from around the room, "so we'll get started at first light. Don't stay up too late. I will be waking you up at the crack of dawn regardless of how tired or hung-over you are."

He flashed an impish grin at the crowd, who laughed and jeered as he finished up. Once it quieted down, he moved back over to where I sat and offered me a hand up. I had finished eating while he was talking, so I took it and eased myself up to my feet.

"You know, I was wondering about something." I glanced at him curiously as I put my plate in the basket. "I just realised while you were talking that the lights down here are still on. How are the lights on when the power grid is offline?"

"I was talking to Rebecca about that earlier, actually." He threaded an arm around my waist casually. "She told me they have a solar-powered generator in case of emergencies."

"Oh." My mood brightened immediately. "So… hot showers?"

"Yes ma'am." He shot me a sideways look, his voice soft enough that only I could hear it over the renewed noise in the room. "It's almost time for bed anyway, so why don't you tuck Priya in, I'll take the dog out, and then we can see where it goes from there."

"I like this plan," I agreed readily, giving him a sideways squeeze before I detached myself from his embrace. I looked at Priyanka, and discovered that she'd finished eating and was watching the two of us with a puzzled look on her face. The moment she realised I was paying attention to her again, her expression brightened. "Bedtime, sweetie. Come on."

"Okies," she answered happily, bounding to her feet. I took her hand and showed her where to put her plate and utensils, then led her out of the room. We wound our way through the passages to one of the communal lavatories so that she could relieve herself, before I took her back to her little sleeping chamber.

There, I helped her to change into a nightie I'd salvaged for her and put in her backpack, gently explaining the difference between night clothes and day clothes. As always, she was a quick study. I was still sitting on the edge of her bed, talking to her, when Michael returned from taking the dog out.

I hadn't even realised he was there until I happened to glance up and noticed him standing in the doorway with his arms crossed, smiling affectionately at the two of us. Suddenly feeling shy, I smiled back and absently tucked a strand of hair back behind my ear.

"Doggie sleep with me?" Priya asked suddenly, looking back and forth between us.

I glanced at Michael, who shrugged. There seemed to be no good reason to deny her request, so I acquiesced. "Sure, sweetie. Call him to you. Say 'come, doggie' and clap your hands so he can hear you."

"Come, doggie!" she promptly cried, clapping her hands enthusiastically. The dog's ears pricked up.

After she called a couple more times, he padded away from Michael's side and went over to the edge of the bed, sniffing curiously.

"Now, say 'up, doggie' so he knows he has to jump up," I instructed. Priya mimicked me obediently. After a few false starts and a little help from the humans, the elderly canine managed to get up on the end of the bed. "There you go. Now, you go to sleep and he'll go to sleep as well."

"Okies," Priyanka answered agreeably. I leaned down and gave her a gentle hug, then she lay down and snuggled herself up under the covers. Michael and I said our goodnights to her and backed out of the room, closing the door behind us.

Then we looked at one another, and I found myself grinning. "So, what was that about a hot shower?"

***

Hours later, I awoke to darkness, my back snuggled comfortably against Michael's firm, warm chest, his arms wrapped like a blanket around me. I could hear the sound of his breathing, slow and even on the back of my neck. Nature was calling, but I didn't really want to get up. I closed my eyes and tried to go back to sleep, but the pressure in my bladder was too uncomfortable. As much as I wanted to stay in bed, I couldn't.

With no other choice, I carefully extracted myself from beneath my sleeping lover's arm, taking my time to avoid waking him. Although the room was pitch black, I'd left a torch beside the bed in case of circumstances like this. I fumbled in the dark and found it, then tiptoed towards the door.

The lights were all off in the hallway outside our room. I had no idea what time it was, except that it was night. Still, a need was a need, so I clicked the torch on and I crept along the corridor towards the nearest bathroom.

A few minutes later, I was on my way back to my room when I accidentally took a wrong turn and ended up in an unfamiliar corridor. Just as I was about to turn myself around and retreat back to an area that I knew, a strange sound reached me and made me hesitate. It was coming from around a bend in the corridor.

Always alert for trouble, I followed the sound until I reached the corner. When I peeked around, I saw a shaft of light cutting through the darkness. The sounds were coming from that doorway. They were strange, animal sounds, grunts and curses, and the sound of flesh striking flesh.

Then there was a woman's cry, strange and strangled, that struck a chord of concern through my heart. I clicked off my torch and hurried forward, my bare feet silent on the cold concrete floor.

With as much stealth as I could, I crept up to the partially open door and snuck a look through. The sight that greeted me was the last thing that I expected. I was so stunned that I stopped and stared for a long second before I retreated and headed back towards my room. There was no one in that room that needed my help... but they might if Jim figured out what was going on.

Not only was his wife cheating on him, but she was doing it in spectacular fashion. I couldn't even imagine taking on two men at a time, let alone big, strapping lads like Tane and Iorangi. One was more than enough for me. Her muffled cries and the look of devilish enjoyment on her face echoed in my head as I fled, trying to put the scene behind me.

I felt a little nauseated by the time I got back to my room. I hadn't seen anything that intense since the one time Harry had convinced me to watch a pornographic video with him. Now, I was left feeling dirty. As I burrowed back into bed and hid safely under Michael's arm, I tried to remind myself that it wasn't my fault. I hadn't encouraged her to cheat on her husband, and I'd only gone to look because I was afraid someone was being hurt.

Even snuggled under the warm, comforting bulk of my sweetheart's body, it took me a long time to get back to sleep after that.

***

When morning came, I woke up feeling guilty and slightly soiled. Normally, my dreams were a happy place, filled with friends, family and the warm, sensual moments that I shared with Michael. After what I had seen the night before, my sleep had been troubled, filled with vague, shadowy human forms playing 'the beast of two backs'.

Well, the beast of three backs, technically. That made it so much worse. In spite of my effort to suppress the outward signs of my disquiet, I shuddered at the thought.

"What's the matter, sweetheart?" Michael asked quietly, just about scaring me out of my skin.

"Nothing," I said quickly, but he knew me too well to let me get away with that.

"Really? I felt you shiver just then. It's not cold, so that means you're brooding." He propped himself up on an elbow and leaned over me to switch on the light, so that he could study my face. "Ah-hah, just as I thought. You look like you kicked a bunny. What did you do?"

"I didn't do anything," I answered glumly; there was no point in lying to Michael when he could read me like a book, "but I saw something last night. I don't know what to do about it."

"What did you see?" he asked, gently capturing a strand of my hair and plucking it out of my face. I cringed, because telling him meant I had to think about it again when I was trying very hard to block it out.

"I got up in the middle of the night to go to the bathroom." I sighed, finding it hard to meet his eye. "On the way back, I got a little lost. I ended up in another part of the building. I saw... I, um..."

"Out with it," he demanded when I hesitated a few seconds too long. My shoulders slumped.

"I saw Mrs Merrit shagging Iorangi and Tane. Now I don't know what to do." I buried my face in the pillow to try and hide my anxiety, but it was a pointless endeavour.

"Wow, that is a pickle." I could hear the disapproving tone in Michael's voice, but I knew it wasn't aimed at me. "We should probably tell Jim—wait, Iorangi *and* Tane?"

"At the same time." I lifted my head and turned to look at him. If I had to suffer, then so did he. It wasn't that they're unattractive people, but there was something so slimy about the whole situation. Even if it weren't for the infidelity aspect, Rebecca Merrit was at least fifteen years older than the younger of the two brothers – that made her old enough to be his mother. An underage teenage mother, but still. The cheating aspect was worse though, and made me feel really sick. "Christ, what do we tell him? Do we tell him? Is it our business?"

"It's our business now," Michael answered grimly, his expression set in a look I hadn't seen before. "If I cheated on you, you'd want someone to tell you, right?"

The logical side of my brain knew he was just using that as an example, but the irrational, emotional half heard those words and promptly went nuttier than a drunk wombat.

"Yes!" I exclaimed. "I mean, no, I mean—oh my God but you'd never do that, right? I'm not sure I could handle it if you—"

"Whoa, whoa, calm down." Michael held his hands up in self-defence, a panic-stricken look crossing his face. "Where did that even come from? You know I'd never play around on you."

"I know, but I don't know – anything could happen. You might start to hate me one day, and then you might cheat on me and then... and then..." And then I burst into tears. The worst part was that I could actually see myself going nuts, and I knew it was completely and utterly without reason. It was like the rational part of me was looking down from above, watching my emotional side go into total overload, without being able to do anything about it.

Poor Michael looked about the same way. His expression was one of utter bewilderment as he struggled in vain to comfort me. Neither of us could quite work out what was going on, until it suddenly hit me. My fit of inexplicable rage the day before, followed by the intense desire to screw his brains out, and now this? There was only one possible explanation.

As suddenly as they had started, the tears stopped. I stared at Michael with wide-eyes, not quite sure how to react. "Oh, my God. Honey, I think I'm premenstrual."

"...What?" He just looked even more bewildered.

"Oh, um... hormonal. I think I'm hormonal." Well, this was an awkward conversation to have with my boyfriend, but he did have a vested interest in that region of my body. "Like, seriously hormonal. As in, I think I'm going to get, um, 'that time of the month' soon."

"Oh." He stared at me for a long second before realisation dawned in his eyes. *"Oh.* You mean…"

"Yeah. I mean that." As soon as I had a name for what was bothering me, I felt much better. Embarrassed, I summoned a weak smile for him and I wiped my eyes. "I'm sorry, I haven't had one in years, so I guess I'm a little unbalanced. I think my body kind of forgot it was female for a while there."

"Thank God, you had me panicking." Michael looked so relieved that for a second I thought he was going to faint. "It's okay, no harm done. That just means that you're recovering and getting healthier again. That's good news." He smiled at me and gave me a hug, which instantly made me feel better.

"I'm so glad you understand." I snuggled up against him, feeling relief like a palpable force. While I wasn't looking forward to dealing with ol' Aunt Flo again, at least I knew it was in the name of the greater good. "Actually, I'm glad I understand, too. It's been so long that I had no idea what was going on at first, but now it all makes sense. You know I'm not usually this irrational. I think it's just been so long that things are a little haywire inside me."

"It does make sense, and it's a good thing. I want you to be healthy." I felt tender fingers running through my hair, and then Michael gently pushed me back to look me in the eye. "In the meantime, I know what will make you feel better."

"For once, I'm sad to say I'm not quite in the mood." I gave him a wry smile.

"What?" He blinked owlishly. "Oh! Oh, no, not that. I mean that I have a present for you."

"A present?" This time it was my turn to look surprised. I thought about it for a second, then tilted my head curiously. "Is it food?" The moment the words were out of my mouth, I suddenly felt stupid. "Wow, I really am premenstrual."

"No, it's not food. It's a real present." Michael laughed and tickled my ribs, drawing a girlish giggle from me. Then he slid out of bed and rose to his feet, padding barefoot over to where our bags sat in a corner. He knelt beside his backpack and dug around in the pockets until he drew out a couple of small, shiny objects that I couldn't quite make out from afar.

"What is that?" I asked, curiosity getting the better of me, but he closed his fist around the shinies before I could get a good look.

"Well, I had an idea. Something Anahera said got me thinking." Michael returned and stood in front of me, dressed only in the boxer-briefs that he usually slept in, and the bandages over his wounds. Gazing down into my eyes, his expression turned serious. "Life is short and brutal. We really have no idea how long we're going to have together. Either one of us could die tomorrow. If that happens, I want the world to know how much I love you."

My breath caught in my throat as he eased himself down onto one knee on the ground in front of me. He opened his hand to show me his gift: a pair of rings. One was simple and delicate, made for a woman's finger. The other was a thicker band, clearly designed for a man. Each ring was threaded onto a delicate silver chain. I stared at them for a moment, and then looked back up at his face. "But I thought..."

"I know. But, I also know that I want you to be my wife one day. No one says we have to get engaged one day and married the next. If we get engaged today then we can wait as long as we want to make that final step." A smile touched his lips, just a faint ghost. "There's more to what we have than just lust, and I think you know it as much as I do. You are my Yin. I want everyone to know it – and most of all, I want you to know it. Marry me, Sandy."

Tears blurred my vision as he spoke, making the rings in his hand seem to dance and sparkle. His logic made sense – and he was right. What I felt for him was so much deeper than lust, deeper than anything I had ever thought I was capable of feeling for another human being.

"I don't know what to say," I whispered, feeling truly stumped for one of the few times in my life.

"Then just say yes. We'll work out the details later." He smiled adoringly at me as he held the rings. I sniffed and tried to blink back my tears so that I could see him clearly, but the harder I tried to keep from crying the more determined they were to come.

"I... I..." Part of me was mad at him for getting me all emotional all over again, but a bigger part of me was so thrilled by the idea. It felt so right. He was The One. Somehow, my instincts had told me that from day one, even if I had ignored them. Now, things had changed. I bit my lip for a moment longer, then drew a deep breath and nodded. "...Yes. Yes, I will marry you. Thank you."

"'Thank you'? I wasn't expecting that." He laughed gently and reached up to place the delicate silver chain that supported my ring around my neck. As he leaned back, he trailed his thumb along the curve of my jaw. "No, sweetheart. Thank you. I don't quite know how I know, but my gut tells me this is meant to be."

"Mine too," I agreed, fussily wiping the tears from my eyes. "It feels strange, though. I mean, marriage is kind of an archaic ritual now, isn't it?"

"It is, yes. But I think marriage now will be different to what it was ten years ago. Everything is different." His thumb followed my hands, brushing away a tear that I hadn't gotten to yet. "All the rules that defined our society are irrelevant now. Now, we make our own rules. No one but you and I can tell us what our marriage is supposed to be."

"That's true." The thought cheered me up. "First rule – I'm not wearing a big, stupid white dress. But there will be food, lots and lots of food. And lots of snuggles, too."

Michael laughed merrily, and eased himself up to sit on the bed beside me. With strong, gentle hands, he dragged me into his lap and cuddled me close, a situation that I was more than happy with given the circumstances. Only once I was comfortably seated on his firm thighs did he take a moment to slip his own chain around his neck.

I found myself watching with interest as the ring it carried settled against his tanned skin. On an impulse, I leaned over and pressed a kiss against his collarbone right beside it. A surge of simple joy passed through me, and I smiled in spite of myself as he arms closed gently around me.

"This does feel right," I murmured, snuggling up contentedly in his arms. "I... I want you to know that I only have eyes for you, Michael. I saw how nervous you were yesterday around all those other men."

"Oh, you noticed that?" I heard him sigh heavily, and felt his fingers running through my hair. "I'm sorry, I was hoping you didn't notice. I did feel a little, I don't know... jealous, I guess. I caught Tane looking at you when you didn't see, and I've caught Hemi at it a few times too."

"There do seem to be a lot more male survivors than female. It's bound to cause trouble one day, particularly with the likes of Mrs Merrit around." I grimaced and tried not to think about the reason why there were more men still alive than women, but unfortunately I knew it well. I was one of the lucky ones, but many were not as fortunate. Without laws to protect us, women like me were vulnerable.

For a moment, we were both silent as we thought over that grim fact. An idea had been forming in the back of my mind, an unexpected idea but one that certainly had merit. It was too early to say anything to anyone, but the more I turned the idea over in my head the more interesting it became.

"We should probably go get this tree sorted," Michael said, breaking the thoughtful silence. I sighed, but he was right. One step at a time.

***

By the time the sun cleared the hills, I was fed, dressed and out in the bush, picking my way carefully through the thick, verdant ferns. Richard and Jim followed in my footsteps, letting me break the trail for them. Jim's arm was bound up in a sling, and Richard had insisted on carrying our gear, so it came down to me to lead. I decided that was the way I preferred it.

"Should be up there a ways," Jim huffed, out of breath from our walk. It had been an awkward trek for all of us, because we were following the line of the river through the heavy bush. The ground beneath our feet was slanted down towards the water's edge, so each step required careful balance. Every so often, a spot that appeared to be solid would turn out to be a mesh of twigs and leaf-litter that gave way underfoot, so I had to choose my path with care. Just to make matters worse, the ground was wet and slippery beneath us; as I'd predicted, it had rained overnight.

"When was the last time you came up here?" I asked, almost as out of breath as Jim was.

"Few years back," he answered, "but we didn't

need it at the time, so we let it be."

"Fair enough. Done that a bit myself," I agreed amiably, trying very hard not to think about the bad news I might have to break to him at some stage. Michael and I agreed that we would try to gently probe him for information when we could, to get a feel for how he'd react. The last thing we wanted to do was put either of them in danger, even if we didn't like what Rebecca had done. We were both keeping an eye out for the right time to do it privately and gently, and if the opportunity arose then whichever one of us was there would take it.

Jim mumbled something unintelligible in response, which I took to mean he wasn't interested in casual conversation. I was fine with that; it was hard enough to focus on where I was putting my feet.

Michael and I had also decided to keep our engagement a secret for the time being. I wore my ring on its chain around my neck, hidden beneath my clothing, but Michael had reluctantly taken his off since he was going to be spending most of his day underwater. It was in my pocket now, nestled safely within the most secure compartment I had.

I suppose, in theory, carrying the rings went against my normal ethics. They were technically dead weight that added to our burdens while contributing nothing, but for once in my life I was okay with that. Even in my most perverse moment, I couldn't bring myself to resent the tiny added weight of an engagement ring from my beloved around my throat. I couldn't even feel it, but knowing it was there made me feel like I was connected to him even when we were separated. When I thought about it that way, it was worth a hundred times its meagre weight in emotional value.

Hiding a secretive smile, I ducked beneath an overhanging branch and scrambled up a shallow ledge that was slippery with leaf mould. The debris was so thick that I didn't even realise the ledge was made of concrete until I was standing on it.

"I think we've got something," I called over my shoulder to the men. With great care, I negotiated the ledge to the far side, and found that it dropped sharply down to the river. A narrow channel of filthy, clogged water ran into the hillside, terminating in a dark, ominous cavern. The ledge turned to a walkway barely wide enough for one person as it wound into the cave's mouth alongside the water.

Eternally vigilant, I brought my shotgun up and slipped the safety off as I made my way down the stairs towards the entrance. I moved with a smooth, practiced step, stealthy yet efficient. When I reached the entrance, I paused to listen, sniffing the air while I waited for my eyes to adjust.

The only sound was the soft tone of water against wood and concrete, but the scent was much more complicated. I could not only smell the forest and the dirt, but also the faint odour of rusted metal, fuel, and decaying flesh. When my eyes adjusted to the dark, I could make out the faint outline of something bobbing in the water below us, which eventually resolved itself into a small boat.

The cave itself was shallow, only just deep enough for the boat, with a slender walkway around the edge. A frayed old rope creaked morosely with the rise and fall of the water, keeping the boat tethered to its mooring. Between the boat and the open river, an old grill gate stood half open, too crusted with rust to go anywhere without significant force.

"We're clear," I called to the men waiting on the walkway above me. I heard their footsteps crunching over the leaf litter, then changing timbre as they descended to join me.

"Hm. We're going to need to get that gate open," Jim pondered, absently rubbing his chin.

"There's a lot of debris in the water, too," I agreed, clicking the safety back on my shotgun. Since Jim couldn't do much more than stand watch, I handed him the weapon and beckoned for Richard to follow me. Together, we moved to the edge of the walkway and knelt down to inspect the junk floating in the water. It was a tangled mess of branches, old trash, and even a few animal bodies. At least, I really hoped they were animal bodies.

"See if you can clear some of this while I take a look at the boat, huh?" I glanced towards Richard. He nodded quietly and set our gear down on a ledge near the boat. While he was busy hunting around for something to scoop the trash out of the water with, I turned my attention to the little bucket of rust that I was loathe to call anything remotely resembling a vehicle. Frankly, I was amazed that it was still afloat.

With great care, I moved around to the side of the dock closest to where it was moored, and lowered myself down to sit on the edge of the concrete. Tentatively, I poked the bottom of the boat with my foot, half expecting it to sink at the lightest touch. To my surprise, it didn't. In fact, the 'rust' came off all over my boot, leaving me a little bit filthy and more than a little confused.

I poked the boat with a wary finger and came away even dirtier; what had first appeared to be rust was actually a thick layer of slime. I wasn't sure if that was a good thing or a bad thing, but under the slime, the little aluminium runabout appeared to be quite solid.

Settling back on my haunches, I considered the evidence I saw and came to the conclusion that the boat must have gotten swamped at some stage in the last decade, probably during a heavy storm or something. With no one to bail it out, the water just sat there until it evaporated, leaving behind a layer of all the crusty things that infested river water during a flood. I judged that it must have happened recently, or perhaps even repeatedly – the gunk was still wet.

Luckily, we had anticipated a certain degree of filth and come equipped. Jim carried a light backpack full of cleaning rags and a few other small things, which he handed to me without a word. I took it, fished out a grotty old towel, and set about the unpleasant task of de-sliming our boat.

Needless to say, it wasn't my favourite task of the year, but at least I wasn't fishing corpses out of the river like Richard had to. I could hear him gagging while I was wiping away the gunk, but he didn't curse or complain at all. I had to admit that I was impressed by his stoicism; in his place, I would have been bitching up a storm.

It took some time to return all of the slime to the water from whence it came, but at last the task was done. I sat back to admire my handiwork. Beneath the slime, the little boat was in surprisingly good condition. It was a small thing, probably only about four metres from bow to stern, with an inboard engine that powered not only the boat's propulsion, but also a pair of light chain winches.

I inched towards the aft to examine the winches, and found that while they wouldn't be strong enough to tear the gates off Fort Knox, they should be more than adequate for what we needed. The chains were rusted, but not so badly that they'd be useless. The steel clasps on the ends screeched faintly with disuse at first, but they still worked.

"Hey Jim. Can you bring me a screwdriver, mate?" I asked, casting a glance back over my shoulder. "Medium-sized, Phillips head."

Jim grunted and went off to do my bidding, while I turned my attention to the housing that protected the motor. It appeared to be watertight, and the last person who'd used the boat had locked that box up tight. The caution of some long-dead mechanic would be our salvation.

It took a bit of lubricant and a great deal of cursing to convince the screws to let me in, but when I finally lifted the lid I was pleased to find the motor in very good condition. The seal had held for all those years, through all those storms, leaving the important mechanical components no worse for wear than any other boat that had been kept in storage for a decade.

That is to say, it wasn't perfect, but it would do for a start.

***

By mid-afternoon, courtesy of some fresh petrol and a new battery, the little boat finally roared to life. Although the noise of the sputtering engine was deafening in the closed space, it felt like the prettiest sound I'd ever heard. Feeling pleased with myself, I reassembled the engine housing and sat myself down in the rear of the boat.

Richard handed the toolkit down to me, then he helped Jim into the boat as well. The rocking motion as the older man walked over and sat down made me tense up, but he didn't seem concerned. While Richard untied the slimy rope that held our craft against the docks, Jim took the wheel in his one good hand and looked over the controls.

Richard had managed to clear away the worst of the debris, and wedged the water-gate open far enough for us to get out. Now, the only thing between us and the freedom of the open river was figuring out how to drive a boat.

The men seemed to know what they were doing, or were at least good at faking it. They fought for a minute before Jim finally relinquished the wheel to Richard and came to sit opposite me in the aft. He was huffing and grumbling so much I had to fight hard to hide my amusement.

There was no time to laugh, though. A few moments later, Richard put the boat into whatever passed for 'in gear' in a floating craft, and we leapt away from the dock. I yelped in surprise and grabbed the edge, half-expecting to hit something at high speed and burst into flames.

Luckily for all of us, he figured out what he was doing before that came to pass. With a little more care this time, he nudged the boat out of the cavern and eased us out into the open river. A pleasant breeze hit us, bringing with it fresh, pleasant scents. It was raining again, just a light drizzle, enough to refresh but not enough to drench.

The wind caught a few strands of my hair that had escaped from my braid, and sent them dancing around my face as we slowly picked up speed. In spite of my initial caution about the unfamiliar sensation of boat travel, I found myself enjoying it. Like riding on the back of a quad bike, it got my heart pumping and adrenaline flooding through my veins.

Unfortunately, thinking about the quad bike brought back memories of Tane, and what I'd seen the night before. I stole a furtive glance at Jim and found him staring off into space, oblivious to my concerns. It seemed so cruel. After all the sacrifices he had made to keep the electricity on all these years, he'd been betrayed by his own wife. I had to talk to him, but not now. Later, in private. No need to humiliate him in front of Richard.

Trying to distract myself before a dark mood could settle in, I watched the trees flash by along the edge of the water, then looked back to admire the ripples we left behind in our wake. It was kind of mind-boggling to think about the fact that it had been ten whole years since any human crafts had troubled the placid waters of the Waikato River. I hoped ours would not be the last.

The more that I thought about it, the more the idea gestating in the back of my mind made sense. The human species – my species – was on the verge of extinction. The only possible way for us to survive was for someone to intervene in the survivor culture that had sprung up over the last decade.

Someone needed to take a hand in the future of humanity. God knows we'd done the same for many other species over the years. I thought about the zoos, where scientists had strived so hard to preserve the most vulnerable animals against their inevitable extinction. Now, it was our turn. Someone had to do it, or there was no guarantee that my kind would live to see another generation.

When I watched Michael with Priya, something

stirred inside me that had lain dormant for a very long time. I was shocked to realise that I did want children one day. When the time came, I knew I could rely on him to be a wonderful father, just the way my own dad had been for me.

Although I had initially rebelled at the idea of having my own offspring, the truth was that perhaps they would help me to fill the hole in my heart that had been so empty since I lost my family a decade ago. But there was a problem. Several problems, in fact. Even if our children were born immune to Ebola-X, there was no guarantee that they'd be safe if we continued to live the way we were.

If I wanted to have my own child one day, then it was my duty to make sure that the world I brought her into was a place where she could grow up, be educated, and live amongst friends. That meant that something had to change, and it had to change within my lifetime.

As our little boat rounded a bend in the river and the massive power station came back into view, I came to a decision. I've never been the kind of person who relies on others to do things for her. It's against my nature.

If I wanted this world to be better, for my children and my children's children, then I would have to change it myself.

Chapter Twenty-One

A cheer erupted from the gaggle of survivors on the river bank as the power station roared to life.

It had taken a week for us to clear the obstruction from the turbines, but at long last we had succeeded. A few hours before, we'd hauled the last of the debris down-river and disposed of it where it would no longer pose a danger to anyone. Now, we stood watching as our victory came together at last.

For the last week, I had struggled to try and get Jim alone for a moment, but it seemed like there was always someone around to get in the way. Although it was frustrating, my temper had calmed down when my hormones settled back into their normal routine. I had patience again, so I bided my time, waiting for the right opportunity.

On the day after we had found the boat, a sharp stab of pain in my lower abdomen had advised me that I'd guessed correctly: my emotional outbursts had been a symptom of an impending visit from Aunt Flo. Although the discomfort — both physical and emotional

— made it much harder to work up the urge to lug around bits of tree, necessity had driven me to keep on trucking. The worst of it had passed now, and the cramps had subsided to a dull ache.

Michael had proven himself to be a real keeper during that week, too. Even though I had been in no mood for sex, he'd been so sweet and understanding that it made me want to cry. He was always on hand to administer kind words, back-rubs, and cuddles when I needed them most. Best of all, he knew without me having to say anything that my condition meant I was often unhappy and in pain; he had made it his duty to be a pillar of comfort and sympathy throughout, and that made it so much easier to deal with.

He was with me now, standing with one arm looped casually around my waist as we watched the power station begin sucking water in through its enormous turbines. Everything seemed to be going fine, but we still observed with avid interest as the station went through its start-up routine. Eventually, it settled into a low, deep thrum that sent vibrations through the ground beneath us and all the way up our legs.

"Big noise," Priyanka whispered theatrically, looking nervous as she hovered nearby. I smiled reassuringly at her and reached over to ruffle her hair, which brought a bright smile to her face. After a solid week in our company, the girl had begun to truly blossom into the lovely young lady she was going to become.

Watching her grow more relaxed and social had been one of the most pleasing experiences I'd felt in a very long time. Although her speech was still a little stunted, she improved every day. She was constantly cheerful and busy; it seemed like she was always rushing about, helping anyone that expressed a need, which was an attitude that quickly endeared her to everyone.

She was no longer afraid of Hemi and the others. Quite the opposite, in fact. I often caught sight of her following one person or another around, looking fascinated by everything that they did. Despite that, she never seemed to get underfoot. There was just something about her sweet-faced innocence and earnest desire to help in that made even the staunchest of us happy to have her around. Looking down at her young face, all I could think was that she deserved so much more than to live out her life as a solitary survivor.

"Well, I guess that's our work here done," Michael rumbled, holding me close against his side.

I nodded thoughtfully and glanced up at him. "It'll be nice to go home. Skye sounded pretty stressed when I spoke to her last night. Maddy's still freaking out pretty badly."

"Agreed. I hope they're okay." He sighed softly and reached up to trail a finger around the curve of my neck, tracing the chain that held my ring. It had taken some time for me to get used to the idea of getting married, but once I'd warmed to the idea… well, let's just say that I had only taken my ring off to bathe. When I looked up at him and saw the flash of silver around his throat, I knew that he felt the same way. On a sudden impulse, I leaned up and pressed my lips to his. Surprised, Michael hesitated for a moment before returning my affections.

Priyanka giggled gleefully, as she often did when we expressed our feelings for one another in front of her.

"Kissie-kissie," she teased, but there was no malice in it so I took no offense. Instead, I teased her right back.

"You just wait, little miss." I waggled a finger at her. "One day you'll meet a boy that you fall in love with. Then, you'll kissie-kissie him, and I'll laugh at you."

"No!" she cried, looking mortified. "Boys, yuck yuck. Boys have bugs."

"Boys do not have bugs!" I laughed, surprised and amused by her outburst. "Who told you that?"

Priyanka looked at Michael with enormous eyes, but said nothing. He stared back at her, looking sheepish. I looked back and forth between them for a moment, then fixed Michael with a pointed stare. It only took a second before he started looking guilty. "I just didn't want to see anyone taking advantage of her."

"So you told her boys have bugs?" I said dryly, fighting the urge to laugh my head off. "That's some solution, honey. Good thinking."

"Hey, give me a break!" Michael put on his best whipped-puppy expression. "I haven't had to deal with a girl going through puberty before – but I know what I was thinking about at her age."

"True." I sighed heavily, and gave him a long,

thoughtful look. "I think we've got some time yet, but one of us should probably give her The Talk at some stage."

"Hey, don't look at me," Michael protested. "When I tried, she ended up thinking that boys have bugs."

"Fine, fine, I'll take care of it." I snorted mockingly, but I wasn't angry at him at all. He was right. I had more experience with teenage girls than he did, since I'd been one. Sure, that felt like it had been a lifetime ago, but I still remembered the hot surge of hormones that had driven me towards anything that remotely resembled a male. That gave me a moment's pause, then I looked back at Michael. "On second thoughts, let's ask Doc to do it. I'm sure he'll be able to traumatise her enough that she'll never want to touch a man, ever."

"Now that sounds like a plan," Michael said with a good-natured laugh.

"In the meantime – do you see what I see?" I asked, raising my eyebrows pointedly.

He blinked, then looked around curiously. "That depends. What do you see?"

"I see Rebecca over there, along with everyone else, so it occurs to me that means Jim must be on his own inside. I should go check on him." I shot another pointed look at Michael, who smiled grimly and withdrew his arm from around my waist.

"Good luck," he murmured. I nodded and touched his hand, then turned and walked away from my little family. Priyanka tried to follow me, but Michael distracted her with something I didn't quite catch before I was out of earshot. The sound of voices faded behind me as I made my way away from the group, and picked my way carefully up the stairs that led back into the depths of the power station.

The door closed heavily behind me, blocking out the sound of the churning turbines, but not the vibrations. I could still feel the tremor beneath my feet as I made my way through the tunnels, and found the set of stairs that led up into the engine room itself.

There, a single figure stood hunched over a control panel, monitoring a mind-boggling array of dials and doohickies. I had no idea how he knew what he was doing, but he seemed to. Jim was so focused that he didn't even seem to notice my approach until I cleared my throat loudly. Only then did he glance up, with a look of annoyance at being interrupted.

"What? Can't you see I'm busy here?" He glared at me. The dirty look gave me a moment's pause, but I braced myself against it.

"Jim, I need to talk to you about something and I wanted to get you alone to do it," I answered calmly, keeping my tone of voice as even as possible despite my annoyance at his attitude. "This is the first time I've managed to all week."

"Christ, what's so important that you have to tell me now, of all times?" He grumbled a few choice words and turned his attention back to the panel in front of him.

"Jim, I just want to know… about you and Rebecca."

As Michael and I had agreed, I chose my words carefully. I didn't want to get Rebecca in trouble – or worse, put her in danger. "I don't know what kind of relationship the two of you have. If she got involved with another man, would you be angry?"

"What?" He froze for a second and stared at me. "That's all? You came all this way and interrupted my work to ask me that? I wouldn't care. I already gave her permission to shag whoever she likes."

"You... I... what?" I stared at him, shocked. "So you already know?"

"Of course I bloody well did!" he snapped. "She asked my permission when your boys arrived, and I agreed. Christ, you think she'd do something like that without my permission?" As though suddenly realising just how much distress I'd been in for the last week, he turned and looked at me. "You were really that worried?"

"Yes," I answered, feeling more and more confused by the second. "I mean, I thought..."

"Aw, Christ." Jim absently scratched at his balding pate and eyed me uncertainly. "Erm... how do I put this? Rebecca is my friend. We've been friends for a very long time, but we're not friends 'like that'. About a year or so after the plague, she was living in Arapuni township while I ran the station. She used to bring me food and stuff, but then some boys from the south started coming by and bothering her. She was getting really scared for her safety, so I convinced her to move in here and be my 'wife', so that I could protect her. It's never been any more than that, though. She ain't my type."

"She's not your type?" I stared at him, bewildered by what I was hearing. "I don't understand. She's a nice lady, and I'm sure she's pretty attractive, if you're that way inclined. What's not to like about... wait..." My eyes widened in surprise when realisation struck me. "Do you mean...?"

"Aye, lass. I'm gay." Jim looked amused by my freshly-caught-fish expression. I could only guess that he got that a lot when he told people.

"But, you don't—"

"I know, I know. I don't look gay, and I don't act gay. I'm homosexual, not a bloody ponce. I'm just a regular Kiwi bloke who happens to prefer other blokes. There's a difference." He glared at me for a moment, right up until I started feeling like a total idiot. It must have shown on my face, because an amused smile suddenly flickered across his lips. "Stereotyping is rarely right on the money, kid. You should know that."

"Damn... I'm sorry, mate." I looked down at my feet, rubbing the back of my neck. "I had some trouble with the blokes down south as well, so I've spent most of the last decade alone. I don't really know how to read people anymore."

"Don't worry about it, lass. You meant well." He brushed my shame aside with a vague gesture. "Just be glad your boyfriend isn't my way inclined, or I'd give you a race for your money."

I smiled shyly, sensing the joke behind his words

despite his deadpan expression.

"Fiancé, actually," I corrected him, reaching up to draw my necklace out from beneath my clothing to show him the ring. "He proposed a few days ago."

To my surprise, Jim looked genuinely pleased. "That's good to hear. You two make a nice couple. You'll work well together, I think."

"I think so, too. He's the only other person that I told about Rebecca, Tane and Iorangi. We didn't want to embarrass you, but I guess it doesn't matter now." I sighed, feeling relieved all of a sudden. "I'm so glad it turns out there was a perfectly reasonable explanation for it. To be honest, it's been tearing me up inside all week thinking that she might have been betraying you with my friends."

"Two of them, huh?" Jim chuckled, a dark sort of chuckle that set my teeth on edge, but he didn't seem to notice. "That little slut. Well, I suppose a girl's gotta do what a girl's gotta do."

"I guess she was a little pent up?" I suggested with as much humour as I could, even though the comment made my inner feminist a little uncomfortable. I'd learned that Jim was a special kind of fish, and that it was best not to take his comments seriously.

"Must be. Now, you get out of here, I have work to do," Jim grumbled and made shooing gestures at me.

"Okay, okay, I'm going," I answered as I retreated towards the door. "Thanks for not killing me."

"It's fine, lass. Thanks for giving a shit," he replied. A moment later I was out the door, and left him in peace. That also left me alone with my thoughts, which were a very confusing place. How on earth was I going to explain this to Michael?

***

It turned out to be easier than I was expecting.

By the time I tracked Michael down, he was back in our room packing our bags in preparation for our departure. It was still fairly early in the day and we were all anxious to get home to our families, so it seemed wise to set off as soon as possible. I plunked myself down on our bed and repeated word-for-word exactly what Jim had told me. Michael stayed quiet the entire time I relayed the conversation, and it wasn't until after I was done that he said anything.

"Well, I suppose that's a relief then," he murmured uncertainly, absently scratching the stubble on his chin that he hadn't gotten around to shaving away.

"Yeah, I guess so. It kind of feels like we got all worked up over nothing now, doesn't it?" I smiled and leaned over to give his scruff a little scritch of my own. Michael gave me an amused glance in return, but didn't complain.

"That's a good thing though, isn't it?" he asked, looking up at me curiously. "I'd rather get worked up and have it turn out to be nothing than break up someone's marriage. Wouldn't you?"

"That's true," I agreed simply, and then slid down off the bed to sit beside him on the floor. "I'm relieved, too. Now we can just go home, and worry about whatever the hell is wrong with Madeline instead."

"She's a kid. Kids have nightmares. Don't worry about it." Michael put his arm around my shoulders and drew me close, planting a reassuring kiss on my cheek. "Once we introduce her to Priyanka, they'll be the best of friends and she'll forget all about fires and scary things. She's just lonely and bored."

"That reminds me, actually." I sighed heavily and reached over to grab my bag so that I could stack my things back into it. "We need to look for some replacement parts for the Hilux on the way back."

"Gotcha covered, sweetheart." Michael smiled and gave me a quick snuggle, catching me by surprise. "I told Hemi and his boys about it the other day. They're going to take us into town to look for parts, and then they'll give us a lift back to the truck. I think he still kind of feels like he owes us for something."

"Well, that'll be handy," I agreed, then glanced up at him curiously. "Will your dog be able to keep up for that long, though?"

"Hemi reckons he can get Alfred up on the front of one of the bikes," he answered cheerfully.

"Alfred?" I laughed in surprise. "You named the poor pooch Alfred?"

"Damn straight, I did." His smile widened into a full grin. "It'll take a little practice, but he should be fine. You know how dogs are about the wind."

I chuckled at the image his words conjured up. "That's true. We should get ourselves some quad bikes." Suddenly, my smile faded. The moment to reveal the first stage of my plan to Michael had arrived without any warning at all. I wasn't prepared, but I decided to plunge ahead anyway. "Actually, I've been pondering something and I want to run it by you. I think that we should talk to Anahera about combining our groups."

Michael blinked like a possum caught in the headlights. "Why?"

"Well, I..." How did I explain this to him? It was a thought that I could barely wrap my head around myself. "Michael, we need to do something for our futures. Not just us personally, but *all* of us. The entire human species. We're not going to be able to survive picking over the bones of this old corpse of a world indefinitely. We need to find somewhere, settle down, and start gathering people. As many people as we can. It needs to be somewhere defensible, so we can grow crops and raise animals. We'll need every hand we can get.

"It's the only way we'll ever be safe, and the only way our children will have the opportunity to live in the kind of world that our parents took for granted. We need to build a sanctuary, and fill it with as many good people as we can find. There's safety in numbers, and if we can build a permanent settlement then we'll have a chance to eventually grow our numbers."

"You want to build a city?" Michael stared at me, stunned. It took me a second to process what he'd said, before the words actually sank in.

"I hadn't thought of it quite like that, but... yes, I

think so." I nodded thoughtfully. "Not build from scratch, though. At least, not to start with. We need to get the first wave of people together before we can think about that, so we'll need to find somewhere safe and secure to house them, somewhere we can grow food and become self-sufficient.

"Once we have a large enough number of people, we won't have to worry about gangs or anything like that anymore, and we can focus on repairing what Ebola-X did to us and planning for the future. Combining our group with Anahera's would give us a solid base to start with. That would give us sixteen people, which is a large enough group that most of the gangs would steer clear of us."

"And once we've got a safe place," Michael said thoughtfully, picking up where I left off, "and enough numbers to protect everyone, then we get word out. We'd attract people from all over, particularly the women and children who are vulnerable out there on their own – like you were."

"Yes, exactly," I nodded, relieved that he understood my idea.

"This is ambitious, Sandy." he looked at me uncertainly. "It'll take a long time, a lot of hard work, and it's dangerous. Are you sure you're up to it?"

"I've got you to help me, right? With you and all the others, I think we can make this dream a reality." I paused for a second, and then shook my head. "No, I *know* that we can make it a reality. We have to. The only other option is to watch our friends and family gradually slide towards barbarism. Think about it, honey. Humanity is the only species that has ever actively attempted to save another species from extinction. It's time that we did it for ourselves."

"That's... really profound." Michael drew a deep breath and let it out slowly, closing his eyes. "I think you're right, though. I think we can do it. Like you said, we have to do it. For Priyanka and Madeline."

"For all the children," I agreed softly, reaching over to take his hand, "including ours, when the time is right."

He looked at me, and it was like a light had come on behind his eyes. Watching that understanding dawn in his expression made all the effort worthwhile. I knew then that I had him, and that he would stand by my side to the end. A slow smile crept across his face, then he drew me into an embrace and held me close. "New New Zealand?"

"What?" I blinked owlishly, before I realised he was offering a name for the city we planned to build. "Oh, no. That's terrible, honey."

"I know," he answered, lifting his head up so that I could see his grin.

"Mocking me already? Sheesh." I made an indignant noise and tilted my chin up defiantly. "You just wait, we'll both be hailed as heroes one day. There will be statues of us in the town square, and school children will have to memorise every detail about our lives."

"Not *every* detail, I hope. Some of those details are pretty X-rated," Michael laughed merrily and dragged me into a kiss. My cheeky answer to that was muffled by his lips, just to prove his point.

Chapter Twenty-Two

"Oi, Sandy!"

At that moment, I was bottoms-up under the dusty bonnet of an ancient ute, so my answer came out muffled. "What?"

"Sandy? Where the hell are you?" The voice drew closer, close enough that I could identify that it belonged to Hemi.

"In here," I called back. Unfortunately, drawing the breath to yell meant I inhaled a good deal of dust, and ended up sneezing. By the time the fit passed, he'd found me.

"Hey, careful there." The youth grinned impishly at me. "You'll sprain something."

"*You'll* sprain something when I get you." I shook my fist at him teasingly. "Anyway, what are you shouting about? I'm a little busy here."

"I was just coming to tell you we found a truck you might be able to scavenge." Hemi leaned around me to get a look at the old ute. I was half way through disconnecting the starter motor to replace the one that

I suspected had died in the Hilux. "You already find what you need?"

"It's all good. I have no way to test this one, so we're better off taking a couple of spares." I beckoned him closer, and ducked back under the bonnet. "Come help me with this one, I could use an extra set of hands."

Hemi came over to help me out. Together, we managed to get the component free and wrapped it up in an old towel to keep the grease from getting everywhere. I put it in my backpack and shouldered it, then we headed out to go see the car he'd found.

When we arrived, I discovered a gaggle of bewildered-looking blokes standing around another old utility, with its hood raised. They were alternately scratching their heads and shooting sneaky glances at one another as they tried to figure out what they were looking at, without giving away that they were completely clueless on all things car-related.

Amused, I shouldered my way through the crowd and leaned over to inspect the engine myself. The starter motor looked fine, so I enlisted the help of a couple of strong hands to extract it. Once the component was out, I wrapped it up and added it to my pack as well, then shooed the guys back towards their bikes.

Ten minutes later, we were on the road at last. The wind streamed through my hair as I clung on to Ropata's waist, enjoying that feeling of freedom. With the bikes at our disposal, I estimated we could be back to the Hilux by midday. Assuming things went well with the repairs, we could be home by just after sunset.

I was looking forward to sleeping in my own bed again, so much so that I could almost feel the soft pillows beneath my cheek already. Although home was wherever Michael was, there was a pleasant familiarity about our old loft that I adored.

The outskirts of Arapuni passed by in a blaze with our quad bike bouncing merrily over the dips and cracks in the road. I heard a yelp from the dog and glanced back to check on him, but he seemed perfectly happy to perch in front of Hemi, panting in the wind.

We slowed as we approached the narrow roadway that passed atop the dam, but I had no time to worry. Before I quite realised where we were, we were across the far side and making our way up the slope on the far side of the river. The corpses of the men Michael had killed in self-defence still lay where they'd fallen the week before. Now, their blood had crusted over and dried, washed and baked by alternating periods of rain and hot sun.

We passed them without stopping, and angled our way up onto the long, flat expanse of road between Arapuni and the ruins of Pukeatua. The sun crept slowly higher in the sky as the kilometres fell behind us.

The sky was clear, a beautiful, breathtakingly-infinite arc of blue dusted with fluffy clouds, but the wind was cool and carried with it the bluster of early autumn. As we passed by, I suddenly realised that the forests on either side of the road had begun to take on their golden-orange coats. Another summer had passed us by, leaving me to wonder what we would do come winter.

Should we wait for spring before we began our venture? Or should we set out immediately to seek a site for our new city? As much as it saddened me, I knew that Ohaupo would not serve for my grand scheme. What we needed was somewhere larger, a bigger town or a small city. More importantly, we needed to get further away from Hamilton.

I had a gut feeling that we would see those abominations again, the living, hunting dead. I felt like we were living on a time limit. If they were determined enough, they would find us in Ohaupo, and then we would have to fight again. The future of our children – born or unborn – rested in our hands, and we couldn't risk that anywhere less than perfect.

South seemed like a logical direction to go. I already knew the areas to avoid, so we could focus on the regions that were unknown. Though, if we could convince Anahera to join us, our combined force would be enough to give any of the gangs pause. The largest I had seen was five or six people; a potentially deadly threat to a lone female armed only with a taser and a small pistol, but not much of a problem to a dozen trained, determined, and well-equipped fighters.

And if I had my way, that's exactly what we'd have in a few days' time.

***

The rain came around mid-morning.

Plump, black clouds rolled in from the west to pelt us with fat droplets that left us shivering and cold. We didn't stop, though it did force us to slow down a bit for everyone's safety. I ended up hiding my face against Ropata's broad back to keep the water from stinging my eyes. The asphalt hissed beneath us and kicked up a spray that made it hazardous for the bikes following us.

Suddenly, there was a clunk and the rain became lighter. I opened my eyes and looked up to discover that we were driving beneath trees, picking our way through the undergrowth at a more sedate pace. The canopy above us filtered the heavy rain into a light mist. It took me a moment to realise that we'd gone off-road, to avoid the same break in the asphalt that had hindered us on the trip eastwards.

The bike bounced nimbly over tree roots and through clumps of ferns, leaving a trail behind us that felt like it was a mile wide. None of the riders seemed to care, and it made some sense. We'd passed Pukeatua about an hour before and seen no sign of the neo-Nazi threat, so they had no reason to assume there were other dangers lurking about.

I was warier, of course – but I always am, suspicion is in my nature. While we rode, I watched the deep shadows of the underbrush for any sign of trouble, but I saw nothing. Ropata and I were in the lead with the others strung out behind us. Eventually, we left the bush and thundered back onto the tarmac again, where we paused to wait for the other riders to catch up.

I sat up straight and looked back, counting heads as the other bikes emerged from the brush until I was satisfied everyone was safe and sound. I waved to Michael and Priyanka reassuringly, and then we were off again, following the curve of the road towards Te Awamutu.

***

The rain passed after a while, though we had to keep our pace relatively sedate on the wet roads. It was a little after midday by the time we reached the outskirts of Te Awamutu. I leaned past Ropata and pointed the way towards where our truck waited for us; a few minutes later, the quad bike crunched to a halt on the gravel at the top of the hill, beside the high steel fence that had served as our little fortress on that first night. By the time the other bikes joined us, I had already hopped off and squeezed through the half-open gate to check on my Hilux.

Everything was as I had left it, even the keys sitting on the driver's seat. No-one had passed by in our absence; our footprints were the only ones visible in the long grass. While I popped the hood and leaned over the engine to start work, I heard the others parking their bikes and fanning out to relieve themselves and organise lunch.

Before we'd left, Rebecca and Jim had thanked us profusely for our help, and given us enough supplies to see us back home safely. To my surprise, neither of them had suggested that they wanted us to stay, or would like to come with us.

At first, I had found that a little strange, but after taking some time to think about, I'd come to realise that Arapuni Power Station was their home. They felt safe and secure there, even if they were alone together. They always had one another, not as lovers but as friends. When it came down to it, companionship and friendship was so much more important than sex anyway. They were comfortable together, and once we left they would continue being comfortable with one another, even if they had enjoyed our visit while it lasted.

Priyanka scampered over to join me while the guys were busy getting lunch ready. She hopped up on the front bumper to get a better vantage point and stood staring intently into the depths of the engine for some time, mimicking me. Eventually, she glanced over at me for guidance. "What we looking at?"

"What *are* we looking at," I corrected gently. "We're looking at an engine. This engine will make the car drive for us, but right now it's broken. We're going to fix it." I looked at her and gave her a smile. "Do you want to help?"

"I will help." Priyanka nodded solemnly, always ready to assist even if she had no idea what she was doing. I couldn't help but be amused by her serious, intense expression, but it was an opportunity to teach her a useful life skill so I snatched it up.

In simple terms, I explained to her what the engine did and named each of the major components for her.

She was a quick study, and repeated the names that I gave her with confidence. After each one, I gave her a brief explanation of what it did. When we reached the starter motor, I went into more detail and told her how I knew that it was broken.

"Is broken because engine no go broom-broom?" she repeated once I was done, simplifying what I'd told her into her stunted English.

"Exactly. So, we're going to take the broken one out, and put a new one in." I opened my pack and removed one of the components, to show her what it looked like.

"Ooh. New one not broken?" She reached out to touch the component, and then sniffed at the grease that came off on her finger.

"I hope this one is not broken – but we'll find out when we put it in. Come over here, I'll show you." I beckoned for her to follow me, and together we bent over the engine and worked to replace the component. Although her inquisitive little fingers sometimes got in the way, it felt important to teach her everything that I could, so I stayed calm and patient, explaining each step as we were doing it.

Eventually, we got the new starter motor in and stood back to admire our handiwork. At some stage, Michael had wandered over to observe what was going on, but I hadn't realised he was there until I felt a gentle hand touch the small of my back. I jumped in surprise and glanced at him. He smiled in return.

"How is it?" he asked softly, in that deep, sultry

rumble he reserved just for me.

"We're about to find out," I answered, absently reaching up to tuck a strand of hair back behind my ear. I froze half way through the gesture when I realised that I was unconsciously flirting with him yet again. Suddenly embarrassed, I glanced away. "Um... would you mind turning the key for me, please?"

"Of course," he answered, barely able to hide the amusement in his voice at my momentary shyness. But, more importantly, he understood me well enough not to mention it. He just gave my back a gentle rub, then moved around to the driver's door and slid in behind the wheel. The engine spluttered for a moment when he turned the keys, but then it roared to life with a deep, throaty growl.

Priyanka squealed in surprise at the loud noise and clapped her hands over her ears. For a second, she looked so utterly terrified that I thought she was going to make a run for it, but she held her ground. She stared at me wide-eyed until I smiled and reached over to ruffle her short hair, the way I often did. She seemed to like it when I did that, and equated it with being praised.

"It's okay, sweetie," I told her, then waited until she took her hands off her ears before I explained further. "That noise just means it's not broken anymore. We fixed it."

"We fixed it? No more broken?" Priya stared suspiciously at the rumbling truck for a long moment while she processed that information. Suddenly, her expression brightened. "Fixed, no more broken. Yay! We fixed it. I helped?" She looked at me with those big, soulful eyes of hers. I couldn't even hope to resist them.

"Absolutely. You're a good helper." I ruffled her hair again and gave her a little hug. "Get your bag, we're going to go for a drive in the car now. Going to go home."

"Go home to where Sandy comes from?" she asked quizzically.

"Yep," I told her gently. "We're going to go back to my home. We have some new friends for you to meet. There's even a nice little girl there that you can play with. She's a bit younger than you, but I think you'll like her."

Priya's expression lit up like a Christmas tree. She nodded rapidly and scampered off to fetch her things. While she was gone, I picked up my backpack and headed over to join Michael. He was just climbing into the truck, but he paused to take my bag and placed it in the passenger's side footwell.

"I'll drive first, so you can eat," he offered, pointing me towards where Hemi and the others were cleaning up the remains of their lunch. I noticed at a glance that they'd set something aside for Priya and me, which made me smile.

"That's sweet of you. Thanks, honey." I looked back at him and reached out to touch his hand. "Are they going to go their own way home?"

"Nah, they're going to escort us back to our place

and stay the night with us, then go home in the morning," Michael answered, closing his hand around my fingers gently. "It'll be after dark by the time we get there. It's too dangerous for them to be driving along that track of theirs in the pitch black."

"Good point. At least the Hilux has proper headlights," I agreed, absently stroking his big fingers. For some reason, the contrast between us never failed to fascinate me in my more introspective moments. I loved every aspect of his body and his mind, no matter how different it was – but it was the differences between us that really intrigued me.

In the six weeks since we'd left our bunker home in Hamilton, his fair skin had turned dark with a smooth tan. On the other hand, I was still pale but had turned into a mass of freckles during the heat of summer, as I usually did. His hair was still jet black, while mine had bleached even blonder in the sun. We couldn't have looked any more different unless one of us turned green – but that was okay, because I loved him for who he was, not what he was. He could have turned into a giant flying spaghetti monster, and I'd probably still love him.

Priyanka scampered back to us with her backpack, the dog bounding along at her heels. Michael and I parted then, to guide our respective charges to their seats in the rear cab of the old truck. I opened the door and helped Priya climb in, then showed her how to fasten her seatbelt.

"What's this for?" she asked curiously, tugging at

the strap as I adjusted it over her shoulder.

"This is a seatbelt. It keeps you safe in case the road gets rough. Make sure you leave it on, but if there's an emergency and you have to take it off, just push this button here." I pointed to the appropriate place, and then gave her a smile and put her bag in her lap. "The doggie doesn't fit in a seatbelt, so you need to make sure he doesn't jump around for me, okay?"

"Okies," Priyanka agreed obediently. She unzipped her backpack and pulled out her old teddy, so that she could cuddle it. On a sudden, overwhelmingly maternal impulse, I leaned over and kissed her forehead, then closed the door and climbed into the front passenger's seat. By the time I was settled, Michael had managed to coax the dog into the back, and opened the window a crack so that he could smell the interesting things we were passing.

Hemi came over to give Priya and me our lunches. The food was nothing exciting, but it was hot and edible so I took it without complaint.

"We'll be right behind you, eh?" Hemi leaned against the sill of my window and looked at us.

"Sweet as," I nodded agreeably. "You know you're always welcome at our place. Not sure where we're going to put you, but we'll figure something out."

"Man, so long as we're not sleeping in the rain, it's all good." Hemi grinned vibrantly, then shoved himself back and went off to gather up his men.

In no time flat, we were back on the road again. We led in the Hilux, since the lads on the bikes had more mobility than we did. We had to pick a path that the truck could handle, so it made sense for them to follow us instead of the other way around.

To my amusement, Priya squealed in mixed delight and terror every time we went over a bump or rolled down a slope. I glanced back at her every so often to check on her, and found her clutching her teddy and staring out the window at the passing scenery with enormous eyes.

The dog, for his part, mostly just slept. Priya's enthusiasm seemed to have exhausted him, which I could understand. She was young and full of energy, while he was elderly and tired. I was pleased to notice that she didn't do anything to wake the dog, and he didn't seem bothered by her noises.

As the hours and kilometres rolled by, I found myself yawning as well. Michael didn't need me to guide him; he remembered the route we'd taken when we had come through before. Despite the jolts that the broken tarmac sent through our vehicle, I lay my head against Michael's firm shoulder and closed my eyes.

Chapter Twenty-Three

It was dark when someone shook me awake.

I opened my eyes, feeling disorientated and groggy, but before I was even fully alert I knew that something was wrong. Michael's shoulder was tense, and I could see him staring intently into the distance.

"What is it?" I whispered, following his gaze. Before he could respond, I saw exactly what had him tense: the horizon was glowing a hellish kind of red. "Oh, God. Please tell me that's just the sunset."

"The sun went down ages ago," he whispered back, his voice taut as a bowstring. "That's not the sunset. That's something else. I don't know what that is."

"It's a fire. A very big fire," I answered with dread certainty, then I stuck my head out the window and yelled Hemi's name.

"We see it!" he shouted back over the noise of the engines. "Pick up the pace; we're right behind you."

I didn't need to convey the message, Michael had heard him as well. He gave me just long enough to brace myself before he put his foot down, and the Hilux leapt forward. Priya squealed in fright at the sudden increase in speed; a quick glance back showed that she was clinging to my seat, holding on for dear life. Then the smell of smoke hit me, and distracted me completely.

"Oh my God, it's big. It's really big," I exclaimed, leaning forward in my seat to try and get a look. We were still a couple of kilometres from Ohaupo, but I could already taste the falling ash on the wind. The truck lurched over a break in the road, almost throwing my head into the dashboard, but I didn't care. My home was on fire. My sister could be in there. It was all that I could do to sit still as we careened faster and faster through the broken streets.

Suddenly, we were passing familiar buildings on the outskirts of town. I knew before we even rounded the corner onto our street that it was our motel burning. Michael slammed on the brakes and threw the truck into park, then we were both out the door. Side by side, we sprinted the last few metres to the front of the building that had been our home, which was now illuminated by a terrible wreathe of flames.

The fire had consumed the front corner of the building above the kitchen, and burnt all along the roof. Fat raindrops began to fall all around us, but it would be too little, too late. I looked at Michael and saw him frozen in shock. I felt the same way, but I had to shake it off.

My sister. My sister might be in there. Oh God,

Skye! I stared at the building, struggling to work out the way to respond.

Suddenly, a memory flashed through my mind. If Skylar had followed my instructions, then there would be hoses and fire-fighting equipment in a nearby building. I turned and ran towards the building, ducking beneath a low-hanging something. In the hellish semi-darkness, I couldn't even tell what it was. Behind me, I heard an explosion as a window blew out, and had to fight down the urge to be sick.

Hold on, Skye – I'm coming!

I vaulted over a half-collapsed fence and dodged around a shattered tree that lay at an odd angle against the side of the house, heading for the porch. I could only pray that Skylar had done as I'd instructed, for her own sake. With my path only lit by the crackling glow of flames, I didn't see the hose sprawled across the ground until I stood on it and slipped. I fell hard, the breath knocked out of me, but I was so focused that I was struggling back to my feet before I even realised that I'd fallen. That was when I heard the muffled sobs of a child crying.

"Maddy? Maddy, is that you?" I whispered into the dark space beneath the porch. "Maddy-monkey, it's Sandy. Are you okay, sweetheart?"

"Miss Sandy?" A little voice answered from the shadows. A moment later, a tiny body flung itself into my arms, sobbing out of control. "Granddaddy's in the fire! Please, please, save Granddaddy. I tried to get the hose to put the fire out, but it's too heavy."

My heart leapt into my throat. "Where's Granddaddy? Is he in his room? Where's Skye?"

"The man took her. Granddaddy's in the garden. The big boy hit him and he fell down, then they hit Miss Skylar and she fell down too." Maddy sobbed in my arms as I struggled to make sense of what she was saying. "Then the man and the boy screamed and yelled, and they picked up Miss Skylar and ran away. But Granddaddy's in there and he's too big for me to lift so I tried to get the hose but—"

"It's okay, sweetie," I interrupted her, hugging her tight. I heard footsteps and familiar male voices, and then a torch beam illuminated us.

"There's a hose here, and some fire extinguishers!" I heard Hemi's voice as they rushed past us, snatching up the fire fighting equipment from under the porch.

"There's a fire hydrant fitting over there, the hose should fit on that," I called over the noise, pointing in the direction of the old blue symbols painted on the pavement to mark the fixture. Hemi shouted something I couldn't hear and ran off in that direction, lugging the hose along between him and a couple of his comrades; I couldn't tell which ones.

Ignoring the pain in my knees and elbows from where I had fallen a moment earlier, I gathered Madeline up in my arms and carried the sobbing child back to our truck. There, I found Priyanka hovering nearby, looking terrified.

"Priya," I called her name breathlessly, pulling

her gaze away from the fire. "I need your help, honey. This is Maddy. I need you to take care of her for me, okay? Stay with the truck if you can, but if you see anyone you don't know I want you to take her, run away, and hide. Do you understand?"

"Okies," Priya whispered, though she was obviously very frightened. I set Maddy back on her feet beside the older girl. As soon as she realised that Madeline was younger than she was, something protective came out in my little foundling. She took Maddy's hand without any further instruction, and led the little girl to hide in the gloom behind the truck, where they were out of sight.

Once the children were safe, I turned back to stare at the fire. I could see the silhouettes of my friends rushing back and forth, and heard the hiss of fire extinguishers and hoses running, but the smoke was thick and black. I remembered from my school days that smoke killed faster than fire ever did. If the doctor was unconscious in there, then we had to get him out before it was too late.

The motel's thick glass doors hung open, with only the faintest trickle of smoke oozing out of the ground floor. I hesitated for a second, then reached into the front seat of the truck and pulled out my backpack. I snatched out a singlet and a bottle of water, soaking the fabric thoroughly before I tied it over my nose and mouth.

"What are you doing?" Michael's voice startled me; I hadn't realised that he was there until he spoke. I glanced back and found him watching me with concern, his face and arms already smudged with soot.

"Doc's in there," I told him. "I'm going to get him out before it's too late, so either help me or get out of my way."

He didn't even bother to reply. In a single smooth movement, he slid his t-shirt up over his head and pulled it off, then grabbed the bottle of water from my hands. He followed me as I turned and ran back towards the burning building, my feet splashing through the puddles left by the rain and Hemi's attempts to fight the fire.

I heard Hemi shouting at us as we ducked through the open door, but I didn't stop to see what he was saying. Every single one of my senses was screaming at me, warning me that what I was doing was dangerous – potentially even lethal – but if I didn't do it then someone was guaranteed to die. Michael was a footstep behind me, forced to run in a half-crouch to keep his head clear of the smoke; his bulk was a hindrance in a situation like that.

There were no flames in the foyer, but the smoke hung thick and heavy in the air. I burst out into the central courtyard, where I could see that the flames had originated from the kitchen and crept up the inside of the building to engulf Skylar's bedroom and the roof above. The back end of the building was still untouched, but the smoke had saturated the area, filling the building in a deadly, billowing black miasma.

Careful to keep my head clear of the smoke as

much as possible, I hurried across the garden. I could feel my feet crushing our precious baby plants, but I didn't care. The plants could be replaced; our friend couldn't.

"Where is he?" Michael's shout sounded like it came from miles away, even though he was right behind me. The noise of the flames was deafening, overwhelming all of my senses.

"Maddy said he was here. She said he was in the garden!" I shouted back, staring around frantically. Our doctor was not a small man, he shouldn't have been that hard to find. "I don't see him. You check the hydroponics room; I'll check the storage room."

I heard a vague grunt of agreement, and footsteps retreating behind me as I hurried in the direction of the room where we kept our spare supplies. The smoke was particularly thick in the doorway, and it took me a second to spot the human figure on the ground in the flickering half-light. I screamed for Michael as I dropped to my knees beside him. Stewart was half-conscious, but he moved weakly when he realised I was there.

"Turn it off." He coughed pathetically, and pointed at the wall. I suddenly realised that he had been trying to reach the main switchboard for the power, on the wall above our supplies. Understanding came a moment later; now that the power had come back on, it had the potential to keep feeding the fire far beyond our control. I leapt up and flicked the rows of switches into the off position as fast as I could.

By the time I was done, Michael had found us, and was already gathering the doctor over his shoulder in a fireman's carry. The doctor was struggling though, frantically trying to tell me something.

"Gas!" he grated, his voice so hoarse I could barely make out what he was saying. "Use that!"

Suddenly I realised that he was pointing at something, something half-hidden beneath the stacks of goods. I followed his finger and realised he was pointing at a huge fire extinguisher, one of the strange ones used for fighting special kinds of fire. I couldn't remember which kind, but I trusted him to know. Whether he was delirious or not, the doctor was a brilliant man. I took the hint, grabbed the extinguisher, then rushed after Michael as he hurried to get the doctor to safety.

In the courtyard, we parted ways. He headed for the exit, while I went for the kitchen. Yanking the safety clip out of the nozzle, I closed to within a few metres of the edge of the flame and pulled the trigger. A spray of thick powder exploded from the tip of the hose, and struck low at the base of the nearest flames. They retreated a few centimetres, and I advanced a few centimetres, focusing my efforts on one step at a time.

I could vaguely see the stove through the inferno, and wondered if that was the source of the fire. It was too hot to tell, though. Everything was melting. Sweat dripped down my skin, and occasionally I had to dance away to avoid getting burned.

Suddenly, a hand grabbed me from behind and

pulled me back. I found the extinguisher snatched from my hand by a pair of strong, dark-haired youths, their faces wrapped in cloth just as mine was. It took a second for me to realise that it was Tane and his brother, who had come to take over from me. Iorangi gave me a shove towards the exit and shouted something that I couldn't make out, but I didn't need to hear it. The gesture was enough.

They'd stripped me of my means to do any good anyway, so I ran for the exit. The smoke had started to thin out, just a little bit enough to be significant. Beyond the exit, I saw Hemi bracing himself against the power of the fire hose he had aimed at our roof. I rushed to help him, but he shooed me away.

"We've got this. Go find your sister!" he yelled over the endless blast of water and the roar of the flames.

I had nothing to say to that.

I turned and ran back towards the Hilux, where I could see shadowy figures crouched around one another on the ground. As I got closer, I could see the two little girls and Michael kneeling beside the doctor, who was struggling to talk around a terrible, hacking cough. He was gesturing towards the north, but by the time I reached them he had lost the ability to speak.

It didn't seem to matter, Michael had heard enough. As soon as he heard me coming, he rose to his feet and turned to me to relay the tale. "He said that two men came wanting to trade this evening. They came from the north, and said they wanted to trade for food, but it was late so Doc tried to send them away.

"One of them panicked and hit him; he's not sure which one. He fell down and passed out for a minute, and when he woke up he heard Skye screaming at the men. Then there was a terrible crash and everyone started yelling. He managed to get into the garden before he passed out. Maddy said she saw the men carry Skylar away."

"So wherever she is, she's alive," I said, my voice husky from the smoke and exertion.

"Yes," he answered, but I could see the look in his eyes, and knew he was as concerned as I was. With good reason. These men could be anyone. They had set fire to our home and kidnapped my sister. They were dangerous. I felt my hands clench up, and I knew that the only way I'd be able to relax was when Skye was safely back home where I could protect her.

"Get your gun. We're going to get her back," I told Michael. My voice came out strangely, ice cold even though the anger I felt was red hot. Without waiting for his response, I discarded my makeshift mask, and dove into the Hilux to find the shotgun. Michael was a second behind me, grabbing his assault rifle out of the back seat. He let out a sharp whistle to call his dog to heel, and then he was a step behind me was I raced off towards the north.

"What are we going to do when we find them?" Michael's voice was urgent and concerned. "We don't know how many there are, or how well armed they are.

They could have us outnumbered."

"First, we find them," I answered breathlessly, flicking my hair back out of my face, "and when we do, we'll improvise."

There was a grunt that told me he didn't quite care for my plan, but he had no choice. I was going whether he liked it or not, so his only option was whether or not he was going to help me. Adrenaline thrummed through my veins as I picked up the pace, my path illuminated by the glow of the fire, and the moon overhead. It was almost full, and its silvery glow cast our world in a strange mixture of black, white, and flame-orange.

Behind me, I heard Michael's feet on the asphalt and the panting of his dog beside him. In just a few minutes, we had passed the run-down old shops that flanked the northern edge of town, and were out in the wild countryside. The noise and smoke from the fire diminished until the only sounds I heard were our own footsteps and harsh breathing. How far had the strangers come? I could only guess – but to my surprise, the dog told us.

Just as we were passing a stand of dense bush, Alfred skidded to a stop and froze, sniffing the air sharply. Michael halted a second later, and the sound of his change in pace alerted me that something was out of place. By the time I returned to them, Michael was kneeling beside the dog and talking to him in the half-gibberish talk that humans instinctively used when talking to animals.

Taking the hint, I slipped the safety off my shotgun and approached the edge of the forest, examining it as best I could in the dim light of the moon. Even with my very human senses, I could see that there was an obvious trail leading deeper into the gloom. Several people had come this way; it was too dark to tell how many or how recently.

Suddenly, a voice pierced the darkness, a female voice raised in a blood-curdling shriek. It wasn't the sound of my sister in pain, though; it was the sound of an unknown woman screaming in fury. She was too far away for me to make out her words, but her anger gave us a fix on their location. I glanced at Michael and nodded; he returned the gesture, then fell in beside me as we crept deeper into the gloom.

Our stealth was unnecessary. The woman was still screaming, yelling abuse at someone that we couldn't see. As we rounded a bend in the narrow pathway, we could see the distant flicker of a camp fire, illuminating a small clearing amongst the trees. I held up a hand to halt Michael, then beckoned for him to follow me as I melted into the shadows beside the path. Together, we inched forward until we crouched between the ferns. Carefully, we parted the fronds so that we could see the scene unfolding in the clearing without being detected.

The woman was starvation thin and furious, with a shock of frizzy brunette hair and weather-worn skin that made it difficult to estimate her age. I couldn't make out the details of her face in the semi-darkness, but it was obvious the target of her ire was a man. She smacked him hard and yelled at him incoherently, then turned away holding her head in her hands.

"You were only supposed to trade!" she wailed, tugging at her hair. The man she'd struck cringed, and backed away. He was tall, but just as skinny as she was, with olive skin and dark hair; his face bore an expression of guilt. A teenage boy stood behind him, looking terrified.

I glanced across the clearing and saw three younger children of different ages huddled together, all looking equally frightened. Between the children and the adults lay a body slumped unconscious on the grass. Even from afar, I recognised the form as Skylar's. Her curly blonde hair fanned out across the grass, but she didn't seem to be restrained in any way.

"I swear, I didn't mean for this to happen," the man protested, holding his hands up in defence.

"I sent you up there to trade for food," the woman yelled, rounding on her husband with fury, "not to set their home on fire and steal their women!"

"It was an accident!" The man backed away, as though fearing another blow. "We panicked when they said no. We just wanted to grab something and run, but she surprised us and the gas cooker she was using got knocked over. What was I supposed to do? Leave her to burn to death?"

"It's my fault," the teenager spoke up suddenly, looking for all the world like he was about to cry. "I hit the old man. I... I was just so hungry, when he said no...

I'm sorry, Mum..."

"Old man?" The woman spun around to face the teenager. "There was an old man? And you left him in there?"

"We couldn't find him." The man jumped to the teenager's defence, though the woman looked so weak from starvation that she probably couldn't have hurt either of them even if she'd wanted to. "We tried, but the smoke was getting too thick and he wasn't where we'd left him."

I glanced to my left at Michael, and saw an expression on his face that looked just the way I felt. This was not what we had expected. These people were not vicious, heartless marauders, but a starving family that had been looking for food. Whether we believed that it was an accident or not, it made sense. Then, suddenly, the dog began to growl.

The fight in the clearing continued unabated, and none of them seemed to have heard the growl. I glanced at Alfred and then at Michael, lifting a brow to ask the silent question. Michael shrugged, but I could just barely see the tension in his shoulders. The dog had heard or smelt something that it didn't like. When I reached out to touch the canine, I found his back was up and he was ready for a fight.

A second later, we heard the shriek.

It was a terrible, blood-curdling screech that froze me to the core, and halted the argument in a heartbeat. It was a noise both Michael and I had heard before, and we both knew very well what it meant. This was a moment that we had dreaded, but now it was here. The predatory dead had come south.

In a split second, we were presented with a choice. We could either grab my sister and run, leaving these people as a human sacrifice to buy us time, or we could try to save the very same people that had almost burnt our home to the ground. None of them had anything that even remotely resembled a weapon. They were completely helpless.

I glanced at the three tiny children, the youngest no older than four. The look on those little faces made the decision for me. If I wanted to save my species, it had to begin with the very thing that makes us human: our ability to cooperate and work together.

Michael was right beside me as I surged to my feet and lunged into the clearing, just as a second and third screech reverberated all around us. The teenager shouted in surprise when he saw us coming, but the noise only attracted the creatures to him. I saw a flicker of movement in the bushes on the opposite side of the clearing; a moment later, I levelled my shotgun and fired from the hip into the brush. A terrible howl told me that the buckshot had struck home.

"Get the kids behind us," I ordered sharply, catching the woman's eye. Without hesitation, she grabbed her son and husband, dragging them over to protect the children. I leapt over my sister's prone form and crouched on the far side of her, staring into the bushes, waiting for the creatures to come.

They didn't come. In fact, they did something

far worse. They stayed hidden, screeching their horrifying noises, without exposing themselves. It was too dark for us to spot them in the undergrowth, unless we got lucky. They could flank us from any direction and our only warning would be if they howled.

"We need to retreat before they get behind us," I told the family. "Grab anything you can't live without – and I expect one of you to carry my sister if you want to live out the night. Do you understand?"

There was a chorus of agreement, followed by a flurry of activity. The people had almost nothing except a couple of small bags of things for the children. I heard a grunt as someone lifted Skye up, but I didn't dare to look away from the forest's edge.

"Michael," I called, waiting until I heard his response before I issued another command. "I want you to lead off. I'll cover the rear. Take them back to town. We'll work things out there."

There was another noise of agreement, and then I heard the sound of his footsteps retreating. I waited until I heard the others hurry off as well, then I back-pedalled after them, keeping an eye on the trees all around us and my ears alert for danger. As soon as I was out of the clearing, I turned and ran as hard as I could.

I caught up with the group a few moments later. With the children slowing them down, they had barely reached the road. There was another shriek, but it was further away now, which gave me a brief flash of hope. In the glow of the moonlight, I dimly saw the man carrying my sister just in front of me, casting fearful glances over his shoulder. I saw the woman stoop and pick up the smallest child. Michael shouldered his rifle and gathered up the next youngest.

We ran as hard as we could, with me in the rear to make sure no one got lost. The sound of harsh breathing and footsteps pounding over the asphalt drowned out everything else. For all our differences, there was one thing that united us, and it was the pure, animal terror of the beast we couldn't see, waiting to devour us if we stopped for a moment to catch our breath. Even the children seemed to understand that to lag behind was to die a horrible death.

Somehow, we made it back to the township. The screeches had faded further and further away, moving off in another direction. By some freak of fate, we had been spared to fight another day. Eventually, we drew to a ragged halt near the Hilux, where the raging fire lit our faces in a devilish glow.

Only then did I have a second to think about what we'd done, and who we had just saved. A heartbeat later, I made up my mind about what to do. The next step to going beyond survival was to find a way to forgive those who had wronged against us. Now was the time to practice what I hoped to one day preach.

"Put the little ones in the truck where we can protect them," I told Michael. He nodded and hurried to obey, opening the door to the rear cab so he could place the little child he was carrying safely inside. The woman hesitated for a moment, and then passed the toddler to him as well. Soon, all five children, including Priyanka and Maddy, were safely inside.

I looked at the man who carried my unconscious sister, and tilted my head towards the truck. Understanding my gesture, he carried her over and placed her gently in the passenger seat, and then stood back, looking at me with uncertainty. All of them were looking at me, I realised suddenly: the two strangers, their teenage son, Michael, Doc, and even the dog. They were waiting for me to say something, to make some monumental decision that would somehow make everything okay.

I drew a deep breath and fumbled with my thoughts for a moment, then looked at the strangers and carefully set an expression on my face that was both firm and kind at the same time. At least, I hoped it was; this whole leadership thing was kind of new to me.

"I don't think I need to tell you what you've done to us here," I gestured behind me, to the building wreathed in flame. Frantic figures ran back and forth, silhouetted against the fire: Hemi and his team, hard at work trying to extinguish the damage these strangers had done. The man and the teenager looked down, guilt clearly written across their faces. The woman glared at them, then looked back at me.

"They weren't meant to do that," she explained, obviously trying hard to keep her anger under control. "I only sent them to trade for food."

"I know. We heard everything." I shook my

head and gave her the faintest of smiles. "Accidents happen, unfortunately. This was an accident. As such, I'm willing to offer you a choice. You can either leave now and take your chances on the road, or we can work out an alternative."

"What kind of alternative?" The woman's expression flickered; the firelight playing across her features made it hard to work out exactly what she was thinking. I took another deep breath and plunged ahead anyway.

"We need friends, miss. I think we both do. Friendship and trust are the only way we can prevent things like this from happening again." I pointed to the car full of children, their little faces ghostly pale as they stared at us through the windows. "It's the only way that we can protect them from the terrible things in the darkness. My alternative is this: stay with us and help us put this right, and then we can look towards the future together – for our children."

The strangers stared at me, looking shocked beyond words by the generosity of my offer. At first, they had no response, so I smiled and sweetened the deal a little. "We have food here, and a real doctor. This man beside me was a police officer, and still lives by the ethos to protect and serve. We are good people, and we're happy to share what we have with other good people, so long as those people are willing to help us in return."

"Help you to do what?" the woman asked softly, her expression flickering between hope and concern.

"To rebuild. To recreate what we lost." I reached out towards her and placed a gentle hand upon her shoulder. "For the sake of the next generation, we have to look to the future and stop living in the ruins of yesterday's world. We have to plan for tomorrow, and work towards a common goal. We have to find something to hope for.

"We've all spent the last ten years scavenging, but if we want to survive another decade, then we have to invest in our future together." I squeezed her shoulder and smiled at her. looking her straight in the eye. "My name is Sandrine McDermott, and I say that merely surviving is no longer enough."

***

To be continued, in The Survivors Book III: Winter.

The Cast

THE NARRATOR
Sandrine "Sandy" McDermott

THE OHAUPO GROUP
Michael Chan
Doctor Stewart Cross
Madeline "Maddy" Cross
Ryan Knowles
Skylar "Skye" McDermott

THE PARATA TRIBE OF LAKE RUATUNA
Anahera Parata
Hemi Parata
Ropata Parata
Iorangi Parata
Tane Parata
Richard Parata

THE ARAPUNI GROUP:
Jim Merrit
Rebecca Merrit

MISCELLANEOUS:
Lee Hawera
Priyanka
Alfred the Stray

DECEASED:
Sophie Chan, niece of Michael.
Dog, member of the Ohaupo group.
Kylie McDermott, mother of Skye & Sandy
Roger McDermott, father of Skye & Sandy
Everyone else in the whole world.
May they rest in peace.

Kiwiana Language Guide

Aotearoa   The Maori name for New Zealand, literally "The Land Of The Long White Cloud".

Bush   Specifically, "native bush". This term refers to an area of native forest, which is characterised by a particularly thick shrub layer dominated by indigenous ferns and bushes – hence the colloquialism. Native bush is often very thick and dark, and can be very difficult to travel through as a result.

Cark It   To die. *Example: "We were half-way to Tauranga when the car carked it."*

G'day   Colloquial version of "Good day".

Hangi   Maori culture, an underground oven used to cook food.

Hongi   Maori culture, the pressing together of the nose and forehead in a greeting. Used in a similar fashion to the handshake in Western culture. Symbolises the mixing of the breath of life integral to Maori folklore.

Kai   Maori, "Food".

Kia Ora   Maori, "Hello".

Kumara   A sweet potato.

Maori   Relating to the original peoples of New Zealand. May be used to refer to their cultural traits (*e.g. "she tried to live by the traditional Maori ways."*), language (*e.g. "he spoke Maori."*) or ethnicity (*e.g. "my grandmother was Maori"*). The Maori culture evolved from Polynesian migrants that arrived in New Zealand around 1,000 years ago.

Mate   A contextually sensitive word that is usually used in place of the word "friend". Can be used sarcastically or in threat just as readily as being used in a friendly fashion, *e.g. "You're going to regret that, mate."*

Pā   Maori, can refer to a village or settlement, but usually describes a hill fort.

Rēwena   Maori, literally "ferment/rise". In terms of bread, it refers to a traditional Maori potato bread.

Credits

Concept & Story:	Victoria L. Dreyer
Editing:	Holly Simmons
Cover Art:	Alais Legrand
Graphic Design:	Alyssa Talboys

***

Financial Support

Prior to the release of this novel, the author ran an online fundraising campaign to help with the costs. Without the generosity of these lovely people, *The Survivors Book II* may not have been possible.

Donna Gray
Hazel Godwin (*Craves The Angst*)
Rachael Babbington
Rebecca Rakes
Rebekah Andrews
Sarah Hayward

And of course, the anonymous donors who requested not to be named. Thank you.

About The Author

Born in Auckland, New Zealand, Victoria Dreyer began her career in the most peculiar of ways – as the writer and illustrator of graphic novels. Although her ultimate dream was always to become a novelist, she spent many years exploring other mediums before finally returning to the one she felt most comfortable with – the written word.

Ms Dreyer is a voracious reader, and in addition to the post-apocalyptic genre she also enjoys reading and writing science fiction, modern fantasy, and the paranormal romance genres. Her primary works include the *Immortelle* series under the moniker Abigail Hawk, and numerous short stories.

She currently resides in West Auckland with several flatmates, a large collection of books, and two very spoilt cats.

CPSIA information can be obtained at www.ICGtesting.com
Printed in the USA
LVOW08s1921140414

381650LV00001B/3/P